THE FLOWERS I DESERVE

TAMARA JERÉE

WATER SIGN BOOKS

AUTHOR'S NOTE

The Flowers I Deserve is an FFF erotic dark fantasy novel. It is only intended for adult readers.

Content notes: death, depression, grief, self-harm (poisoning), lesbophobia, animal bite, blood, injury detail, explicit sexual content, sexual relationships between a king and her servants, obsessive relationships, voyeurism, knife play, piercing, choking, unnegotiated bondage.

I

HOME

ONE

W HEN A MONTH PASSED without word from Ma, I went into the woods.

The earl's letter rasped in the pocket of my dress. It had arrived not with the regular post, as Ma's letters did, but with a well-dressed man on a tall black stallion. My father had broken with the wax seal and wept without reading the news. Before the letter, I had never known who my mother worked for. Now, so armed, I had a plan.

Dusk stained the sky in wounded hues, a rust of old blood at the horizon and purple dark above. Fevered air parched my throat. Flies buzzed over a small husk of matted fur. My skin crawled at their feasting, and I hurried to put the scene behind me. Holding my skirt in one hand, I waded through the coarse underbrush, the layers of woods that had died in the drought. Footpaths had vanished long ago. Thorns scratched at my legs and snagged my hem. I wouldn't be able to hide that I had strayed from the farm's safer soil. Overhead, the pines were bare, their branches wretched fingers grasping the dying sky.

I knew the brightest poisons because there were no competitors to their beauty in such a barren land. The bushes flourished from cracked red earth. White flowers beckoned, their petals impossibly dotted with dew, their cordate leaves glossy green. I'd never picked one of hell's flowers, was always under Da's watchful eye when I ventured outside, and now hesitated at the precipice of my choice.

Ma, what flower overcame your spirit? Was the devil who brought you here the one to take your spirit home? Had they missed you?

Did they miss me?

I was torn between the leaf and the flower. A morbid choice. I snatched a flower, held it to my face, let the yellow stamen tickle my nose. Its petals formed a shallow cup with a shock of violet where they joined at the center. I plucked the petals as if playing a schoolyard game. *He loves me, he loves me not.* I stacked them neatly on my tongue. The last petal—*he loves me*. It seemed a good omen.

Mild flavors of bitter and green were all that came of my careful chewing. I expected poison to taste like a warning. This was as sedate as the cleric's tinctures for cough and fever. I glared down at the flower bush. Perhaps the elders were wrong. I plucked a leaf and held it to the moonlight, turned it so that its gloss caught the light. What a silly scene to look back on, a girl judging her poisoner and finding them inadequate. I tucked the leaf under my tongue and ventured farther into the dark woods in the hope of finding a better ally for my experiment.

I hadn't walked for long before a simple breath became a labor. The land was flat here and yet I felt I'd run up a hill. I stumbled and fell against a desiccated pine. It'd been hollowed by burrowing insects, turned pockmarked and brittle, and its branches snapped at my weight. A sympathetic pang tugged my chest. Or maybe it was plain and simple pain, my body's alarm confused for emotion. I couldn't feel my feet. I sucked in a breath and turned my face to the sky. The stars whirled in a dance I had never seen them perform. The whole sky was going to fall if they kept moving like that. Going so fast, they made the air hot. Sweat trickled down my temples. I wished for a breeze. Maybe I had walked farther than I thought. I turned to start home. Some of the stars had already made it to earth. They floated in the bushes. I couldn't feel my face. Or maybe I couldn't feel my hands that touched it. Eventually, I was only looking at the sky. I had a good view of it there in the dirt, though I didn't remember lying down. Then, the stars went out.

The clouds were thin and drawn over the moon, and this sky meant that I was not at home. We'd had no clouds in weeks, and the air in this new place was sweet with the scent of thriving green. Yet I could glimpse only a small box of sky.

Bedposts and the velvet hanging from them shielded the world from me and me from the world. A necessary modesty. I crossed my arms over my bare chest and startled at the blanket of red beneath me, not a blanket at all but a weave of flowers on their vines. I'd never seen varieties like this—slender petals bursting into pom-poms; a chalice of spider-thin petals; a delicate crimson maw, pinked at the center. Having overcome my fear once, it was easy to reach again, to trail my fingers along the reddening blush at a flower's edge. I pinched a stem with the intent of plucking it free, and it was here that I paused. I didn't want to disturb anything in this place. These flowers were unlike any I'd met before, turning to me as though I were a small sun. When I touched them, I knew their devotion and wouldn't betray it.

I was bending to the face of a bloom when the curtain stirred. I froze. A slender, fine-boned hand slipped through and caught the fabric, opening me to a featureless black where the sky did not continue. I couldn't see who held the curtain, only the flare of her red skirt where she stood to the side. Still, her gaze burned from the dark.

I called to her and received no answer. My breaths rose. I thought to go to her but didn't know why she watched me, whether she was appraising or admiring. A tickle at my wrist called me back to the flowers. As one, the vines shifted on a wave, curving over my thighs and capturing my waist. My first instinct was to pull away, but I'd moved too late. The flowers pulled me down like a lover. Heat bloomed across my skin. The woman still watched me. I felt her attention, rapt and unashamed even as the grip of the vines turned firm and encouraged my legs open.

I'd had dreams of this tenor before, ones that woke me hot and slick, but never so vivid, never so lucid. I would meet a shadowed lover whose body I could never see because we were not meant to know each other's bodies. I would meet a selfless lover who I was afraid to touch because their body was a mirror. But these dreams never grew flowers, never introduced the thrill of binding and surrender.

Overhead, a flash of white winged past. It was not a bird but a figure. I tensed in the cradle of the vines, and they curved tentatively across my body, their touch a question. The figure circled lower in the square of sky, too swift to determine any features. Did this being watch me in turn? Did they judge me? I lost sight of them in the circle of the moon.

I wanted to ask the woman whether she'd seen this miracle with me and turned to find she'd drawn nearer to the curtain. Another realization opened like borderland springtimes of years past—when the cloud-dark of a storm is burned clear by the all-seeing sun. My dream lovers were never men or women or anyone.

Now, a woman.

I saw one brown and eager eye before the vines were around my throat and I was sinking into them and they into me.

MY REVELATION DRIFTED FROM me like something cast out on the pond, something rippling away. When I reached to recapture it, the water had gone, and a basin of parched earth widened before me. A voice called from the farmhouse behind. My body was too heavy to rise and answer, too heavy to stand at all. I groaned. The sun was big. Da's face eclipsed the light.

I rolled over in bed. Da's face looked down upon me again. With him, a young Restorationist cleric I had never seen. I thought he was a new dream. His veil of white feathers fell just to the chin. His jaw worked as he spoke, and I had the urge to pull the veil apart. All the wisdom I sought was the face underneath. This was my first blasphemous thought and so soon after waking. The poison had made short work of corrupting me.

The three of us were crowded into my bedroom, its sturdy pine furniture and walls built by my father's hands. It was too small a room for two men—a holy cleric of the great angel and my humble father. Though I couldn't see the cleric's eyes, the intensity of his gaze weighed on me. I rolled away from their scrutiny. Da's exhale was long and relieved. Why was it still so hot?

"Carlotta?" he said hopefully. "How do you feel, dear?"

I mumbled an answer and shielded my eyes with my forearm. The daylight was so bright for this time of night. Maybe all the stars had crashed down.

"The worst has passed," came the cleric's voice. "Ensure she has water and rest. She'll return to herself."

My father's shadow left me. "You speak so confidently." There was an edge to his voice I'd never heard before. "Do you often find girls lost in the woods with deadly plants in their mouths?"

"Perhaps we should step into the hall, sir? Allow your daughter to continue resting."

Da's heavy sigh came again. His boots tramped across the floor. The door shut. I did not want him to go. I pushed myself to sitting and squinted against the stabbing light. I swung my feet to the floor. I did not trust my body to bear my weight. I stretched my hands flat and crawled to the door. I'd drawn breath to call for Da when the cleric's voice resumed, somber in the hall. I set my ear to the door.

"Your daughter pressed through on her own strength. By the time I found her, most would be dead, and even if one survived so long, my medicines would not be enough to pull them back from the brink." A long pause. "Do you understand what I'm telling you, sir?" A longer pause, then a hesitant prompting. "Her mother shares her condition, yes?"

Da offered nothing that I could hear.

"I see."

"We just learned of her passing. I didn't know Carlotta would take the news this way. I didn't know she would try to . . ." Another sigh, as if the past hours were bad air he needed to clear from his lungs. "I didn't know young people could think of their own deaths like this."

"If your daughter understood her mother's condition and how it has supported the two of you, consider that she was not trying to kill herself but the opposite. She's a smart girl, you've said. And now, she has proof of her power. Look out for her."

"I've failed once. I don't intend to let it happen again."

"If you ever have need of it, my order would be honored to shelter your daughter. Her gift is a sign that the fallen angel is remembering who they are. Girls like her—they're the only ones who can encounter the evil of the world and emerge unscathed."

I tensed. The Restorationists' views were considered heretical. But Da didn't take a side. He didn't like any religious talk. If not for the aristocracy's demand for our gift—and, therefore, their selfish protection of us—the Clerical Order of Angelic Retribution would've ensured we had no place in society. If one were to ask a northern Retributionist, they'd say that Ma had a devil inside her, that the souls of poison girls were birthed in hell and shepherded to earth by an ill spirit. Such care on the part of these devils only to later do nothing to forestall her early death or any poison girl's death. What evil was so neglectful of its plots?

Of the two clerical orders, only the heretical Order of Angelic Restoration believed the fallen angel still walked the earth and could be returned to their twin in heaven. For them, the rise of poison girls was prophecy fulfilled. Our immunity could cleanse earth's evil through sacrifice. Humanity's atonement was our true purpose. We could unmake the grief that had burdened the wings of the fallen twin. But Da would not engage with what he couldn't prove with his own hands.

"Thank you for your help," he said simply, his voice absent its usual warmth.

"Certainly. And Mr. Bridge? If I may be frank, you should tell your daughter what she is as soon as you can. There are people who would promise her anything to protect their own lives. Do not let her make another hasty decision. Poison girls are—"

"Respectfully, dear cleric, do not use that term in my house."

"Of course. Excuse me." He cleared his throat. "What would you prefer?"

"We needn't speak of it."

"I understand your reluctance, but denial will not protect her."

An acknowledging grunt was all I heard from my father before their steps and conversation receded. I slumped with my back to the door. Gold light pierced the lace curtains, another gift from Ma. I looked too long, and pain lanced behind my eyes. I squeezed them shut and saw spots. My throat was parched, my limbs heavy, but through the discomfort, grim elation suffused my body.

I had done it. I was a poison girl.

Above me, the doorknob rattled. Da called my name, a note of alarm in his voice.

"I'm here," I said, my voice strange to me. Distant, papery. I would become letters too, like Ma.

"Please open the door."

"But it's unlocked," I said.

He tried again, said my name in a tone short on patience. He was rarely impatient with me. I wondered at this. I stood. This took a long time. I walked my hands up the door, leaning my weight into it as I did. Once upright, I opened the door.

Da's eyes were wide. The floor rushed forward. I fell into his arms. He carried me back to bed and sat in the little rocking chair beside, head in his hands. I watched him through the curve of the water glass on my little table. My father was a tall man. It was strange to see him folded up so small. Unlike many of the men in our town, my father still had smooth and unscarred brown skin. He had not had to labor so hard in withering heat over land that did not want to yield. He'd kept his long hair too. It still fell in dense locks down to his waist. He said Ma fell in love with his hair. That's why he never cut it even though the style for men of our class was cropped close to the scalp. Only aristocrats braided their hair or allowed it to grow long enough to lock.

"You scared me, Carlotta," he said, his face still in his hands.

"I'm sorry." I was. My plan had been to return before he woke. There wasn't supposed to be worrying.

He shook his head, but it was a slow, whole-body sway. "No. It's my job to guard you. I am sorry."

I turned this over. Da had never apologized to me. He'd never needed to. "I'm a poison girl," I said because suddenly this felt like the only thing I could know for certain. "I'm going to write to Earl Huxley and take Ma's place."

Da startled upright. Anger crunched his face. "You are not a poison girl. Do you understand? You will speak that name to no one, and you will not hold it for yourself. Huxley will take nothing more from my family."

I'd never heard him express any negativity toward my mother's gifts or her employer. The change shocked me. I turned away from him. I wanted to cry. Da had never been angry with me. A chasm opened between us where none had been before. Poison girls could not die, I wanted to reassure him, because I had survived this once.

I thought to remind him of Ma's letters, all of them pressed and perfumed with petals, the neat squares of poetry in every envelope. She'd become a humble student of the day's aesthetic. Through her, I had studied too.

Each poem was more fantastical than the last. A meditation on the beauty of an innocent flower. Meter that revived the rhythm of heels upon a ballroom floor. Odes to lush landscapes that, to a girl raised at the forgotten edge of a kingdom, were hopelessly distant. I read these poems and grew an ache that never left my chest. The world harbored soft places. Lands where flowers could be symbols of beauty instead of danger. The earth beyond was rich with green. I'd give anything to know it. I wanted Da to understand.

"Carlotta." Da had moved. He was kneeling at the bedside now. He took my hand in his. "There are things about the world you don't understand. And that's my fault. I wanted you to be happy, and so there's much I never told you."

I turned my head on the pillow. My face was still numb, so I didn't know what expression I was making. "Matteo told me Ma would die. We were still children. He was the sort of boy who'd smear clay in girls' hair after the rains."

I'd hoped that what had been revealed to me was only the cruelty of a boy and nothing more. I wanted to return to the reality where Ma was immune to everything always and forever.

Da bowed his face. Was that shame? Regret? I still think about it now. It's one of my sharpest memories of him. Maybe he was praying to Ma. If I were to believe in someone I'd never seen, it would always be Ma. The clerics' twin angel in the heavens was broken and so far away.

"Why can't I call myself what I am?" I was proud of this newfound resistance to nature and men's schemes. Though I lay in bed half numb and half in pain, I was powerful. I'd never had anything so special to claim as my own.

"It is not respectable."

"Ma saved the earl's life. She's as honorable as any knight."

"It is not respectable for women to have such dangerous professions."

"The king is a woman."

"She is not respectable. And nothing like a woman. Here, drink," added Da, wrapping my fingers around the glass as if I'd forgotten how.

I wouldn't let him distract me. I needed to understand. "What if I don't care about being respectable?"

Da looked at me as if he'd found a suspicious bud among his seedlings.

I pressed on with my logic. "Ma wasn't respectable, but you still married her. The king isn't respectable, but she's still the king. If I can have love and power, why do I need respectability?"

"You'll understand when you're older." He stood. "Drink, rest. I'll bring your dinner."

A wave of feeling swept through me. I hadn't cried when the earl's man arrived on our step. I was all action: swipe the letter, craft a plan. I was done crying. I was done being a girl. I wanted to be something that could scream loud enough for the world to hear. I wanted to be like the king—nothing like a woman. Respected but not respectable. Hell where my gender should be.

I sat up too fast. My head pounded. "I can understand now!"

Da's face tensed as though he would chastise me, but he exhaled the fight before it could brew. "She wanted so badly to see you, Carlotta," he said instead.

I held my breath, like any movement would threaten what he was about to reveal.

"She was arranging for months to come home and welcome you to your eighteenth year. It's an important one for daughters of the aristocracy, and so much time with them solidified it as a concept in her mind. But the earl's new trade ventures on the king's behalf mean he's attracted enemies, people who think he's furthering Vinstrum's demise by working for the cursed king. In the months leading up to your mother's death"—Da laced his hands and nodded again as if fortifying himself—"she lost her colleagues one by one. Only one other woman, a good friend, still worked with her."

He stepped delicately when talking about Ma as a poison girl if he talked about her at all. This moment was a gift. I wanted to hear more and didn't know the right question. If I chose wrong, he would close up again.

To think she had almost returned to me.

"I cannot even know where she's been laid to rest—as if I would dig up the body for answers! The earl won't divulge anything. He thinks truth will bring more harm to his house." Da continued of his own accord, an overflow of grief loosing his words. "Much is shifting, Carlotta. I'd rather not see you caught in it."

Violence was still shocking, even when it wasn't on the scale of war. After the last great battles decimated the continent, the kingdoms agreed to an end to violent conflict, hence the popularity of subtler methods for disposing of one's enemies and the aristocracy's rising demand for the company of poison girls.

I was already caught in this shifting tide by virtue of my talents, because I was my mother's daughter, because I wanted to know the world beyond the borderlands. Without Ma, we would have died on this farm. I would take any path that led me out. A short life in comfort was preferable to a short life in struggle. This was simple. Propriety be damned.

Da stood as if resting had made him weary. "Huxley has promised the pay he owes your mother within the week. Then we have a choice. If we're careful, it could see us through the year, but families who have the means are already fleeing the village. The augurs foretell an angrier land and sky."

"Then we go north," I said immediately. What was the consideration? Where was his hesitation?

"Safe passage would cost us all we have, and in the north, the aristocracy owns everything. The land we worked and the home we lived in would never be ours again. It would be hard."

"But I could—"

"No!" Da's voice was a startling boom. When he saw my expression, he smoothed his own, unclenched his fist, and exhaled long. "I'm sorry," he said quietly. "We did this because we had you to care for. Both our families disowned us when they found out about her condition. There's no need to repeat this pain."

"You never told me."

"It didn't matter. It was done." He reached for the door. "I'll be in the field."

I made the most of my days with Ma's poetry and the books of verse she'd sent us. My favorite was a thin volume that collected the work of Phaela Mirrors, the king's royal poet. She was seen in society only once a year during the winter feast where she would debut her new work before disappearing into the castle until next solstice. I was close to Ma this way, reading the words I knew she'd read and loved.

After a fortnight, Da turned gloomy when the earl's representative made no appearance with the promised coin. Our only visitor was my teacher arriving at our door to ask after me. This was a critical juncture, and I shouldn't fall behind in my studies—unless my hand was promised to someone? she inquired. This suggestion floated up through the floorboards. I wanted to hiss. I wanted to put my fist through the window.

This rage was a new companion, a fever drained down into my chest that never left. It fed on where my grief lived and grew even larger, eclipsed and erased the feeling that birthed it. I didn't know how to hold a feeling so hot. Tentatively, I considered an alliance. It was with fire that northerners survived the winters.

"She's just lost her mother," I heard Da explain, begging more time for me. "I wrote to you."

"Excuse my frankness, but I speak as a daughter who also lost her mother young. Your late wife provided a unique shelter for Carlotta, but the world will not be so kind. She must learn this. She needs to apply herself to something other than her poems."

What had I imagined for my future? Silly and impossible things. I'd imagined going to visit Ma during the winter solstice. I'd imagined a chance meeting with Mirrors wherein she'd be so taken by a slip of poetry I just so happened to have tucked up my sleeve that she would take me on as a pupil immediately. I'd dreamed of artistic sponsorship and royal balls. A life devoted to my art. I did not want marriage, and yet my parents had worked to place me in one of the few southern schools that would prepare me for a fine husband. I was a farmer's daughter who was destined for a sheltered life. I was a poison girl's daughter destined for a respectable role. I was supposed to transcend both my parents and make them proud.

In my dreams, the pond rippled, the truth sometimes near and sometimes far. I did not want marriage.

I did not want men.

"I will talk to her," Da said in the same flat voice he had used with the cleric.

"She needs guidance right now. Realism," my teacher continued as Da walked her down the steps.

"Thank you," Da said, the reply automatic and distant.

I did not break my window. I sat at it and looked down at my teacher eyeing the flowers growing unchecked around the porch and preparing to hatch their white buds. I didn't remember them being so tall yesterday, but the poisonous ones grew overnight, leading people to wake the next morning believing they'd been cursed by a devil passing through. My teacher shivered in the heat before lecturing my father for his negligence. She said the angel would not look kindly upon him for this. She called him Alessio with the same authority she used in the classroom, as though they were not the same age. I felt his name as a jolt. No one called my father anything. Not our neighbors or the vendors at the market. Speaking a name was an intention to draw someone close, but everyone knew Da—knew Alessio—as the man who had married a cursed woman, and who would want to draw such a person close?

"What does it matter?" Da said. I barely caught his words, but the defeat in them was clear. "Neither I nor my daughter are fools enough to touch them."

The lie came so easily to him. I was happily the fool.

"It's the principle of it all." My teacher's voice was passionate even at a distance. "We shouldn't have our daughters around such things. Yours especially."

"Mine? Is that so." He stared past my teacher. I thought he might challenge her but only promised my return to school before leaving her surrounded by poison in the sun.

Phaela Mirrors was born in the year of drowning feathers 2586, making her exactly twenty-five years senior to me, a daughter born in the year of dusk feathers 2611. Both of us were only children and daughters of poison girls, but unlike me, Mirrors was a member of the aristocracy and had already published her first poems when she was sixteen.

On grief, sixteen-year-old Mirrors wrote,

I braid my hair
as you showed me
as I have
always
done and will
continue

I sit
at the same
table and eat
the same foods

I am
living still

It's unknown who inspired the lines. Desperate for the solace of common experience, I searched for the date of her mother's death. I could never confirm the time.

I went down to the porch and picked a bouquet of the white flowers for my bedside.

THREE

T HE DAY I RETURNED to school dressed in pink silk, King Emelia the Deathless declared it a day of mourning for another lost poison girl. Her name was Elizabeth River, and she was the sixth.

The mothers in the schoolyard traded scandalized whispers, let slip a bitter laugh. "How can she declare such days?" one said. "She herself demonstrated that she feels no pain."

A more solemn voice added, "I heard she mourns them like wives."

"They behave nothing like a wife should. Don't dignify them with the title," replied another. "She is a devil, and her girls are cursed. What love is to be had?"

At this, the circle of gossipers dropped their voices and drew together, trading sharp looks and laughing behind their hands.

My chest burned. Beside me, my father's face was a mask. He never greeted the other parents with more than a polite nod. That day, he wouldn't meet their eyes. I hated to see him shrink. Ma had loved us! She'd had so much love and done everything for love. What did they know of us? The mothers hushed as we passed on the way to the door. Da caught me glaring and wedged himself between me and the other parents, ushering me on.

"Where is your respect?" he said under his breath.

"I will find it when they deserve it," I hissed.

He sighed and didn't fight my retort. He had stopped fighting me at all and now wouldn't meet my gaze either. I was something else to tire him.

The lace hem of my dress was already stained red by the dusty clay roads, and sweat pooled at the small of my back. I was hot and embarrassed. Da had protested the dress before we left. It was my favorite, I had said. Ma had it made for me. It was inappropriate, Da had said. No matter that it was a gift from Ma. We were still in mourning. And did I really wish to call more attention to myself with an ostentatiously northern style? Our clothes were made to hang loosely and catch the breeze, the better to endure the heat. Northern styles were too structured to be comfortable in borderland heat and were shaped to the body in a way that made the elders *tsk*. I couldn't tell whether we drew looks because of my long absence or my dress or because news of my mother's death had spread. I had thought the dress would feel like armor. Instead, I felt small. I wished again that I could be like the king.

Everyone knew the story of her ascension like a tale from myth. On her first day, she earned her epithet, its durability trialed publicly by the assassin at her self-coronation. The king dug the crossbow bolt from her bloodied eye with as little affect as removing a splinter from her thumb, pausing in her speech only to rip the sleeve from her dress and tie a makeshift eye patch.

Several artists were so struck by this description of the king, a single bloody tear on her cheek and the power of the crown freshly upon her, that they were driven to their canvases. The clerics—themselves at odds since the Restorationists' heretical split a century ago—were reunited by moral concern, declaring the resulting paintings so beautiful as to be blasphemous. A devil should not be depicted lovingly.

After this, no one attempted such a direct assassination, but the fact that King Emelia kept poison girls like every other aristocrat meant she wasn't completely immune to death. The mothers' prejudice kept them from the truth. If she could die, she could be hurt.

Da and I walked in silence to the third and largest building among the cluster of high-ceilinged clay structures that comprised the village campus. They'd been built before wooden structures became the dominant trend, though the drought saw newer buildings returning to the old way. Around us, slender pines struggled. Fallen needles cushioned our steps. Beside the schoolyard, a cornfield languished. Desiccated stalks rustled in the wind.

In the meager shade, Da drew me to the side of the schoolhouse door and put his hands on my shoulders. "I will be back in the afternoon. Do not leave without me."

I studied his face. He'd never been so stern about how I walked home. I glanced at the mothers without turning my head, a quick flick of the eyes. Did they know I was like my ma? How often was immunity inherited?

Da's hands squeezed. "Carlotta."

"I understand," I said. Over Da's shoulder, I watched the other students file inside. No one dared look at me while Da was here. They'd save their taunts for when our parents were away.

"When classes are over, do not talk to anyone. Do not take anything offered to you."

Now I looked at his face again. "What would anyone have to give to me?" *Why* would anyone give anything to me? The borderlands were not a kind or abundant place. People barely had enough for themselves.

"I need you to promise," said Da. A drop of sweat fell from his temple to his chin.

I wanted to tell him he was scaring me. I wanted him to take me back home. Instead, I promised.

He squeezed my shoulder one last time. "We love you, Carlotta," he said, the same as he always did, speaking for Ma and himself. He turned to go.

"Da," I whispered, but the knot of grief in my throat choked the sound.

Any other day, I would have hurried out of the sun and into the cool refuge of the schoolhouse, but today, I could only watch Da's retreating back, how our neighbors flinched and shied away from even him. He'd knowingly taken a cursed wife, and even her death could not absolve him.

A pair of sisters marched for the door, giggling at something shared between them. I stepped back from their approach. They'd make a show of giving me a wide berth otherwise.

I was naive to think deferring to their personal space would be enough.

Their giggles turned vicious as they passed. In unison, they crossed their wrists over their chests, fanning their hands up to their shoulders in a mocking imitation of the Retributionist gesture of angelic protection. They wiggled their fingers as though to ensure I noticed their wings and would feel sufficiently banished, though no believer would dare this sort of irreverence.

Only one family in our village were true Retributionist converts. The ways of the angelic orders weren't fully embraced this far south, most families preferring the earth wisdom of our long farming history.

Yet my peers knew enough of the northerners' superstitious rituals to taunt me.

Twinned grief and rage seethed. I took an instinctive step forward, my clenched fists aching to grasp and shake and tear. I wanted to pry their wrists out of that silly pose and shove them into the dirt. But what would that prove with all these eyes on me? I harbored the evil potential they'd always suspected. Wretched Carlotta couldn't even grieve like a normal girl.

The sisters squealed and ducked inside. The parents were dispersing. I stood alone in the heat again.

Did the king's mourning feel like mine, like anger? Did she want to hurt the ones who hurt her?

I wanted the power to declare a day of anger.

I squeezed into the sliver of shade offered by the roof. This late in the morning, the sun burned the skin, but I didn't have the will to face the girls inside. I lingered and listened to the class settle. I contemplated staying outside until Da returned, but it was too hot to sit and too hot to stand.

A small voice said my name.

I turned to find another girl squeezing into the shade. "Carlotta, isn't it?" she asked, her smile shy. She wore a linen dress in a conservative shade of green, a faded hue that I'd think was the result of sun bleaching if not for how common it was.

I hugged my book of poems to my chest. "Yes," I said.

It was silly to ask my name. We had all been in the same small class since primary school. No one moved to the borderlands, only away. No one except for Lady Reed, famous among us for securing a sickly aristocratic husband who left her with the funding to return home and establish her school, providing other borderland girls with a chance at the life she had lived.

"I'm Isabella," the girl offered.

"I know."

Her smile was very stiff.

"You don't have to talk to me," I said. "People will stare."

Somehow, this softened her. "That's okay. I've decided I don't care." She took another step, bringing us close as friends. "I'm sorry about your mother," she said.

I saw her for the first time, saw past the conservative dress and the penitent scalp-shorn hair. She was broader and curvier than I, with high cheekbones and bright, hooded eyes. Her dark skin was blemishless, as though the angel themself ensured her beauty.

"Your family are Retributionists," I said, though her friendliness alone made me doubt what I'd been certain of for years. "You should hate my mother and me more than the other girls do."

Isabella's family were our closest neighbors, but we never paid visits to their farm or exchanged help during harvests like so many did. It was well known that her brother left to join a temple in the north.

"I'm not like them," she said.

"Then . . . what are you like?"

The entire world existed in dichotomies—Retributionists or Restorationists, the righteous or the cursed.

She searched my face. "Maybe I'm most like you."

I gave a little shake of my head. She couldn't be confessing that she was a poison girl. And how could she know about me? Was there something to intuit in my face?

"Oh." Her expression shifted, a spark of recognition widening her eyes. "I didn't mean . . ."

I backed away from her.

She caught my sleeve. "Wait, Carlotta." She drew close again and lowered her voice. "I won't say anything, I promise. I promise."

I measured her look again, more warily this time. Da had told me not to talk to anyone.

"My brother's rhetoric around the dinner table frightened me by the end," she said. "I can't be certain about the king or her nature, but I do know you. We've sat together in the same room for years. That is enough for me to be sorry for your loss."

Her hand rested on my arm. It burned more than the sun.

"You shouldn't touch me," I whispered but couldn't pull away.

She laced our fingers.

⸺❖⸺

Landlocked Vinstrum was a narrow stretch of country squeezed between larger mining nations that guarded access to the major rivers and northern lakes. Arga, the mightiest of these kingdoms, separated us from the continent's trade.

I couldn't imagine the abundance of water I saw on the map was real, not when our village rationed what we had for drinking. Though we were a nation of farmers, planting had become futile in the borderlands. None of the old methods worked. Nothing about nature was predictable from month to month. What was irrigation without water? What did soil health matter when farmers were going mad in their fields?

More and more families had come to depend on the king's caravans for aid. At first, no one would take the food. It spoiled in the wagons. Then desperation won out over fears of curses. Now, windstorms to our north had delayed the caravans. Our king had been maneuvering for Vinstrum's use of the waterways since her strange rise to power, but no ruler would bargain with her. That she was a woman was the least of their concerns. To those in power, entering a treaty with her was as good as signing a pact with a devil.

But Phaela Mirrors, who wrote of love and loss and loneliness, had been in the king's service for decades now. She was still seen in society. Still healthy and sharp enough to debut new work. Surely, if the castle was rising from hell as the rumors claimed, she would not be so sound of mind.

I read through class—my book atop the desk, eyes intent on the poems. Despite my teacher's conviction during her home visit, the worst I received for this was a frown. I'd taken my usual seat at the rear of the classroom by the wall. I liked to peer out of the tall windows; my view, a dead field, would be a tragic sight if every other field didn't share the same fate.

Whenever Reed turned her back, Isabella would cast a glance over her shoulder, find me still reading, and smile. I wasn't used to receiving smiles or returning them. The first time, I was too late, and Isabella had already turned away. The second time, I grimaced.

We weren't the only unfocused students. The sisters stole glances at Isabella and passed notes under their desks. No one raised their hands. No one volunteered to complete the budgeting figures for the imaginary household we were running. I glanced out the window to the dead cornfield again, and when I looked back, the sisters' staring had turned to glaring.

Reed sensed our restlessness and cut the lesson short, dismissing us for the day. While the other students filed out to sit under the trees, Reed watched me with a pinched face and beckoned me to her.

"Am I in trouble?" I asked innocently.

She frowned at my dress. "How have you found your first day back?"

"It's fine." I didn't like this conversation. I couldn't guess what she wanted.

"I worried it would be a hard day to return," she said, clasping her hands in front of her. "The news about the king's poison girl must hurt after your recent loss."

"I don't think about the king," I said because it was easiest.

She nodded to the book in my hand. "You'll complete your studies this winter. What are your aspirations after school?"

"I don't know," I said, though I did know. I knew it loudly.

"You're not asked to work your fields. Your hand is not yet promised in marriage despite your peers' successes. Your father is aging and can't care for you forever. A girl like you must start thinking of these things."

I hated her tone. Though I said I had no aspirations, I hated that she believed this was the truth, that I was a silly girl who couldn't think of the dire future.

"I have!" I snapped, gripping my book. "I mean," I added, consciously smoothing out my voice, "I have thought about it."

"And?" she prompted, waving a hand at me.

Da's warning crowded my thoughts. "My da knows. That's all that matters."

Reed's face flickered through several emotions. Eyebrows up, mouth upturned, though not in a smile. "I see," she said. "Your inheritance is unfortunate but not your life's inevitable path. You could travel north. With your education, if you apply yourself, a family might take you in as a tutor."

I held my book to my chest. A shield. "Thank you for your concern," I said, turning my back to her.

I stood beside the door where Da had left me that morning and kept my head down so I wouldn't accidentally catch anyone's gaze. Thumbing back to the first page of Mirrors's collection, I mouthed, *I am living still*. I held the book gently so as not to set a bend in the pages or break the spine, but I wasn't reading. I was thinking about the king and how we were both in mourning together, though she'd never know it. I was thinking about Isabella and hoping she might notice me again. Perhaps we might walk home together.

A rush of girls exited the schoolhouse, voices high, laughing. One knocked into my shoulder. I caught myself but was holding Mirrors with such care that the book tumbled into the dirt, pages crushed beneath the weight of its open cover. I dashed to retrieve it and was pulled up short. Something tore. A breeze brushed my arm where there had been silk before. Before I could understand what had happened, a hand snatched Mirrors from the ground. A shove hit my back. Bright pain burst my nose and lip. Breath was knocked from my chest. Pine needles stabbed my hands. The dirt so close. I spit the grime from my mouth and saw red.

I cast around for my book and found girls' feet. Pink silk, ragged at the edges, dangled from a hand. I pushed myself up. Looked the girl before me up and down. Olive linen dress. Long braids tied back with a scarf at her crown. A proud nose. In her hands, my book and my torn dress. The book and the dress my mother had given to me. My mother who was gone and who I would never see. The only things I had left of her. Words and silk.

I lunged, took the girl and myself back down in the dirt. The circle of students scattered with a cry. The fever again. I tore at the girl, my book and dress forgotten. As I burned hot, I tore at her scarf and hair, the things that I knew meant something to every girl. My hands hated her face.

Screaming. Hands on my arms hauling me up, restraining me. The fever roared. I couldn't feel my face. I couldn't feel my hands. Then the world came back.

People fled from me, mothers shielding their girls in retreat. Other faces looked on in shock and disgust. I laughed. Blood dripped down my chin. Metallic body sludge. The girl who took my things cried over mere scratches, sobbing as if she'd never seen blood well to the surface of her skin. She was lucky I'd been pulled away. I wanted to make a bruised fruit of her face. No one would take anything from me again. The world tilted. The hands on me were mean again. I tried to shrug them off. They dug in.

I tilted my head to the sky and let the blood run thick down my throat. No clouds today, only heat. My dress was soggy in my armpits. Could the twin angel see me now? Was I still a blessing as the cleric said?

Beyond the uproar of mothers and daughters, a tall man on a tall horse dismounted. This horse was white. I wondered at its coat, pristine despite the clay roads. I heard none of the yelling directed at me. I only saw the man, how he arrived and parted the crowd with his presence alone. How students and parents alike looked up at him bewildered and then startled. He wore a smart riding coat and high shiny boots. Intricately patterned braids against his scalp. Thick, noble brows. Light-brown skin. I couldn't guess his age. Young in the way that aristocrats and those close to them seemed until they weren't.

He stepped over the screaming girl with the ruined face as though she were something small and disgusting in his path. Not a glance, only the greatest care for the rich leather of his shoes. He grinned at me. I thought he might bow and ask me to dance.

"I'll take her," he said in a high accent that inspired immediate compliance.

The hands left me. I swayed. I tasted petals on my tongue. My book was in the horseman's hand. He offered me his arm. I took it on instinct and averted my eyes. Stares bored into me. *Bad girl. Mad Girl.* I would do it again!

The man offered me a canteen from his saddlebags and ordered me to drink. I drank. The water was miraculously cool. I spilled it down my chin. I emptied the canteen. He raised an eyebrow and took it back. He found another and splashed water over a handkerchief. I let him wipe at my face. I felt like a child. The cloth was a balm to my hot skin.

"Earl Huxley sends his condolences to your family," said the man.

I opened my eyes. I didn't realize I'd closed them.

"He'd like to extend an offer of employment at his estate. Consider it a standing invitation for when you complete your studies."

I stared at the man and his regal face. Blue eyes. I had never seen eyes so electric. I worried they might see too much. His words reached me slowly.

"Employment? Doing what?"

My lip was too big. My nose clotted with blood.

The man's mouth quirked. "I would say you could be a guard. You have the strength of one. But you fight like a common brawler."

"I'm to fight?"

"No, dear girl." The man chuckled. "You're a poison girl like your mother, yes?"

My body felt far away. "What do you call the white flowers? The ones with the violet star in the center? I've felt odd ever since."

The man's eyes sparked. "You're immune to florals?"

"I think so. I ate a few."

"A few!"

"Was that wrong?"

The man's teeth were very straight and white. I couldn't read his smile. He threw the bloody handkerchief to the ground. Guilt squeezed my chest. Had I ruined such fine fabric? Did he not intend to keep it?

"You're exceptionally gifted," he said.

No one had ever told me that.

"I write poetry too," I said because I thought this could matter to the man. It'd never mattered to anyone else but Ma.

He returned my book to my hands. "The earl would personally see to it that you could continue your studies. If you wished, he could bring the finest mentors to the estate."

"Could I meet Phaela Mirrors?" I asked. "Did you know my—"

"*Carlotta!*" Da's bellow ripped my fantasies from me. He was far down the road, so distant that I couldn't make out his face.

The horseman's smile fell. He folded a slip of creamy paper into my hand. "You're destined for more than this small place could offer. If you ever have need of it, the earl's home is open to you." He hauled himself up into the saddle.

I reached for him. He couldn't leave. This was the future I wanted, and if he left, he would take it with him.

"I want to go now," I said with my bruised lip and fevered brain.

Da was running, closing in with long strides. The horse snorted and pawed the ground.

"Soon," said the man.

My father was upon us. I didn't miss the glare between the men—the horseman up high looking down his nose, Da's chin raised in defiance. He angled himself between me and the horseman.

"You've come to deliver my late wife's pay, I expect?" Da said tightly.

"This is a tumultuous time," the horseman replied, "and Earl Huxley is a busy man with a large estate to manage."

"I'm owed my wife's wages." Da caught the horse's reins and lowered his voice to a simmer. The horse huffed but otherwise remained as coolly unbothered as its rider. "Huxley is late, and my wife is dead. Damn his estate! And damn you for whispering rotten promises in my daughter's ear. Deliver this death allowance, and I won't write again."

The horseman slapped Da's hand away. Chin tilted to the horizon, he spurred the horse on, and I watched him thunder away down the road, taking our promised futures with him. I clenched the slip of paper in my fist, scared Da might discover it and rip it away.

Da cupped my face in his hands, glanced to the small crowd of onlookers and back to me. My teacher came forward, her face stony. The bloody handkerchief was still at our feet. Da noticed me noticing it and examined me—bruised face, ripped dress, bloodied silk.

"She hurt me," I explained, "so I hurt her back."

Reed stopped before she reached us, grasped the cord around her neck, and drew a talisman from where it'd been hidden beneath her dress. Her eyes shone with tears, but she trembled with fury. "You're as good as the king," she hissed, holding the talisman against me like a ward. "A devil lives in you!"

The circle of green glass caught the light as it swung on its cord, spearing sunlight into my eyes. My head pounded. The rage leapt back to my chest. To hold a ward against the living! I coughed up a nasty laugh. I stepped forward to snatch the talisman from her. *I am living still!*

Da caught me. "We're going home," he said, steering me away from the schoolyard.

I lunged to retrieve the fine, bloody handkerchief. I'd wash it, and it would be mine. I tripped over my feet, and Da put an arm around my shoulders, ushering us fast down the road. I cast a glance over my shoulder. It was the last time I would see my teacher.

She held her hands skyward. How funny. The cleric said I was the special one. I didn't need anyone to intercede. I'd entreat the angel myself.

Da said nothing to me during the two hot miles home, only squeezed my hand while I held my fatal wish in the other. On this walk, as on every walk, we passed abandoned fields of skeletal maize stalks. Most had been burned by the sun. Some had been burned by fire. I'd never seen it happen, but everyone knew the smoke that would cloud the sky. Everyone knew a farmer who didn't merely give up but who harbored enough malice for the land that spited him to set it ablaze.

Sweat clung my dress to me by the time we arrived home. I unclenched my fist to find the horseman's note damp and bloodstained from the handkerchief, the ink indecipherably smeared.

FOUR

A WEEK LATER, THE well-dressed man on the tall black stallion returned. Or maybe it was a different man and a different stallion. I imagined the wealthy could have as many of these as they wanted. I saw him from my bedroom window. Before I could reach the door, Da sent him away. My rush downstairs had made my body light, and the floor turned unsteady. I slouched against the wall and watched Da pass. He wouldn't look at me. We didn't meet for dinner that night or breakfast the next morning. Da had given up on me. So be it.

I locked myself in my room. I tried to read and couldn't. I tried to write and couldn't. What more was there to say? Eventually, hunger brought clarity. Da thought I had given up on him. I would prove to him otherwise. I would make something simple to bring us back together.

Pawing through our cabinets, I found the empty flour jar, three spilled grains of rice, and a wedge of stale flatbread spotted with dark mold. I retreated upstairs and admired my perfect flowers until my breaths steadied.

Ma's death allowance never appeared. A new wave of extraordinary heat swept across the south of the kingdom, and I saw no one on the road in front of our house. Rainless thunderstorms tore the skies at night, and I tore apart my dresses with equal measures of boredom and hatred. Piled at my bedside—strips of taffeta and lengths of lace and a deconstructed mourning dress. By candlelight and lightning flash, I stitched them into one, alternating fabric until I had a monstrosity of a garment. Flamboyant pink hitched to mourning gray, haphazard ribbon and lace demarcating the border between celebration and solemnity. I was no seamstress. I was good at nothing, as my teacher had implied. My stitches bunched and joined at odd angles. The dress was not pretty, but it was undeniably striking. I would feel everything, all the good and bad I deserved; I would carry it against my skin. I slept with pricked thumbs and new blisters and was satisfied.

Snapping branches startled me awake. Heavy from sleep, I trudged to the window and looked down to see my father pacing circles around the dead pine in front of the house. He'd consider a branch, test its height, then rip it free of the trunk. He continued this way until none remained in his reach. On the sunburned earth, he lined them up and considered them once more. I pulled the curtains across the window and retreated to my bed. The sight unnerved me. This was no farmers' work that I'd ever seen.

I dozed on and off through the day, waking drenched in sweat to snaps in the yard. I curled in on myself. The sun set. I waited for the creak that signaled my father's boot on the step, but it never came. Chest tight, I went to the window. Da stood beneath the stripped tree, his back to the house. The moon was full and high that night in an unclouded sky, casting the tree's long, dead shadow across the cracked ground. Bruised blue on silver. The moon traveled through the sky and Da remained still. My teacher's glass talisman flashed in my memory. I returned to my bed and plucked a petal from one of my flowers. They remained as radiant as when I'd cut them, just as I thought they would.

I needed to forget this vision of my father. I took the petal on my tongue, and like a friend, the flower pulled me softly under.

Da was gone when I woke. His room was empty. He was not in the field. The branches he'd lined up in the yard were nowhere to be found. It was noon, and the tree had no shadow, but I could feel it reaching, long and cold, from that night. I stood where Da had, and despite the sweltering heat, I could have stayed there forever. My head throbbed in time with my heartbeat, the lingering proof of the petal's mercy.

A man came down the path, his feathered veil swaying with each step. The wind had disappeared with the storms, but his white robe billowed as he walked, not a bit of skin exposed. He called out to me, and I studied his approach. He moved like someone humble and yet above the world at once, able to hurry despite the heat, no stain of sweat on his clerical garb. A satchel slouched heavy on his hip but did not impede his pace.

"You'll burn if you stay out!" he said, unfolding a white parasol. He held it over my head, and his loose sleeve slipped down to his elbow. I marveled at his dark and holy skin. "Is your father at the market?"

I stared at him. I couldn't speak.

"Poor girl! You need water! Shall we go inside?" he asked, gesturing to the door with his free hand.

I was startled to find the house still standing behind me. At the porch, the white blooms thrived. The cleric offered his arm as the horseman had and guided me past them as though they were fanged and lurking things. We went inside.

With all the shutters closed against the sun, it was dark but not much cooler. I navigated the familiar shadows. My grip on the cleric's arm changed. In the transition from light to dark, I was the only one who could lead. He fumbled through the kitchen and pulled out a chair for me. When I continued to stand dazedly, he prompted me with a soft "Please, miss." The petals were very strong. I sat. I folded my hands atop the pine table my father had built before I was born, before the trees died of thirst, before carpentry—like agriculture—became another bygone skill.

Defeated by the emptiness of our cabinets, the cleric returned to me. "Your father must be at the market?" he said hopefully.

"It is very hot," I said, "for the market." My voice sounded far away, these words spoken by some distant but preserved piece of me that still practiced the basic decorum of answering when spoken to. "And I've seen no traders on the road."

"When did you last eat? Drink?"

What an interesting consideration! I turned to look the cleric in the eyes and met his veil, impassive and soft. I thought of kissing it.

The cleric unpacked his satchel, setting a small bundle of bread and dried fruits on the table along with a jar of water. I licked my lips and noticed for the first time how cracked they were, how dry my tongue.

"Please, miss," he prompted again.

My hands shook as I lifted the water to my mouth. How amazing that these men could procure water! Despite the veil, I felt the intensity of his gaze as I drank, then inhaled this small feast.

"I hope you can forgive me for attending the village gossip, but I heard you were dismissed from school."

The dry morsel of bread in my mouth was suddenly a stone. I stood, my chair scraping across the floor. I would go upstairs. "I'm sure Da will be home soon," I said, though the truth settled at once. I was alone.

I broke out in a new sweat. Not from heat but fear. I had lost Ma, and that meant Da could die too. Was he already dead and had I continued on, as oblivious in my living as before? Was I about to send away the last person in the world who might care for me?

My scarf was damp against my forehead. I tore it off. Sweat drenched the underarms of my dress. I wanted out of my skin, out of my body.

"I'm not here with judgment," the cleric said behind me. "These are hard times for all. I only wanted to see how you fared after our first meeting."

I hadn't given much thought to how I fared. Thinking would make things worse. I preferred to sleep and, maybe, to dream.

"If you ever have need of it, the doors of the angel's monastery are open to you. I can assure you'd be respected and provided for."

I recalled the horseman and grinned. My lip cracked. I tested it with my tongue and tasted blood. Why marry as my father wanted me to when men would appear with better promises?

"What would be my duties? At the monastery?" I asked.

"Our medicines can only do so much against poisoning, and growing the staples for our remedies is harder with each year. With your help, we could continue to care for the villagers' health while using precious water for other crops."

"The villagers would not touch me."

"People will set much aside in matters of life or death."

I thought of the smudged note, still under my pillow like a wish. Would my horseman return? I would never complete my studies now. Did my unfinished education endanger the earl's offer? I pored over the ruined strip of paper in the secret hours of the night and wanted to cry. Surely another horseman would visit. I only needed to intercept him before Da could. *If Da was even . . .*

"I'll consider it."

"I understand your mother served the aristocracy and that you might also have hopes in that vein, but be warned—by allowing a devil on the throne, the rich have made themselves willing servants of hell."

I clenched my teeth so I didn't laugh. I didn't care who I served, and I cared even less who the ones I served allied themselves with. Upstanding morals had saved no one in the borderlands. At least the king and those in her castle did not have to scrape together a life in the dust.

I leaned toward the cleric. "Do you know much about the king?"

Contempt overtook the cleric's mild voice. "King Eric cursed us with her. A kingdom as small and stricken as ours cannot hope to match the military power of our neighbors, so Eric looked below for answers."

"And summoned King Emelia?"

"Summoned her father. I won't speak that evil name here. When the contract went bad, as all deals with hell do, the duke took Eric's soul but couldn't be bothered with the other half of the deal and so sent his daughter to rule Eric's forfeit kingdom."

"Do you truly believe she's as terrible as they say? She must care about the borderlands and the water. Otherwise, she wouldn't send her caravans or maneuver for our access to the big rivers."

The cleric's veil didn't stir. I felt his judgement. Then, with a wave of his hand, his mild voice returned. "Put the king and her ways out of your mind. Nothing good can come of what devils are up to. All we can and must do is fortify our hearts."

But my thirst was not slaked. "I've heard the king is too beautiful to look upon."

Standing, the cleric brushed the nonexistent creases from his robe. "Then it is good we do not have to see her. Let's speak of her no more. It's bad luck to dwell on matters of the below. Do not call their attention to you." He clasped my hands in his, and I jumped at the contact. His skin was cool and smooth, and I was embarrassed by my sweaty palms. "I implore you to seek the shelter of the angel. Their wings are expansive enough to shield us all. Through them, someone as blessed as you could arrive at the holy knowing that only clerics aspire—"

The front door banged down the hall. The cleric jerked away from me as if caught in sin.

My mouth was dry. "Da?" I called, my heartbeat throbbing in my temples.

I listened for his boots or the creak of the floor, but only a growing shadow signaled his approach. His silhouette filled the kitchen doorway. On his back, a heavy bundle distorted the shape of him. My blood rushed in my ears.

"Did you go to the market?" I asked.

Da stepped into the candlelit glow of the room. The light cast shadows in the hollows of his face, and I startled at the sight of them. Surely only a week could have passed, yet his weariness had advanced in months. Dark circles bloomed under his eyes. Sunken cheeks made his frown harsh.

"To what do we owe your visit, dear cleric?" He sighed, throwing the lumpy bundle on the table. It was the same pale canvas sack he brought to market, but he always took such care in the packing and arranging so as not to injure any of the most perishable items. Even in the gloom, I could see red dirt staining the canvas, as if he'd dragged it behind him the entire way home. Its contents stuck out at odd, piercing angles made stranger in the candle's guttering light.

The cleric hastily repacked his own satchel. "I thought to check in on Carlotta," he said. The veil did not turn toward my father. "News in the village spreads quickly."

Da crossed his arms and leaned back against the counter. "I didn't know you traded in rumors, cleric."

"I was just on my way." He patted my shoulder. "Be good, dear girl."

We listened to the cleric's retreat. The door closed silence into the house. Da and I stood across from each other, unmoving.

"What did you find at the market?" I asked, forcing cheer into my voice. Maybe, if I could play at normal well enough, this bad week would recede.

I did not like the way my father looked or the way he looked at me. I was happy to have the table between us. When he didn't move or speak, I untied the cord at the mouth of the sack, my hands shaking as I did. Da watched me closely but said nothing. Inside, I didn't find any of the usual treats he hauled back home for us. I didn't understand what I was seeing and stepped back, unsettled by the dark matrix within.

"What's this?" I asked sharply.

"The tree is growing, Carlotta," he said. His lips barely moved as he spoke, but his eyes held the flame of the candle. "I've been watching it grow."

I wanted to call the cleric back. I inched toward the door. I thought of farmers going mad in their fields.

"The merchants would not take the branches, but they're good quality. Sturdy. I built this house from pine. I know wood."

"But this isn't lumber, Da," I said. "The trees have been dead for years."

He shook his head solemnly. "Not dead." He reached into the sack and withdrew a branch as long as my arm. "Here."

I backed away.

His whisper was insistent, like we had a new family secret. "Here, Carlotta."

I shook my head.

"Here," he repeated, holding the branch with both hands like an offering.

I studied him, then looked at the branch. I drew closer.

This wasn't from the pines in the yard at all. This was from my parents' magnolia on the hill. A single impossible bud dotted the end of the branch.

FIVE

O N THE DAY MY father would die, I heard him laughing in
the yard. It was the kind of laugh one could choke on,
high and straining for air, its own kind of purging. I'd never
heard him make such a noise.

Somewhere in my room, a fly buzzed. The sound made me
itch. I sat up. The edges of my sight blackened. My heartbeat
pulsed in my temples, the sound coursing through my ears. A
tickle on the back of my hand made me glance down. Fresh red
droplets stained my skin. I wiped my nose on the gray stripe of
my dress. At my bedside, my flowers were still so pretty.

Yesterday, I'd walked the mile to Isabella's farm only to
find the house deserted. Their front door was unlatched. Dust
swirled in the entryway. Inside, I clenched my fist and felt
Isabella's hand in mine again. Though I knew the drought had
driven them away, I also felt to blame. I shouldn't have talked to
Isabella. I shouldn't have hoped.

Their cabinets of course were empty. Anyone fleeing north
would've taken the last of their food with them. I'd gone to the
house with no clear purpose because my purpose was everything,
my entire small world—please see me, please help my father. The
monastery was too long a walk to make without water, the village
just as far in the opposite direction.

Regardless, I decided I would see the king. When people weren't whispering about my mother or me, they were whispering about the king. I grew an affinity for her. What evil had the king committed that the cleric found so unspeakable? She was a woman who loved women, and she loved too many of them at once. Years of gossip told me this was the true difference that set her and the neighboring kings apart in the eyes of the people. I needed to know someone who could endure their judgment and continue brazenly on. I needed something to hope for.

On the heels of heat and drought, quiet came to suffocate us No sounds in the yard. From the road. In the house. The world was empty, as if everyone had been swept away by the storm and only we remained. Fear rooted me to where I sat on the edge of my bed. I'd never felt foreboding as a physical force that must be overcome like the wind. My heart beat fast. Pain raked its claws inside my ribs. I doubled over and fought to breathe. I wondered whether people could die from nothing at all, whether feelings were lethal. I balled my fists against my chest. A primal, childish urge to cry for my mother overwhelmed me, but I couldn't picture her face, had no memory of ever being held by her, didn't know what her voice sounded like. Even though I had her letters as proof of her care for me, to my body it was as if she'd never existed. I wanted to be embraced by someone who'd always been a ghost.

As all storms did, this one spun itself out, though I didn't know how long I held my chest and sobbed without tears. I wanted to sleep for months. Instead, I dragged myself upright. I needed to find Da. I needed to take him to the clerics. Yes. They would know how to heal whatever had overcome him. No matter that it was too far. No matter that Da didn't believe in their angel. I needed to get him away from the farm and its hopeless air.

Down the stairs. Out the door. Sunlight was a slap in the face, as if the sun had drifted closer to the earth while I dreamed. I stood stunned by its rays, squinting, forearm across my eyes. In the still yard, the tree had been picked of its branches again, though the pruning went higher than a man could reach. It looked wounded like this, scabbed where the branches had been torn away. I retreated and passed through the kitchen and out the back door. The outdoors was disturbingly bright again. I squinted across the barren field. No sign of Da, but the barn door was cracked. New flower bushes had sprung up around it overnight. I'd forgotten my slippers, and the ground was hot. I hurried. Blood dripped from my nose and stained my lips. Flies buzzed in my face, seeking the sweat on my brow.

I didn't make it inside the barn. Neither had Da. The door was ajar as if he'd opened it and immediately fallen. Only his boot protruded into the light. The rest of his body lay shadowed inside. His ankle had swollen to a bruised purple. I knelt—to do what? My hand hovered there, uncertain.

"Da?" I whispered, as if perhaps he was sleeping.

In answer, a snake the color of the bruise slipped from the shadow of the barn door. I froze with my hand outstretched. The snake's dark scales rippled a pearlescent sheen as he rose to flick his black tongue at me. At his neck, proud spines protruded like a cat's mane. His eyes were a pale and ghostly green.

The snake flicked his tongue against my finger and wound his way up my arm, cool scales a balm in the heat.

"You can rest now, Da," I said, but the words were hollow.

I felt how artificial my rules of the universe had been. Da couldn't die because I'd needed him. Da couldn't die because Ma was already gone. My first impulse at being disproven was petulance because it was safer than grief. Da's death and him denying me a pretty bauble became the same. My raw heart could give me nothing else, not then. The burden of our survival had transferred to me—because I hadn't appreciated how Da had carried it? Because I wasn't worthy of his protection any longer?

Time would tell whether his spirit had chosen this form to haunt me or guard me. I deserved what I deserved.

"I know you dislike them, but we're going to see the clerics," I explained.

The snake constricted on my upper arm. I imagined it was a protest. I turned away from my father's old body. After such a transformation, it was bad luck to stay here. I returned to my room one last time to pack all my books of poetry into a little bag. I'd carry the spirits of both my parents with me. Da slithered up into my hair and around my bun. The nosebleed was bad now, and my hands looked as if I'd killed some small creature. I found a cloth in the kitchen and held it to my face to staunch the bleeding. This was how I departed for my new life.

Wind kicked dust into my hair, my eyes, my mouth. The sky was clouded the same red as the cracked earth, dirtying the sunrays. I wouldn't make it to the monastery. I walked on. The wind picked up, the world turned hazy, and I lost the horizon, but a flash of white cut through the storm where I thought it might be. I imagined an elder cleric's long veil, but no, there was so much white.

Wings descended upon me. With outstretched hands, the angel froze the storm in their grasp. Through a haze of suspended dust, I searched for their face, for a benevolent gaze. I suddenly wanted the cleric's stories to be true. I wanted to witness something holy with my father.

II

HOLY

SIX

T HE CLERICS SAID I would've been lost to the dust storm
without the divine guidance that led them to me. But I'd
lived, and now I hadn't seen the borderland sun in five years.

I nestled deeper into my bed, a nest of sun-bleached linens and
petals and shed snake skins. I wouldn't leave until late evening
to sit with my flowers in the garden under the softer light of the
moon—unless the clerics delivered a poisoned one to me.

A purge meant I wouldn't recover until the following night.
Perhaps even the morning after that if the cause was some berry
my body didn't favor. Most often children came in poisoned
this way and seizing, having wandered from the sight of their
caretakers and been captivated by the first bright thing they saw.
Who could resist red's allure? Adults were likely those who'd
resorted to foraging and misidentified a root or mushroom
they'd added to their basket. Roots left me with the most
vivid dreams for nights. Mushrooms muted my waking hours.
I couldn't read or write after mushrooms, though my mind
buzzed with ideas. Berries were the most agitating. I could not
sit still, and the need for constant movement was so exhausting
it made me cry.

Floral poisonings were rare. People knew well enough to leave
flowers alone. Flowers were for one's enemies.

The Clerical Order of Angelic Restoration were not enemies of the Retributionists as some mistakenly believed, though one could be forgiven for that misunderstanding. A century wasn't much time for a deep ideological wound to scab. The rift was wide, and the witnesses to it still lived their long lives. I'd met several elders who told me they were excommunicated from the clerical summit for the hope or hubris of believing they could restore a broken angel to their home in the sky.

To the Restorationists, my rescue was an omen. I was a symbol. A poison girl's talent, when set to the enlightened duty of atonement, could help balance the sin of the world and unburden the fallen angel so that they could remember themself, recover their scattered feathers, reunite with their twin in heaven, and become the angel who watched over the earth once more. Then, with the blight of all our wars healed, we could live in bliss forever after.

This belief was heretical to the first and older Order of Angelic Retribution, which preached that poison girls had no hope of redemption and were another expression of the failing world. The fallen angel's task was not to return to heaven but to wake and judge the sinful, eliminating us from the earth so that only the holy remained.

Da hadn't liked talk of sin. I understood why now. Regardless of which clerical doctrine one chose, Ma could never be human within it. We either rose or fell. We were mythical. We couldn't stand like people with our feet on the ground.

With the drought, the Restorationists abandoned the southern monastery to join their singular northern one. Of course, I'd gone with my rescuers. They said I'd been blessed with a vision and accepted my ideas for my spiritual atonement like commands from the angel themself: I wanted a room with no windows, a small plot of the garden for my daily labor, Tuesdays reserved for my silence, seven mourning dresses made in the southern style, and for none of the poisoned to ever thank me. Within this structure, I wrote my sad poems and ate humble food and whispered to my deadly flowers under moonlight. Da continued to grow and shed his skin, and we were content and wanted for nothing, just as the cleric had promised.

Scuffling and crying echoed down the hall, and I sat up to light a second pillar candle for the clerics to see by. Then torchlight cracked into my room. Two clerics carried in a woman on the verge of fainting—or dying. Her head swayed, long braids swinging free of her scarf. Her eyes rolled back in her head. I slipped from bed and knelt on the floor, resting my forehead against the cool stone and extending my hands in front of me. Around my neck, Da stirred, smooth scales fresh from a recent shed gliding down my arm. He often looped around my forearm and presided over the purge.

Accustomed to my process, the clerics delivered the woman gently to the floor and said nothing about how she'd come to the monastery or what she'd consumed. These stories were distracting. My body would know the truth. Their steps retreated, and my door groaned shut. Only then did I reach for the woman. I sat with my legs folded beneath me and my eyes closed. Faces were also distracting. The poisoned would not remember me, and I didn't want to remember them. I had yet to fail, but when I inevitably did, I didn't want to invite a haunting. One soul stuck to me already.

I felt in the dark and found the woman's hand, trailed my fingertips up her arm and found her heart, her throat, her mouth. Resting my left hand over her forehead and pressing my right thumb to her lips, I began my work.

Saving someone from poisoning was easiest if they were not poisoned to begin with. This was how most poison girls worked—how my mother had worked, I now understood. It was easiest to act as a shield for others, to test the world and determine if it was safe before everyone proceeded with their lives. Purging poison from one's own body was infinitely easier than locating it within another and drawing the effects into oneself. At the monastery, all of my work was the latter. I knew poisons like friends: the colors they wore, how they moved, where they liked to linger and settle. I retraced my way from the woman's lips to her breastbone, splayed my fingers, pressed down. Within her: palpitating heart, constricting chest, stuttering lungs. I opened myself to the poison like welcoming home a toxic lover and let the pain seize me, fold me. I sucked in a breath, dimly aware of my cheek on the woman's chest, how our hearts synchronized a frantic rhythm. I sank deeper, turned feverish. It was always at this point, when my pain equalized with the poisoned's, that I thought it would capsize me into death's arms.

Da squeezed my wrist, grounding me through the wave. This sort of purge was locating a tight fist in a dark room and prying the fingers open to rescue the bleeding heart inside. My breath seized. One last push, birthing the poisoned back into the life they had always lived.

The clerics were kind to always tuck me back into bed after the purge, when I was unconscious and brimming with another's misfortune. I woke with Da's weight curled on my chest, the second candle snuffed, and the woman gone. I hoped she had survived. That was the only question I ever asked the clerics afterward, the only thing I needed to know.

I couldn't save my mother or father, and no amount of resurrecting others would return my parents to the world as they had been. I knew this. Still, I tallied the saved as if the number held any meaning, as if I might be able to return home after my service and find it untouched by disaster.

The clerics offered little guidance beyond vague encouragement. When would I have suffered enough to cleanse my soul of its sinful inheritance? When would the fallen twin angel notice all my good work and consider a return to heaven? There was no number at which either of us ascended. Five years had passed, and I wasn't sure whether what I was doing at the monastery was atonement. I didn't think one could grow bored with atonement.

My favorite part of monastic life was midweek temple, my only window into the outside world. Restorationist temples were humble—a roofless circle of columns all that demarcated sacred space. We performed our rites under moonlight that shone silvery on the clerics' veils, and I fantasized about pledging myself to the angel just so I could feel something so soft on my face.

Seekers who favored the Restorationists' view of a gentle awakened angel made the trek to our little alcove of the mountain, bringing rumors from merchants who'd recently departed the capital for the countryside. I hugged the perimeter of the temple, slipping behind columns to eavesdrop on their nervous conversation. The castle was sourcing larger than usual quantities of food as though for a banquet, though no one knew the occasion. The great grandchildren of the original castle's architect estimated the castle was a foot taller than it was this time last year, owing to the hellish growths protruding from the masonry. The merchants who delivered goods to the castle reported that none of the king's dead poison girls were actually buried in the castle's cemetery, giving rise to rumors that the king must've performed some unholy ritual to disappear the bodies. And so on.

I kept a close record of any mention of poison girls—with special attention to the king's—and recited these bits of information for the duration of temple until I could hurry back to my room and scribble what I'd learned in my journal.

Questions I had no way of learning the answers to: How many poison girls lived in the kingdom, and how many were in the king's service at once? What I did know: The king had declared two days of mourning since my arrival at the monastery. I was the only one who observed.

New moon temple arrived a week later without pilgrims to observe it. I waited at the pass with the head cleric, wind ruffling the feathers of her veil and harassing the flame of her torch, to welcome our nonexistent visitors. In keeping with clerical tradition, she did not have a personal name, only an astrological title denoting her position, but privately, I thought of her as Marta.

Tonight, Marta was troubled.

Five years of living with veiled holy people possessed of frustratingly measured voices meant I'd learned other ways to read emotion—the way one curled their shoulders or bent their head, an agitated flick of the veil when one swallowed a scoff, when a usually brisk cleric slowed or a patient cleric hurried.

Tonight, Marta's left hand held her right side, a clutch that betrayed pain or anxiety. She never crossed her arms, always clasping her hands serenely in front of her or letting them rest by her sides.

Nothing moved on the path, and nothing moved in the woods below. This had never happened. The trek to the monastery could be hard on the valley's elders, but those who had the means always brought a horse or cart to ensure all who wanted could attend. I walked a few paces beyond the cleric and her flame for a better look at the village, but where I was used to seeing a host of twinkling lights, only a few burned valiantly against the night.

Over the wind, Marta called to me. Above us, a din broke out near the temple. A shout, protestations, and an inhuman shriek. I felt I had no distance from it, as if someone had ambushed me with a hot needle to my ears. I clapped my hands against my head but could not escape. Then quiet. When I remembered the rest of my body, I was crumpled in the path. Marta, having rallied before me, cast our torch down into the rocky shadows below and pulled me out of the open.

Marta was not warm, none of the clerics were, but now she held me to her as if I were her own child. The contact was as much a shock as our danger. Was it only when she feared she might lose me that I became a girl worth protecting?

"Stay out of sight. I will find the others."

"What was that?" I demanded.

The wind ripped at her veil, exposing a chin, a cheek. "I don't know."

"Then—"

"*Stay*." And she disappeared up the dark, twisting path.

I counted to ten and followed. The billowing white robe and trousers of the clerics was a beacon in the dark. I let her gain a lead and hoped my mourning dress was enough to hide me if she glanced back. A woman's voice drifted down from our alcove, her words chopped by the wind. The speaker was unfamiliar to me, but she carried on at ease as if she was used to entertaining. Where the head cleric took the direct path to the temple, I took the one that split higher, overlooking the temple and courtyard gardens. The torches were still lit in preparation to receive pilgrims, and within their glow, the monastery's fifteen clerics stood holding a line against an invading army of two.

A knight in imposing black armor stood at attention behind a woman in a shimmering red ballgown and lace opera gloves who looked ready to burst into song. Where the borderlands favored earth-toned garments, monastery and valley life was lived in austere neutrals. In neither of my lives had I seen someone so extravagant as this woman. I wondered how she had arrived. To venture up a mountain in a ballgown! She was powerful in her finery. My fear melted at the sight of her. I'd never seen a woman with such long hair locked as men wore it. She styled it in a pile atop her head save for two locks left loose at either temple. A queen, I thought. Only her crown was missing.

"Is a civil conversation coercion?" she asked theatrically, pacing the cleric's battle line. "I fail to see how my invitation is so nefarious when you're guilty of exactly what you accuse the king of—trapping a poor girl without recourse." She raised her voice, calling for me. "Carlotta, my dear!"

Hearing my name in her mouth, I remembered the beating heart in my chest and the breath in my lungs. *I am living still!* My old dreams returned to warm me. I stood, I thought, to call out to her.

"She will not speak with you."

The head cleric advanced into the torchlight, and upon seeing her, the line of clerics regrouped to encircle the woman and her knight.

"Carlotta has lived with us for five years," Marta continued. "She's remained devoted to her work and saved hundreds of lives. If you take her, the valley will suffer."

"I'm not *taking* her. I'm *inviting* her to a party! The king wishes to show her appreciation for our kingdom's poison girls, honoring precisely the hard work you've praised Carlotta for."

"She would woo Carlotta away from us."

The woman tapped the breastplate of her statuesque knight with an elegant finger, and the clerics flinched, though I'd never seen the knight move. Like an ornamental piece in a grand hall, it seemed hollow and harmless. I stared at it, the torch flames dancing on the black mirrored faceplate, the vengeful curve of the helm, and knew the knight couldn't be a knight at all. It was magic. Around my neck, Da hissed a warning and slipped down into my sleeve.

"Perhaps, as I have said, we should let the lady in question choose?" said the red woman, turning to pin me with her gaze as if she had seen me all along.

The clerics' veils followed her line of sight, and Marta broke from the circle as if she could grab me down from the ledge herself.

She placed her hands over her heart, a silent plea. I bent to find a handhold, and she shook her head. "Don't," she whispered, her veil stirring with her breath.

I turned my back to her to pick my way down the slope of rock, choosing carefully where I stepped only to have my footing crumble as I reached the bottom. Marta caught me with a soft *oof* and I found myself staring up into the face of the red woman. So near, her attention burned me.

Her eyes held the fervent glimmer of a cleric's after a vision. Her lips quirked in a grin ready to bite. If the king had clerics devoted to her cause of decadence and secrecy, this woman was one of the chosen. Gold eyelids. Long black lashes. Full red lips. She extended her hand, and I took it, let her steady me and pull me up. "Carlotta," she said, her tongue caressing the syllables of my name. I stared. She stroked my cheek, and I flinched at the fine texture of her lace glove. "Oh, you're the prettiest poison girl I've ever seen! Not even these dull clothes can rob your beauty. The king will *adore* you! Here." And she drew a small roll of paper from her cleavage. My face turned hot. The paper was warm. "If you'd like to attend the ball, you have only to sign this. We'll see to it that you have a personal escort to the castle."

The wind died, our mountain holding its breath with the clerics. I didn't look at them, wouldn't allow guilt to burden my heart. They must've known I couldn't refuse this. A chance to see the king! To meet other poison girls! A little world made just for us when I had never felt a part of this one.

I was still unworthy of the monastery's inner rooms despite the clerics' promises that I'd one day, through my sacrifice, ascend to the purity needed to enter them. And what would I find once I was there? Would it have been worth these years? The king did not require atonement of her girls, didn't weigh the purity of their souls against angel feathers. They were beloved as queens.

I wanted to feel beloved.

I asked for the red woman's name, and she took my hand in hers, raising it to her mouth for a kiss and staining my skin a scandalous carmine. Her lips curved as if she knew her own name to be a delicious secret. "Meet me in a fortnight, and you will know."

Facing the clerics once more, she dropped into a deep curtsy. It was so deferential, I wondered whether she mocked them. Head bowed, she thanked them for their audience and, without a backward glance, made for the path to the valley. While all our attention was on her dazzling performance, the black knight vanished.

Seventh Starlight Seeker, otherwise known as the head cleric and—affectionately—Marta, stood in the door to my room and wrung her hands. She'd exhausted every indirect suggestion that I not attend the king's ball and was too much of a cleric to directly tell me what she wanted me to do.

Fifth Starlight Wanderer, the cleric who had witnessed my first purge and the only one to have known my father before his transformation, stood gravely by my wardrobe. I knew he was standing gravely because at any minor disruption to the monastery's routine, he'd declare it proof of my key role in restoration. Since the red woman's departure, he'd been quiet.

I held the invitation gingerly in my hands, remembering the horseman's ruined note from years ago. I wouldn't suffer the same loss again. This time, I would have my entrance into aristocratic society. I would wear a pretty dress and eat rich food and forget about my past for one night. I would make myself into someone new and worthy of the king's attention.

I would meet my peers, and their fellowship would prove I didn't bear the weight of sacrifice alone.

Finally, Fifth Wanderer spoke. "The ball presents a great opportunity for us." If the head cleric heard him, there was no indication. Given no protest from her, he stepped forward, drawing a small vial from the sleeve of his robe. He held it out to me, and I took it, studying the white powder inside.

"Fifth!" the head cleric hissed. She glanced behind her and shut the door in a hurry. "If an assassination attempt is traced back to the monastery, it will be the end of the Restorationists. King Eric would have razed this temple and the valley to quell any threat of treachery. Imagine what *she* could do if provoked. We put everyone at risk, not just us."

"But if we succeed—" he started with conviction.

The head cleric cut him off, reciting the mission. "We work patiently in service to the angel. We teach our pilgrims how to find the lost feathers, and we reassemble the wings." Her veil flicked toward me. "We are healers," she huffed. "Do not put Carlotta in this position."

"Carlotta is the only one who *could*. The king will be at her most vulnerable when surrounded by poison girls. She wouldn't suspect them, and few have Carlotta's talent for extraction. This is our chance to wipe a great evil from the earth. The scale of such a rebalancing could change our world overnight."

I rolled the vial in my palm, realization settling. "This is my weeping luna from my garden?" I asked.

The clerics' veils turned to me.

"You *crushed* my flowers?" I asked, voice rising.

"It's one of few poisons she's vulnerable to," Fifth Wanderer tried to reason. "I didn't hurt the bush. I took only one clipping."

My heartbeat roared in my ears. My body shook. "My flowers are mine!"

It was a nonsensical thing to say. I didn't know how to speak in that moment, only that something big and threatening had crashed over me. Why had I been asked to assassinate the king with my own flowers when I only wanted to be beautiful and adored for one night? Why could I not have this one wish? I despised my life.

Why was the entire world about who was evil and how to survive them? The borderlands had died. An entire swath of land gone forever. That was evil, but no simple assassination would bring back the dead earth.

"See reason, Carlotta," the cleric pleaded, kneeling where I sat.

The head cleric crossed her arms—crossed them!—but didn't intervene. Was she persuaded to this terrible plot so quickly?

"This is the world we've been working to create," Fifth Wanderer continued. "We restore the angel, and with them, every lost soul. You'd see your parents again."

"How dare you speak of them," I hissed.

No angel was coming to save us. There was no angel. What ideal being would require me to endure so much pain? Five years. It'd been five years! And misery before that. Da was right. It was too easy for clerics to make claims when they didn't have to shoulder the burden.

I tossed the vial into my mess of bedclothes and stood. It felt good to tower over someone. I wanted to hurt him. I wanted someone to hurt the way I did.

"You should've left me to die with the borderlands," I said and was delighted by his flinch, that twitch of the veil and ruffled feathers, a full-body flicker of doubt.

I strode from my room and back into the night, the invitation clutched in my hand. The garden was the only place in the monastery that felt like mine, and my body guided me to my corner of the courtyard on instinct. I settled among the flower bushes, lying flat in the dirt with the little roll of paper pressed to my breastbone. My heart beat beneath my hands as I watched the dark sky. No one followed me. Nothing stirred.

I imagined myself wearing the red woman's dress, how the ballroom chandeliers would catch its shimmer. I imagined the sisterly embrace of my fellow poison girls, how the eldest among us might cup my face and tell me that the years of pain were behind me and I could be happy now, on this night. I imagined that the king would extend her hand, compliment my features as the red woman had, and invite me to dance.

This was where the vision broke. I didn't know how to dance or even what the king looked like. Rumors abounded, of course, but the only consistent traits among them were that she was very tall and wore no crown.

Taking up the invitation again, I slipped my finger under the red seal. It broke with a pop of sparks and hiss of smoke, and Da curled tight on my wrist. "It's okay," I soothed. "It's just magic." As if magic were always simple and harmless. When had I ever encountered it? The invitation took on a new thrill. I rolled onto my belly and angled the paper so that it caught the best of the light.

Dearest Carlotta, it began, the written words an intimate whisper at my ear. *It is with pleasure and gratitude that I announce my first annual ball in honor of our kingdom's poison girls. I am moved by your valiant devotion. Through your gifts, we flourish, and all of us at the helm of this kingdom have lived too long in a state of complacence and expectation of this sacrifice. Your commitment must no longer be taken for granted. My late and beloved Anne inspired this celebration, and it is in dedication to her memory that I extend this invitation to all of you.*

Your presence honors me.

It was signed simply, *Emelia*. I stared at the signature, unadorned and without title, like the king had stepped down from her throne to meet me eye to eye. It was personal and unguarded, that bare first name, and I wanted to depart immediately. The red woman said I only needed to sign if I wanted to attend, and my hand ached for a pen. The ink melted into the paper and presented me with a blank page. New words floated to the surface. This ink was freshly red.

To ensure my invitation safely reached your hands, I made a small sacrifice. To reach me, would you return it in kind?

Da hissed, startling me back to awareness of the garden. He wound tight around my wrist, constricting until I couldn't move my hand.

"Stop! Stop it!" I tried to pry him loose.

He struck out as if to bite, and I narrowly jerked my hand away. In all our years at the monastery, he'd never behaved so erratically. I'd never been afraid of him. I shook my wrist, demanded that he release me. My fingertips prickled and went numb.

"Stop!" I screamed, on the verge of tears, and this time, the bite landed. I went still. Pain was slow to register. I stared numbly at my hands, at the blood welling up from the bite. Running footsteps echoed toward me. Blood dappled the paper, and it caught fire as if tossed in a hearth. I cried and dove to smother the flames, but hands caught me and pulled me away from where the letter smoldered to ash. My chest was hollowed by the sight.

Someone shook me. Someone waved a hand before my face. Someone repeated my name. I blinked.

"What happened?" This was Marta, her veil inches from my face.

If I had to stay on this mountain, I would throw myself off of it.

A cleric bent to examine my hand. Another called for bandages.

I shook. I grit my teeth. "Leave me alone!"

The courtyard went still.

I shouldered around Marta and knelt where the letter had been, scooping the ashes into my hands. Nothing was left to salvage; I knew this, had seen it burn. My tears turned into sobbing turned into howling. The monastery had not seemed so terrible until I was presented with such a sparkling exit. Who, twice in a life, received once-in-a-lifetime invitations and saw them ruined? Who but me? I was cursed, surely. There was no other explanation. A dead mother who cursed me. A father who haunted me—because I was fundamentally bad? Because I had failed him? A dead homeland that the world had forgotten even before drought took it. A cleric who rescued me only to deliver me into this. Five years of torturous saviorship was not atonement enough. How long was I meant to live in the grip of misery, saving every life but my own? Thinking hurt, and I needed not to think.

With soot-streaked hands, I grabbed for the nearest flower, heedless of its thorns. The clerics cried out. I bit into the white bloom, tearing it free of its stem. Da could not stop me. No one would stop me. I would sleep.

Someone wrenched the stem from my hands, but it was too late. The petals were in my mouth. Dear bitter, dear sting. I couldn't move my tongue, but I could laugh. I opened my empty fist and found thorny bites along my palm. The cleric who'd grabbed at me dropped the stem. They had matching wounds, their palm speckled with blood. Reality blurred. I had only ever eaten single petals when I sought blankness. Never an entire flower. How interesting! How fast my flowers were! I was very heavy and growing heavier. It took so many holy hands to buoy me. White feathers closed out the sky.

Weeping luna, hold me.

SEVEN

H umming woke me. Stars above. Stone below. Turning my head took every effort. "She's awake!" someone exclaimed. The humming stuttered. Blue candles flickered. A circle of veils surrounded me.

Marta, kneeling at the crown of my head, cupped my face and murmured fervent praises to the angel. She smudged cool, perfumed clay on my forehead, and that's when I noticed the fever, hot and sticky deep in my bones. I sighed and reached for her. She swiped at the tears on her chin and squeezed my hand. I liked this, the simple comfort of hand-holding.

With my other hand, I felt the grooves in the stone. We were at the temple's heart. The clerics had placed my body atop the angel's carved sigil as we did when praying for the sick. I was not sick. I'd been sleeping.

"My dear girl, my dear girl," Marta repeated like a stricken mother. "Oh, I thought I'd lost you."

Lost me? My flowers never hurt me, not for long.

Too much to keep eyes open. I lost the stars.

⬥

A strong waft of incense revived me. Irritation spiked through me. Why wouldn't they let me rest?

A brittle snake skin crunched under me and disintegrated. I was back in my room. Marta was here again, patient and faithful as always. I lacked these core qualities. I could never have been one of them.

"Oh, Carlotta," she sighed as if we'd been mid-conversation and I'd said something that made her weary.

"Was that borderland clay?" I asked her.

"Some of the very last." She shifted where she sat at my bedside. "Do you remember what happened after you rejected Fifth Wanderer's proposal?"

"Of course," I snapped, upset by the memory I had worked so hard to escape. I stared at the ceiling and avoided her veil.

"We were scared," Marta said, her voice wavering with emotion, "that you meant to kill yourself."

Startled, I looked at her fully, how she clasped her hands tightly upon her lap.

"How would I have done that? Why would you think that?"

"Even you can exceed your limits. Every girl eventually meets a poison too strong for her. An entire bloom of weeping luna—it's enough to kill a dozen hearty men in an instant. You must see why we were scared."

"I only meant to sleep for a long time."

Marta kneaded her hands, then bowed her head. "I often forget you're not one of us. There's a reason we don't invite people as young as you to take the veil. We all grieved the borderlands in our own way, but I didn't realize how your sadness endured. Your reaction to the king's messenger showed me how vibrant you can be. I want to make your life here better. You have only to tell me what you need."

The only answer was to let me go. For all the clerics' rituals, there was no purifying me. When I regained my strength, I would go into the world. I had no belongings or prospects, but I would go. What was a place of healing for others had eroded something in me.

"Fifth Wanderer doesn't love me. He only loves what I can do and what I could symbolize. To know me would mean losing hope." I hesitated. "Maybe even faith."

Marta was still for a long moment. I was sure I offended her. I hoped I had. "What do you mean?" she asked, her tone maddeningly even.

"I'm not here out of any goodwill. I'm here because I've grown too tired to move, and you offered me shelter. That's all. I would go with anyone who told me I was special and offered me a life."

"And now that is the king?"

"She intrigues me."

"So you will leave us?"

I watched the ceiling. Could one walk to the castle and simply knock on its doors? I would try.

"I hope you find the right poison girl," I said.

"If the king accepted you, we would have word in a few short months that you're dead."

I reached toward her, palm up, seeking. After a moment, she clasped our hands. Recalling how she grasped me on the path and in the temple as if I were her own cherished child, I asked, "Did you ever think of yourself as a mother to me?" I wanted to know whether there was some affection hidden beneath the veil that I had missed, some softness I could retroactively use to blanket my memories of this place.

"If I did, I haven't been a good one. May the angel forgive me. It was all in service to their restoration."

This answer was unsatisfying, so I said, "I've been a sacrifice."

"If that is how you feel, it is good that you go."

I prodded again. "Into death? That's what you said waits for me."

Marta indulged a rare huff of frustration but kept hold of my hand. "Into whatever life you want to make. I am not a mother, and you are not a girl. We are both seekers in our own way and bear the same responsibility to find our way as we know how."

I patted the bed with my free hand, searching for scales. "Fine," I said, closing this boring conversation about feeling and intention. She would never give me the answer I wanted, which was an emotional one. I wanted someone to beg for me to stay or profess their love. Anything less no longer felt worth my time. I had lived a whole life of bland and measured talk. "Where's my da?"

"We thought, after what happened, it would be best to let him roam the garden."

"No. He'll worry about me."

Marta stood. "I see. I'll fetch him for you."

Though I wanted Da, the ease with which she could leave angered me. I wanted to see her cry again.

My door groaned closed, and I was bereft.

I almost hated how I regained my strength. The clerics stopped fussing over me and grew distant once news spread of my desire to leave. Da seemed once again at ease, content to loop around my neck or my arm during the day or curl on my chest when I rested.

Two pinpricks at my palm's fate line were all that remained of the bite.

My flower had worked. I'd slept for a long time, just as I'd hoped. The moon was again growing full in the sky. But what had the red woman said? The king's ball in a fortnight? I was sorely out of time and sure I'd miss it. I hated the clerics, but I hated my impulses more. Perhaps, if I'd bothered to cultivate their maddening calm, I would've realized that the letter was *a* way, but hopefully not the *only* way.

I braided my hair in neat rows, twining a red cosmos bloom into the hair at my ear. The tails of my braids I pulled over my shoulder. They nearly reached my waist now. The scraps of old pink silk that remained I looped and tied around my hairline, leaving the bloom free. Maybe it was silly to uphold this old farmers' tradition—that it was bad luck for hair to fall in one's face while working or traveling—but even now I felt bare without it. I packed my poetry and journals once more, cushioning them with a spare dress. My future couldn't be so far. It couldn't always be out of reach. I tucked away the Mirrors collection last, a puzzling wave of nostalgia washing over me. I hadn't loved the farm where I first read these poems, but I longed for the uncomplicated dreams I'd entertained back then: my mother and Mirrors and a grand chance at mentorship. The dream had not survived wholly intact. Nothing had. But pieces remained. Mirrors must still be alive. The valley gossip would've brought news of her death to me. I gathered my scraps of hope like this, reasoning coolly as the clerics did. If I had no absolute proof of disaster, I must move forward. The clerical orders had existed thus far with only scattered feathers as hope. My pages did the same for me. With my dreams so enshrined, I closed the door to the room that had been mine for five years.

Outside, the clerics waited for me in a solemn line, their backs to the courtyard garden. Marta, though she was the head cleric, was far from the oldest. Even the elders had lined up to see me, their feathery veils thrown over their shoulders and looped over their arms so as to not drag on the ground. I rarely saw them. We never spoke. I was surprised they would gather to see me off. I knew Marta by her height and her hands, the only exposed skin on a cleric's body. Hers were a practical, square shape with blunt fingertips. Very borderland hands.

Sentimentality crowded my mouth, and I swallowed it down with the building lump in my throat. What was this? I wanted to leave. There was nothing to miss and only my happiness to be gained. Effortfully, I smoothed the tension from my face as I approached Marta. *Breathe, dear girl*, she'd said to me often in our first months here, when the recollection of my final days in the borderlands made me so sick I thought I might die. I'd arrived here a crying, shaking mess, plagued by nightmares that left me numb and blurred at the edges. Something so simple as breathing was impossible when my chest felt bound by an iron cage, when my entire body hurt always. Marta would hold my hands in her square ones and breathe audibly until the worst of these episodes subsided.

Now, Marta offered her hands once more, and I let her hold me and refused to cry. I thought of many things to say and said none of them. I kissed her cheek and met feathers. She pressed a hand against her face, and I saw how it trembled. Plucking a feather free from the end of her veil, she folded it, brilliantly white, into my hand. Then she let me go as if she could bear to touch me no more.

"I'm not a pilgrim," I said, squeezing the feather in my fist.

"No," she said.

"You're not going to try and convince me to stay?"

"No."

"Will you miss me?"

"You would enjoy knowing that I miss you?"

"Yes, very much."

"Even though we are not supposed to become attached as such?"

"Yes."

"Even though this kind of missing would hurt me? Even though this worry would never end? Even though it would distract from my duties as head cleric?"

"I would write to you."

"Do not make me an empty promise. Don't you dare, Carlotta."

I studied my intention, searching for the emptiness Marta suspected me of. "But I do want to write," I said. It was the closest I would ever come to sending a letter home.

A pause. "If I await your letter, I must resign as head cleric."

Her declaration sent a ripple down the line of clerics to either side of her. Marta's serenely clasped hands were now clenched tight.

"I will write," I promised.

Her hands flew to her chest as if to staunch a wound. The clerics broke their line. The elders converged on her with demands. I was crowded out. Shouting, I pushed back, fighting my way to Marta. I found her shaking under the barrage of questions and threw my arms around her. I shouted an apology into the linen of her robe, belatedly declared my love of her, promised that I would update her weekly.

"Go, you foolish girl, on with your life," she huffed, attempting to shepherd me down the corridor and out of the uproar.

"You said I wasn't a girl," I reminded her.

Her hand on my back was firm. "Then stop acting like one. Go!"

The clerics receded from me, an agitated wave of white bending around the corner toward the prayer rooms. I stood alone and breathed and breathed. I would walk down the mountain alone. Down the road alone. Into the valley's village alone. I was alone, and the knowledge briefly rooted me to the spot. I had never been left to make such a sweeping decision about my life and only then felt the weight of it. The realization threatened to push me out of my body. I found my plot in the garden and picked one of each flower—lavender, celadon, and ivory—seeing their colors as if they were new, feeling the wind tumble down the mountain, breathing the damp granite on the air. Running my thumb against the underside of a thorn, I left the courtyard and passed the unlit temple and embarked down the path.

III

HEIGHTS

EIGHT

D AWN BLOOMED WHEN I neared the end of the mountain path. Just below, where the grass turned lush and the road properly began, a black carriage drawn by a black horse and guarded by a black knight stood in wait. Elation and relief flooded me. It was as if the red woman had never departed after our meeting those weeks ago, as if she'd simply skipped back down the mountain and passed this time in her carriage with a book in hand. I quickened my pace, sliding precariously on the loose gravel as I navigated the last hairpin turns of the path.

Next to the ajar door, the knight stood as I had last seen them, cold and misplaced, as if someone had come out into the middle of the wilderness to arrange a suit of armor for viewing. The red woman's arrival had been so surreal that I doubted my first perception of the knight. If I drew close enough, I would surely see the subtle rise and fall of the breastplate, hear a stir of breath in the helm. Unsure of how to greet a knight, I dropped into a curtsy and introduced myself. No acknowledgment followed. I peered into the mirror of the dark faceplate and found a warped version of myself. My limbs were stretched and starved, my face broken on the metal's harsh angle. I looked away. Da turned restless in my sleeve. I thought of calling for the red woman but didn't know her name.

I greeted the door and again received no acknowledgment. I rose to my tiptoes and attempted to peer through the windows, but a black curtain was drawn across them. I called again, peering into the sliver of darkness. Nothing stirred, and I stepped away, circling the vehicle.

The horse's black coat was enviously sleek, and its bearing reminded me of the noble horses that the earl's men had arrived on. Unlike those horses, a strange iteration of blinders completely covered its eyes. It conjured the effect of a muzzle on a feral dog, the implication that a horse's sight was as dangerous as a predator's teeth. I shrank from it, though like its knight, the horse didn't move, didn't react to my presence at all.

I sat on the carriage step and waited for the red woman to return. Though return from where, I wasn't sure. We were miles from the village still. The closest settlement was the monastery. I glanced up at the knight, who still did not move, and wished for some instruction, an explanation of what was proper to do.

Birdsong didn't come this morning. No wind stirred the grass. I grew ill at ease in the too-still air beside the too-still knight and watched them from the corner of my eye, not yet restless enough to abandon my manners. They carried no sword, no visible weapons anywhere. Their armor, with its spines and horns, had disguised this fact until now. I averted my eyes again. The sky grew bright. No sign of the red woman—or anyone. The horse never pawed the ground or flicked its tail. The knight never seemed weary of standing or silence. I had, however, arrived at the end of my patience.

I threw open the carriage door. Two plush benches decorated in embroidered velvet and red satin adorned the interior. Heavy drapes blotted out the window on the opposite side. I peered into the trees, then at the knight once more. No one disapproved, so I stepped inside.

The door shut, plunging me into darkness. I felt along the edges but could find no latch. Throwing the curtains aside, I saw the knight had vanished. The carriage lurched forward. I fell into the mound of cushions with a startled yelp, and Da curled tight on my shoulder.

"We're okay. We're safe," I assured him automatically, struggling upright out of the pillows.

Safety didn't seem entirely provable, but neither did I feel unsafe. My thoughts spun, but I couldn't chase them to their conclusions. My eyelids grew heavy, then my limbs. I lay down.

A match hissed. Clothes rustled. I turned to follow the sound but could see nothing. Tension banded my head. I imagined the horse and the straps that crossed its face. *A blindfold.* Light bled in around the edges. I thought to reach for it but didn't get far. Soft rope bound my arms against my chest, wrists crossed over my breastbone, only loose enough to demonstrate consideration. I stilled and waited, tracking back through my most recent memories. *I left the monastery. I waited through early morning. I entered the carriage. I slept.*

A shadow fell over me, and I tensed. A clink of porcelain followed. The air was pleasantly warm. My dress was gone.

Another rustle of fabric, a presence drawing close.

"You're safe with me." The woman's deep voice possessed the easy confidence of one accustomed to giving orders. "Would you indulge me in identifying this?"

Her cool hand palmed the nape of my neck. A warm teacup pressed against my mouth. The scent of flowers steamed the air.

Instinct took over again, and I moved to take the cup in my hands. The ropes strained. With the woman so near, with only her command to guide me, the pull of my bindings was a novel thrill. I parted my lips and let the tea wash over my tongue.

Soft pale-pink flower. Bright aftertaste aspiring to berry. Blooming in my mind's eye. Livid violet spots on an innocent blush. Slim, angular leaves on a hairy white stem.

The tea dried my throat and numbed the tip of my tongue.

"King's bane," I pronounced.

An appraising hum.

It didn't kill outright. Anyone so poisoned would feel only vague malaise. It'd be a slow decline that required regular administration to be fatal. So named because for decades it was the poison of choice for targeting vigilant, paranoid monarchs. Its subtle yet pleasant taste made it easy to slip into desserts and teas, masked under the stronger flavor of mundane fruits and flowers. In this blend, hibiscus, rosehips, and raspberry provided cover.

"You're sensitive," the woman noted approvingly. Somewhere behind me and to the side, the teacup clinked again. "I had only a single petal distributed through five pounds of tea."

The pad of a thumb met my lips. Fingers brushed along my jaw, tilting my face upward. I held my breath. Though I couldn't see her, the silent judgment of her gaze was a weight. She was near enough that I could smell her perfume—flowery green supported by pale misty base notes. Warmth ghosted across my cheek, and I panicked. I didn't know how I could survive the aftermath of a kiss from someone like her. Mercifully, she withdrew.

Her touch came next at the small of my back. She settled behind me and drew me against her chest. The familiarity of the embrace startled me. My comfort startled me—as if every evening I surrendered to her just like this. The embroidery of her bodice chaffed against my skin. Little beads, perhaps. Tiny crystals. "I'm so happy to welcome you, Carlotta. All of us are."

I allowed myself what I wanted. I relaxed against her. Inexplicably, I trusted her.

"There," she whispered, smiling against my neck. The touch of her lips set off a frisson of pleasure that shot deep in my belly and prickled my skin. Lust had always been a private thing that resided fully in my imagination, appearing only in the deep hours of the night when I was alone in my bed. Thus confined for so long, the barest touch was enough to set me ablaze.

The woman laughed, though not unkindly. She smoothed her hands down my upper arms, calming the gooseflesh there. Instinct bade me to cross my arms over my chest, but of course they already were. I'd never been at the mercy of someone like this before. I didn't know I could like it.

An old dream came rippling back on the water of memory.

"Isn't it interesting," the woman said, noting my attempt, "that you try to shield yourself from your desires? Did the clerics teach you that?"

Her touch was so light I almost thought I imagined it—a teasing brush over the hardened bud of my nipple. But it was enough to scatter my thoughts. She had asked a question . . . I couldn't recall it enough to form a response.

"As soon as I heard about you, I knew I had to have you," she continued. "A monastery girl seemed such a rare delight."

She kissed my jaw, my neck, unhurried and lingering as she did, as if she knew time stopped for her amusement. My heart beat fast with need. My breath couldn't sate my lungs. The soft wet heat of her mouth dragged a whimper from my throat.

"Please—" I began.

"Have patience," she said, voice low and teasing at my ear.

I nodded. My thoughts spun.

"I want to hear you. A nod is never sufficient."

"Yes," I stammered. "I'm sorry."

"Yes *what*, Carlotta dear?" she prompted.

I floundered for an answer. It arrived like a secret whispered in my ear, a sacred knowledge she only now saw fit for me to know. Her hands wandered down my body to the heat that built between my thighs. I let my head fall back against her, sighed. "Yes, my king."

A bolt of pleasure ripped me awake. Clenching and wet between my thighs. A full-body flush of heat. I bit down on my cry. Swallowed it whole. Habit.

Countless nights passed this way—fingers slick against my swollen flesh, imagining the attention of some impossible and lovely woman, how she might praise me if I pleased her. I always felt cheated at the end, the frustration of smothering the last bright flame.

But I was not at the monastery anymore.

It was still dark. My body had wrung itself out. I felt boneless in a way I never did when I touched myself. This was vivid, visionary. Beyond my imagination and yet of it.

I recalled the king's lips and shivered and could not move.

Hooves on stone called me back to the present—the carriage and my journey. I groped in the dark, feeling for the walls, the door. I found the curtains and pushed them aside.

Moonlight rippled over lake water. Beyond, a castle clawed into the sky like a spined beast birthed from the black diamond heart of the earth. Pale light glinted across the crude facets of its surface.

Where the clouds thinned, towers winked in and out of being. Stone faded into the very night. Behind the illusory masonry, more spires and walls stood guard until they too became nothing and were replaced. The castle breathed moonglow. Its walls advanced, spires raised, only to fade and retreat and begin again.

This place was my destination.

Though my shoulders ached from crouching at the little window, I could not look away. I didn't want to miss this arrival.

As we disembarked from the bridge, my anticipation built at the prospect of rounding the lake. So much water! Fantasies crowded my thoughts. I pictured returning during the day to sit on a bank of lush grasses and see bright fish beneath the water's surface. I pressed my face to the window and wanted beauty.

Murky waves lapped at a bank of jagged black stones. Nothing grew within the lake's vicinity. It was all gray and black and silver, this place, like someone had come through long ago and leached the color and herded all life away. My hope of rainbow-finned fish withered. I couldn't even imagine daylight. This didn't seem like a place that would let the sun rise. A daydream of myself on those hostile rocks now captured me, how they'd stab with every step. The water would be cold. Traders from the frozen north described ice to borderlanders as a potentially lethal substance that steals warmth with a touch. I no longer struggled to imagine something so deathly closing over my head, of breathing in the gray water and turning heavy, sinking down. I let the curtain fall back across the window and sat stiffly at the edge of the bench.

Scales slithered across my lap.

"Da!" I exclaimed, taking him up and returning him to his place around my neck. I had forgotten him. He moved slowly and had grown cold. I brushed my fingers along his scales and was soothed. Not everything had changed. I wasn't alone. I listened to the water and the hooves, and then the water faded and the ground canted up. I returned to the window. All the castle's precarious stone loomed above me, its shadows absolute. I shrank from it. I thought of Marta. I had asked too much. I had abandoned her, and now I was here.

I pounded my fist against the front wall, hoping the driver might hear me from their perch. I called and received no answer. I hadn't imagined a door without a latch. There was nothing, not even a seam where the door met the wall. A wild thought took me—that I would be eternally trapped here, that the carriage would ascend forever into stony oblivion and my journey would never end. Even worse, that this was a dream I wouldn't wake up from, that I wouldn't have even the refuge of my fantasies about the king. Just up and onward forever.

In the distance, a murmur of voices and a faint serenade of strings hummed beneath the wind. I launched myself back to the window, and the carriage slowed.

The castle's great facade loomed, sleek black doors like polished glass set into the dark stone. Gold light spilled from within. At each side, those faceless knights stood. Just inside, I glimpsed a party decked in unmatched finery. Rippling dresses swept the floor, and glittering gems adorned throats. Lace-gloved hands held crystal glasses aloft. The carriage rounded a trail of similarly fine vehicles, and this decadent vision was lost to me, replaced by the beheaded statue of a man. The crowned head still lay at its feet, blank eyes cursed to stare eternally up into the clouded sky. I knew him as King Eric, recognizing the broad nose and proud cheekbones from sketches in my history books. Striking that someone had not removed this tribute to the fallen king, choosing instead to let him remain disgraced and identifiable. Nothing honoring our current king had been installed to replace it.

The carriage rolled to a stop. The door opened. I threw myself out into the free air, casting a glance over my shoulder to see there had never been a driver. Only the horse. And no sign of the knight who'd stood guard. I hurried past the line of carriages—stately ivory and ostentatious red and demure black—and sucked the strange new air into my lungs. It tasted of a looming storm strongly distilled, as though the lightning had been delayed and delayed and tarnished the air. Even at the monastery, I'd never felt such a biting wind. A vicious gust pushed me back, followed by eerie stillness that left me in freefall. I marched a determined path to the door and warmth. The steps into the grand hall were rough, as if some giant had hewed them—a contrast to the doors, as carefully crafted as mirrors, and all the finery within. I stumbled up the rest of the way, my arms wrapped tight against my body, and only paused to see that the knights would not finally break form and bar my way.

Gold engulfed me—gold light, great gold chandelier, gold fabrics swishing past, gold wine in crystal glasses, gold veins threading through the stone floor. I turned round and round and round. My eyes stung with tears. I found a serving girl before me, a gold tray in her hands. I grabbed one of the crystal glasses and tipped it back. White fruits fizzed on my tongue, stinging when the drink hit the back of my throat and alchemizing to heat in my belly. I giggled and held the glass to the light to admire all its facets.

"I can take that for you, miss," the girl offered.

I clutched the glass close and backed away from her. "I'd like to keep it, if I'm allowed."

Her eyes widened. She looked me up and down. I hurried away. There was so much to see, and I needed to find the red woman. I hoped I had not missed much of the start of the celebration, the king, or the royal poet. My books thumped at my hip as I walked, my thumb hooked in the strap of my satchel. The meeting I had dreamed of my entire life must be at hand. I would see Mirrors after she performed her newest work, and I would tell her how much her poetry had sustained my mother—had sustained me—and gift her one of my poems as thanks. I hoped she might like it and see me as an artist in her lineage.

Around the hall, guests clustered in groups and pairs. A trio of women whispered among each other, laughing behind their hands. Some of the women had paired off, had looped their arms around each other or else combed their fingers through their companion's hair and dusted kisses along their cheeks. On their lips. I watched these displays from the periphery of my vision. I meant to hurry on but couldn't look away. My toe caught the train of a woman's dress. I lost the glass in my hand and next saw it in pieces, shards glittering across the floor. The room turned to me. One of the serving girls rushed in with a broom, the only one in the whole room who moved. Finally, one of the ladies stepped to me.

"Are you well?" she asked, looking me up and down the way the serving girl had, as if she didn't know how I fit among them. She was a northerner, the sharp bridge of her nose and even sharper accent a giveaway. I glanced around, truly seeing all these fine people for the first time. All of them northerners, including the aristocrats I only then noticed, a stiff group hugging the left wall and looking vaguely suspicious about the proceedings. How difficult for them!—to be in attendance not by virtue of their own excellence but on account of their *servants*; because, without these servants, they could not survive, couldn't so much as raise a fork on their own. Here they were, the people whose need for protection controlled the fates of families like mine, people who could make excuse after excuse for missing pay while fathers died in the heat. I tasted acid. I took a step toward them.

"Miss?" the woman prompted again.

I looked at her.

"Are you well?" she repeated, her companion hanging back. The woman she'd kissed!

"I'm a poison girl," I said in answer to her unasked question.

"I see." She frowned, darted a glance at the aristocrats. "What is your name? What estate holds your contract?"

"My contract?"

"For your services."

"I don't have anything like that."

At my reply, she looked to the other women as if pleading for help. They turned away from her, back to their conversations and drinks and plates of small food, all of it more interesting than a borderland girl in a threadbare mourning dress.

"Carlotta, my dear!" A dramatic high voice cut through the murmur of the party. Again, the room's attention turned, this time following the entrance of a woman in a daring red dress. I'd never seen a style like it—a trailing hem at the rear that arched up in front to reveal calf and ankle and the sharp points of her heels.

The cut caused a stir, scandal rippling outward with her as the beating red heart. I smiled so wide I thought my face might crack in two. The woman embraced me like a long-lost friend, the spice of her perfume tickling my nose.

"I hope your journey was not too arduous. The way to visit you was grueling. I can only imagine how you must feel." She cupped my face in her hands as if it were a rare and precious jewel, and I loved her. She continued, "We were so happy to receive your response to the invitation."

"My response?" I echoed, recalling blood, fire, and ash.

"Your reply was decisive. The king received it before I returned to her."

"But my invitation. It burned."

"As intended. A little blood is all it ever takes to reach her." She paused, tipped her head in thought. "True of most magic, really, and you bleed well, according to the king." She looped her arm through mine. "If you'd like to change from your travel attire, I have a gown just for you."

That she excused my dress as travel attire was all too gracious. I nodded eagerly, and she swept me toward a set of doors I'd missed just below the grand staircase.

Amidst the jewel tones and metallic shine of the gowns we passed, a modest woman stood out. Her dress was an earthy green that reminded me of home, the cut more conservative than even the serving girls' dresses—but what drew my attention most of all was her round face, so much like mine and those of the women of the borderlands: strong brows, flat nose bridge, a delicate gap between the front teeth. She must've been twenty or thirty years my senior, my mother's age had she still lived. Her thick braids were tied atop her head with shining ringlets left to frame the sides of her face. But for all her beauty, she stood apart from her fellow poison girls like a severe headmistress.

"Who is she?" I asked the red woman.

She followed my gaze and clicked her tongue. "Delfina. Earl Huxley's last loyal poison girl."

The man's name landed upon my body like a cataclysm. I couldn't breathe or I was breathing too fast. Where I hadn't been aware of my heart before, it now fluttered like a trapped thing. Could the red woman feel how I shook?

"The last?" I asked.

"He's had trouble retaining them of late."

My body moved of its own accord, the red woman's voice fading behind me. Delfina raised her chin at my determined approach. Her stiff posture calcified into a shield.

"Did you know a poison girl named Priscilla Bridge?" I asked.

The name roused something in her, something she hid behind a raised brow. I grasped her arm. She was my answer, and I would not let her go.

"Please, she was my mother," I insisted. "She died five years ago."

Delfina attempted to pull away, a frown creasing her smooth face. "If she was a poison girl, you know her fate. Let go of me."

Her borderland accent was unmistakable, slower and warmer, but it had steeped long in these northern lands and integrated the clipped vowels.

I held tight. "You look her age," I insisted. "You would've known her."

"You're hurting me."

"Please. I never knew her."

I found no sympathy on the woman's face, and when she wrenched away, my hope went with her.

"You embarrass us," she hissed, "like you've just crawled out of the dirt."

Hands fluttered over my shoulders, and I noticed the room—everyone staring at me again. My body settled on not breathing. In the silence, my heartbeat was loud in my ears. I thought the rejection would drown me.

"We were on our way," the red woman excused us, steering me back on course.

NINE

T HE RED WOMAN AND I walked the castle's half-lit corridors and shadowy staircases in silence, the gilded allure fading the farther we ventured. I wondered whether the red woman was lost in her own thoughts or respectfully leaving me to mine. If it was the latter, I wished she wouldn't. I'd had five years of quiet and needed no more time to sink in my private guilt, but the monastery had conditioned me well, and so I sank. I'd just arrived and had already made a poor impression on a room of my peers, on the very people I thought would understand me most, on the one person most like me.

Worse, I continued to stain the reputation of the borderlands.

The red woman did not speak but rested a steadying hand upon my back. Her touch lifted me from the mire of my thoughts, and I was grateful to her. She returned my shy smile, and I was dazzled by her beauty again. I needed to be worthy of her regard. I needed her to know I could be strong and steady, and so I kept my anxieties to myself.

After one too many dusty stairways and not a soul in sight, I almost doubted that we were in the same castle, but that was how it had been from the outside too—a curious mismatch of disrepair and opulence. Luxury redoubled once we entered the red woman's rooms, a stark contrast within and without. She seemed to see none of it, how extraordinary her everyday was, and sat me at her vanity while I stole glances about the room.

Velvet drapes shielded us from the weak gray light of the outdoors, and layers of ornate carpets blanketed the floors. The wallpaper, of course, was red. The ceilings were vaulted stone. Uncanny flames burned high in the hearth. They had no fuel that I could see and spiraled in a column as though corralled by some magician. The same dark spices I'd smelled on the woman's skin perfumed her room as well, a strong red essence without florals or softer notes to mellow it. A large four-poster bed dominated the space behind me, all ruffled decadence and more silken pillows than I had ever seen at once.

Heat flushed my face if I thought too much of it—how the red woman might recline there at the close of the day, how her hair might fall across those pillows, how her curves might sharpen in the candlelight's chiaroscuro play. Was she inclined to other women like some of the guests downstairs? Might she take a lover here? I bit down on my tongue to clear the image, to maintain a neutral gaze that could meet hers in the mirror. My head clear, the borderland woman's rebuke drifted back. Not even the thrilling privilege of sitting at the red woman's vanity in her private rooms could dispel the shame for long.

She frowned at me and brushed her fingertips down my neck, pulling gently at my dress's neckline as if she'd found a stain. "The king has settled on her intentions for you, I see," she said, turning my chin to the side so that I might see the bruise she indicated.

I shivered at the sight of it, impossible proof that the king had tasted my skin. I blinked at her reflection, then turned in the little chair to look up at the real red woman. "The king appeared to me in a dream, except I didn't know who she was," I said. "And it seems it . . . wasn't a dream?"

"She's capable of many feats," the woman said, setting out pots of rouge and powder before disappearing behind an accordioned screen.

"And her intentions?" I called.

"She would make you a royal poison girl, of course."

I looked back to my reflection and the bruise, passing my hand over it in wonder. The king wanted *me*, wanted me to stay here, wanted me as hers.

"But I do," I said, "want to be a poison girl. Here, that is."

The red woman appeared again from behind her screen, a spark of delight in her eyes. "Then you must tell her. You're the first new girl the king's desired since we lost Anne. Even before Emelia slipped into melancholy, it'd become difficult to court newcomers to our life here, especially when taking up a contract with the minor aristocracy is less of a risk."

Anne—the name from the king's invitation, this celebration tonight in her memory. And Emelia! How the red woman so casually referred to our king. I wondered at their relationship and this passing mention of a melancholic affliction. It was so at odds with the rumors of a monstrous and cruel creature hiding in a woman's skin. I wanted to know more, but it seemed improper to ask about the king's health when we hadn't yet been introduced.

Recalling the question from the woman downstairs, I asked, "What is this about contracts?"

"Oh, the king never asks her girls to sign one," the red woman said with a wave of her hand before disappearing again behind the screen. "Her survival requires true loyalty from those around her. If a poison girl no longer feels her devotion to sacrifice, she's free to leave. It's better this way. To let a poison girl grow bitter or fearful is a danger we cannot afford."

"Is she as the rumors say?" I asked.

Behind the screen came the sound of closing drawers and the rustle of fabric. "You'll need to be more specific, dear."

"That the king is an ageless spirit from another realm, that she loves women as men do, that she takes her poison girls as wives," I said.

"Owing to her vulnerabilities and the necessity of trust, Emelia is inclined toward those who protect her. To your first question, I should let the king explain herself."

The red woman reappeared carrying an airy white dress made almost entirely of lace. My remaining questions scattered at the sight of it. She bade me stand and held it against me. I swallowed. In the borderlands, only clerics wore white. A color so vulnerable to the grime of daily living, it was considered bad luck. Only those blessed by the angel could keep such a color as pristine as it deserved.

"You dislike it," said the red woman.

"No! I was only surprised. It's not a color we wear at home."

"We've many dresses to choose from. You can have a look and decide what suits you."

I hugged the dress to me as she moved to take it away. "I like your selection."

Her pleased smile warmed me. I wanted to make her smile like that again and again. "Shall we get you changed?" she suggested, her fingers an admiring brush along my jaw. "I'll assist you with the buttons."

Scales wound up my sleeve and around my shoulder, and the red woman jerked away with a yelp.

"Oh! He's harmless. He's mine." I rushed to reassured her, though only one of those things was true. I'd been bitten not so long ago. The tender moment broken, I returned the dress to the red woman and coaxed Da the rest of the way from my sleeve. I carried him to the chair. He looped over the back, purple scales gleaming in the low light. The red woman watched in wary fascination.

"May I ask why you keep a serpent on your person?" she asked lightly.

The clerics had never asked me to explain Da, and I worried that if I tried, her opinion of me might fall. Borderlanders were too often characterized as dull and superstitious by the rest of the kingdom, and a woman seeming to befriend a venomous snake—one that had killed her father—might be considered a dull thing to do. Explaining that the snake carried my late father's soul would only cast me as superstitious. There was no way forward.

"I lost everything to the drought five years ago," I said and hoped an allusion to personal tragedy would be enough for propriety to override curiosity.

"I see," she said, a slight frown wrinkling her brow. "Know that we've experienced many singular happenings here in the castle. No one would shun you for yours."

A flutter of hope cleared the knot in my chest. "Thank you," I whispered. Perhaps, if the king did want me here, I could belong. I'd only needed a place as strange as me, a poison-eater snake-keeper with no ties to speak of.

The red woman offered me her hand, and I took it, allowing her to lead me to the other side of the screen. A towering wardrobe and tall filigreed mirror stood in the corner. Dress forms—one bare and two with half-sewn red gowns—took up the rest of the space.

"You're a seamstress!" I exclaimed, admiring the intricate beadwork on one of the skirts.

"It's a necessary hobby, both the king and I sharing unconventional taste."

"You make the king's dresses too! What an honor."

"Indeed." Her hands came to rest on my hips, and she turned me to face her. "And it would be an honor to dress you for the evening's celebration as well."

I nodded, unable to speak with her close like this, her hands warm through the fabric of my dress. She walked an appraising circle around me, her eyebrow arched in a look I couldn't parse. She set the white lace dress aside.

"Your dress has no laces or buttons," she said as if perplexed.

"No. It's not custom. It's cut loose so that it doesn't need any."

She stepped back to me as if on a dare, gathering the skirt of my dress in her hands. "How delightful," she murmured, her gaze locked to mine as she lifted the skirt higher.

My breath caught in my throat. I struggled to relax my shoulders. We stood like this but a brief moment, breathing each other's air, her lips so close to mine, and then the dress was over my head. I emerged to her stepping away with my old mourning dress in her hands. For five years I had rotated through five identical dresses. Now was time to let them go. Time to live a new life. Mourning would always be with me. I thought, when I stopped missing Ma, when I stopped feeling the cascade of losses that started with hers, I would be able to set the gray dresses aside, but that time had never come.

The red woman studied my old dress with an expert's eye, considering it with a level of care that warmed me to her all over again. The pieces I still had of my home were not something to be disdained or discarded, not with her. She arranged it over the bare dress form.

My gown decided, the red woman turned to painting and powdering my face. I sat politely through the tickle of her brushes, ready to meet this polished version of myself. Southern women didn't often bother with makeup, it being an expensive luxury that one was liable to sweat away within the first hour of the workday.

This was one of the few gifts I had asked for as a girl and been outright denied. *When you're older, perhaps*, Ma had written.

I barely recognized my face when the red woman stepped away and allowed me to look in the mirror once more.

"You dislike it," she said again, a fretful pout to her lips.

Awestruck, I raised a hand to my cheek only to return it to my lap when I remembered I might smudge her hard work. "Not at all! I—"

I loved it. I loved *me*, this newer, shinier Carlotta who could match the women downstairs and hold my head just as high. I hadn't known my lips were this shape, had never thought much about them until they were painted so red. Heart-shaped, the bow of my top lip pronounced. So shadowed and lined in black, my eyes seemed miraculously larger. Some magic she'd worked with her brushes made my cheekbones appear sharper, feline, as if I could hunt something down.

Then there was the dress itself—its plunging neckline, the V of white lace that framed my cleavage. The king's bite was on full display. I was shy to flaunt something so private, but she assured me there was nothing to be ashamed of, that the king would enjoy the statement.

I looked up at her. "What statement would that be?"

She rested her hands atop my shoulders and smiled—sharp, feline, as if she too could hunt something down. "That you claim her in return."

Upon stepping back into the corridor, I suppressed a shiver. My new dress was no protection in the chill, the air nipping at my skin as though I wore nothing at all. The red woman took my hand, and Da shifted restlessly in the bell of my sleeve.

It seemed the castle had rearranged itself after our first journey, or else my memory of the way we'd come was embarrassingly poor. I struggled to walk down the steps in the tall shoes the red woman had insisted upon, clinging to her for dear life and holding my skirt in my other hand so as not to sweep up the dust. After two harrowing staircases, the red woman realized her error.

"You've never worn these before, have you?" she asked gently, apologizing for her assumption.

"No, but I *like* them."

I almost matched the red woman's height.

"Not too much farther," she reassured me.

Finally, we emerged into a wide, well-lit corridor congruent with the first room I'd seen. Paintings of battle and repose lined the walls, the gilt frames and their figures larger than life. I craned my head back to take in the whole of them. In one piece, a woman reclined nude on a chaise longue, sunlight in the halo of her hair and a book dangling unread from her hand. Across from her, an angel was impaled on a spear, the blade bursting from their chest as if they'd fallen a long way to land precisely there. The artist had chosen an angle that rendered the figure headless, their back arched over the instrument of their destruction. Broken wings dragged the ground. A verdant field served as the background, the world caught in the innocent blush of spring. Nothing in the frame suggested what had led to the startling brutality of the central image.

This isn't my fault, I thought when I looked at it and was taken aback by how I'd made a masterpiece so personal.

"Do you know it?" the red woman asked beside me.

I glanced at her, the question lost.

"The painting," she clarified.

"My father wasn't religious," I said because this seemed like the kind of morbid myth that belonged to the north.

"And you yourself? When I first heard rumors of a poison girl living among the clerics, I didn't believe it."

"I don't think I am, no."

"And yet you lived there for years."

"They rescued me after my father died during the drought. I needed shelter, and they offered shelter. They left me alone to write and grieve. That was all I needed."

The red woman was quiet.

"Why does the king keep it?" I asked, nodding to the painting.

"This is the only safe place for it," the red woman said. "Beatrisa Saber became infamous after its showing, which is just another way of saying the Retributionists despise her. She's been the king's favorite artist ever since. Her contemporary work isn't so bluntly provocative, but her reputation precedes her. A saccharine landscape would garner suspicion if it bore her signature. I never miss Saber's exhibitions. They're quite the event."

I observed the painting with new eyes. Guilt receded. My injuries had primed me to see an attack. Saber was one of us.

"Let's not linger, shall we?" said the red woman, and it was only once we'd turned away that Da's grip on my wrist relaxed.

Two knights stood across from each other at the end of the corridor. The red woman breezed past them. I hesitated again. Though they never seemed to look anywhere in particular, their presence still unsettled me.

Quietly, as though raising my voice might incite them, I asked, "Are they real? I mean—are there people inside them?"

As the question left my mouth, the red woman tapped the great doors with a finger. They swung open at her touch. Warmth and light and music crashed into me. All the world's colors paraded on dresses. Five years at the monastery had diminished my imagination. These miraculous hues! These singing strings! Beyond the celebrants, an imposing throne towered over the revelry. No one looked in its direction. No one stood near the dais. I wondered whether the notes of the waltz could even penetrate the air around it. I couldn't look away.

The throne exuded old energy, a grudge festering in the stone. I felt I'd walked in on some horrible scene, that King Eric's head had rolled down those steps only moments before we arrived and no one but I had noticed. Made of the same glassy black stone as the castle's facade, the throne's back climbed the wall like ivy, enlivened and determined.

The rumors were true. The castle was growing.

I blinked hard. I grasped for the red woman and her name and came up short. I turned in the crowd. I found Delfina's gaze. She stood only feet from me. People passed obliviously between us. Her face was inscrutable. How long had she observed me? No one else seemed to recognize me as the girl from before, transformed as I was by the red woman. Delfina shook her head and receded into the crowd.

In the center of the room, the waltz whirled on, women leading women across the shining floor. I pushed to the edge of the dance floor to watch them. The couples pressed together as they were, their voluminous skirts blurred into one extravagant garment as they turned. I could've watched them for ages, and then, as though the musicians had been dropped off a cliff one by one, the song crashed to an abrupt end. Couples broke away from each other. The crowd parted, and the room was cleaved in two. Loud silence rang in my ears.

In the grand doorway, in a black slip of a dress, the king stood. She wore no crown and needed none. Ivory horns curved back from her forehead and arched up to deadly points. Flowering vines grew along their length, blossoms of violet and crimson a bright warning. Taller than even the tallest men in my village, she loomed. Her dress was a second skin that trailed like shadow. This was the red woman's design. *Unconventional*, she'd said. It was. If the red woman's dress was a minor scandal, the king's was reputation ruining. Her first step—barefoot, silent—revealed the high cut at the side of the dress, a flash of thigh.

Her origins were impossible to place. She looked neither northern nor southern. Warm brown skin was our only common feature. Her hair was red as her flowers, swept over one shoulder and done in braids that trailed with her dress. The face that looked down on us was long and angular as a mask. Her neck, long. Limbs, long.

Our king surveyed the room as if she were already bored of the party she'd just arrived to, bored to find so many people in attendance at her behest, bored of all the beautiful people in their beautiful clothes. Of everyone, she paused before me. I stopped breathing. She pinched my chin between her thumb and forefinger. The corner of her mouth twitched as if she'd discovered something distasteful, my face a spoiled fruit amidst a feast. And that's when I noticed—everyone stood with their head bowed. Everyone but I.

Horror spiked through me. Scales flashed up my arm.

"Da!" I screamed, my cry echoing sharp.

He dangled from the king's hand, his fangs deep in her palm.

Her eyes gleamed, boredom replaced with intrigue. She let me go and raised her hand to better observe him. "Were you born of serpents, Carlotta?"

Murmurs rippled through the room followed by poorly stifled snickers. A few attendees dared a sidelong glance at me. The king's tone was neutral, but still people sought to mock the dull borderland girl. They were suddenly all too close and far too many. Though tears stung my eyes, I wanted to use my fists. How dare they be so proud! How dare they laugh at my tragedy, my loss, my life, my family, my home—

"Quiet," the king demanded, her voice barely raised and yet its bite as deadly as Da's.

My red swell of anger spun itself out. The room stilled again. I could salvage this first impression. I could save Da.

"No, my king," I answered, holding my head high under the weight of the room's attention. "This snake carries my father's spirit and watches over me."

"Ah," she sighed, flexing her hand as if to rid it of an ache. "He's venomous."

"I can help," I offered. "I'm sorry. He only tries to protect me."

The king raised her other hand to Da, and all I could see was how sharp and red her nails were, how they could tear a small throat.

"Don't hurt him," I pleaded.

The king looked down her nose. "Don't command me."

She pinched the hinge of the snake's jaws and pried the fangs from her flesh, lowering him gently into my waiting palms. Da flattened the spines collaring his neck and did not move. I placed him around my neck, and he curled there. The king took my hand in her bleeding one.

"Sit with me," she said, her invitation clearing the moment's tension. I hadn't offended her. Da hadn't bitten her. We were starting anew.

Hand in hand with the king, I walked down the aisle of the kingdom's aristocracy and the women who protected them, their heads bowed to us. Satisfaction warmed me at the sight. I wished I were as tall as the king so I could glare down at them. Shivery with nerves, I looked to the king, her gaze trained on the throne, unfocused as though she were seeing through it. I'd misunderstood her expression before. She wasn't bored. She was burdened.

I recalled the red woman's mention of the king's melancholy and wondered how long ago it'd begun. I took a steadying breath and allowed her to guide me up the dais steps to that forbidding throne. At my first wobbling steps, she raised an eyebrow, a twitch of amusement in her features there and gone. Graciously, she offered her arm to steady me.

Upon reaching the throne, the king sat easily. She moved as though unobserved, as though she had no image to uphold—one elbow upon the arm of the throne, chin cradled in her hand, a slight slouch in her spine as if her horns had become too heavy to bear. I didn't want to touch the stone. I stared, wide eyed, suddenly confused as to her invitation. How could I sit with her when there was only the one terrible seat? Sensing my trepidation, she tugged me into her lap and hugged me against her. A full-body blush overtook me.

Her voice was a deep hum against my ear. "Relax," she murmured, just as she had in the dream.

With a wave of her hand, the music resumed, and the party stuttered back to life, guests trying either very hard not to look at us or staring openly. Three women did not rejoin the party, skirting its edge and pausing in their whispering only to raise narrowed eyes to me.

"My king . . ." I started.

"Pay them no mind. They're contracted to minor aristocracy who do nothing of note but inherit land forever and ever and have not even the enterprise to do anything useful with it when much of the kingdom is in the grip of a drought. You'll find that not all poison girls are refined enough to rise above petty jealousies, nor sensible enough to refrain from making their personal insecurities about others." She trailed her nails down my spine like appreciating a finely bred cat. "If your only discomfort lies in what others will think or say, abandon it," she said, staring resolutely forward. "That fear will not serve you. What do you feel when you set it aside?"

I rested my head against her chest and closed my eyes. Listened to the slow beat of her heart, sank into the heat of her around me, breathed freely and unburdened. Her scent was the same as in the dream, a naked bloom of flowers supported by ethereal white base notes. "I'm happy with you, my king. I can scarcely believe I'm here and that you chose me. I'm excited. Hopeful." A part of me that I didn't know could be still stilled—the restless and ravenous heart that ensured I made it here. Here I had everything I needed. I could rest. "I hope I can honor and protect you with my skills, like your poison girls before me."

"Your gifts," the king corrected.

Her face was so near. Big, honeyed-brown eyes. Rows of sharp teeth like the frightening creatures from traders' stories of giant meat-eating fish. She wore no jewelry, no powder or paints, no adornments. I wanted to test her long pointed ears with a fingertip.

"My king?" I whispered.

"You have a gift, Carlotta. Let no one call it anything else." She sat back, grew distant again.

Finally, the whispering women tired of staring and disbanded. I watched the serving girls in their simple black dresses balancing their trays of sparkling wine. From where I sat so high, the women's dresses looked like carnations when they turned in their dance.

"Which of the poison girls are yours?" I asked eagerly.

"Oh." The king roused from her thoughts. "She couldn't attend tonight."

I looked out over the crowd and hoped the king couldn't read my surprise. Only a single poison girl protected our king? When lesser aristocrats might employ several of us? And this single girl absent on the very night the king had chosen to celebrate us? I thought back to the tallies I kept in my journal. It was never announced when the king took a new girl, only when one was lost. I weighed my next question but didn't have to ask it.

The king continued, "She's recovering from an attempt made against me only yesterday. I was sitting with her through the evening and lost the time."

I recast the king's entrance, her manner and dress. If her poison girl had taken ill yesterday, it meant the king had not eaten today. By now, she would undoubtedly feel the effects of her fast. Her disaffected attitude, while she wore it easily, was a shield to grief and fear. To nurse an ailing poison girl on the day of a celebration such as this!

"Will she be okay?" I asked softly, daring to place my hand over the king's.

She noted my attempt at comfort with an appreciative smile. "Meredith will make a full recovery, I'm certain. I look forward to introducing you soon. You'll make lovely companions."

"I'd be honored to meet her."

I wondered what sort of woman she was, how long she'd been with the king, what she'd have thought of this night. If she was not here, then I would serve the king in her stead.

"The venom, my king," I reminded her. "Allow me to help you."

She offered her hand for my examination. It was not swollen. The red pinpricks from Da's fangs were so faded that I nearly missed them. "No need." She resettled her chin upon her hand. "It is an annoyance, not a vulnerability. Belladonna, foxglove, hemlock, jessamine, oleander, and wolfsbane," she listed blandly, "are not concerns to me. Blades and arrows are not concerns to me. It's the undying white flowers that I must remain vigilant of." The king looked out over her party again as though she saw a trial to be endured. "Would you allow me to show you the garden?"

I felt as if she'd offered me her crown. "Yes, my king!"

TEN

A
LL THE BEAUTY I'D longed for on my journey up to the castle was cradled in its courtyard garden: trees cultivated from across the continent, flower bushes in colors I had never seen, ancient stone figures overlooking it all. A central pond hosted glittering creatures—serpentine fish that I could not coax Da out of my sleeve to see. The path was narrow and winding, its course plotted for optimal sightseeing rather than efficient crossing. The paving stones seemed original to the castle, a light gray that hadn't yet been overtaken by the glassy black rock growing elsewhere. With the courtyard walls shielding us from the north's winds, it was pleasant here. Ghostly flames bobbed on the breeze, their light casting the garden in a soft glow.

"What are they?" I asked, cupping one in my hands as it drifted close and finding it surprisingly heatless.

The king hummed thoughtfully. "Some might call it hellfire. It is, most literally, fire from my home."

"It's so delicate!"

"It has many forms. It's not always demure."

She scooped the little flame from my hands and blew as if nursing a campfire to life. It spun larger, growing hearty as a torch. Now, its heat radiated. The king corralled it in her hands, gesturing in wide sweeping arcs until it formed a perfect spinning orb.

My squeak of delight surprised me almost as much as the king's performance. The fire lit a daring spark in her eyes and drew a sharp smile to her face, revitalizing the weary monarch I'd met in the throne room. She held the fire high and tipped her head back, pouring the light down her throat like molten gold. I gasped, but the king's bold feat came as easy to her as tipping back a glass of wine. A brief and sudden darkness settled until, into her cupped hands, the king blew a small and heatless flame, the great fire rendered harmless once more.

A nervous giggle bubbled up from my throat. Earnest laughter followed. In all my daydreams of the king, I never expected to meet a powerful woman interested in using that power to amuse *me*.

"One of my favorite tricks as a child," the king said, returning the fire to me.

I cradled it and tried to imagine a place where children not only played with fire but mastered it. "So what they say is true, that you're from another world."

The king laughed. "Yes, and it is a beautiful one. The rumors always fail to mention this."

I knew another surge of longing. "Won't you tell me about it?" I asked. I felt her height again. To meet her gaze, I tipped my head back the same as when I'd admired her art. How could anyone despise her? She was magnificent, a figure stepped out of our neighbors' mythology of lost titanic gods.

King Emelia contemplated the earth the same way others would gather their thoughts by looking to the sky. "The story you know is the one from clerical lore, a passing mention in the old scrolls of a city so wicked that the earth swallowed it up. Our great city should not be conflated with that one. It did not fall. It was built as all cities are, with spirit and labor. It is a marvel of architecture, a star in the earth, and yet the clerics call it fallen. Our lives are not dictated by the sun, and so the city is always awake. The city has no name because it is the only one that matters. We have different lights and different time. We welcome drifting spirits who decide to call our groves and forests home. Our trade is in intangible things like wishes and names rather than goods. It is the only reason to maintain any connection to this world. There's valor and prestige in locating a dire wish and arranging a pact. So began my story here in this castle. Are these the things you wanted to know?"

"I want to know everything, my king."

This earned me a smile.

"Are we . . ." I began hastily, filling the gaps between stories as I spoke. "Are the spirits of poison girls the wanderers from your city? Do you bring our souls to earth like the stories say? And the white flowers, the ones we're immune to, are they from your home as well?"

Now the king's smile fell, and her attention left me. She stared out over her magnificent garden, and I knew my questions were the wrong ones.

"There's no truth in the Retributionist scrolls is there?" I asked, half hopeful and half fearful.

I thought of Fifth Wanderer and Seventh Seeker. The Restorationists had lost the clerical summit for their heresy, and the elders among them still grieved losing that holy site to the Retributionists, but what had all their heartache been for? Their practice was nothing without the foundation the Retributionists had set a thousand years ago, and that foundation crumbled now in the span of seconds. No evil lived in the earth, only more people and their dreams.

King Emelia's gaze alighted on me again. "Does your soul enter hell when you fall asleep?"

"N-no," I stammered, taken aback to hear her reference an old Retributionist belief. "At least, I don't think so."

My flicker of doubt turned her grin wicked and lovely. "I would envy you such ease if it were true. I'm not even so connected to my home. Rest assured that the only realm you're bound to is your own."

"Then . . . where are the flowers from? Do you know?"

The king set her hand upon my shoulder and slipped into the shadows at my back. I made to turn with her, but she braced my arms and held me so that I looked over the garden.

"Where do any flowers come from?" she asked quietly.

I worried I didn't have the answer, that there was some riddle only a cleverer girl could solve. But I was a farmer's daughter, and though estranged from the labor of our ancestors, I knew the answer in my heart and had known it all along. In my sleeve, Da was still. "From their seeds, from this earth," I answered. "The dangerous flowers and the beautiful ones alike are all ours."

It was part of what Da had been saying all along, but he'd been the only person I knew brave enough to believe it. After five years with the clerics, I'd come away with no great insight into the angel. I had little conviction about the old stories, but unlike Da, those stories had defined my life, my worth. I could never fully turn away from them. Now, King Emelia showed me how I might.

"Such fuss has been made over creating an adversary for their angel. In the city, this was curious news when it finally reached us. We'd been trading in bargains with the surface long before the first cleric set down his words. Only recently have we all become evil and only on certain soil. What an unfortunate era for my first expedition."

The king released me and resumed her walk down the path. When I wobbled after her, she stopped. "You should sit," she suggested, offering her arm again and leading us to a stone bench at a bend in the path.

I sat, still cupping my flame. To my shock, the king knelt before me.

"My king—" I started.

"Your comfort is important to me. Despite what the worst of the rumors claim, I am not cruel to my poison girls unless they have asked me to be and it pleases them." Taking my ankle in one hand, she removed my shoe and kissed the arch of my foot before turning to the second. I watched in awe, heat blooming in my face. "It is because of the sacrifices of poison girls that I am alive and that we are fortunate to meet. Allow me to appreciate you."

"Thank you," I whispered when she was done.

She rested her head upon my knee. "When I asked about your father, it wasn't my intention to embarrass you," she said, looking out over the garden. I wished I could see her face. "This world still surprises me, and I am always learning something about its possibilities. If you had told me yes, that your parents were serpents and you were human, I would have believed you. It wouldn't be unusual, were you from my home."

"May I ask why you left it?"

"You may," she said and paused. "I didn't want to leave, but contracts signed in blood are irrevocable. During the wars, my predecessor forged a pact with Duke Emlochnon, my father. His kingdom in exchange for military might so long as he lived. But my predecessor was a fool who in turn made my father a fool. At the time of King Eric's early death, all he had achieved was the ruin of his own state. There was nothing for my father to inherit, but the pact demanded his attention to the throne. Sending me was his loophole."

"And so you're unable to return?"

"My hope is that I repair the kingdom's land and legacy, make it something my father sees as worth the deal he stuck."

"And then?"

The king finally turned to face me, her hand on my thigh. "Then my father takes the throne, and I am free to live my life."

"What would become of Vinstrum?"

"My father enjoys his political games, but he is a serious man. There is value in allies, something King Eric failed to understand. The kingdom would not return to the poverty of his reign. I will see to that." The king took my hands, swallowed the little flame, and kissed my palms. I hadn't appreciated how much light it cast. Without it, the garden was suddenly too dark. "What troubles you?"

What troubled me? I would be long dead before any of what the king described came to pass. I had no family, would have no children. I had no stake in the future. I was tethered to nothing, a woman who could choose to sacrifice herself in pursuit of fleeting luxury. Perhaps I would fall ill tomorrow, and this night would be all I had. What trouble? What future?

"I could not go home even if I wanted. The borderlands are dead. I am not troubled."

The king studied my hands in hers. A frown passed over her face. "Is there nothing else you want?"

"Ever since I discovered my gift, I knew I would serve as a poison girl. This is what I want."

"Some poison girls have served me for a year. Others for a week. It is rare, with the number of people who want me dead, for anyone to survive their first year. Before you taste anything for me, I will ask you again if there is nothing else you want. You may sleep here tonight without expectation. Consider what this life would demand of you."

"Yes, my king," I murmured.

She stood, and I looked again down the path. In the center, a black four-legged beast waited. I hadn't heard its approach, had been so enchanted by the king that I hadn't noticed anything at all. It was still as the garden's statues, but I knew it watched us. My heart thundered in my chest.

"What is that?" I whispered, not daring to move.

"Don't be afraid," the king said. "It's only curious."

She held her hand out to me, and I took it, allowing her to lead me to the creature. Its build reminded me of the borderland's wild dogs, but its wiry coat was stretched taught over its bones, so emaciated that its joints pressed close to the skin. As we drew closer, a second set of forelimbs became visible, too many and too long for its body. The skull was uncannily human with sharp ears too tall for its face. Across its eyes, it wore the same apparatus as the horse that had drawn my carriage.

I hung back warily while the king picked a sturdy red fruit from a tree at the path's edge. The creature's ears swiveled at the snap of the branch, but it didn't move. Setting the tips of her nails against the fruit, the king tore it in two with her bare hands. Red juice dripped and stained her skin. She handed me a bleeding half. Burgundy gems studded the white pulp of the fruit.

"Don't be afraid," the king said again, crouching beside the creature. She stroked one hand along its skull and offered the fruit half. It curled a long muscular tongue around the fruit and took it into its mouth, juice dripping from its jowls as it chewed. "They're sensitive," the king explained. "All of the animals I brought from home are. Even after all these years, they never fully adapted to the environment. Hence these." She fit a finger under the straps of the apparatus that covered its eyes. "They become overwhelmed at the sight of this world. Its light is too bright, and they can navigate by means other than sight. I don't think they understand they've been transplanted, and I can't bear to see them confused. Early in my reign, most of the spirits my father sent with me departed for home. Only a few remain. They are steadfastly loyal and a comfort to me. I hope you will grow to love them too."

"Your knights," I said, clutching my half of the fruit. "Are they spirits too?"

"Of a different sort. They follow simple commands to watch and protect. Unlike my hounds and horses, they can be dangerous. They won't engage without cause, but it is safest if you pay them no mind." She beckoned me closer. "Would you like to introduce yourself?"

I approached and held out the fruit. Up close, I could count its ribs. The hound licked my hands, found the fruit, and wrapped its tongue around the offering. Red seeds scattered at its feet as it chewed.

"Will it not eat enough?" I asked.

"They eat, but their bodies don't change. We all appear different here than we do at home, and the spirits have little reason to change their bodies for the sake of others' comfort."

I thought the hound might follow us as we continued down the path, but when I glanced behind me, it had disappeared. We rounded the pond and walked down a short series of steps.

The king pointed out a balcony on the eastern wall. "At night, when I need the peace of the garden but don't want to leave Meredith while she sleeps, I step out there."

Was that where the king had been earlier this evening, where Meredith at this very moment still fought to purge the poison from her body?

"May I ask how long she's been with you?"

"Eleven months."

"And the poison—was she able to identify it before she fell ill?"

Now the king gave me a questioning look. "No. It took her swiftly. Florals again, I suspect. Though we are lucky it wasn't weeping luna this time. I've lost too many girls to it."

"If you let me see her, I can help."

The king paused. Her expression was unreadable.

I continued, "When I lived with the clerics, they brought me poisoned villagers. I'm able to draw the sickness of others into myself, and flowers do not harm me, at least not more than anything else would."

"We thought the valley people's claims of a miracle healer were exaggerated."

"I wouldn't describe my work as miraculous, but it is not exaggerated."

The king glanced to the balcony again, hesitated. "I am wary of trading one sick poison girl for another."

"Are you certain Meredith will survive?"

The king's gaze bored into me. Finally, she relented as if it pained her. "No. I cannot be."

"Then allow me to help."

"You've just arrived."

"And if I can prevent it, I would not let another poison girl die."

The king showed me to a room silvery with moonlight. It was decorated like a princess's chamber, pink frills and pale lace turned solemn and wan. In a large bed rested a small woman, the blankets pulled up to her chin. Freckles dotted her nose and cheeks. Her black curls were loose across the satiny pillows. Her hand was cold, but her chest still rose and fell. An impulse took me. I clasped her hand in mine, not for any divining purpose but because I wanted to.

Hundreds of faithful had passed through my care, but I'd never noticed how soft skin could be.

Behind me, the king loomed close, an agitated shadow. I couldn't move without brushing her. I suspected she didn't like me seeing Meredith this way, that a poison girl so incapacitated was akin to personal weakness, a wound that she wanted to immediately hide away.

"What do you think?" she asked.

"I'll need to feel more of her."

The king reached past me to turn down the blankets, her body pressed against my back. Meredith wore a simple cotton gown, little pink flowers embroidered at the neckline. A macabre choice for a poison girl, though I supposed northerners did not grow up with the same pervasively fatal associations as borderlanders.

"Are you very certain of this?" the king asked over my shoulder.

"If weeping luna has not killed me, then it will take a knife," I said, holding her gaze.

At this, she stepped back. "I will believe you," she said, frowning down at where Meredith lay.

Before tonight, I'd never met another poison girl, let alone attempted this method of purging with someone who shared my gift. I snuffed the flicker of doubt and let my intuition guide me. Every step of this path had been a stumble in the dark, of feeling for the walls and finding none. I planted my hands on either side of Meredith, climbing up to straddle her hips. Forehead to forehead, I bent to her, cradling the back of her neck in my hands and resting my thumbs on her cheeks. She exhaled; I inhaled, drawing her breath into me. Da understood my intention and stirred. A squeeze at my wrist grounded me in the present, in my own body, even as I sank into Meredith.

This wasn't weeping luna. It was another white flower. Crowded spiked petals. Angry, sharp pistil—red like it'd just tasted blood.

I'd never needed to speak while drawing out poison and found my face numb and my tongue heavy. Already, I was too weak to sit up.

"Sybil's plight," I slurred and felt the king's hand on my back. "It's sybil's plight."

Unfortunates who befell its influence were cursed to eternal sleep; the white bloom so named after an ill-fated girl so overworked she declared to the twilight that she wanted nothing more than a good long rest. A spirit heard her, though the stories differ in the nature of the spirit. Sometimes it's a lord of the below in the guise of a bat. Sometimes it's one of the restless dead enamored by her beauty. They offer her a white flower and say she has only to put its petals under her pillow and some under her mistress's pillow and she will find respite from her lady's ceaseless demands. Sybil does, and the next morning, her mistress is discovered dead. The daughter finds the petals and accuses Sybil of working malicious energy—of having made a pact with a devil. When Sybil goes in search of the spirit and tells them of her troubles, they invite her to take the rest she had wished for. Having no more means, Sybil wearily assents. Here too, the tellings differ. Is Sybil cursed to an eternal sleep, lost forever to the woods? Or is she, like her mistress, dead? I wanted to think she took the spirit's hand and was led to a new world where every night she fell into a pleasant sleep and took naps as she pleased in the afternoon sun and all her dreams were sunset hued and rimed in gold.

A headache bloomed in time with my slowed heartbeat. Moonlight flickered and went out. Or I couldn't open my eyes. Couldn't draw a full breath. *Meredith, find Meredith.* I sank into the slick of her. She was lovely inside, pink and lush. Her blood leapt at my touch, and she opened to me, encouraged me deeper, guided me to where she hurt. I found the threads of poison cobwebbing through her chest and growing as fast as she fought it off. Ugly stalemate. I tore the web. Her chest expanded. A gasp of breath. A heady exhale. I breathed it in. Sweet girl. There. Unbound, she could fight.

ELEVEN

I RUBBED MY EYES, and my hands came away red. I jolted upright. Beyond a fading headache, I felt no pain. Red dotted my dress too, though upon calmer inspection, the staining was lighter than blood. I studied my hands again, licked my fingertips. Sweet.

Last night drifted back—the king and her throne, the garden and the fire, the hound and the red fruit. I hadn't thought to taste it, had been too awed or intimidated by everything around me. I sat where Meredith had lain, alone in a bed much too big for me. If she was gone, must she have recovered?

Daylight shone as a sharp line between the bed curtains. I petted the pillows, scrunched the heavy blankets in my hands, and admired the floral whorls carved into the headboard, tracing the patterns under my fingertips.

I was here in the castle.

I turned over the pillows and blankets again, searching for scales. Losing something in this bed was too easy. For a fleeting moment, I almost missed my narrow monastery bed and its thin cotton sheet, how my feet would dangle over the edge if I stretched. No getting lost. No getting tangled in sheets made of finer fabric than my dresses. After a purge at the monastery, Da would always curl on my chest, but today I couldn't find him. He was gone. I clawed the sheets away from the mattress, wedged my hand into the small gap at the headboard. I was making a mess. My breath came faster. Da would not leave me. Da would never, ever leave.

Beyond the curtains, a gasp punctured the silence. I froze. A sigh followed, stretching to a whimper, a breathy "My king." I had once pleaded for her like that, blindfolded, the aftertaste of poison on my tongue.

On my hands and knees, I crept to a gap in the curtains. I hadn't meant to spy, though what else had I expected to see? Lovely Meredith stood against the wall with her head thrown back, painted lips parted on a moan. Her bodice slouched low, exposing her trembling, flushed chest. She held her immaculate skirts at her waist, hands fisted in the taffeta. Our king, leisurely in her ministrations, knelt between her legs. She held Meredith's leg over her shoulder, one hand gripping the plush flesh of her thigh, the other pinning her hip against the wall.

Meredith's cries shook me like an epiphany. I wanted her the way the king had her. I wanted the king to take me with the same devotion she lavished upon Meredith, as if she would halt the machinery of an entire kingdom to savor this moment. My breath quickened at the sight of them locked together. Heat twisted low in my belly. *I should look away.*

I didn't. Meredith's eyes fluttered open, her unfocused gaze sharpening when she spied me. Thoroughly shamed, I thought to retreat, but then she smiled, slow and pleasure-drunk, her tongue making a lascivious sweep of her full lips. I longed to kiss her and remembered that she was the king's, not mine. We were both, foremost, the king's. How soon might she ask me to open my legs for her and how often? Could I please her as Meredith did?

Again, she moaned for the king, though her gaze remained trained on me. She wanted me to see her, wanted me to enjoy her. Heat dripped down my thighs. I longed to touch myself where I swelled and ached. I wanted the pleasure that Meredith flaunted.

I could do nothing but watch her come undone. Pleasure arched her. Her mouth filled with *my king, my king*, with utter devotion. So spent, she let her skirts fall. The king towered again. Meredith blinked up at her, and I knew that look. One night in these walls was all it took to understand. Here she was, a woman I'd dragged from the threshold of death mere hours ago and ready to tread the line again. When my turn came to answer the king's question, when she asked me whether there was anything else I desired, I'd say *no* and welcome my own end. I knew because I felt it already as a thorn in my heart.

The king cupped Meredith's face in her hands, kissed her forehead and cheeks. "I could not have lost you," she said, though this was our purpose, to lose ourselves so she might continue. She helped Meredith back into her dress, her attention on the laces as focused as a cleric attending the angel's altar. With a last kiss upon her shoulder, the king said, "Wait for me at the table."

Meredith dropped into a deep curtsy, her head bowed. "Yes, my king," she returned as if she hadn't gasped and moaned under the king's attention only a moment ago.

I retreated from the curtain. The door opened and closed. Steps advanced toward the bed, and the king parted the curtain. Her dress was black again today, though of a more traditional northern cut. Ruched black flowers were tucked among the flounces of a floor-length skirt. The neckline's severe pleats emphasized her angular features.

She observed me knowingly. "Meredith succeeded in waking you, I see."

"It's no problem," I said too breathily, self-conscious of the heat still between my thighs. There was nothing to say after the look Meredith had given me.

The king took my chin again, forcing me to meet her gaze. She rested a hand on the bed and leaned close, her attention slipping down to where I'd worried my bottom lip swollen. She smelled like Meredith, and when she kissed me, she tasted of Meredith. We shared her between us like this, and my hunger for them both sharpened.

"Thank you for returning her to me," the king said against my lips. "I'm certain she'll find a way to show her appreciation to you."

I wanted to throw my arms around her neck and pull her back into a kiss. I wanted to beg her to touch me. I wanted her to push me down on the bed and order me as she pleased.

She saw my naked desire and withdrew. "Don't doubt that I want you. But I've found the drama of ceremony heightens my pleasure, especially with my new girls. I still have guests to entertain, and it'd be the perfect moment to properly introduce you as mine. Would that please you?"

Her words were a balm. "Yes, my king," I answered.

She considered me, her gaze roving over my stained dress and disheveled braids. "You've not eaten since your arrival?"

So I hadn't, I realized only as she said it. I'd been so enchanted that my body had forgotten its needs. "No, my king."

"We will feast today," she said with a flash of teeth. "I'll send Lenora to help you bathe and dress."

No one had ever helped me with such a simple and personal task, but then I remembered the north's complicated garments and thought better of declining. I likely couldn't find my way out of my current dress.

"Thank you—and a question, if I may ask it."

"You may."

"My da. I can't find him." I held my wrist where he'd been last. "I remember having him here when I helped Meredith. He makes sure I wake up."

"Ah, yes." The king's lips quirked down. "He grew agitated and would not let anyone near while you were unconscious. For the safety of my staff, I took him to the courtyard."

"Is he well? Has anyone seen him today?"

The king came close again and took my face in her hands. "I would not let any harm come to something precious to you."

My heart beat fast. Were I at the monastery, I would've demanded him brought to me. I would've neglected my duties to find him. Ma was dead. I needed to look after Da's spirit. It had adhered to the snake for a reason. I couldn't abandon him again. I couldn't let him die again.

The king stroked my cheek. "We all have our ghosts, Carlotta. They make their demands, some of which we must heed, but you're the one who lives. Why are you here?" she asked in the same voice from the dream, low and exacting.

"You sent for me, my king," I answered and knew it wouldn't satisfy her. It didn't satisfy me.

"Why are you here?" she asked again, "in the bed of my only surviving poison girl, wet for her and desperate for my touch?"

"I . . ."

A wry smile revealed her teeth. "Why are you, a devoted servant of the angel, here in this evil house and eager for your own corruption?"

My skin burned with each question. I struggled to hold the flame of her unblinking gaze but knew that I must.

She rose to her full height. "I will meet you at the table," she said and let the curtain fall.

Lenora was my age, a northern girl with a kind round face that set me at ease. She wore her hair like Meredith did, ringlets spilling loose down her back. Her figure was thin and boyish, her arms toned from work like the women of my village. I liked her immediately, and I could tell from her talkativeness that she liked me too.

The basin was a pool grand enough to swim in, and the water smelled of mint and lemongrass—a plant I'd never heard of. My eyes had filled with tears. So much water for the purpose of bathing alone! Lenora had held my hands and reassured me that we had plenty of water for drinking elsewhere and that one wouldn't want to drink this water anyway. It owed its milky aventurine hue to the minerals in the stone, she said. Wonderful for the skin, though unpleasant on the palate. And no, the pond in the garden was not for drinking either but for aesthetics. Here too the black stone grew, veining through the arches and columns above us. I was about to ask about it when Lenora spoke first.

"I wish I could be a royal poison girl," she said. She kept working on my hair as she spoke, her fingers combing through my wet curls. "You're so lucky."

In a way, I did feel lucky—to have survived and survived again, to have been chosen. And luck did not imply the absence of heartache, only a strike of fortune. I passed over the matter of my luck and said, "How long have you worked for the king?"

"A plague took my family five years ago, and I applied to be a handmaiden here. The castle has become a haven for me. Most of us share a story of fleeing misfortune into this community. I cannot protect the king as you do, but supporting your work brings me pride."

A castle full of orphans and otherwise tragic women was all that propped up our kingdom. It would be funny if I weren't so personally invested.

"Does the king often host celebrations like this?" I asked.

"No, this is the first." Lenora's fingers snagged in a tangle, and she apologized. "Your hair is beautiful. It's very thick!"

So Da had said when he braided my hair. He said it was like Ma's.

"Thank you," I said, unable to receive the compliment with more warmth. Then, "Why is she hosting it now?"

Lenora's hands slowed, and her contemplation stretched. "It was a surprise to us all when she announced it. She's been . . . ill of late."

So the red woman had mentioned. I reached for her name again only to come up with conspicuous nothingness. Had she really never introduced herself? Had I forgotten the name of someone so unforgettable? I stopped trying to think of her, and half my question returned.

"I heard she was taken with melancholy."

"You've met Meredith, yes? The girls are saying you revived her."

I could only think of Meredith as I'd seen her this morning, of the heat in her gaze. "I did."

"Did she mention anything to you? About the past months?"

"We haven't yet had a proper conversation."

"I see." Another maddening pause. I couldn't place the cause of her hesitation.

I turned to face her. Her eyes went wide, her hands still hovering where they'd been in my hair a moment before. The water lapped at our shoulders.

"What happened?"

Lenora lowered her hands into the water. "For as long as I've known her, the king has kept three poison girls. Of late, her ability to weather the losses has suffered. Meredith has been her only poison girl for months. The king ate less and less. We were all scared for her. We rarely saw her. She stopped coming to the table and only took meals in her room, requesting rare meat and pomegranates and not much else. Then one day, Meredith emerged and said there would be a celebration. So you see, Meredith has your answer." She set her hands on my shoulders to turn me again. "Please, I should finish your hair. We shouldn't keep the king waiting."

"She mentioned a ceremony to introduce me," I said.

"Oh, yes! Your first taste of your new life." Lenora seemed relieved for the change in topic. "Customarily, only the king and your fellow royal poison girls would be present for first tastings, but because of Anne's celebration, you'll have all the kingdom's poison girls to welcome you. You're so lucky," she said again.

I was lucky that I had Lenora to escort me to the great hall. As when the red woman had shown me to the throne room, I couldn't tell inner from outer walls, upper floors from lower floors. It seemed we climbed one staircase only to descend another shortly after. Each corridor was as identical and deserted as the last with long stretches without any doorways. For the castle to be so full of guests, there were no signs of life. No echoes of footsteps. No snatches of conversation.

"Your sense of direction is impressive," I commented.

Lenora's smile was sympathetic. "The original inhabitant of the castle was paranoid, as monarchs are, and only trusted his family to oversee the design. It was to be intentionally unintuitive in case of a breach. King Emelia's presence has intensified the effect of the original design, but don't worry. Once you're bound to her, you'll have clarity."

"Outside, people say the castle is growing. Or rising from hell."

Lenora giggled. "Well, it *is* growing. Over the years, it has fit itself to King Emelia's tastes and her mental states through no exertion on her part."

We found another grand corridor lined with paintings as tall as the high ceilings, and I took it as my clue that we neared our destination. If this were a pattern and if the castle reflected its king, all the public-facing rooms would connect to extravagant corridors like this.

Lenora stopped before two glassy black doors framed by a marble tableau of unearthly creatures. Some were locked in combat, teeth or swords at each other's throats; others tangled in ecstatic postures. An orgiastic meeting, one body indistinguishable from another, crowned the arch of the doors. The scene did nothing to calm my building nerves.

Lenora placed a supportive hand on my back and murmured reassurances. She patted my hair and dress again as though checking that an arrangement in a vase was just so before presenting it to its recipient. This dress, of course, was beautiful and white again—feathered lace dipping low at the neckline, a mad froth of skirts flaring from the waist. I liked the bracing undergarment she'd laced me into. It held me steady and tall, and I was thankful for all help in this. Yet I also felt an unexpected sting of longing for my southern dresses, their earth tones and light fabrics and breezy silhouettes. I attempted to run my fingers through my braids, and my hand closed around air. Lenora had taken down my usual style and done one circlet in a big dramatic braid around my head. I'd liked it when she showed me, but now I had nothing to occupy my hands.

For all the talk of a gathered party, I could hear nothing on the other side of the door.

"You're beautiful, miss," Lenora soothed me. "You'll do well for the king, I'm certain."

Questions crowded my mind, but Lenora had already grasped the sculpted golden handle—an arched winged creature—and was leading me through the doors.

Warm, fragrant air and the din of a dozen conversations washed over us. At the end of the hall, a hearth wide and high enough to accommodate a dancing couple burned with the same disciplined column of fire I'd seen in the red woman's room. The ceiling's vaulted height was too dizzying to fathom, its entire length painted with the same violent, indulgent scene as was carved into the marble arch outside. Battles among beastly winged people transitioned to wild lovemaking and back again, all of them trapped in a relentless cycle of excess. Below the heavy chandelier, the kingdom's poison girls sat around a long table of shining black stone laden with glazed meat and glistening fruit. Women leaned on each other's shoulders or fed tiny forkfuls of meat to their conversation partners. Meaningful looks passed across the table, hands meeting to hold in the middle. At the head of the party, in a chair that could only be described as a small throne, King Emelia overshadowed it all. Our gazes locked, and she stood, a small but proud smile gracing her lips. Silence fell.

Every poison girl rose to her feet. The floor between us stretched to an eternity, and only a foggy sense of decorum kept me from running to my king. I watched her watching me. My smile was too wide, but I could do nothing to stop it. I forgot about my stiff dress and the ceremony. I forgot about the concerns I'd had beyond these walls and the losses that had driven me here. There was only my King Emelia and I, a fresh sacrifice to her deathless reign.

She took my hand as I reached her and pulled me close. My heart was too fast. I was sick with delight. Meredith set a golden tray before us: four crystal chalices, three full, the fourth empty; a delicate silver blade. Down the long table, dozens of beautiful faces peered at me. And the king overwhelmed me with the flowery scent of the garden that clung to her, the warmth of her body against mine, and how she looked at me—as if I alone could sustain her.

"She's perfect. Thank you, Lenora," the king said, admiring me all the while.

She guided me before the table, to the tray Meredith had set. I saw the knife again. Too dainty for the intention of cutting meat. Too wicked a profile for spreads. The king said something to our audience, an introduction, her musings on the role of royal poison girls as sacred companions. I stared at the chalices. Guessed at their contents. One filled with water. One filled with milk. One filled with wine. One empty. The king raised her hand to my neck, her thumb and forefinger in the soft underside of my jaw. Meredith's eyes gleamed with hunger, a feral mirror of our meeting in the bedroom. She wanted to bite and draw blood. Her gaze flicked from the king's face to mine, expectant, waiting for a signal to strike. I looked away from her. I was too hot now, my back flush against the king like this, her hand against my throat. Above, through the frame of the chandelier, the beastly soldiers lapped blood from their lovers' wounds.

Meredith took the water from the tray, and as one, each poison girl raised an identical glass I hadn't noticed before. "To your life, Carlotta," they recited in unison, all of them watching with expectant smiles.

I searched for the borderland woman among them and couldn't spot her. Meredith tipped the chalice against my lips, and I opened for her. The water's chill shocked me, so cold that it burned down my throat. I drained the glass and shivered.

"To your life," the king echoed, her murmur slithering under my skin.

The painting shifted. Lovers raised swords.

"To your strength, Carlotta," the poison girls chanted next, and Meredith brought the second chalice to my lips.

It was milk—mildly sweet and too thick. I gagged, but Meredith kept pouring, her eyes alight.

"To your strength," said the king, her voice a breath against my ear.

The party gave a final cheer, wine held high. "To your happiness, Carlotta!"

Meredith brought the third chalice. This wasn't the golden wine served last night. This was deep red and so bitter it dried my tongue.

She kissed my cheek. "To your happiness," Meredith said in the king's voice. The poison girls stood with their empty wineglasses, faces now solemn as if this had been an entirely different sort of ceremony all along.

Meredith took up the knife and the empty chalice.

"My king," I whispered.

Her gaze was on the knife. "You're doing so well, my dear," she murmured. "Do you trust the hunger that brought you here?"

This had always been the path. Here were my aspirations before me, finally in reach. I didn't fear poison or death. What was a knife?

"Yes, my king," I answered.

"Good." She took my wrist in her other hand, holding my arm out to Meredith and her knife. "It will not hurt. Look, if you are bold."

In the soft bend at my elbow, Meredith found a vein and opened it. I gasped, more from shock at the sight of my blood spilling free than from any real pain. I watched it run and worried the chalice was too big, that I would faint before I filled it and disappoint the king. A war raged across the painting above her now, lovers declaring sides, and she herself had changed. I didn't think a mouth could be so wide. This was a jaw that could unhinge and swallow prey whole.

Wet heat across my skin drew my attention back to Meredith. She lapped at the cut she'd made, her lips red with blood and smeared rouge. The same pleasured look from before softened her features, her gaze half lidded and distant.

"How is she?" the king asked, trading my wrist for the stem of the chalice.

Rapt, Meredith watched the king raise my blood to her lips and answered, "The best we've had."

The king swirled my blood in the chalice, inhaled, and drank.

The room melted and thrummed, her sated hum shivering through the stone. It was the sigh at my ear and the moan in my throat. We breathed as one, every poison girl. Frescoes smeared into riotous color above. Candlelight stretched. Meredith's lips were on my throat, my hands in her hair, our kisses blurry. Her heat, the king's, and the cold stone around us. Through them, I knew the castle as a body like our bodies—its contours and longings. The corridors heaved with our breaths. The painted subjects in their frames gasped and writhed.

As suddenly as it had dissolved, reality snapped solid. Meredith flinched as if from a bright light and hid her face in the crook of my shoulder. The poison girls at the table blinked dazedly, all of them entangled and draped across laps, dresses rumpled, a hand beneath a skirt, long hair in a firm fist, lips kiss swollen. The king lowered the empty chalice.

"The best," she agreed.

TWELVE

T HE KING CARRIED ME to her bedchamber. The way glittered with clusters of black stone where walls met floor and ceiling, growing thicker the farther we went. The view was enchanting by candlelight, like descending into a magical cave even as we climbed the stairs. I went with my arms around her neck and my head nestled against her chest.

Beside us, Meredith held a plate of tiny delights: a flowering green vegetable roasted and drizzled with red sauce, thin cuts of smoked red meat, pale cheeses aged with dried herbs, and rosy fruits in alien shapes.

"What did the clerics feed you?" the king asked.

"We had oats mostly, brought to us by the villagers. Potatoes, sometimes. Apples after the harvest."

The king clicked her tongue. "They know nothing. Poor thing. You bleed monthly, don't you?"

"Yes."

"Then we cannot allow you to eat like a goat."

Meredith giggled.

"The door, please, Meredith," the king prompted, and I peered over my shoulder to find another set of doors like the ones downstairs. The knights stood at either side. Despite the king's reassurance about her companion spirits, a tinge of unease still gripped me at the sight of them. Meredith didn't spare so much as a glance. She balanced the plate and shouldered open the doors.

Cavernous and black as night, the king's chamber seemed of another world. Here, the black stone had taken over entirely—smooth along the floors and rippling up the irregular walls. Stalactite clusters hung from the vaulted ceiling. Fat candles dripped wax from little alcoves or from where they'd been set upon the flatter protrusions in the floor. The room glittered with their flames, every surface a dark mirror for their light. As in Meredith's room, glass doors overlooked a courtyard balcony, but I wasn't sure whether these opened anymore. Stone crusted over the hinges and spread along the threshold, creeping up the glass.

Though entire homes in my village could fit within this single room, it lacked the trappings and comforts of a personal chamber save for the giant bed. Its frame grew up from the floor or—just as likely—the wood had been swallowed and encased in stone. Luxurious crimson and cream linens did impressive work softening the space: Tufted pillows and white furs and velvety throws spilled from the bed. Immaculate embroidered pieces had been unceremoniously abandoned on the floor to be stepped on.

In all this extravagant softness, the king arranged me on a mountain of pillows as if setting a precious gem into its case. Meredith curled against me and lay her head on my belly. I followed the impulse to drape my arm over her and was surprised by how natural it felt, how we fit together. Seeing us like this eased the last lines of tension from the king's posture, and she settled on my left, taking the plate Meredith had brought into her lap. The king fed me little morsels of food from her hands, admiring me as if this was the purpose she kept me for. I'd never had a meal so varied and rich, not even when Da was able to bring home small delicacies from the market. I hummed through my first bites, happy to close my eyes and savor this—the food, the king's attention, Meredith's comforting weight. The meats were seasoned with smoky spices uncommon to the borderlands. The many seeds of the conical berries were a surprise and then a delight. The cheese was strongly aromatic, the herbs mellowed upon tasting by its creamy density.

The king left the strange vegetable for last, unconcerned by how the sauce coated her hands as she plucked it apart. I liked the precise flex of her long fingers. I liked watching her unmake something just for me. Beneath the sauce's tart sugar, the leaves had their own subtle sweetness, a perfectly roasted balance to the vegetable's bitter crunch. The flower gone, the king set the plate aside and held her fingers to my lips. I licked the sauce from her skin, taking a finger, two, into my mouth and sucking away the last of the sweetness. I tested the sharp edge of her nails with my tongue, admired the structure of her fingers with my mouth. The king's eyes fluttered briefly closed. Meredith's weight shifted lower. The king's gaze flicked to her and darkened. She took her fingers from my mouth and cupped my chin.

"Might we have another taste of you?" she asked.

Her question was enough to summon a pulse of heat between my legs. I clenched around nothing.

"Yes, my king," I breathed.

She looked to Meredith again, her eyes bright with anticipation. I wanted to see Meredith's face, wanted to know whether she wore that same look from before, but when I shifted, the king pinned me.

"Look only at me," she said and leaned close as if to bite. "Tonight, your pleasure is mine."

Meredith pushed my skirts up around my hips. Cool air tightened my skin against the feverish kisses she laid on the insides of my thighs.

I blinked up at the king, my thoughts momentarily too scattered to speak. "Yes, my king."

"You will not be timid. Open your legs properly so that Meredith can admire you."

I breathed fast. My lungs fought against the constriction of my laces. The anticipation from the dream was true, and now I was here in my body and under her command. "Yes, my king," I whispered and obeyed.

"Good girl." She lifted my wrist to her lips and breathed against the soft skin like savoring a bouquet. I admired how she admired me. I was something to revel in.

Meredith's touch was a mirror of hers, worshipfully soft in her attention. She trailed her fingers through the slick of my arousal and up to the sensitive bud at the apex. I gasped and arched, reminded myself that this was real and that I was allowed to feel it. There would be no more shadowed lovers. I was here now. Meredith explored me gently, pressing, circling, finding what made me hum, chasing the rhythm that made me roll my hips into her touch. She turned her face against my thigh and whispered sweet praises into my skin. The king nodded to something—a wordless question—and Meredith's fingers slipped inside me. I bit down on a cry. I hated the way I'd conditioned myself in the monastery.

King Emelia gave me a searching look. "You have the blood of a woman destined to be a royal poison girl, and my poison girls do not shrink from pleasure. I want to hear you."

She took my wrists in one hand and cupped my chin again with the other, watching. I burned under her gaze. A tight coil of heat built low in my belly. Meredith bit the inside of my thigh and sighed into me. She added a finger, stretching me open. I swallowed a moan. I was so wet for her I could hear it.

"Do not deny me," urged the king. "I want to hear you."

At her words, Meredith crooked her fingers and angled her thumb against me. A bright burst of pleasure shot through me. I whimpered.

"Know you're beautiful like this," said the king. "You'll learn to bend for me, to break if you must."

Then Meredith's mouth was upon me, and I forgot what it was to be self-conscious. A cry ripped from me. My hips bucked against her. She held my thighs and moaned, her pleasure vibrating through my flesh.

"My king," I gasped.

The world snapped. My body arched. Released. Trembled under the obliterating wash of sensation. I trembled with it. Meredith was close now and offering her hand to the king as if she had unearthed something precious. She bore nothing but my slick arousal. I watched the king lick the taste of me from her fingers, how Meredith had that ravenous look in her eyes again, her lips and chin still wet.

"She's so good, my king. She's—" Meredith glanced down at me, wild fervor in her eyes. "She's perfection."

"Yes." The king kissed Meredith's palm. "Hold her."

The air was hot between us, that delirious swell of energy from the great hall doubling back. The room distorted, black and glitter bending everywhere I looked. My head was in Meredith's lap and emptied as if I'd stood too fast. She petted my hair, my cheek. "We're so happy you came to us, Carlotta," she murmured. The candles shone in her eyes. The king was kneeling between my legs. I opened myself for her. Her tongue was lavish. I would bend, break.

I didn't dream. My imagination could've offered me nothing better than what King Emelia had bestowed. I had everything I'd ever longed for: to be pretty and adored among other pretty things deserving of adoration. And yet, when I woke, my first thoughts were of home.

I had forgotten Da, though I promised myself I would never. I had forgotten Ma's poetry as soon as I'd arrived, abandoning the last of her gifts to me in a room I didn't know the way back to. Guilt squeezed my chest. My parents, they had adored me. I'd known this. Of course I'd known this. Why, then, did it suddenly feel like an unbearable weight?

I sat up. I was free of my dress though didn't remember changing out of it. A white nightgown identical to Meredith's hung from my shoulders. And there she slumbered beside me, her soft body curled around where I'd lain. The assembly of candles burned on. The king was gone. I swung my feet over the edge of the bed and stopped. I was watched. I glanced back at Meredith still asleep. My feet hovered only inches from the floor, but something so simple as getting out of bed no longer felt safe or correct. This wasn't a room where anything could hide, and yet I found myself scanning the walls.

Shining black against shining black, one of the knights stood at the wall opposite the foot of the bed. I startled when I made it out—wicked helm, sharp epaulettes—because I'd been staring at it all along.

This one was different. The knights always faced straight ahead. They never turned their heads, and yet this one had, its faceplate at an angle to its body. Watching me. My heartbeat readied for a chase that didn't happen. We stared at each other. Had it been here since we entered? Had I been so enchanted that I'd missed it?

It is safest if you pay them no mind, the king had said. I tore my gaze away and leapt to my feet.

"Carlotta?" Meredith's voice was crinkled from sleep. She raised herself from the nest of pillows. Her ringlets were crushed. "Where are you going? Please don't leave me."

"I need to find the garden," I said. "Where is the king?"

Meredith squinted at the balcony doors. "It's night. Why do you need the garden at night? Come back to bed. The king wanders."

Mournful gray had pervaded the sky since my arrival, so dark that I hadn't noticed how truly late the hour was. How had we slept through the last half of the day? I must've stared so long that my confusion showed on my face.

"Our welcome can be tiring for a new poison girl," Meredith said, now awake enough to smirk. "Hence why you should come back to bed."

I wanted to. How easy it'd be to let her fold me into her arms and take me back to those downy pillows.

"I need to find my da," I explained.

Meredith frowned.

"I mean—the king said she took my snake to the garden."

Her frown deepened only to clear with a splutter of laughter. "I can't fathom what the hell you mean, and that sounds like a terrible euphemism, but *finally* an interesting new girl."

Out in the corridors, things had changed. The dark and neglected corners I'd met on every journey so far had vanished. New sconces were lit and adequately spaced. Spiraling vines reminiscent of the ones gracing King Emelia's horns were set in stone relief, their patterns curving down archways and columns. When I leaned close to admire the lifelike detail on a stone bud, it blossomed, petals unfurling toward my outstretched hand.

Meredith cupped the flower, and the stone blushed pink, transmuting into soft life. She took a shuddering breath and plucked it from the vine. She sighed, tears spilling down her smiling cheeks. She tucked the bloom behind my ear and kissed me, throwing her arms around my neck. "Our king is happy again."

No one had ever looked at me as she did, as if I had arrived bearing the dawn cupped in my palms. I thought it had all been the heat of the ceremony, but the look in her eyes was true. She thought I had done this, that I could sway the heart of a king.

As we descended the stairs, I found Meredith wasn't leading me. We walked side by side as peers, two people who individually understood the way to their destination. Upon crossing the threshold of the king's chamber, clarity had settled, the whole of the castle opening up to me as if I finally held the map. The garden wasn't far. I was no longer lost.

The lower corridors were alight with merriment, the poison girls from the great hall having continued on without us and spilling through the castle's arteries. Women passed in rumpled dresses, once immaculate updos slouching and frizzing. Some had abandoned their dresses altogether. They leaned unselfconsciously into friends or lovers, laughing wide mouthed and slopping the contents of their cups upon the floors. As a red arc missed her, Meredith squealed delightedly and dragged me through the throng.

I was dizzied by the loosed bodices and loose lips, gossip flowing as freely as the wine. To the left: one woman marching to another, a slap. To the right: five women on the floor in a pool of silks, their mouths kiss swollen and rouge smudged along necks. Soft skin, sweet wine, and a clash of perfumes dampened the air. Temple could never compare to this. The clerics' liturgies were nothing to this babel of poison girls, all the singing and giggling and shouting harmonizing into one uproarious voice. This was the gathering of pilgrims I wanted. These seekers I understood.

Around a corner where the din faded, a woman stood nude and alone, contemplating the painting of the speared angel. She held a crystal plate of grapes and tore them fast from the vine, watching the gory scene with the same rapt attention of a cat tracking its prey. Her hands, mouth, and eyes moved in twitches—fruit to mouth, eyes right left right. The painting was alive only to her.

I paused at her back, an uncertain question on my lips, and Meredith pulled me along.

"She's had a good flower," Meredith murmured. "Let her be."

"A good flower?" I echoed.

She paused thoughtfully. "Poison girls have found gentler uses for some flowers. In small amounts, certain varietals can be diluted into calming tonics. Select pollens bestow visions or light the world in new colors. It's like dreaming while awake, though only some enjoy these journeys."

I turned to watch the woman over my shoulder. She did not notice us.

Outside, the crisp air was refreshing as a cool cloth to the face. The quiet pressed into my ears. Clouds had overtaken the moon, dimming its light as though a gauzy curtain had been pulled across it. Grateful for the king's small lights, I captured one of the flames as it drifted close on a breeze. This side of the garden was different than where I'd visited my first night. Pale trees sheltered the path of the western entrance, their boughs pleached into arches overhead. Vines grew up the length of the trunks and into the canopy. In the low light, it was nearly impossible to tell which flowers belonged to the vines and which to the trees themselves.

"Tell me again what we're looking for," said Meredith, taking my hand in hers.

Giddy delight buzzed through me at the simple comfort of the gesture—*here I am, linking myself to you*. Upon my arrival, I'd been so focused on whether the king wanted me that I hadn't considered how much I longed for the company of a fellow poison girl.

"I *am* quite lovely, I know," Meredith teased when I continued to stare, speechless, at her.

I ducked my head and stifled a laugh. An odd feeling took up in my belly, something awkward and fluttering. Staring determinedly ahead, I led her down the path. Her searching gaze burned my face, but I didn't look at her. I wanted to share the story of what had happened to me, and I needed her to understand.

"Do you know about the drought in the borderlands?" I asked.

"Not much," she admitted. "The Perch cities are only concerned with themselves. Any news about the wider kingdom or continent is filtered through how it may help or harm us. Years ago, all the talk was about the failing maize harvests in the south, presented as an issue for bakers needing to source different grains."

My heart twisted. "I see." Our life-consuming tragedy framed only as a minor inconvenience of distribution.

Meredith squeezed my hand. "But I know it's more than that. If you want to tell me."

The trees had changed. The short ones with the sturdy red fruits grew along the path. *Pomegranates* Lenora had called them. My search would be frustrating, possibly futile. I could walk the entire garden and never see Da, especially in this light. He could be anywhere, under anything, twined in any branch. I ventured off the path and into the tall flowering grasses. Meredith followed.

"My mother was a poison girl," I said, taking up a stick and parting the grass before I stepped. "I never knew her, but she sent her earnings home to my da to support us. Because of her, it took longer for us to feel how desperate things had become. Then, just before the dust storms began, she died. The lord she was contracted to never paid us what we were promised—some large final sum that was to be distributed upon her death. My da tried to coax our fields back to life, but they'd been abandoned too long, and they wouldn't have yielded soon enough to feed us. Dead maize was everywhere. It became all you could see. Farmers started leaving for the north if they had family to take them in. The day I left our farm was the day I found my da dead in the barn."

Meredith's tone was light as tiptoes. "And he's since become a snake?"

"*He* isn't the snake, but it carries his soul and his will. I think it sensed his suffering and relieved him. You'll understand when you meet. He could not be mistaken for a common animal."

"I see."

"He has tried to protect me and been a constant companion."

"And so then you found the castle?"

"I was rescued by the Clerical Order of Angelic Restoration. They left the borderlands for their northern monastery and took me to live with them. I've been there these past five years, helping the valley folk the way I helped you."

"A monastery girl! The real thing!" Meredith exclaimed.

"What do you mean?" I asked, looking at her now.

"It is a common fantasy people have. Something about the clerical garb and the feathers and . . ." She hummed thoughtfully. "Touching divinity." Here she gave a mischievous quirk of her eyebrow. "We kept costumes of the veil on hand for when patrons requested it."

"A fantasy of playing dress-up?" I asked.

"Oh, sweet thing, you *are* from a monastery, aren't you?"

"Yes." I frowned. "As I've said. Though I never pledged the veil."

Tangled in the shelter of the pondside fronds, two women startled as we passed. I had almost missed them in the dark and startled in return. Meredith did not, staring at the woman who lay beneath her partner. Her bodice was rucked down, her skirts pushed up. Again, I felt unmannered but couldn't glance away. Is that how I'd looked only hours before under Meredith and the king?

The alarm in the woman's eyes cleared, and she smiled indulgently, reaching out to us in silent invitation. Her partner trailed kisses down her chest and thrust into her so that she gasped and arched her back. Meredith went to them, kneeling to kiss the woman in the grass and whispering something in her ear that made her breath catch. The woman's partner lay a tentative hand on Meredith's back, and when she turned to her, hunger alight in her eyes, the woman slipped the sleeve of Meredith's nightgown down her shoulder. I hadn't known anyone could look so at ease and confident at once in these states of half undress, a painting come to life—all artfully rumpled fabric and soft skin and loose postures.

I bit my lip, felt silly standing there as the woman took Meredith's nipple into her mouth and made her sigh. She slid her hand under the second sleeve, and Meredith's gown fell limp around her waist. The moonlight loved her with its glow. Seeing her so revealed, the woman in the grass rose to dust kisses along Meredith's neck, taking a fistful of her beautiful ringlets in hand and pulling her head back to expose the line of her throat. Those were bruising kisses. She would mark her the way I wanted to; they would take her apart, and yet I was too timid to step forward and claim her. The chorus of their sighs filled the night air, and Meredith trembled there on her knees. Then her glassy gaze slid to me.

"My Carlotta," she breathed. "Do you not want me?"

Her plea pulled me to her like a hypnotic spell, and I knelt with the other women who worshipped her. Her eyes darkened. Her breaths came fast. I cupped her face, and she looked at me as a dying person might, as if I were her last hope.

"Please, Carlotta," she said, and I kissed her as she came undone, moaning into my mouth.

The after was blurry—skin against skin and someone's dress and soft murmurs. Waking from their dreamy stupor, the couple returned to each other with renewed zeal, and we left them to continue on our way.

"Is everyone so free here?" I asked.

"Our lives are often short," Meredith said, leaning into me as we walked. "We could let fear and grief define us if we let them, but so many of us come from pasts where we were shunned or suffered. Why let it continue when we could love each other abundantly?"

The courtyard lulled me with its bobbing lights and foreign plants, with how pleasure could hide in the grasses. Overhead, the moon now threw its light against the swift-moving clouds, forming mysterious silver shapes where it cut through the shadows. I cast my gaze high and low, seeking a glimmer of dark scales.

"What was your life before the castle?" I asked.

Meredith hummed. "People will pay a pretty coin to bed a poison girl, at least in the Perch cities. Morbid curiosity made for a good living, and I liked that I wasn't tied to some insufferable lord or lady. I had freedom in a world that often doesn't afford as much to commoners like us. I could be happy."

"If you were happy with your life and freedom, how did you come to the king?"

A mysterious smile crossed her face. "The lady of the house said a very important patron had requested me, that it was a woman, and that she'd asked I wear a blindfold for the duration of our meeting. It wasn't a wholly unusual request. For some patrons, it's a power fantasy. Others, especially the noblewomen, simply want their anonymity. I couldn't have guessed the king had discovered me and sent Phaela in her stead."

Phaela! I shivered at the name. Questions piled on my tongue. Why would the king send her royal poet? What had she been like? Did Meredith see her often? But I didn't want to seem too provincial, didn't want to interrupt when Meredith was inviting me into her past.

"Phaela sat with me very politely and asked questions about my life and what I wanted. It was an interview. Then she left. She visited twice more. The third time, at the end, she asked me to remove the blindfold and promised me everything. That's why I left. I was happy enough, but I'd never felt so intensely adored. And I had my little cousins to think of. The king has promised that they'll be financially cared for. Pledged it in blood. No one else would do something like that for me. And so I would do anything for her."

Sacrifice ran in our veins. I thought of Ma.

"Have you seen your cousins since you came here?"

"Oh yes! Twice before the king fell ill. We hosted them here at the castle. If you have family, you should say something. The king wants us to be happy."

I did not have family, of course. I felt a strange relief for Meredith's cousins, then anger at my own lack, fresh as when I lost Ma. She had been planning to visit me, and Earl Huxley had kept her away. I breathed deep and dismissed the memory. I didn't want to be upset, not here with Meredith, not so soon. My anger was poisonous, and I wanted to stave it off as long as I could.

Silver moonlight. Breathe.

Blue grass. Breathe.

The wind blew a lovely fall of curls across Meredith's face. *Breathe.* Her hand in mine. A treasure.

I puzzled over her previous comment. "And in your work, you found people wanted to have sex with clerics?"

A laugh burst from her. "You've caught on!"

"But . . ." I thought of Seventh Starlight Seeker and Fifth Starlight Wanderer and couldn't help my frown. "Clerics are astoundingly withdrawn and uncharismatic. If you say anything with too much emotion, they will reply with esoteric reassurances about the angel."

Meredith was doubled over now. I worried she might suffocate on her laughter. "Fantasies are not about *reality*," she managed. "Of course you'd find nothing of interest in a cleric. You know them too well."

"If it is not about reality, then what is it about?"

With a cleansing sigh, she sobered and set her hands upon my shoulders. "The tension between the forbidden and the sacred," she answered, her gaze now intense as if to make up for her overflow of mirth. "An unknowable link between the earth and the heavens." She smoothed her hands up my neck. "And a desire to possess what is pure." She lifted my chin, making some evaluation of me. "I think, having met you, I can finally see the appeal in it."

"I am not pure," I said because I was close to squirming under her stare.

"No," she said, her lips quirking in a smile. "Or you wouldn't have come here. But you are rare, and the king collects rare, pretty things. For someone who's lived as long as her, novelty is a great prize."

"So many have served her. How could we amuse her?"

Meredith let me go and continued our walk. "I think she's compelled by the story of a woman. She found me like she found you, through rumors. I think it appeals to her when a poison girl makes her own way or chooses an unconventional path. It's hard to do, and she says it gives us intriguing character. Though sometimes, she slips and says *flavor*."

We came upon a plot of violet flowers, and I sank down among them. The long petals didn't arrange themselves in a neat radius but swooped high and low with the exuberance of a lady kicking up the flounce of her skirts. Like so many plants in the courtyard, I'd never seen them before and didn't know their name. I considered asking but let it be. There would always be time for flowers. Where was Da? Meredith joined me in the grass, settling her head upon my lap. How late was it now? I was tired. Perhaps Meredith was right and we should have stayed in bed. But then, this had been a lovely walk.

I decided to tell her as much, said, "Thank you for coming with me."

"I'm happy to. I've been alone for many months." Meredith threaded our hands again, unable to let me go for more than a moment. "The king was here, of course, but she was not herself."

"How so?"

A faraway look crossed her. She kissed my knuckles and held my hand against her chest. How intimate—right there, her heartbeat. The moonlight continued its play. The bulbs of fire flickered on the breeze. Shadow pooled in the hollows of Meredith's face.

"The king is everything to me. It hurts to see her hurt. I can't dwell on it. Right now, I'm happy."

THIRTEEN

I WOKE IN THE grass, my nightgown dew damp and the warm weight of a hand on my side. My shoulder ached. The sky had cleared to a civil shade of gray. The air smelled watery and green. Flecks of soil clung to my cheek as I sat up. And here was the king! With an indulgent smile on her face and a bundle of blankets in her lap. She was resplendent in a black gown, its bodice wicked and cutting. As daring as the dress she'd worn on the evening of my arrival, this one's neckline plunged in a steep V, its point terminating just above her navel. Between the black silk, a mesmerizing strip of skin and the proud curve of her breasts. No necklace again, the sharp jut of her collarbones adornment enough.

Like a fool, I hurried to brush the dirt from my face and straighten the awkward twist in my gown. Futile. I was an embarrassment. Beside me, Meredith stirred under King Emelia's touch, the bewilderment on her face mirroring how I felt.

"I leave the two of you alone and you become wild women, curling together in the grass like lost kittens," the king teased, fluttering blankets around our shoulders. "This will be the final blow to my reputation. I cannot even provide beds to my poison girls."

Meredith clutched her blanket about her shoulders and yawned. "I quite enjoy my bed. I'm sorry to have missed it."

The king turned Meredith's head to better inspect the bruises along her neck, their coloring flagrant in the dawn light. "You seem to have enjoyed yourself regardless," she noted.

Another yawn. "Yes. Some of the visiting poison girls were down by the pond. We interrupted them."

"And they tired you so thoroughly that you fell asleep in the grass?"

Meredith boldly took the king's wrist, kissing the hand that had held her. "We woke long enough for a pleasant stroll before sleep took us again."

"How do you fare, my Carlotta?" the king asked, absently petting Meredith's curls. She leaned into the touch, as catlike as we'd been accused of.

I passed a hand over where Meredith had made her ceremonial cut only hours ago and inspected the skin. It had already healed into a scar. "I'm well, my king. We ventured out to find my da," I said, worrying the tasseled edge of my wool blanket.

"I see." She closed her eyes, sinking a sharp hand into the earth. Her head turned this way and that, as though she were scanning the horizon. "He's in the hellebores," she said, rising. "Come."

Like shabby strays, we followed her. The hellebores were arresting, their petals so deep a red they were nearly black. I didn't venture among them, instead squatting at their border. I reached my hands into the flowers, and they stirred, a shivering disturbance among the leaves winding its way toward me. Meredith made a little sound of surprise when Da looped himself over my arm.

"You must stop biting," I chided even as tears turned the sight of him blurry. "No one here means us any harm."

Meredith peered over my shoulder. "I've never seen one like that," she said admiringly. "Those scales!"

His spines flared.

"Meredith, love," the king warned, pulling her away.

My chest seized. "Da, you must be cordial. This is our home now."

He disappeared into the shelter of the blanket, and my peaceful morning suddenly clouded.

"Perhaps he will come around in time," the king tried to soothe me, though she still hung back with Meredith.

He would not come around. His last concern before his death was that I not follow my mother's path in pledging my life to an aristocrat. This will, more than anything, guided the snake. When I stood, Da slithered back into the hellebores as though I had never cared to visit at all.

I did not understand why we were using so much water to bathe again today when I had bathed yesterday. I did not like Lenora's plan for my hair. I wanted to do it myself in a long southern style. She said it looked so pretty, and why didn't I ever wear it loose? I bit my tongue until I tasted blood.

Across from us, Meredith flirted with her handmaiden, Winifred, and regaled her with the story of how she'd come by her love bites. Their giggling and splashing grated on my nerves.

"Is something the matter, miss?" Lenora asked.

The terrible feeling that had been welling up in my chest since the garden broke, and I would drown in it publicly if I didn't escape. I hauled myself up out of the pool with an inelegant splash, slipping on the wet stone and landing on a knee in a burst of pain. I hissed a curse and limped for the stairs. Dripping and naked, I didn't know what to do once I reached the landing. I felt again like a small and silly girl. As I was still beneath the castle's main floors,

I doubted I would encounter anyone aside from the handmaidens and so wandered down what I supposed was a servants' hallway until I found a door. Inside was a small closet stacked with fresh linens. I let myself in and closed the door so that I was alone in the dark. On the cold floor, I hugged my knees to my chest and cried until I shook with it. A thin wail leaked from my mouth, defying my need for breath. On and on it went, a weak exhale of sound that I hadn't the power to stop.

A knock came at the door. I couldn't answer. The door opened, gray light flooding in from the high, narrow windows beyond. Someone cocooned me in a plush robe, pulling its hood up over my wet hair. She sat with me patiently until, eventually, the sound stopped. I couldn't look at her.

"The first days are hard for every poison girl," came Meredith's voice. "Beautiful and thrilling, but hard too."

My face was leaky and swollen. I hid it in the robe. Meredith settled beside me and pulled me into her. Oh, she was so soft and warm. My body recommitted itself to crying with renewed vigor, and I gritted my teeth through it like a disgusting task I'd been forced to see to completion.

Gently, Meredith asked, "You never got to properly mourn them, did you?"

I was all action! Swipe the letter! Craft a plan! I was dehydrated delusions and visions. The angel had never appeared to me. There was no one above to receive my atonement. To what end had I done anything? My parents were already dead.

"So many women come here fleeing their guilt," Meredith said. "You made your way with the options available to you, and there are rarely many."

But if I had not left Da to labor in the field alone, perhaps he wouldn't have been bitten, and if he hadn't been bitten, perhaps we could have gone north together. Because I had abandoned him, he was trapped between life and death, aware only enough to know that I continued to disappoint his final wishes.

Meredith hushed the tide of guilt. "No one is healed by visions of a future that didn't happen."

"Then what?" I asked miserably.

She turned my face to her and smoothed all my wet hair. I wanted to hide away my grief-ugly face, but she held my chin as the king might. The door was still cracked from her entry, leaving a slice of light to find her eyes.

"Only a certain kind of woman comes here. She's been called selfish or mad and dismissed. She's eternally out of place. Perhaps it has turned her melancholy. But she knows she's deserving of all the things society will not give her. That fire is rare, and the king senses it. That is why she's courted you here."

Meredith kissed my tear-stained cheeks. I flinched when she licked the salt from them, a breathy moan in her throat as when she'd tasted my blood. The sound unlocked something in me.

"Only women like us are capable of true devotion," she continued, a new edge in her tone. I understood how she could so easily wield a knife. How she could cut me open. "Only women like us can fully appreciate the beauty of our king and understand why she must be protected. That is your purpose now, not an imagined debt to your past. Grieve, but do not let guilt diminish you. Yes?"

I nodded at her prompting; my tears were mesmerized away.

"Good." Her kiss was hard, and I opened to it. If there was an ember on her tongue, I would let her burn me. I knew why the king had chosen her. "Tell Lenora what you want—how you'd like your hair, how you want to dress. We are seeing off our fellow poison girls today, and the king will no doubt ask you for your first tasting. It is important that you feel confident. You are here because it's what you have yearned for. The king has delivered it. Let her enjoy you. Yes?"

"Yes," I echoed, trembling in the wake of her kiss.

I was disappointed when I asked for redseed oil only to be met with confusion. Even at the monastery we could procure a bottle or two, but the tree must not favor the soil so far north. Lenora offered a honey gold oil instead and watched intently as I sectioned my hair for twists. I asked for a green dress, one that did not require the cinching undergarment. I'd liked how it held me up, but today I wanted something familiar. Lenora's smile was nervous, but still she said, "I'll do my best, miss," and left me to my hair.

I'd been shown to a bedchamber down the corridor from Meredith's and now sat before my very own vanity. All the castle's small staff lived along a hall of repurposed guest rooms, every door its own color, to reflect, I imagined, something about the woman who lived within. My furniture was bright as ivory—the wardrobe with its tall doors and carved floral motifs, the little writing desk with its neat stack of drawers, and of course the bed fit for a queen. A sedate painting of a field took up one wall, the blurry and bright impression of a landscape dwarfed by its heavy gold frame. The walls were papered satiny blue, the whole room promising as a spring sky.

I was halfway through twisting out my hair when Lenora returned, that pinch of nerves still on her face. She bowed apologetically, offering a pale-green dress in her arms. "It is not the style anymore to have so plain a skirt. Ladies prefer the defined bodice and waist . . ." Lenora trailed off as I rose from the vanity to take the dress from her.

It was not quite the flowing garments I was used to, but it maintained a loose shape where it fell from the bust, most of its fussy ornamentation in the puff of the sleeves.

"I love it," I said, running my hands over the taffeta.

Lenora exhaled, her usual smile settling back into place. She apologized for not being able to find a matching scarf in time but offered a silk ribbon to tie back my hair. I appreciated her thoughtfulness and thanked her for it.

The scarf of the borderlands was a symbol of its farmers, women who could not be bothered with the inconvenience of hair falling into their eyes as they worked. The style grew beyond its practical origins, taken up by all southern women as a statement of resilience and pride. I had never thought so much of it until now that I was outside the borderlands, now that it was gone. When I had settled in, I would ask for fabric and make my scarf. I ached for a defining feature of my identity, for a connection to my home.

Lenora buttoned me into my dress. I looped the ribbon around my twists, tying them so that they fell to the middle of my back.

"You look very pretty, miss," said Lenora proudly. "The king will be happy to see you."

The fluttering sensation took up in my belly again. "What is the first tasting like?" I asked.

"It is the first time you will pledge your life to King Emelia, a pledge you will renew daily. Every meal is solemn and joyous. It is the most sacred practice within our walls and a tradition you're blessed to join. You'll take the first bites from her plate, a sampling of everything on offer. The king will await your judgment, and you will declare the start of the meal."

I watched my reflection in the vanity and nodded.

"Most women have a bit of nerves the first time. King Emelia won't judge you for it," Lenora said. "You'll sit at her right hand with Meredith and enjoy your meal together. Today will be busy with the king seeing off her guests and settling her next plans with some of the ladies and lords, but don't think she's forgotten you. In the evening after the first tasting, she always seeks the company of her new poison girl."

Desire and fear shivered through me. I smoothed my hands down my dress and didn't ask the tangle of questions that leapt to mind. Only then did I realize how comforting Meredith's presence had been, a buffer between me and the king. Tonight, it seemed she'd take me to bed alone. Of everything she could command, she wanted precious time with me. I allowed the thought to settle my nerves. I was worthy of this. I could deserve a king's attention. I could please and protect her.

In the corridor, Meredith waited for us with her handmaiden, Winifred, a girl so enamored in Meredith's presence that she startled when my door closed. I swallowed my laugh. I understood. I sympathized.

Meredith's dress was almost as mean as the king's—red like a wound, its lace somehow brash. Her silhouette stung. Winifred had pinned her ringlets so that they cascaded down one shoulder, her hair the softest thing about her. Rubies shone in her ears. Meredith looked me up and down, her judgment swift and satisfied. She took my hand as if it were a longtime possession of hers, and so linked, we arrived at the doors of the great hall.

Faced once again with the threatening scene arching the doors—those dreadful creatures murdering their way to a summit of pleasure—a shadow overtook my happiness. I'd been so preoccupied on my first visit, thinking only of myself and my future, that I hadn't felt the weight of the room's history. How many poison girls had stood where I did now? I shivered their ghostly hands away and clasped Meredith's tighter. We could not die. Nothing had ever killed me. I had saved Meredith once and would do so again, as many times as fate demanded it.

Meredith eyed me. Our handmaidens pushed open the doors. "Savor everything," she whispered.

FOURTEEN

I WANTED THE ARISTOCRATS gone. I'd never given any consideration to where they'd been all this time and wanted to continue in my ignorance of them. This was our table, our hall, our castle. Our haven, a world for poison girls alone. The noblewomen were distinguishable from the poison girls by how they hid their mouths behind fans, their contempt plain. They loathed Meredith. They loathed King Emelia—for many things though, in this moment, chiefly for treating us as queens.

King Emelia rose from her chair for us, and so they too were forced to rise. The aristocrats' silence was absolute and simmering, gazes rapturous with hate or lust or both. Meredith surveyed the room like a huntress settling on her targets, her smile all violent glee. The king's aura had iced, the spark of warmth in her eyes reserved only for us. The red woman, just as stoic, stood with her at the honored left-hand chair. At the sight of her, I wanted to shout and point. I had not imagined her! Here she was!—the woman I had been trying and failing to mention.

With the weight of the room's attention upon us, we reached our king. She kissed our cheeks in turn, this small gesture a refuge under scrutiny. I wanted to fold into her and cocoon our private world, but this moment was what my younger self had only dreamed of. I would not retreat when my place was finally set. If I could not make myself worthy of an angel, I would make myself worthy of a king.

"You look divine," she whispered, a glint of mischief in her eye.

The cruel rumors about the king were laughable now that I knew her, all of them unenlightened speculation on something we could never understand. She was like our distant moon, our enduring mountains. She had existed long before us and would exist after us. People loved to worship ancient, grand, unknowable things, and she would be mine. My angel, though whole and unbroken.

She pulled me against her so that we faced the table together and bade our company sit. Her voice hummed through my body and echoed down from the ceiling, charged as a thundercloud. Meredith gave my hand a final squeeze and took one of the two empty chairs to the king's right. At the left, the red woman regarded me, a small and knowing smile on her face. She nodded when I met her gaze.

The king and I remained standing as servants materialized with extravagant silver trays of food, removing cloches to reveal more novel vegetables in artistic arrangements. Honeyed spiced carrots circled scalloped potatoes. Thin cuts of meat wrapped the stalks of a green spear-like vegetable. Flaky pie crusts enfolded salty cheeses and leafy greens. Loaves of dense, spicy bread cooled fresh from the ovens. Three servants wheeled in a giant bowl of tangy red soup. And finally, the offering that lifted shocked murmurs from even the most reticent guest—braised rosy meat, the flesh flaky and unlike any animal I had seen before.

The king smiled as though some calculated risk at the gambling table had paid off. "Salmon, a fish. A gift from our neighbor, King Marcus of Arga."

The shock heightened. All I could think of was water. Lakes so big that warships could sail across them. Networks of rivers like vital arteries. Blue abundance that had been closed to Vinstrum since King Eric's reign.

An immediate hush fell as the king spoke again. "Our tentative negotiations have lasted this past year. I'll soon send an emissary to Arga for closing formalities. I have hope that this is the start of a new age for Vinstrum, one of open trade and water's prosperity. Today, we celebrate this beginning and welcome Carlotta, my newest poison girl. Her gift is exceptional, even among poison girls, and I'm honored to have her by my side as I chart a new path for Vinstrum."

My heart thrilled at this news. We could travel, couldn't we? Oh, to see a new kingdom! To see the great lakes! It was said they had shores like the sea, white sands that stretched for miles. I would walk there with King Emelia as her guard. I, not so long ago a girl who couldn't imagine life beyond the borderlands. We would have water.

A servant set an immaculately prepared plate before us, and I was happy King Emelia held me against our company's appraising glances. I knew their questions. How, they wanted to ask, could a borderland girl be so exceptional? I lifted my chin and rested my hand over where King Emelia held my waist. I had what I wanted. Now I looked down on them all.

King Emelia's lips brushed my ear. "Is there nothing else you desire, my Carlotta?" she asked, though the answer was in the question. We both knew I was hers, had known from the start. The asking was a formality.

"Nothing, my king," I promised.

Her hand squeezed, nails biting into my hip. "Then the first taste of your new life awaits you."

She released me. I stepped to the table. The room was so quiet I could hear the breath in my lungs. A long line of expectant faces stared. This would be a perfect meal to undermine, to poison. We all knew it. I looked to Meredith. *Savor*, she mouthed as though we had plotted something devious together. I was grateful for her. All I could do was enjoy this meal as any other.

An intimidating selection of utensils were set to the left and right of the plate. I chose what seemed logical, taking up the largest spoon for the smooth red soup. Pomegranate again. Tart and savory. An artful spray of garnish floated atop—spiraling orange threads that crunched like carrot and sharp herbs I couldn't identify. Harmless. I nibbled at the pie, stabbed at a morsel of hard cheese, broke the crust from the loaf, sliced a bit of green stalk. I closed my eyes and savored. The spread was a perfect tour of textures. I wanted to meet our chefs and kiss their cheeks.

The fish I saved for last. My audience leaned in as though I might divine something in its flesh. It was so delicate I didn't need the knife. Its flavor was the most unadorned, simple salt and a spray of citrus all that met my tongue, the natural flavors of the fish itself intended to shine through. This was the taste of the lake, fresh and blue, and I, a servant, the first in Vinstrum to know it. Tears blurred the faces before me. With a trembling hand, I set down my fork and wiped them away. I exhaled.

"It is safe, my king," I pronounced.

At my word, the poison girls conducted their own tastings as formalities. They ate slow and contemplated, watching each other chew and delaying the aristocrats' first tastes of the fish. Several poison girls took bigger bites than were strictly necessary. Someone dared to huff, but no one would openly rush or chastise us in the king's presence. Meredith looked as though she might burst into laughter and ducked her head. Soon, the ladies and lords grew restless, their entitlement ruined by their greater demand for safety. I bit my lip. The red woman looked on serenely. The king petted my hair and let us have our amusement. At length, the poison girls set down their forks.

The king proceeded as though nothing of note had happened. "Please enjoy this gift from our new allies," she said, beginning our feast.

Along the walls, the servants traded relieved smiles. I was happy to sit beside Meredith and out of the spotlight, happy that the meal had been untampered.

"You're radiant," Meredith said to me, and I realized I was smiling too. She kissed the back of my hand as a lord might, her manner all flirtation. "What a grand initiation. Congratulations."

"Congratulations indeed," the red woman said.

She clasped the king's hand atop the table, and I tried not to stare. She couldn't be another poison girl, and Vinstrum had no queen. Another answer scintillated at the edge of my thoughts only to stun me and vanish when I tried to grasp it. The red woman smiled sympathetically as if she often had this effect on others.

"Emelia," she said, her tone a gentle nudge. The sound of the king's name in her mouth, so vulnerable without her title to guard it, still skewered me with its intimacy.

"Forgive me," said the king. Embarrassment looked odd on her like a dress that didn't fit. "Carlotta, allow me to properly introduce you to Phaela Mirrors, my favorite poet and oldest companion."

Her name expanded like my internal map of the castle, there as if it had always been. It was a treasure chest pried open at last only to reveal a puzzle within. Phaela Mirrors, born to a poison girl in the year of drowning feathers, was twenty-five years my senior. The woman across from me was five years older at most.

"No need to draw attention to my age," Phaela teased.

The king smoothed her thumb against the back of Phaela's hand. "I'm only stating how long I've loved you."

"So I'm to let you get away with it?"

"You've allowed me worse things."

"Everyone must have her limits."

Meredith hummed pointedly. "And this is where you draw yours, Phaela?"

While I'd been so entranced by the king and the mystery of our royal poet, Meredith had started on her food. Only flakes remained of the little pie. She licked her knife so obscenely that I didn't know whether to stare or avert my eyes.

"Careful, my dear," the king warned, a spark of amusement in her eyes.

"Yes, careful," echoed Phaela, though this second meaning was lost to me.

The king took Meredith's knife as though this was the topic of concern.

Phaela turned her full attention back to me. "I've composed a sonnet in honor of you joining us. It's part of a crown I'm drafting, and I'd love your blessing to debut it as part of my recital today."

I blinked at her. My reality turned unreal. Her casual offer was wilder than even my childhood dreams of meeting her with a poem of mine conveniently tucked up my sleeve. Could Ma have ever imagined this when she folded all those verses against her letters? Look where her introduction had led me!

I swallowed against the knot in my throat and nodded. "I'd love to hear it," I said. "My ma loved your work and ensured I knew it."

"Might I have known her?"

I shook my head. Oh, if only clearing grief were so easy, to shake it off like water, to deny it. "No. She was only a poison girl."

Phaela's face pinched as though I had hurt her. "Never speak of your mother or yourself with that diminishing word," she said gently. "My mother was a poison girl as well. You are beauty, hope, and strength. The world would be lost without your light. That is why we are all here now, to celebrate your lives and pay respect to the dead. Do you write to your mother?"

Confusion slowed my answer. "No. She's passed."

"So has mine, but I still write. It's good exercise. Wounds do not hurt less for ignoring them."

"I'll try it," I promised.

Meredith cleared her plate first. Despite this being the most perfect meal I'd ever tasted, I couldn't eat. My stomach was a fist. I was happy and sad. Excited and nervous. I worried that my picked-over plate might be read as some slight and resolved to apologize personally to the chef and the kitchen staff. The fish had gone over well. A lord down the table inquired after the name. When I didn't finish mine, Meredith asked whether I was well before eating it from my plate.

The king rose, and conversation around the table stuttered, faces turning to see whether she had another shocking announcement. Instead, she beckoned to me, and I followed her from the room.

Breathing was easier in the corridor, in its quiet and neutral air.

"I'm sorry, my king," I apologized immediately.

"At least half of my poison girls are unable to eat after their first tasting. You've nothing to apologize for. Sometimes, getting away from the table settles the nerves. If you find later that your appetite has returned, Lenora can bring a meal to your room."

"Thank you, my king."

"Let us walk," she said. "We have time before Phaela recites, and it's best to approach her work with a clear mind."

Had the corridor's paintings changed again, or was I always so nervous here that I could never set their order and details? We passed still-life paintings of bouquets and loose sheaves of paper, scenes of women enjoying literature in the nude—pacing gardens or salons. No bloodied angels or devils at war disturbed the calm. I imagined a crew of servants emerging every evening to change the paintings out of their heavy frames.

"Do you know what Phaela will read?" I asked. "Does she show you her drafts?"

"Oh no. She hides these pages when I visit her. They're a gift, she says. My only crown."

We came to a set of stairs and turned back.

"If I may ask—where is your crown? Why don't you wear it?"

"It was lost when my predecessor fell. My father does not trifle with those who offend him, and his wrath is swift," she answered dispassionately. "The crown melted upon Eric's head."

I flinched at the image. The beheading of his stone likeness was merciful by comparison.

Though she watched me, her gaze was distant and cold, her thoughts elsewhere. "Do you think I should wear one?"

"No, my king." I pretended to observe the paintings. "One of my first thoughts when I met you was that you needed none. You are . . ." It was silly to tell the king she was beautiful—she knew this, of course—and now I knew she had been so miserable that night at the thought of losing Meredith.

"Yes?" she prompted, my stumbling having brought a glint of amusement back to her eyes. "What am I?"

"Well, you are beautiful," I said, the simple thoughts I'd resolved to keep to myself spilling out in the absence of anything more eloquent. "I couldn't look away from you."

The king laughed, big and echoing and generous, and I was mesmerized anew. I'd seen only twitches of amusement thus far, a quirk of her lips here and there. Never such genuine and unrestrained mirth. I loved that I could look up and see all her rows of teeth, how she seemed softer for it, joy having lowered her guard.

"No, you couldn't. Only a florist would be so charmingly impudent. Or dare call me beautiful."

"A florist, my king?"

She hummed. "Do you use another word in the borderlands?"

"A word for . . . ?"

"You have never found a man interesting in your life. Your peers' fancies over boys puzzled you. But there was perhaps a girl in your class, a neighbor you hated or loved who made your heart beat madly. You've come to understand your friendships with other girls were intense and one-sided. The thought of marriage, when others proposed it as an inevitability of your life, provoked rage or despair you couldn't rationalize," she said. "These are the experiences of a florist."

Isabella's face, forgotten so long ago, returned with startling clarity. I felt the hot borderland sun on my back. My hand twitched at the memory of our laced fingers.

"And so she is a poison girl?" I asked.

Another laugh. "Not every florist turns out to be a poison girl, and not all poison girls are florists. One is a gift and perhaps a profession. The other is a way to describe who you spend your life with or take to bed."

I received this word as one would a startling and precious flower, its bloom placed lovingly into my hands.

"I see," I said. I considered her definition. "Then the fable of weeping luna is also a tale of florists?"

I liked the gleam that came into the king's eye. "Is it?"

Now I hesitated. "Not as written, not explicitly. It's a cautionary tale about the destructive nature of selfish desire."

"Are Cordelia and Felicity selfish?"

Their story was our most well-known literary tragedy: women born to rival aristocratic families who found fellowship in the woods' neutral ground before discovering their respective houses. "Only as much as it is selfish to want true companionship. But as written, yes."

"And their desire destructive?"

Her question gave me pause. "Yes, as written."

How could it be anything but? On discovering the truth, the families rushed to secure marriage proposals to distract their daughters from their blossoming and forbidden friendship. Their efforts were disastrous. Desperate not to be separated, both women died in a foolish and convoluted plot that hinged on a decoction of weeping luna and a fatal miscommunication.

They were the first poison girls, mythic in their folly, the spiritual mothers of us all—two women who would rather continue their girlhood meetings picking flowers than be properly married, with hubris enough to believe they could leverage floral tinctures and a fledgling understanding of their gifts to fabricate their deaths and run away together. Blame was cast on the herbalist who had aided them and supplied the poison. Felicity misunderstood the woman's advice and imbibed too much of her tincture. Cordelia, on discovering her friend—her lover, the woman she loved!—truly dead, drank the rest and joined her. Their families were shattered and sank deeper into their feud, each blaming the other for their girls' deaths.

The flower acquired its name after the events, when in the woods between their families' estates, on the moon marking the anniversary of Cordelia's and Felicity's deaths, it was said their spirits wandered the night crying and seeking each other.

For so long, I'd found solace in a tragedy. It was the only story I knew in which two women so ardently loved each other, and though it was a dreadful and cautionary tale, I loved it where I should have been fearful. When had I ever heeded a warning?

The king saw my epiphany and continued her questioning. "Do you believe the stories about me and the judgements attending them are true?"

"No, of course not," I disagreed vigorously.

"And are the stories told about you, that you have taken in and told to yourself, true?"

I dropped my gaze to the floor. I was different, I wanted to say. But to do that, I would have to talk about what I'd done, and I didn't want the king to think poorly of me.

"I don't want them to be, my king," I answered.

A fascinating scent, bracing and bitter, perfumed the great hall upon our return. Around the table, servants poured a dark and fragrant drink into white teacups. Pleased murmurs spread down the table as more guests sampled it, nibbling on the accompanying little cakes and biscuits between sips.

Meredith had already drained half her cup despite the heavy plume of steam. Loath to burn my tongue, I patiently blew on mine.

"Another import from Arga, this gift by way of Harsper," the king was explaining of the drink's origins. *Coffee*, she called it, originating in the southwestern kingdoms of which Harsper was one. "I'd be remiss not to thank Earl Huxley," she announced, "for his expertise in arranging the trade."

My hands burned. Meredith pried the teacup from them and dabbed at me with her napkin. I barely felt her fussing, fixated as I was on the congratulatory murmurs down the table and the man at the center of them. Delfina sat on his left, a noblewoman at the right. He hadn't caught my attention earlier because he was unremarkable and boring, all his evil behind such an unassuming facade. High on his own importance, he nodded to his fellow lords in acknowledgment, a satisfied upturn at the corner of his mouth. He did not quite smirk. That would be too unbecoming, though he wanted to. I wished the servants hadn't cleared my setting, wished I still had my knife.

"What's wrong?" Meredith hissed in my ear.

He'd been with us at the table this entire time, had observed my first tasting. Did he recognize my name when the king introduced me? Had he seen my mother in my face?

I'd been a foolish girl. Here he finally was—the man I'd been so desperate to pledge my life to years ago, the man who had tried to court me away from my father while knowing he never intended to do right by my mother.

If he stayed in the castle any longer, I would find him and take what was mine.

Meredith shook me. I blinked, looked at her. Her lips formed my name. She held my hands so gently, wiping the spilled coffee from them. She was perfect and kind, and I was happy to look upon her instead. Taking my unused napkin from the table, she folded it discreetly over the stain on my lap.

"Are you well?" she asked, squeezing my shoulder.

Someone—the king, Phaela, Meredith—had summoned a servant. She pressed a cool bundle against where my hand reddened. Meredith thanked her in my stead, and the servant hurried to wipe away the spill on the table.

My attention drifted back to Huxley. Damn the knife. I would put the sugar spoon through his eye.

"My dear."

I raised my eyes to the king. Huxley had fooled her. Huxley's offers were false promises. I had not been able to save Da, but I would save her from him.

"Yes, my king?" I answered and found my voice weak.

"You're faint. Allow me to escort you to your room."

"No," I said too fast. "No, my king," I corrected. "I need to hear the sonnets. They will restore me."

The king glanced to Phaela as if for permission. I had never seen her do that, didn't know she could look uncertain, didn't know she could defer. What was Phaela to her?

The red woman, the royal poet, my summoner—she studied me. She had seen me grasp Delfina. She knew my loss. She understood.

"Let me read to her," she said and stood.

The room hushed with the anticipation of a gift to be bestowed.

I expected pages in her hands, but Phaela's crown was kept safe in her mind. The embroidered beads on her dress glittered when she took a breath. She was magnificent. I sat back in my chair and watched her golden aura expand as she recited like a cleric in temple, with command and reverence entwined. If only Ma could hear her. Her words were sacred. I breathed them in and placed my burned hand over my burning chest.

FIFTEEN

I STOOD WITH MEREDITH on the castle wall and peered down from the long-unused battlements. The onyx had grown to encase the crenellations, forming a serrated veneer over the original stone like the lower half of a monster's jaw. Cruel wind stung our faces and ripped at our dresses, and my knee hurt from my fall earlier in the day. Meredith had suggested our perch, saying it was the best way to see everyone as they departed. The carriages lined up as I had seen them the night of my arrival, stately coaches and well-bred horses choreographed in their descent, perfectly spaced. The king stood on the castle steps to see her guests off, and the lords and ladies stopped to share a final word before boarding for home. Even from our height, I could tell the exchanges were so brief as to be perfunctory. One could not snub the king.

Despite her insistence on watching the farewells, Meredith leaned carelessly against the crenellations and looked at me. "Back at the table—what happened?" she asked.

The clouds were swirling to a darker gray. In the borderlands, this sky would precede a storm, but here, I didn't know what it meant. The sky was always stormy, and it had never rained. I didn't realize how adrift I would feel in losing the ability to discern nature's simplest messages.

"One of the lord's faces reminded me of my da," I said. It wasn't untrue, but I knew how Meredith would misunderstand it, and I felt bad lying to her.

"I've known women who had similar nervous attacks. They're common among us. No one will judge you for them. How should I help if one comes again?"

I shook my head. "You're very kind, but I'd rather not think of it now. It makes me ill."

Her eyes searched mine as if she wished to ask more, but she turned back to the scene below.

Earl Huxley's carriage was the last to leave. He lagged behind the others, the tail of the procession disappearing as he stood with the king. Delfina stood behind him, her head bowed. Hate and sympathy welled in me. I hated her for choosing him, and I understood. The king nodded to something Huxley said. I tore myself away from the wall and marched for the steps. Meredith trailed haltingly behind me, and when I ignored her, she let me go.

I considered going down to the kitchen and asking after what was left of the afternoon's feast, but upon returning to my bedchamber, I fell into a restless sleep and only roused when a knock came at my door. Color had drained from the room. Gray shapes floated in the almost dark. I lay still and felt divorced from reality. Strange to fall asleep in a room that was mine but held nothing of me. Strange to call a space in this castle my own. Strange, after so much ceremony, to wake alone.

The knock came again.

"Yes?" I called, and Lenora cracked the door.

"I've brought you food, miss," she said. "I heard you were unwell this afternoon."

I couldn't think of how to respond to this. The afternoon seemed so far away, as though I had lived it long ago and not mere hours before. Lenora set about lighting candles, and I gave up on a reply, the silence having stretched too long.

My body was heavy as though I'd eaten a petal. I wished I hadn't fallen asleep. I'd neglected to change out of my stained dress and was now embarrassed to have company. I went to one of the velvet chairs, and Lenora took up the one across from me, setting a plate on the little table between us. She wore the same worried look as Meredith had. I felt guilty for being a cause of concern and tried to make polite conversation, asking about the kitchen staff and telling her to pass on my compliments and gratitude. She seemed relieved when I cleared my plate and took it again when she stood.

"I'll return to prepare you for the king," she said, a spark of excitement in her eye.

Alone again, I paced the room. Opened the curtains on a gray dusk and closed them again. Tried in vain to unbutton my stained dress. In the end, I retired to the balcony and breathed deeply of the cool air. Novelty and glamour had fueled every moment until now. I had never been alone—Meredith or King Emelia or Phaela there to stroke my cheek or hold my hand and tell me how lovely I was. I hadn't had time to brew insecurities. Without their sparkling mirrors, I was myself again.

I couldn't think too hard of what the king might want from me. When she came to me, I would know.

"Nerves, miss?"

I startled and found Lenora behind me. "Some," I admitted.

She joined me. "Your presence has the entire castle in bloom. The king is already taken with you. Tonight is an opportunity to deepen your bond. That's all. Enjoy your time together." She drew me inside and closed the doors. Lowering her voice to a conspiratorial whisper, she said, "You will *love* what Phaela's made for you."

On the bed, Lenora had laid a sheer gown with flowing lace sleeves as long as the garment itself. Buttoned silk cuffs gathered the lace into dramatic bells at the wrists. A band of ribbon under the bust ruched the short skirt into delicate ripples. An enticing cross of straps laced the back. Matching stockings and garters were set beside the gown, all of it black.

Savor everything.

I allowed my hunger to rise and held it close like a flame. The gown was light as air when I took it into my hands, its fabric a magic trick.

Lenora watched me with a satisfied smile. "Shall we get you changed?"

Though I now understood that Lenora's help would be a constant feature of my life in the castle, I was still unused to the casual intimacy of her role. Tonight, there was a new charge between us. Had I been too self-conscious to notice it before, too dizzied by the simple fact of having someone undress and bathe me, of suddenly being above the drudgery of my own maintenance? *I wish I could be a poison girl*, she'd told me. Her touch lingered as though I were a ritual item to be purified for the altar. The brush of her fingers was reverent. She cinched the laces at my back, and gooseflesh broke out on my arms. Her hands came to rest on my shoulders. I waited for a word from her, a whisper, a question. I tensed with anticipation. She pressed a kiss to the nape of my neck, so soft I almost doubted it.

"Lenora?" I ventured.

"Yes, miss?" Her words ghosted across my skin, her lips still so close.

"Do you want me?"

Was any pleasure forbidden in this place? Was this a forbidden question?

"I want to please the king, and you are a conduit. I hope she will see your beauty and think of me, even for a moment."

Lenora rolled a stocking and knelt at my feet so that the only work I had was to step into it. I did. Her knuckles brushed up my skin. She paused at my knee. Her hands clenched. My first thought was an unfortunate snag in the fabric, but no, the issue wasn't with Phaela's work but with me. Lenora set her fingertips against my skin as though I were some prized and tragically damaged possession, something that cut when broken. I imagined her kneeling to gather a shattered saucer, a chalice, a mirror, how gingerly she'd pinch a dangerous edge.

"You've a nasty bruise, miss," she said. "I worried when you fell. You must be careful."

"I've endured worse. I can hardly feel it," I lied. It hurt when I walked. Hurt when I sat. It hurt in that persistently dull and aching way that reminded me I lived in a body.

"It may not bother you, but King Emelia is quite anxious and particular, especially when it comes to her poison girls. As much as is possible, you must maintain yourself with the same care given to the king's most valued possessions. You're among them now." She fastened my stockings and stepped back to admire me. I was her project. I'd made her proud. "Come sit," she added, hands coming to rest on the chair at the vanity.

Astonishing—to wear an entire garment that felt like nothing against the skin and be so transformed by it, to wear clothing to enhance the suggestion of not wearing it. The earrings Lenora chose for me were heavier than the whole ensemble, the glittering black pendants extravagant as a chandelier. She powdered and lined my eyes as Phaela had, and the smudge of dark pigment turned my face luminous.

I leaned into my reflection and traced a finger down the glass. I was unreal, a living shadow among shadows. I was a vengeful goddess of long-lost lore.

"How do you feel?" Lenora asked quietly.

She'd been transformed too, a twilight guide to hand me over to the night.

"I feel good," I answered, flattening the swell of my feelings into those simple words.

She bowed her head. In her long black dress, her edges were indistinct until she moved. "I'll find the king. Have a good night, miss."

She left me again. I looked back to the mirror. Turned slow. Leaned close enough to see the scatter of candlelight in my eyes. *Savor.* It seemed vain to admire myself like this, to study my own curves in a new light, but Phaela's work was such that I couldn't look away.

"So it fits." In the doorway, the designer herself stood, stoic and appraising. I couldn't tell whether she was judging her work or me. She was still dressed as she'd been at the banquet, but my lost satchel now dangled from her shoulder. It was so faded and homely against her finery that I was embarrassed to have brought it here.

"The gown is beautiful. Thank you. And for your art and your sonnets this afternoon."

"I'm grateful you were there to hear them." She handed off my things. "Your bag has the heft of paper."

"Yes," I answered shyly.

"Your words or others'?"

This was the moment I'd dreamed of for years. A poem up the sleeve.

"Both."

"Good." The small word was a thrill. "Do you share your work?"

"Not as of yet. But I'd like to." *If you were my only audience forever, that would be enough.*

"When you've had time to settle and reflect, deliver your favorite couplet. That will tell me everything I need."

Her request was cryptic and terrifying. I nodded and didn't dare ask more. Phaela was different than the red woman. Her dramatic, effusive flair had dropped like a cape untied. She hadn't aged, though now I could see her years, the love and loss of decades. I held my poems against my chest, waiting for what she'd actually come to deliver.

"Know that Meredith and I worked hard to bring you here, to entice Emelia from the depths of her melancholy so that she might look at you and find hope." Phaela caught one of my twists in her hand and trailed her fingers down its length. "Do not disappoint us. Don't disappoint her."

I held my poems tighter. "I wouldn't."

"Good," she said again and finally smiled, a little of the red woman's warmth shining through once more. "I look forward to your work."

I watched her leave. I couldn't take any more visitors. I busied myself stowing my notebooks away in the desk and thought better of it, thought of how the king might find me. I sat at the little table as I had with Lenora and waited. Even breathing made me restless, made me think too much of the monastery, of Marta. *Breathe, dear girl.*

The king's voice rang clear through the door, my own name enchanting as a spell. My heart leapt. I jumped to my feet.

"Yes, my king," I answered.

Seeing her was like waking again—settling into the world anew. She'd changed into a regal slip of a dress that flowed like water with her step, its unbroken length enhancing her height. Over top, a satiny robe billowed in her wake. Though black as always, this was the softest thing I'd seen her wear, a setting aside of her armor just for me.

Two handmaidens flanked her. One carried a tea set on a tray. The other held a red clamshell box.

The king greeted me with a mysterious smile and a simple, "Good evening."

"Good evening, my king," I returned.

She swept past me, and my skin ached for her touch. The handmaidens placed their items on the table. I stared at the box.

"Cold will set in tonight," the king said. I was so dazzled by her entry that I only then noticed the little flame dancing in her hand. She knelt before the hearth and coaxed the fire into one of the spinning columns I'd seen elsewhere in the castle. "Freda and Aline," she addressed her handmaidens without turning. "Thank you. You may go."

The women curtsied in unison and filed from the room, shutting the door soundlessly behind them. I clenched my hands together. The king continued to study the fire, and my attention drifted back to the lacquered box.

"How have you found your room? Is there anything you desire? Anything you'd see changed?" the king asked. Finally, she met my gaze.

Relief flooded me. "No, my king. It's perfect." I grasped for something to expound upon, something that would mark my thoughtfulness and gratitude, but here we were, alone again, this privacy more intimate than the garden. My thoughts tumbled over each other until all but the simplest sentences were broken. "The space is generous."

A smile tugged at the king's lips as though I had done something endearing. "And your dresses. Phaela and Lenora both have mentioned you're accustomed to a different style."

"Oh! I meant nothing against what I've been provided. It's all so perfect."

The king left her post by the hearth and took the chair across from me. I watched blankly as she poured our tea into gilded little cups. Too late, it occurred to me that I should have offered, that this was something a handmaiden might do.

"Please. Sit," she said, gesturing to my chair.

I hadn't remembered I was standing. I sat. My knee protested.

"Do you take sugar?"

"Yes, my king."

She pinched a cube between her red nails and dropped it into my cup. The tea was almost as red. The king didn't sweeten her own. She held her cup and saucer but did not drink, looking expectantly to me. I took my cup and breathed in a curl of steam. Pomegranate again, forward and bold. A nutty, earthy scent as the base and a mellow, honeyed middle layer. Nothing alarmed me from the scent, so I took a sip. Tart and sweet as expected. A tisane. It lacked the astringent effect a true tea would have on the palate. Brightness lingered on my tongue.

"It's safe, my king."

She hummed, took a small sip. "Phaela has already sketched some designs for you to approve. It will take some time to furnish a new wardrobe, but she works fast."

I blinked. "I'd never make such a demand of her."

"She enjoys new patterns and styles. Your comfort is no imposition."

I sipped my tea. I couldn't square Phaela's warm offerings with her exacting demands. "She's been so generous to me. I'll have to thank her next time I see her."

"See that you do. She thrives on appreciation. Though that's true of most."

I cradled my tea in my lap. "And for you, my king? You've lived and reigned so long."

She drained her tea and poured a fresh cup. A smile, grim and startling, overtook her face. It stretched too far, revealed too many teeth. "It's good I'm not given to seeking praise. There would be no way forward." When I thought she was on the cusp of laughter, she schooled her face back to its customary mask. I wondered how much of her early time in our world had been spent approximating and mastering our expressions, how much effort she spent on this conscious smoothing. "My poison girls are my hope. This role requires painful things of you," she said, "and though I require your sacrifice, I also want your happiness for as long as I may have it. That is all I need."

The king watched me finish my cup and waited for me to set it back into its saucer and the saucer upon the table. She studied me openly as she hadn't before, her gaze slipping from my face as though she'd noticed my dress for the first time. I held still as though even my breathing might be an unwelcome disruption. I didn't need air, not when she looked at me.

She took the red box into her hands. "I enjoy adorning my poison girls. It hurts only a moment, and the pain will bring you closer to me and place you within the lineage of royal poison girls. Would you join us?"

I felt my heartbeat in my throat and a surge of anticipation in my chest. There was no reality in which I'd deny her. "Yes, my king."

"Lie down on the bed for me," she said. The heat in her gaze did not reach her voice. It was the same tone she might use with the other staff, detached and polite.

Standing was surreal. The candles twinkled. My dress resettled around my body, light as a dream. All was the same, but the king's command, as much as I'd expected it, had made me unsteady. I returned to the bed I had napped in only an hour ago, its wrinkles smoothed by Lenora, and found it significant where I hadn't before. I felt my handmaiden's presence like a ghost, her quiet intensity guiding me. I arranged myself with Lenora's conscientiousness, smoothing my skirt, fanning my hair out over the pillow, resting my hands loose at my sides.

The king did not hurry. She remained at her seat and finished her tea as though I weren't waiting for her. In the silence, without her gaze on me, my nerves wound me tense. The click of her teacup in its saucer was enough to startle me. Her shadow fell across the bed. I swore it had weight, swore it was her spirit itself pressing down on me, testing where I might be weak. I stared up at her wonderingly, my breaths and heart fast under the pressure of her observation. Her face retained its stoic mask, but I was reassured by the ember in her eyes. Still, she didn't touch me.

"Lift your skirt to your hips," she said. "Remove your thong."

A shiver took me. I did as she instructed, hooking a thumb in the strip of fabric at my waist and tugging it down over my legs. It'd been barely enough to cover my sex, its backless design lending to the feeling of having worn nothing at all. I waited with my knees apart, my heart a frantic flutter in my chest.

The king's face revealed little, and yet she asked me how I felt.

"I trust your plans for me," I said, my thoughts so loud that I was barely able to summon more than a whisper.

Her mouth quirked. "And I am honored. But you've not answered my question."

My breath, my heart, the prickle in my skin all told me *fear*. But I wanted her and whatever she would give me. The unknown of this new place, of what my service to her might bring, made my blood hot, made each draw of breath hungrier than the last. And there was my answer.

"I need you, my king. That's all I feel."

Finally, a smile, a sedate flash of teeth. She settled at the end of the bed. A latch clicked. I glanced down. The red box was open, but I couldn't see inside for its lid. The king's gaze locked to mine. "This time, it is best if you don't look," she said. "Focus on your breaths. Shall I blindfold you again?"

I looked to the canopy above. "Only if it pleases you."

My answer earned an appreciative hum. She shifted. The box snapped closed. I held my breath.

"Relax, my dear." I felt the warmth of her skin, imagined a cheek against my knee. "This is a gift. A small pain for an eternal adornment."

She touched me, though not in the way I'd expected. There was a tug at the thin hood of skin above my clit, an odd and testing stretch.

"Take a breath for me," she said, and I obeyed, my thoughts spinning.

A sharp pinch. A deep gasp. My body clenched. Nails in palms.

"Good girl," the king murmured. "You did well."

Already the pain had subsided to a dull ache, but my body remained electrified, charged and hypersensitized in the aftermath of something like a lightning strike. The king pushed my knees back. A wordless plea reached my lips. A whimper. Her nails dug into my thighs. She held me open to her.

"The greatest pain is past," she said. "You're with us now."

Candles melted in an instant. Fire licked across the floor. The damask curtains went up next. There was no smoke, only endless engulfing flame, the bed a pyre waiting to catch. Far away, like a fluttering heart or a guttering fire, something old groaned—ancient as a curse but not as aged as the castle itself. It contained knowledge I could open if I just overcame the flaring ache in my belly. Ash coated my tongue. Gold dripped into my eyes. I blinked them clear, but the taste of death lingered in my mouth. Women stared from the flaming dark. The starved longing in their gazes burned where the fire did not. They'd lain beneath the king like this, had loved her and let it destroy them. I met their eyes, and the circle of them advanced, steps measured and reverent as attendants of a royal ceremony. Unlinking their hands, they reached for me, a dozen specters seeking a living body. They found my warmth and sighed. They grasped my hands and combed their fingers through my hair and stroked my cheeks. They teased my nipples and dug their fingers into my thighs. Their touch was cold, and yet I warmed to their welcome. As one body, they captured mine, and when I sighed, they chorused my pleasure back to me. An impossible scent perfumed the air—a warning of cardamom and sage.

All the spirits were beautiful, but even the dead looked to one woman in particular. She wore gold rings in her hair like a queen, single braids long at her temples and a flare of magnificent curls as a crown. She pillowed my head in her lap and watched me with eyes as black and glittering as the castle's stone, the flames caught in their gleam. Their reflection leapt and flickered. I thought she would kiss me, but she paused with our lips inches apart. She would not fulfill me.

When I sighed, she stole my breath, breathing my air like a heady draught. When I cried out, the hand between her legs quickened. The ghosts hummed, pressing in like greedy subjects. Their queen trembled with her want, with mine. When she'd drawn what she wanted from my body, when her back arched and her head fell back, the cord of tension between us snapped. The spirits vanished. I emerged from their cold haze to find my hand clutching one of King Emelia's horns. I'd crushed her red flowers under my palm. Shaking, I withdrew my hand. Petals flaked from my skin like old blood.

The vision of fire burned itself out. King Emelia's grip relaxed, nails leaving starry pinpricks of sensation where they'd dug into my skin. I couldn't register it as pain anymore, not when I had experienced something far greater. My face was wet. My cunt dripped. Her fingers were inside me. It was mad to moan for her as I did, but she had broken me as she promised, and I was desperate as the dead.

Not even my own body was gentle with me. Release didn't come with a soft unraveling. It struck like a blow, emptying me as the pain had. I could feel no more, endure no more. Mercifully, the king gathered me into her lap. I trembled against her, curled into her soft warmth, and let her bear my weight. This castle was full of the dead, and now they had seen me. I tucked my head under the king's chin and held her tight.

"You have nothing to fear from them," the king soothed. "You are all part of the castle now and all of you mine. You did well tonight."

I liked how she stroked my back. I liked how her praise rumbled through her chest. I thought I might cry again, not from any pain or fear but for another kind of release.

"Thank you, my king," I said, relieved to have done this for her.

The king pulled away, and I whimpered unbecomingly, too frayed for inhibition.

She kissed my forehead and cheeks. "I'm not abandoning you, my dear," she reassured. At the basin in the corner of the room, she poured fresh water, dampening a cloth and returning to wipe my face. "You made a beautiful mess of your makeup," she murmured. The cloth came away blackened. She left with it and prepared another cup of tea for me. I was surprised to find it still hot.

"Drink," the king insisted.

I drank. She poured another, offered it to me, and finally held me once more.

Late in the night or early in the morning, I fell asleep in her arms. My body spent, I dreamed of nothing, not even the dead women.

Sixteen

I WOKE ALONE, THE covers pulled up to my chin and the fire still spinning in the hearth. Gray light bled around the edges of the curtains. It could be any time of day. The pillows beside me were still perfectly fluffed, the blankets smooth. The king had not slept here, and I still felt the hands of the dead.

Borderland elders would say I'd been marked by death. Clerics would sequester me and perform a full moon of purification rites. My skin would be scrubbed with clay and salt. My hair would be shorn. The elders would've given me a pebble of basalt to hold under my tongue for a fortnight before I could safely speak to the living without passing on my cursed fate. But this was the remedy given to an otherwise pure woman who was haunted. Once one was found to be a poison girl, few saw the need to help.

For the Clerical Order of Angelic Retribution, a cursed fate was simply the lot of a poison girl. There was no purification to be done because a poison girl was simply another symptom of a world in need of judgment.

What would Ma have done with me? Was the Huxley estate as rapturously haunted as this?

The coverlet fell from my shoulders as I sat, and I found I wore nothing. I pushed the bedclothes away and felt cautiously between my legs. My fingers met something small as a ring and just as smooth. I couldn't see it in the gloom. I went to the vanity and lit a candle.

There, glittering among the dark curls, were two black gems. I tested the jewelry again, braver in my exploration. Hidden beneath the thin hood of skin, a short curved bar nestled against my clit. At the barest pressure, a delicious shiver overtook me, my body more sensitive than before. The king had pierced me, the secret adornment just for us. Heat flushed me. I dipped a finger into the fresh slick between my thighs and wished the king hadn't left.

Cold hands braced my hips from behind. My heart raced at the touch. A woman, her eyes luminously black, watched me in the mirror's refection. She'd come from nowhere, a shadow from shadow, her bare body flush against mine. Her grin was startlingly white.

"We were honored to welcome you last night," she said. "I needed to see you again."

She kissed my neck with her cold lips, cupped my breasts in her cold hands. A shiver ripped through me, and she giggled. I should've been afraid of her. I should've feared everything in this place—its creatures and rituals, the architecture itself—yet I opened myself to it. I chose to open again. The king wasn't afraid of her dead poison girls. She was one with the dark magic of this place. She was its magic. Now I was too.

"Who are you?" I asked.

She twisted my hair into her fist and sucked gently at my neck. I let her. I was already cursed, already haunted. Already transformed. Her breath chilled me. She nudged my feet wider.

"When you come," she said against my skin, "call me Anne."

A noise of surprise died in my throat. Her cold hands held my shoulders as she bent me over the vanity, and I allowed her guidance.

I planted my hands flat. Waiting, she loomed behind me. I held her gaze in the mirror. My pulse fluttered at my throat.

"Your desire called me." Her hand slipped between my legs. "You're so warm," she moaned, as if my warmth was a gleaming thing she could steal.

My thighs trembled. My skin burned at her touch. Ice, this was ice. My breath hissed through clenched teeth.

"Because you have the onyx, I can finally reach you," she said. "I saw you arrive, how you sat in King Emelia's lap and everyone watched. Even the living envied you."

The stun of Anne's chill melted. She pulled my hair until my spine protested, my neck and back at a strained angle. I swallowed with effort. In my reflection, the light from the candle carved my body into planes of glow and shadow. Gold on my neck and the peaks of my shoulders. Hollow dark in my eyes and the dip of my collarbones. Anne's eyes gleamed. She thrust into me until all resistance melted from my body, until my mouth dropped open on a sigh.

"Look at you," she cooed to the mirror. Her grin turned devious as though she'd discovered a secret about me. She put her elbow in my spine. I dropped to the vanity. The little crystal jars and pots of powders rattled. Something shattered on the floor. Held against the cold wood, I bit down on a moan. In this position, I couldn't see Anne anymore. I didn't need to. My body chased its need. I canted my hips up to her, ignored the flush in my chest, banished the thought of how undignified I must look. My breath fogged on the varnish. I let her have me.

Anne's thrusts were quick and rough. She added a finger, two, did not slow her pace. I bucked against her, and she shoved me back down.

"Quiet," she hissed, though I didn't realize I'd made a sound. "I see why the king loves you. Talented. Pliant on the surface, or at least with her, at least when there's pleasure to be had. But you have a dark heart like the rest of us."

I ached under her. My back pinched. I couldn't think of a reply.

She finished me as though she hated me—for my living, for yielding to her so readily. Her voice was at my ear again, darkly sweet. "What did I tell you to do when you come?"

She stroked me through the crest of pleasure, insistent and focused. I gasped sharp, exhaled her name. Her eyes gleamed like the onyx. She never blinked.

"Louder. I know the king has taught you how."

"Anne—"

She reduced me to my breaths, each one for her until she had wrung every sigh from my body. Her hands left me. I pressed my forehead to the vanity and couldn't move. My head felt starry.

The world intruded with a knock at the door. Light cracked into the room. I lifted myself from the vanity, legs unsteady, wet cooling on my thighs. Anne was nowhere. Silhouetted by the hall's light, Lenora regarded me from the doorway. I held a hand against the glare. She closed the door silently and came to me. A square of gold shone behind my eyes when I blinked.

"You'll catch a chill," she said, settling the robe she carried around my shoulders. She didn't tie it closed, only held the sash in her hands. She smelled like soap and was close enough to kiss. Her gaze slid up my body until she met my eyes. Her lips parted. She took a sip of breath. "Does the ring suit you?"

"Yes," I answered, my voice lowered to the same intimate hush as hers.

"Good." She tied the robe, fingers working slow over the sash. "I'll escort you to the baths. King Emelia is waiting for you."

The king had never disrobed in my presence. I almost didn't expect her to, imagined her standing by as a solemn observer. Instead, upon reaching the pools, she let her slip drop unceremoniously to the stone floor, the satin pooling richly at her feet. I clutched my robe and stared. She was tall, yes, I'd known, but the curve of her spine confirmed additional notches of vertebrae. With a roll of her shoulders, she seemed at once more serpentine, a natural comfort in the gesture that she withheld in company, opting instead for an approximation of our more limited range of motion. The muscle in her legs did not follow the usual composition either. She was eerily smooth and uniform, as though her skin was not stretched over muscle and bone but something machined and precise, elegant and tapering lines moving as one. As I watched, her arms took on this same quality as if a glamour had dropped. Her skin was poreless and hairless like something other than skin entirely. An animal part of me was unsettled by her alien beauty, a deep and instinctual fear in response to perfection.

She studied me and, when I didn't recoil, reached for my robe and dropped it to the stone. Both of us revealed, she led me into the pool, holding my gaze with each step. We waded deep. Her braids floated atop the water like a fatal spill of blood.

Her touch was a new language for this moment—a hand over my heart as if it were a beloved creature she could hold, a kiss to my palm as though everything I'd ever held were sacred, a soft stroke down my spine like a promise to bear whatever burdened me. The warm water lapped at our skin, and for a long time she held me against her and said nothing. She could lull me back to sleep this way while I stood up to my shoulders in water.

"You've met Anne," she said finally.

"Yes."

The king stroked my hair, though she didn't look at me now. A memory clouded her face. "She did not pass quietly."

I thought of Ma. Who would go quietly? And who around them could stand it? I had survived, and I would avenge Ma if I could.

Gently, I asked, "Anne's death left you and Meredith alone, didn't it?"

This was what neither Phaela nor Meredith would tell me—the catalyst for the king's withdrawal and fear, the reason she'd rather have wasted away than court a new poison girl. And now I was the first to arrive and a curiosity for a ghost whose wrath had nowhere to go.

The king raised her gaze to the ceiling like a supplicant pleading to the angel. The sight of her almost made me regret my question. Visions like these roused the clerics to prophesy. She looked like an ancient statue made flesh, as if she belonged in her art collection with all those terrifying yet beautiful subjects. Then her smile, disconcerting and strained, broke again. "Our days of tragedy are past," she declared. "Let us enjoy this time."

SEVENTEEN

A s Phaela dressed me in her newest creation, fussing with pins and adjusting the last stitches, I thought about Anne and her ghost, the castle's legacy, and—now—mine. On my first night, Phaela told me poison girls were free to leave the castle if the burden of their duty ever became too much to bear, but who, after serving the king for even a moment, could stand to leave? She had meant it when she'd looked Meredith in the eyes and told her she couldn't lose her.

Phaela's dress forms wore only neat folds of fabric with sketches pinned to their chests. In her paper visions, the dresses flowed like creatures who lived on currents of air or water, all effortless freedom. I wished I could feel as light.

As Phaela frowned over her work, I stifled a yawn and tried not to fidget. "Forgive me. I didn't sleep long."

She dropped a handful of pins into a little dish. They clinked sweetly into a pile and glinted in the light. "That's how it is at the beginning. Emelia tries to be mindful, but daily slumber remains incomprehensible to her."

"She doesn't sleep?"

"Every few months, she will trance for an hour or two as is natural to her people." Phaela pinched the shoulders of my dress and stepped back to study its drape. "She says our sleeping makes her lonely. Don't feel slighted if she's gone when you wake."

"It was odd to find her gone," I admitted.

Phaela laid a sympathetic hand against my cheek, but the tenderness in her touch didn't reach her face. *Do not disappoint us.* "You'll find she shows her care in other ways. Now. How does your dress feel?"

With my arms spread wide, the dress was geometric, sleeves left draping and undefined to join the main body in a bold clash of angles. But when I walked, the dress fluttered, sleeves winglike in my wake. Bright-yellow thread zigzagged joyously across the coppery red linen, organic in its path. It was the closest thing I'd seen to home since I arrived—the linen the color of our clay, the yellow the color of our maize. Phaela presented me with a square of matching fabric, and I clutched it to my chest. A matching scarf to tie back my hair!

The buoyant gratitude from the eve of my arrival returned. I thanked her, and she smiled as the red woman had. I liked this look on her, could almost forget that she was someone I could disappoint. Someone who demanded things of me. She sat me at her vanity and took up her brushes again.

As the first swipes tickled my skin, I hesitated, asked softly, "Am I to be so adorned every day? Our guests have gone."

"Emelia will have you sit for your first portrait session today. A painter is arriving from the city shortly after breakfast."

I held still as to not disrupt her work, a little sound of surprise all I could give.

"Don't worry. It will be a good likeness. Emelia would not tolerate less."

The post arrived to the great hall's table on a silver tray carried by a servant wearing conspicuously thick leather gloves. Wax seals bearing imperious crests in every color dotted the envelopes. Meredith set about opening them without so much as a glance at the king, and I startled at the pop of the first seal. I knew nothing of life in a castle, but opening royal correspondence seemed like a punishable breach of privacy. Across the table, Phaela sensed my confusion and explained that poisons lurked not only in foods. Papers and linens were choice ferries for noxious powders and perfumes. I was startled to recall the powdered luna Fifth Wanderer had attempted to smuggle with me—it seemed already a lifetime ago—and banished the memory as if the others might see it on my face and deem me the treacherous one.

The king shifted from her languorous perch at the head of the table to something more approximately upright. We'd not seen each other since the bath, and she had not remarked when I entered, apparently lost in her study of the painted scene above us. I already missed her ready compliments on my dress, but it didn't seem a targeted slight. Rather, I worried. Until now, at the mention of poison, she'd seemed utterly removed from us, lost to some thought so deep that not even Phaela's greeting touch to her shoulder could rouse her. Some rumors were true, and a monarch who could mourn her poison girls was a vulnerable one indeed.

"A few decades past," the king related as though she'd been engaged all along, "there was a noblewoman notorious for gifting poisoned gloves to those she wanted to dispose of. The trend started in Arga of all places. Their plots are most inventive. I'm glad to have their favor."

Meredith, having completed her assessment, passed the first envelope to the head of the table.

The king wrinkled her face at the gold seal and unfolded the paper in a huff. "Gold wax is for the insecure."

Meredith passed a letter to me and opened her second.

"We're aware of your prejudices," Phaela sighed as though this was a worn sentiment.

The king shot her a look, and Phaela smiled coyly down at her journal. "What do you think of Carlotta's new dress? I stayed up all night to complete it."

Over her letter, the king's gaze slid to me. Her brows relaxed. She set the paper aside, its transgression forgotten, and appraised me as if I were one of her paintings. I held my chin higher so I wouldn't avert my eyes. A look from her could still burn me.

"Stand," she said.

I stood.

"Turn," she said.

I turned.

Her gaze swept me up and down, a satisfied smile finally tugging her lips. "Exquisite, as always."

Meredith handed up another letter to the king. I found mine embarrassingly crumpled in my hand and pressed it flat against the table. The king grinned and said nothing, returning to her correspondence.

We went on like that until the meal arrived, the only sound that of rustling paper—Phaela bent over her journal, the king reading, Meredith and I sifting for treachery. After all the guests we'd entertained over the past days, this felt like the quiet company of a household in its daily rhythms. I almost forgot there was any danger at all.

The morning closed, and King Emelia's vulnerability went with it. Her regal stride returned, her spine dignified. Each of her crowning flowers was a fresh shade of red, the petals in new shapes and arrangements than the night before. She held my hand as we walked, and it was easy as ever to relax into her warm regard. I allowed her to lead me down the stretch of gallery-like corridors, all their gold and glaze and glass dazzling.

"Your knee was not so bruised when you came to me," she said.

I stared up at her, so awed by the paintings and sculpted ladies that I didn't immediately understand her question. "No, my king," I answered.

"Then how did you come by it?"

"I slipped on the way from my bath yesterday. I was careless."

Her tone was soft. "You don't have the look of a careless person."

"I was upset after visiting my da."

"I see." This answer seemed to relieve her. Her stiff poise melted, the curve of her neck uncannily sinuous when she looked down at me. "The castle has never been hostile to my poison girls. I worried something had been unkind to you."

The doors to the throne room glided open at the king's approach, but I stood rooted to the threshold. I clenched her hand. That animal sense prickled again, the weight of being watched.

The knight on my left looked at me. I knew it was looking at me because its body faced the corridor but its helmet did not. Its helmet faced me.

Mirrored in the black faceplate, my starved body stared back at me again—head giant and warped, limbs emaciated and overlong. My eyes were big and waterlogged. A twist of disgust blocked my throat. I patted my face and felt estranged from the soft skin under my palm, imagined it peeling away when I withdrew my hand to reveal the knight's vision. They were determined to see me as this ghastly Carlotta even though Phaela and King Emelia had assured me I was beautiful.

"Come, my dear," the king said, her hand on my back ushering me forward.

The doors closed. The thread of tension between me and the knight snapped. My image righted, but I was changed by what it'd shown me, foggier and paler than before.

I'd not returned to the throne room since the night of my arrival. Without all the ladies and their big dresses, without the music warming the air, without the bubbly shimmer of the wine, the room didn't breathe. Every noise was doubled or swallowed. Its ceiling was so high that when I looked up, I felt I was falling. I swayed against the king, and she folded me to her.

Setting up at the foot of the dais, the painter peeked at us around her canvas. She was so small in the cavernous space, like a singular stalk of maize planted and abandoned in the middle of a wide empty field. A spark of recognition lit her lined face, and she set her paints aside to greet the king with a deep curtsy. "It is an honor to return to the castle. How are you, my king?" she asked, gazing up as though the angel themself greeted her. She had a deep, wise voice that I liked, and her open adoration of King Emelia set me at ease. She'd dressed plainly in a frock and wore her hair like Phaela in the long-locked style I had only associated with noblemen before arriving to the castle. She'd gathered the locks at the nape of her neck, and they swayed beautifully when she moved. Her only adornments were a gold ring in her nose and bangles that chimed at her wrist.

Some of the fog drifted from my thoughts as I looked at her, and I realized I had missed her exchange with the king, had missed all but her name.

"You painted the angel!" I exclaimed out of turn and was immediately embarrassed.

The king and the painter only laughed. I relaxed again.

"Indeed," Beatrisa said. "Do you know the clerics wanted me to stand trial for my blasphemy?"

"I wouldn't have let them touch you," said King Emelia, a restrained edge to her tone I'd never heard before.

"The new artist collectives have thrived with your support." Beatrisa canted her head in thought, and the two women shared a heavy look between them. "You cannot fight the Retributionists and charm the aristocracy alone. Look what it has cost you. Phaela—"

"Phaela lives," King Emelia cut in. "And has chosen to stay at my side."

Beatrisa softened her approach. "Have you heard from your father? Will he aid you?"

"I don't need his aid, and he would not offer it."

"I see." Beatrisa's attention landed on me once more, and she relented. "And now we have Carlotta here to protect you."

"She's done well for me already." Pride lightened King Emelia's voice. "Carlotta healed Meredith on her first evening here."

I found the king's adoring gaze and was stunned again that it was for me—how the ever-present tension in her jaw relaxed, how the weariness behind her focus lifted.

"*Healed* Meredith?" Beatrisa echoed.

"I can draw the effects of a poisoning into myself," I told her.

"Amazing." Beatrisa stepped to me as if to better see the work I'd done these past years. "And to be so lovely in addition to your exceptional gift." She cupped my face as if it were already a prized and precious work of art. The bangles clicked at my ear. Her perfume wafted over me. I basked in her attention. "Where did you find her?"

The king smiled proudly. "A Restorationist monastery."

Beatrisa's eyes widened. "Phaela did well."

"She did." Nodding to me, the king added, "As always, you're welcome to arrange her as you like."

"Shall we?" Beatrisa asked eagerly.

Hand in hand—the king on my left and Beatrisa on my right—we ascended the dais steps, the throne our impending destination. I felt we'd entered another ceremony with me as the centerpiece, a private coronation. What an honor to take the throne alone!

They helped me up the last stair, and a shiver ripped through me when I sat. I regretted my dress. Linen was not made for such cold stone.

I swallowed and looked to the king. She offered a reassuring smile and watched Beatrisa fuss over me. "Your only job is to relax."

But the throne was King Emelia's. My toes barely touched the floor. The back of the chair was so far away and the seat wide enough to accommodate another woman beside me. I cast about for something to say, some polite small talk to distract from my discomfort.

"How many of the king's poison girls have you painted?" I asked as Beatrisa tilted my head and arranged my dress and set my hand on my lap just so.

"You'll be my tenth," she answered.

To this, the king said fondly, "I would not trust anyone else to capture the likenesses of my poison girls."

"Where are the others displayed?" I asked. For all the works I had seen in the halls, none of them were portraits.

"You must hold still, my dear," the king reminded me.

The painter's thumb swiped over my lip, her gaze intent on my mouth as she tilted my chin down once more. "Here," she said, rising. "Perfect."

Her cloud of perfume left me.

"Does every poison girl in the kingdom sit for her portrait?" I asked, thinking of Ma, hoping that finally, somewhere, I could look upon her face.

Beatrisa studied me with a new emotion. "The portraits are one of the king's traditions as far as I understand. Why do you ask?"

"My mother was a poison girl."

Sympathy softened her smile. My chest tightened before she even spoke. "Then I know she was beautiful. I would've been honored to capture her likeness."

I bit my lip. Beatrisa's words were as kind as the clerics', and somehow this hurt more. In my early days at the monastery, I lived with a fissure under my breastbone that would open at even the happiest memory. It threatened me again now. Seventh Seeker would squeeze my shoulders and guide me through my bodily grief, her veil sweeping soft against my cheek as we counted our breaths together. I cleared my lungs.

"I will do my best for you," Beatrisa said. It was all that was in her power to promise.

I thanked her. I smiled. At my side, the king's shadow was magnetic, and I longed to turn to her. I knew her gaze, and it hurt not to return it. Beatrisa, though, free to look up at her, smiled at whatever she saw, grinned full and conspiring. Together, they descended the short steps and left me alone.

A hand braced my back. I tensed, but the hand simply held the small of my back as a dance partner might. It did not move again, and if not for its cool pressure, I would have done my best to dismiss it. Beatrisa disappeared behind her canvas, and the scratch of her pencil filled the air. She peeked at me between loose, broad strokes. King Emelia loomed over her shoulder and watched the sketch progress. Beatrisa was stronger than I. I couldn't imagine creating anything with the king observing so intently, and yet she worked completely at ease.

Down the armrest, a manicured hand curved over the stone. Her nails were blunt and buffed to a shine. If I'd been permitted to move, I could have peeked over the throne's edge and seen a girl crouched there. She laid her hand over mine as though in confidence. Cold again.

Beatrisa scratched away at her canvas, and I allowed the sound to soothe me. Time passed in this way: the artist making her judgments and adjustments, the king pacing serenely behind, and I with relaxing as my only burden. I alternately turned my eyes to the inky sweep of the king's dress, the mist beyond the windows, and the chandelier's glitter. The hand over mine shifted, its thumb tracing affectionate circles against my skin.

At length, the king paused and turned to the door. It burst open moments later. Meredith strode in as though fresh from the thrill of a hunt, a letter raised triumphantly in her hand. Phaela followed unhurriedly, her posture formal as a headmistress's.

Meredith dropped into a deep curtsy before the king. "The white crow arrived!" she exclaimed, presenting the letter with both hands.

Even from the throne's distance, I couldn't mistake the gleam in the king's eye as she received the letter. "My gratitude, Meredith," she said, setting the point of a finger under the girl's chin and tilting her face to her.

Meredith stood on her toes to meet the king. They lingered in their kiss, but upon breaking away, the king was singularly focused on the letter. She withdrew to the door with Phaela, trading brisk words between them, and Meredith was left to clench her hands in her skirts, her face still angled longingly toward the king. She bit her lip and took two agitated steps in their wake before her gaze alighted on me. Her expression cleared, and she came to the dais.

"You look like a queen up there," Meredith complimented me, her smile wide, her entire body still animated from the delivery of whatever good news had taken the king from us.

Before I could reply, two servants entered with a late afternoon tea service, and Beatrisa officially adjourned us to stretch and refresh ourselves. Sometime during the interruption, my extra hands had left me. I stood gratefully. A stiff ache renewed in my knee from disuse. Meredith bounded up the steps to take my hand and lead me back to mortal ground. She settled primly on the bottom step, and the servants set two golden trays between us, one for tea and one for biscuits, cakes, and fruits.

"Oh, I *loved* having my portrait done," Meredith sighed, settling back on her elbows as the servants left us. "King Emelia could watch me for hours more and I'd still not have enough of her attention. *Sometimes,*" she added, leaning in for a conspiratorial whisper, "she'd stand absolutely still and watch me without blinking. And you know how intense a look from her can be. It was torture to sit still when she would tease me like that." She gave a giddy little shiver. "We'd barely make it back to her bedchamber after my sessions. She ripped one of my dresses, and Phaela was cross with her for an entire *day.*"

"It's not been so heated as that," I admitted.

"Oh, not *yet.*" Meredith's gaze dropped briefly to my lips. "She learns what gets under your skin. Then you will meet your undoing." She opened the lid of our kettle and peered in at the tea, inhaling deeply of the plume of steam that rose. "Delightful. We have a white tea today."

She cradled the porcelain kettle to pour our cups, and I studied her delicate hands: broad palms though not squared like mine, a confident and steady grip, nails neatly rounded to points but for the index and middle of her left hand which were blunted. I wondered at this. Meredith was too particular about her appearance for it to be anything but intentional.

"What happened to your nails?" I asked.

Meredith startled and turned her hands over at once as though grime might have spontaneously attacked her. After a thorough investigation, she frowned and asked what I meant. When I explained, she laughed. "A lady must always think of her lovers," she said. "Though I did allow mine to grow evenly for a time before you arrived." She dropped two cubes of sugar into her cup, adding, "King Emelia doesn't enjoy penetration of any sort."

Meredith stirred her tea with a petite spoon while I settled into the abrupt turn of our conversation. I'd never known anyone who could speak so casually and plainly about sexual preferences. Village girls whispered and giggled about their dalliances with boys, but it was always that—a whisper and never a declaration.

"Oh, you admire me," Meredith said, grinning. "I love being admired." Her tongue caressed the back of her teeth on the word *love*, her lips forming an *O* of drama around the word, and I was mesmerized. "Do keep looking at me like that."

I couldn't help my laugh. "Yes, I know now how you love to be looked at."

We giggled over our cooling tea, and I was struck again by the realization that I was having an experience I had never had before, one so mundane that I could have found anywhere but never had.

"I'm very glad to be here with you," I said when we had worn through our mirth.

Meredith's face cleared. "I'm very glad you came to us. I was enthralled by blood and sex magic last I told you, but I did mean it."

I ducked my head and stifled another giggle before we fell into fits again. We'd been so lost in our conversation that we hadn't touched our treats.

Eating or drinking without the motions of ceremony seemed wrong. How quickly I'd become accustomed to the castle's rituals. I said as much, and Meredith took a little cake from my side of the tray. "I will protect you," she declared, flirtatious and earnest at once. She bit into the cake with a flourish, leaving a fine dusting of sugar to powder her lips. She chewed methodically and allowed a thoughtful frown. I loved her performance, loved watching her throat as she swallowed, how her pink lips pursed and her tongue swept away the sugar. "It is safe, my Carlotta," she declared, holding the other half of the cake to my lips. I allowed her to place it on my tongue, and she watched me chew with the same rapt fascination I had bestowed upon her. Her attention was so distracting that I could taste nothing as long as I looked at her. I glanced down at the tray. The cake was dense and crumbled fast. Its flavor was understated—butter, sugar, and salt a perfect accompaniment to any tea.

I sipped my tea and realized I'd forgotten sugar. No matter. It seemed too late now. "Where is your portrait?" I asked. "I'd love to see it."

Meredith took her time with a biscuit. "Oh. I'm not sure where it is."

I forgot my tea in my hands. "Did King Emelia never let you see it?"

"I saw it when it was done, of course. I just don't know where it's displayed. And anyway"—she quirked her brow—"I have my choice of many fine mirrors."

"But have you seen any of the others, then? Of the poison girls before you?"

Meredith shrugged helplessly. "There are so many girls," she said as though this was an answer.

I finished my tea. Meredith poured another cup.

"Who is the white crow?" I asked next.

Meredith hummed around a mouthful of biscuit. "King Marcus sends his letters by crow. We've been waiting on word from him. He's invited King Emelia to meet him on Arga's soil. As much as it is a great display of trust and goodwill, it has also been . . . a complicated request, though critical in solidifying their alliance." She cleared her throat. "You've not told me about your night with the king."

"My . . ." I trailed off. I had almost forgotten about the ghosts and their hands.

"It is castle tradition to regale your fellow poison girls with the details of your passionate night. We all feel each other come, after all, so I at least know you took the ring. And I heard you from down the corridor."

My mouth opened, but I found no reply.

The servants bustled through the door ahead of Beatrisa. I'd missed her leaving but was glad for it given the conversation's turn. The servants took our trays, and Meredith snatched a last biscuit away, thanking them as she did. The women giggled and told her how nice her hair was today and how pretty her dress. Meredith found something about each of them to compliment in turn, and they left nudging each other and whispering excitedly.

"You're as admired as the king," I commented.

Meredith flipped her curls over her shoulder and struck a little pose just to make me laugh again. "And you will be so adored once they know you. I'm certain of it. You're already my favorite girl."

"You're flattering me."

The charm of her smile slipped for only a moment. "And if I am? You're too lovely to resist."

EIGHTEEN

KING EMELIA DID NOT return for the remainder of my session, but Meredith kept me company, reclining on the stairs with her needlepoint.

"Are you the embroiderer of all the king's pillows?" I asked, reinstalled and statue still on the throne. The forbidding cold from before seemed a distant and minor discomfort now. As with the rest of the castle, I had only needed a proper introduction for it to let down its guard.

Her gaze flicked up to me. "Do you like them?"

"I'm sorry to say I was distracted last I saw them."

Meredith snorted, and I swallowed another laugh. I wanted to keep amusing her. Is this what infatuation was? Prodding at someone's attention and hoping she found you clever?

"I will sew some little pillows for your bed," she offered, attention on her thread, "and hope to distract you from those too."

Right as I thought my back could stand it no longer, Beatrisa called our session for the day and thanked me for my energy and dedication. I was eager to see our progress, but she didn't offer her work, and I worried it would be rude to presume. Meredith stretched as though she'd been the one posing for half the day.

"We have some hours before dinner," she said, catching my hand. "Shall we return to the garden? Or go for a bracing walk along the wall? Retire to one of the salons?"

"There is a library, isn't there?" I asked.

Meredith's smile slipped again. I worried she found my request boring or, worse, pathetic, to be excited for something so simple as a library. Her mountain cities had several of the kingdom's greatest. My village, when it had existed, had none. The only books to borrow were from the schoolhouse's singular shelf, and I had read them all multiple times over. I treasured every book Ma sent to us because it was something new, something I would never have had without her.

"I should've known," Meredith said, rescuing her smile. "You are an admirer of Phaela."

We waded through the courtyard and its new mist—gray above, gray below—and entered a door to the south. A flight of stairs flourished, stone flowers in the arched ceiling blooming heavy with color as we climbed through pale light. Down the corridor, the castle anticipated our path. Broad-leafed vines snaked down as though on an overflowing trellis. Meredith reached for the leaves as we passed, greeting them with gentle touches.

Nothing grew near the great onyx doors. Meredith lingered down the corridor admiring the plants and took her time returning to my side. Wan light from the opposite windows reflected bright on the glassy stone, casting us as shadowy silhouettes in its reflection. Like the great hall's doors downstairs, a marble arch framed these. I leaned close, trailing my fingers down a carving of a lithe creature with gossamer wings and petite horns.

"What are these?" I asked. They seemed less shocking than the figures downstairs.

"They are pixies," Meredith answered. "Tiny devilish spirits from the king's home."

Little bodies swarmed upward, vying for an overflowing chalice at the arch's apex. The scene was so sharp with detail that I missed where their competition turned to violence. The pixies who'd arrived in the chalice's shadow bit and tore at each other's wings, forbidding the closest from reaching the chalice's waters. Those stripped of their wings lay broken beneath the chalice, reduced to lapping at the ground for what had been spilled.

Upon deciphering the image, I took a step back.

Meredith, unbothered, spared only a glance at the maimed pixies. "Hell delights in its grim myths. Shall we find your book?"

Inside, it was dark but for the gray light through the narrow windows, too high and far away to be of any use. Gloomy shelves towered around us and pressed in close. Meredith went confidently forward, finding and striking a match. Her face glowed with the light of a candle when she turned to me.

"If you want to have a proper look, let one of the servants know. They'll light the chandelier for you beforehand."

With our small light, we perused the shelves, all of them tall enough to require a ladder for the highest volumes. At the end of our row and set into the southeast corner, an iron stair spiraled up to a narrow second level where light glinted off glass cabinets. Meredith pulled me gently away when I started toward it.

"You'll want the poetry over here," she said, nodding to the shelves set along the back wall.

I followed, glancing over my shoulder at the stair and the cabinets. I could not see into their glass from down here.

"Phaela's work is along this shelf," Meredith said, pointing to a row of thin black volumes with gold titles on the spines.

The cabinets forgotten at once, I pressed close to read the titles by the light of her candle. "Are these all of them?" I asked. "All of her works?"

"Aside from the in-progress poems, yes."

"Am I allowed to . . . Can I—" I gestured to the spines.

Meredith giggled. "You can take them off the shelf, yes."

"I didn't know there were so many."

I took the first and held it lightly in my upturned palms. Had Ma read this one? She could rarely send entire volumes and so had transcribed her favorites in her own hand. I didn't know what collections most poems came from, which books might contain familiar lines.

"Have you read this one?" I asked.

"I'm not so devoted a follower as you," she said in a tone that made me glance up. I had never heard Meredith shy. "Perhaps you'd read your favorites to me someday."

By candlelight, Meredith's golden skin was angelic. The glow caught in the sleek black of her curls like a gathering of stars. I'd discovered a universe to fall into. Her mouth parted on an unsaid word.

Gathering myself, I managed, "I'd love to. Anytime. Perhaps this evening—or even now, if there's time, if something appeals."

Again, Meredith giggled. My heart beat anew at the little note of amusement.

"I trust your recommendation," she said.

When Ma sent new books or poems she copied down, I'd read them to Da after our dinner. We had poets from the kingdom's Heart and Perch cities and a smattering who were popular enough to be imported from the lake kingdoms to our north. I was happy to collect poems from anywhere. But when I had asked for Ma to send a borderland poet next, she said there were none. Or at least none who had been widely published. I wrote my reply and ripped up the page and started again. An overwhelming but unnamable feeling rooted in me, my first awareness of a shame that would grow over many years. Eventually, I managed a reply to Ma. I promised her that I would be our first poet. She said I would make her very proud.

The candle flickered between Meredith and me.

Other titles along the shelf—*Dressed in Silver*, *Poisonworker Prayer*. I pulled the second and set it atop the first I'd taken. Its title made me shiver. My palms were hot. I would read them in my room where it was less grim and, having dreamed with Phaela's work under my pillow, compose my couplet.

"If it isn't wrong to ask," I began, keeping my voice low as though someone might overhear, "do you know why Phaela doesn't age?"

"I understand she's part of the castle in a way," Meredith answered. "She came to the king after her mother's death and never left."

"She's like the ghosts."

"She is something between."

"How do you mean?"

Meredith faced the shelf and, in doing so, took the light from me. "The ghosts are bound by their pasts. Phaela seems untethered from past and future. She lives to serve the king, but unlike us, her servitude is so fundamental as to have rewritten the laws of her name. People struggle to properly see or recall her unless King Emelia invites them to."

"It was the same for me when I came here," I said, relieved to have someone recognize the phenomenon.

"For me too." Meredith nodded to the stack of volumes in my hand. "You have your selections?"

"I think I'm to study with Phaela," I said, an even more surreal prospect now that I understood her nature. "She wants me to compose a couplet for her."

Meredith's expression brightened, and I was glad for it. "How lucky for you! She doesn't take on pupils. What will be your subject?"

My mother seemed the obvious choice, the link between us, the reason I'd been enamored of this place. Both of us being daughters of poison girls, Phaela would sympathize, wouldn't she? She'd understand the intention behind the words. But as I turned over the idea, I grew less certain. Would it seem I was seeking an easy route? Worse, could I ever write of my mother and honor her distant life? For Ma, the lines would have to be perfect, and I was a dilettante who could not yet weather critique on something so precious.

But here was Meredith haloed in candlelight. At once, my worry cleared.

"If you'd permit me . . ."

Meredith smiled slowly and knowingly.

The fluttering in my belly took up again, and I pressed valiantly on. "I'd honor you with my pen."

"I'm to be your muse?"

"If it pleases you."

She came to me with her candle, drew so close I could snuff the flame with a breath. "It does." She reached past me for the table, bringing our bodies flush together as she set the candle safely away. Her hands held my face, a thumb swiping over my cheek. Only now in the quiet dark I catalogued the small callouses on her hands—one on the left thumb and another on the index finger, signs of her devotion to her own craft. I loved that something so delicate as her needlepoint could leave a mark.

I rested my hands on her hips and wished her softness weren't shielded by so many stiff layers. Would she allow me to unlace her as the king had?

Our lips met in our first private kiss, gentle at first, then Meredith's relieved sigh set off a frisson that rocked through me like fate. King Emelia and Phaela had brought me here through their power and mystery. Everything was possible because of them, but Meredith was the earth itself—magnetic, grounding, true. When magic had spun itself out, she remained.

I opened to the soft explorations of her tongue and dared to nip at her bottom lip, thrilled at how her flesh gave between my teeth. I needed what I had been too shy to claim before. Meredith tipped her head back invitingly, baring the fading kisses our guests had left. I lost myself against her sweet skin. Memorized her pulse, just there under my lips. Collected her little sighs like precious gems on my tongue.

"I need—" I started, and "I want—" she began. Breathy laughs, a tangle of arms. Meredith shifted and took a handful of my skirt in her hand, bunching the fabric at my hip. The cool library air whispered around my ankles, and I stilled.

"I want to feel your ring," she murmured against my ear.

I nodded against her. She lifted my skirt, palm gliding over my bare thigh. I shivered despite the heat between us.

"Now look at me," she said, one hand under my chin while the other slipped between my legs.

Finding me wet, she curved her fingers into me, and I clenched around her, suddenly unsteady on my feet. Mesmerized, I watched her expression clear then slacken with pleasure as though she'd lain back on her pillows and touched herself. A whimper dropped from my lips, and Meredith echoed. Her breath was in my lungs. My voice was in her throat. My head swam.

I gripped the table. A current had caught us. Meredith swayed into me, just as unsteady. I wrapped my arms around her, and we went down together, her on top of me, my back hitting the table.

I stared up at her, awed by the black of her pupils blown wide, her curls mussed and wild from my hands. Her breaths were deep and shaky, each inhale straining her chest against her dress. In the candle's shadow play with her body curved over mine, she looked like a mythological hero undone.

"Um, miss?" a timid voice came from the dark.

At the end of the row of shelves, Winifred stood with her eyes averted. Lenora stood with her, looking on unashamed, her professional demeanor unruffled.

"King Emelia requires you both at the table," Lenora said crisply.

Meredith withdrew her fingers, and I hurried to settle and smooth my skirt. My legs shook under my weight.

"Of course," Meredith said primly, licking the taste of me from her fingers. She arched an eyebrow and linked our hands as though we'd only been found reclining for a chat in the garden. "Shall we?"

We entered the great hall to Phaela and King Emelia conversing as intensely as we had last seen them, their heads inclined over a scattering of papers. Beatrisa had joined their strategizing. The king was the first to turn at the sound of our entry, glancing up with an agitated frown as though she had been interrupted in her study. It was enough to bring me up short, suddenly and anxiously certain that our tardiness had disappointed the king. Meredith, however, dropped my hand and cried out with glee.

"Oh, my Rangford, how I've missed you!" she exclaimed, throwing her arms around the hound at the king's side. "My darling fellow!"

Startled by the king herself, I'd missed the imposing creature standing at attention beside her chair. It defied all earthly logic, statue still even as Meredith threw her weight against it in an embrace. She might as well have hugged one of the sculptures in the corridor for all it seemed affected. Meredith flopped down to the floor beside it and hung her arms around its neck, kissing its fanged snout as one might nuzzle a kitten.

"Do you have—?" she began, looking up hopefully at the king.

King Emelia's expression softened, and she handed down a slice of pomegranate to Meredith. Finally, the hound reacted, opening its great jaws and seizing the fruit with its tongue.

"You will stain your dress," Phaela warned, her tone weary as though she'd uttered these exact words many times.

Meredith scurried out of the way, giggling as seeds scattered upon the floor.

"I'm sorry I couldn't stay for more of your sitting," the king said, her gaze on me once more. "I trust you two had a fine afternoon. Meredith has developed a habit of arriving to the table before me these past months. It's good to see her occupied."

Tugging me into my seat beside her, Meredith said, "Carlotta is going to write a poem about me. It will be about how beautiful I am, won't it?"

Replies fled my mind. We had an audience now. I nodded to her flirtation and could think of nothing clever.

At Phaela's side across from us, Beatrisa smiled. "It's good to be back in the castle again and see you all in good spirits. I worried when you didn't summon me that you'd found no one to take on who suited you."

Phaela busied herself with bundling their papers away and handing them off to a servant.

"It was a long search," said the king. "I've had to be more exacting in my choices."

Five wineglasses were set before Meredith and me. While a servant poured a brightly scented golden vintage, others busied themselves serving food. Meredith struck up such a lively conversation with our wine pourer that, by the third glass, the woman was holding in her laughter and telling Meredith to hush or risk a spill. This evening brought more novel vegetables and a new gift from the lake: tough green buds sprinkled with crushed nuts and dried berries, a salad of tender plum-colored leaves drizzled with a piquant green sauce, and—finally—a pale pink curl of fish with a hard red tail drowned in buttery cream.

Beatrisa placed a hand over her heart as though she'd received a great gift. "You've not even signed your treaty!"

King Emelia's smile was satisfied. "It bodes well, doesn't it?"

Meredith and I took small sips of wine from three of the glasses before us, and at our nods, the servants redistributed them to King Emelia, Phaela, and Beatrisa. The wine's dry sugar lingered on my tongue, and I wanted another sip immediately. It tasted like a surprise of white grapes from the summer market—back before the drought, when water was still heavy in the air.

"Carlotta?" Meredith rested her hand on the arm of my chair. She wore that look from before, the one from when I had spilled coffee over my dress and left her at the wall.

At the head of the table, the king watched me expectantly. I hurried to her, taking little bites from her plate without tasting. The wine was still bright on my tongue.

"It is safe, my king," I declared.

Her nails trailed down my spine, and her gaze lingered. "Thank you, Carlotta," she dismissed me.

Upon completing her assessment of Phaela's and Beatrisa's plates, Meredith rejoined me on our side of the table. I liked the meal once I settled—the chewy tanginess of the dried berries in contrast with the crunch of the nuts, the surprising spice of the vinaigrette, the simple and salty pleasure of butter. This fish had a heartier texture than the first but one that I enjoyed all the same. Overzealous, Meredith popped a whole little fish into her mouth only to immediately scrunch her face upon chewing. Her muted flailing brought the king's political talk up short.

"You must remove the tails, my dear," King Emelia said. "Prawns are shellfish."

A servant appeared at Meredith's side with a fresh handkerchief to spare her the embarrassment of spitting the tail back to her plate. Her mouth free of the shell, Meredith apologized profusely, her golden cheeks flushing red. The servant bit down on her smile and hurried away with the wadded handkerchief.

"How was I to know fish could have shells?" Meredith muttered, gazing warily at the prawns as though she'd been betrayed.

"The water holds many surprises," the king said evenly, though her eyes gleamed with amusement.

Happy to dwell in the evening's flavors, I lost track of the conversation around treaties, timelines, and travel. One name turned my attention to the topic at hand.

"I will send for Earl Huxley, of course," the king said in reply to one of Beatrisa's questions. "The counsel of the merchant families has proven invaluable. Your time here may overlap. I'd be happy to make introductions."

I looked up from my plate. "When will he arrive?"

At my first words of the meal, everyone turned to me. I avoided Phaela's gaze.

The king considered. "I have just written him. My hope is within the month, barring any prior arrangements he may have with business partners."

Delfina would return within the month. Hope flooded me. I could try for a better impression. Over an extended stay, there'd be no way for us to avoid each other.

The king tilted her head. "What concerns you?"

I clasped my hands beneath the table. "I briefly met one of his poison girls my first evening here. I hoped to see her again." The king waited as if knowing there was more to my reply, and I couldn't help a glance at Phaela. So she hadn't mentioned my outburst? Reluctantly, I added, "She's from the borderlands too."

Delfina's final words still rattled shamefully in my mind. *Like you've just crawled out of the dirt.* I would prove to her that I belonged in this world just like her. I would gain her respect, her friendship. Then, she would tell me the truth.

And with it, I would protect the king from Huxley's treachery.

"I see." King Emelia's expression eased. I braced for a pitying look from her and was relieved when her face remained neutral. "The older woman, yes?"

Phaela and Beatrisa fell into laughter at this, and the king's eyes widened in bewilderment.

"Who is old to you?" Phaela asked. "She is certainly not older than either of *us*."

The women continued laughing like old friends, and the king stared on, flustered and admiring at once. I'd never seen her so, didn't know monarchs could gracefully stand for their mistakes to be laughed at, and felt privileged to witness another casual intimacy between them.

"I meant," the king amended, "that she has renewed her contract for longer than the average poison girl."

Which meant Ma's service had not been average either. She'd had barely more than forty years when we received Huxley's letter. Delfina, like Ma, was working for the benefit of someone other than herself, and that made her desperate to maintain her contract.

"Of course she has," I said, unthinking, only feeling.

Again, everyone turned to me. I clenched my hands under the table. My frantic heartbeat made me sick. I wanted to sob or smash something. Preferably both at once. Instead, I breathed and held myself still. I would not storm out! I would not cause another scene! I relaxed my expression into something smooth and empty even as heat raged in my chest. The clerics would be proud if I'd not so deeply disappointed them.

Why was no one speaking? I was so calm. I could endure whatever they said next. I would not disappoint the king as I had disappointed my teacher and my father and my clerics and perhaps, worst of all, my mother. I'd be better here. I would do what I was supposed to do. I would be what I was supposed to be. That was why I had come. So I wouldn't be evil or exalted anymore. So I would be just a poison girl among other poison girls. Nothing more and nothing less.

Meredith placed a cautious hand on the arm of my chair. She looked at me as though I weren't calm, and so to prove her wrong I very calmly stood and bowed to the king and calmly asked if I might be excused.

The king frowned but nodded her assent.

My back to them, the ache in my chest broke open. I could scarcely breathe through it, thought I might suffocate and collapse on the floor of the great hall, but I made it through the onyx doors and into the ornate corridor and away from anyone who might see me cry.

Nineteen

D AMP HAD SETTLED INTO the grass from the afternoon's mist, and thin clouds swathed the moon. I lay with a hand in the hellebores and the other against my breastbone. Even at night, the grass was quiet, absent of little crawling, buzzing, gnawing things. I'd missed this fact of the garden until now, had been too enamored of its unchanging perfection. Nothing but the wind moved here. Did anything here truly live? What was a garden that didn't see seasons? Annuals that never bid their farewells, perennials that never rested through winter? I'd thought maybe this place would feel like home, or the way home used to feel, with all its green leaves and dark soil, but these plants didn't ask for labor, only admiration.

Soothed by my unaccompanied presence, Da slithered from the flowers and curled across my chest. In the silver quiet of the garden, I could imagine we'd fallen into our old routine—a poisoning, a purge, a revival. Serpent and tether, Da's spirit anchored me to the earth when my body was too overcome, whether with poison or my own volatile heart. The dew chilled my back. I breathed and watched the sky pass through night. By the time I heard the king's hem rustling in the grass, my fever had left me.

Da coiled tight as though he would strike but instead made a swift retreat to the hellebores. I took my first breath without his comforting weight and watched the king observe the starless sky. Her ivory horns framed the moon, and from my lowly position against the earth, I cast her as a venerated goddess, a figure beyond even heaven and the angel. She was a religion for me alone. The flowers against her hair were violet and electric, their petals disks that absorbed moonlight. Finally, she started toward the path.

"Come," she said.

Careful not to trample the trail of her dress where it rippled over the grass, I hurried after her. She led us to the pond. Peaceful as candlelight, little flames danced on the water's surface and floated along like leaves. Their light reflected on the creatures below, glittering across a rainbow of scales as they arced through the dark. The king contemplated this display, but her gaze was far away.

A breeze chilled the damp fabric against my back, and my shiver drew the king's attention. She unclasped her cloak and settled its velvety weight over my shoulders, enveloping me in her white perfume. Where the garment's length swept elegantly about her ankles, it pooled unflatteringly at my feet, rumpled like stately drapes in a plain and low-ceilinged room. And yet the king paused to admire me.

"You said you didn't care about the borderlands," she said gently.

"I wanted not to care," I admitted. "While I had my da and our home, all I thought about was escaping north. I spent my entire childhood dreaming of elsewhere. Now there's no home to go back to."

The king didn't reply, and I kept talking, on and on like a hidden well suddenly tapped.

"The clerics said our fighting made the angel sad and ruined the land, that poison grows in place of woods or crops because it's what our spirits have sown. That's why poison girls are sacred—because we're the only ones blessed to survive in the new world. That's why there are more of us now. The angel made it so. At least that's what my clerics believed because they thought I could be good.

"Da said there were simpler explanations. He said the droughts were only seasons and knew this one would pass. No need to believe in so much. But the drought lasted. Every year, with the same conviction, he said it would break. He believed in the sky itself, that everything would turn right and we'd finally have enough rain. Now both my parents are dead, and there is nothing beautiful left there even though it's where they fell in love. Da said Ma proposed to him at a great magnolia on a hill. At the start of the drought, he would trek up the hill with water. That's how much he loved my ma. He wouldn't let the tree die, but eventually, even we couldn't spare the water. The tree was dead most of my life. I don't think he ever had the heart to tell Ma, and she never came home, so to her, the tree could always be alive."

For a long while, the king said nothing, and I hated how I'd rambled.

"This tree you mentioned has a flower?" she asked eventually.

"One of few that remained safe," I said.

"Sit please," she said, and I followed her command. Amidst a luxurious pool of velvet, I waited. "Are you able to picture this tree?" she asked. "Can you still feel its shade? Do you know the scent of its flower?"

I nodded.

"I would return it to you if you'd allow me."

I stared up at her wonderingly, and she sat with me in the grass. I thought, with how she held my face, that she might kiss me, but instead she instructed me to close my eyes, to remember this tree and others like it, to feel the leaves under my fingertips and press my hand against the bark. As a girl, I had collected the leaves when they fell, admiring their waxy sturdiness and broad shape. *Bigger than my hands*, I had exclaimed to Da. *Big as saucers!*

"What majestic creatures," the king sighed.

At the sound of her voice, I opened my eyes. The king gazed skyward, her attention rapt, as though one of the trees rose behind me. She smiled full and wide, her glee revealing too many teeth, cheeks splitting along a heretofore invisible seam. Her eyes had gone black as the night, and she was beautiful.

"Feel the soil," she breathed, her hand grasping my wrist and guiding me to the earth. "Imagine rooting deep. Imagine opening, blooming."

I saw the scaled layers of a green seed pod, the white spear tip of a flower bud.

"Deeper," the king urged. "Do not be timid."

By the pond, the ground was cool and the soil loose. It was easy to sink my hands into the dirt. The roots of the grass tickled my fingers, and I imagined overturning fresh dark earth, of planting something new. The garden recognized me, its leaves turning to me as though I were the sun. A years-old dream resurfaced, one in which the flowers had claimed me, one in which the moon had looked on just like this. Wind whispered through the courtyard to sigh against my face, and the water of the pond rose against its bank, lapping toward us like a longing hand.

The king's forehead fell to my shoulder. She shook as if from exertion and slumped away from me, her braids dragging the ground and curtaining her face. My cocoon of euphoria ruptured.

"My king—"

She heaved as though sick. I hurried to her. She turned her face from me, but in her hand, a black mass dripped through her fingers. Clutching it, she dragged herself to her feet and made for the pond. She moved as though injured, in slow and lurching strides. Bile stained the grass where she'd hunched. I peered closer. Red seeds shone in the viscous black. I thought of pinching one in my fingers.

The king knelt at the pond. I approached her cautiously, staring over her shoulder for a glimpse of what she held beneath the water. She wiped her mouth with the back of a hand before submerging it again. Pond water soaked her dress, but she seemed not to care. I kept my distance, and finally, she looked to me, offering a fresh green seedpod in her palm. I startled at the sight of it, wanted to ask how she'd done it, but her weariness shocked me more. I went to her and didn't think, only braced her shoulders and guided her head into my lap. She allowed me and stayed. I cupped the hand that held the magnolia pod, wondering at its realness, at her long sharp hand nestled in mine.

King Emelia's voice rasped when she spoke. "My father sent me here, a place where I risk a true death, in the hopes of hardening my spirit. I reminded him too much of my mother—mediating pixie disputes, fostering injured hounds, tending the outland orchards. It wasn't work fit for someone of our station. I should've been at his side as he guided his court. Now I am chained to this castle so I must focus, so I can't *gallivant about*, as my father says. Until I satisfy him, I cannot leave this realm or these walls. This garden is all I have."

Rumor speculated that the king was strengthened by some evil root within the castle, that this was why no one had ever seen her beyond its walls. The truth was more terrible. This was why she dealt so closely with Huxley, to have a hand in the world beyond the castle.

I tried to picture the king in her home realm, no longer a king and perhaps not so old among her people if her father could command her life as he did. I tried to imagine a father who did not care whether his child risked death, who would even cast her into danger and turn his back. A father so unlike mine. It was good that the duke had not taken the throne after Eric. Someone like him would have no sympathy for the borderlands. Someone like him wouldn't weaken himself for the hope in a handful of seeds. I wanted him never to come here.

I didn't know what to say, and now I understood the king's silence after my confession. Like her, all I could offer was a question.

"You've made all the plants here?" I asked.

"Yes," she said. "Poison girls have beautifully vivid memories for plants. Over the years, I've also been gifted memories from merchants and bards who've traveled the continent. At first, I was disheartened that nothing from my home would take root here. I've been told the skies over the castle are uncommonly dark for this realm, though it is still much too bright for the gardens I used to cultivate. I've made my peace with it, as I have with the other attendants of kingship. Now I'm proud of all I've managed to grow."

I found my hand in the king's hair, combing absently through her sleek braids as she spoke. Like her flowers, the color of her hair was different at night, less blood red and more wine dark, less violent and more indulgent. I had forgotten myself, done too much savoring of late. She was still my king. Meekly, I withdrew my hand.

Her eyes shut as though I pained her. She caught my wrist. "Please. Do not withdraw your tenderness from me."

Breath caught in my chest. I lowered my hand back to her hair, felt the motion in slices of time—fingers curled apologetically against my palm to a slow blooming out toward my sun. For an eternity, I reached for her. I met her in an instant. Nothing had changed, and I was awestruck. Touch was a miracle.

King Emelia's countenance smoothed. "This realm changed my body when I entered it. I knew hunger for the first time. I grew more teeth and developed new cravings. At home, we eat only for pleasure, but here, I found that I weakened within a day if I did not eat. Then, eating itself was not enough. I craved flesh. I wanted it bloody and rare. It became an exciting new indulgence."

"That is how I feel here. Overcome by new indulgences."

"Yes. So we are." A wry smile tugged her lips. She shifted to better look at me, and the arch of her horn fitted neatly over the curve of my thigh. "Tell me more of the borderlands and the plants you loved there. Help me imagine that I am free to visit one day."

Of course, I told her of the maize and how tall it grew, the games children played in the fields, and the dolls we made of its husks. The first husk doll I ever made was a poison girl named after my mother. I made a friend for her who was also a poison girl because even when I was small I understood no one would want to befriend a poison girl if she weren't one herself, and I didn't want the doll I named after my mother to be lonely.

The king took my hand and placed it over her heart. "These stalks, they're taller than you?"

"Yes," I giggled. "At harvest time."

She grinned. "Taller than I?"

"No, my king," I said and dared to kiss her sharp smile.

We passed an hour telling stories in the garden until I began to doze and King Emelia regained her strength. The clouds rallied and overtook the moon. Swept up into the king's arms, I was asleep before we reached the castle stairs.

The next morning, the sound of rummaging pulled me from sleep. Perhaps it was the king come to check on me—but then, she had handmaidens and servants to move and carry things. Perhaps it was Lenora here to ready me for the day, but she always greeted me.

A groan of protest rose in my throat at the slide and *thunk* of a closing drawer. How late had the king and I stayed in the garden? I remembered gathering her small braids into a single larger one, how she'd plucked a flower from those that adorned her horns and tucked it behind my ear. I remembered *Do not withdraw your tenderness from me*. I was warm and my bed was soft and my dreams had been sweet, though I couldn't remember them now. I rolled over and pulled my covers higher. The noise persisted and now sounded like the riffling of pages. Alarm flung me upright.

There, at my desk, Anne stood flipping through my journals.

I charged out of bed, awake at once. "Stop that!" I cried, swiping a little book from her.

She scowled as though she meant to quarrel with me, her black eyes glinting before she broke into laughter. The gaunt hollows of her face filled in. Her brown skin regained lively color and an enviable glow. When she looked at me next, the whites of her eyes were clear, her irises dark brown. She set a hand upon her hip and appraised me in my thin nightgown. She wore nothing, as before, and seemed freer for it.

Anne was a wisp of a woman. I hadn't noticed at our first meeting, not with her behind me in the shadows, not when her hands had been so fierce. She wore her dark hair in thin braids as King Emelia did, though hers only reached her hips. Her face was small and the mischief in her features big. She reminded me of the pixies.

"I wanted to know what sort of woman you are," she said. "And then I found this." She pinched a white feather in her fingers, once the most magnificent in Seventh Seeker's veil. Now, neglected at the bottom of my bag, its shaft was broken and its barbs askew. How had I forgotten her last precious offering to me? I felt Anne's question doubly. What sort of woman did it make me?

I held out my hands. "Please," I whispered, begging for its return.

Anne pouted mockingly. "Are you so faithful? Perhaps King Emelia would like to know how you fill your journals with prayers to an angel invented by the men who want us dead."

My heart thundered, dread thawing to anger. I bit the insides of my cheeks. I hated that I'd ever written those prayers because I hated that I'd ever been so lonely and desperate. I hated that I'd had to lose so much.

"Those journals are old," I said. "I was confused." I racked my mind for what might sway her. "Seventh Seeker was kind to me. That's why I keep the feather."

I found myself delineating Retributionists from Restorationists, explaining the latter's view of poison girls as redeemers for a lost world. I told her about the monastery and the clerics, how I'd once been a savior, and Fifth Wanderer's belief that my invitation here was another opportunity to cleanse the world.

"I'm not what they thought I was or what you think I am," I said.

Anne withered as I fought my way toward an explanation, her cheeks growing sunken and her ribs sharpening under the skin. Her black eyes narrowed. "Then what are you if not a poor assassin?"

"I'm just a poison girl like you." I considered, added, "Please do not make me leave."

Anne clutched the feather in her bony fist before relinquishing it to me. It was even more rumpled than before, as though she'd wrung out any holy light it might've had. What were the cleric's feathers if a dead girl's anger could ruin them? How had they ever seemed like more than common bird feathers?

"If you betray us," said Anne, "you may find a cup of tea that proves how much of a savior you are."

"It would be better to cut my throat."

Anne's eyes widened a fraction. Her laugh startled me, and she was pretty again. "You are not a poison girl like me, Carlotta Bridge."

TWENTY

EACH MORNING, I SAT for my portrait, and each morning Meredith brought me a new flower from her walk in the garden. She made such a habit of keeping me company during my sessions that our handmaidens began piling pillows by the throne for the sake of her comfort. The king was absent for much of the day. I missed the concentrated attention that'd come with my induction, though I knew we could not go on that way forever. We reconvened at the dining table where we often met a new merchant or aristocrat happy to share their counsel. Earl Huxley did not appear, and I grew restless though a month had not yet passed.

Meredith and I took to spending our afternoons in her bed. I loved her body as much as I had when I'd first beheld her and adored her more with each passing day. The mole on her breastbone and the tight curl of hair at her temple were treasures. The scrunch of her nose before she spilled into giggles was a gift. When I first tasted her, I thought it would kill me. I thought I would die. She laughed and held me.

I wrote in the garden when the fog abated and sometimes at my little desk and woke in the middle of the night to set a line by candlelight, Anne looming over my shoulder as I did. Most often, though, I wrote wherever Meredith was—in the little chairs on her balcony, in the wide empty parlors where she took her tea and frowned over her latest needlepoint composition. I studied her as if readying to paint a portrait of my own from memory, but for all my watching, it proved impossible to hold the image of her in my mind as soon as we parted.

Phaela assigned and accepted my poems when King Emelia didn't require her, sometimes humming at my compositions as though she'd taken a sip of middling wine. "Don't despair," she would say. "Everything can be taught." She treated my poems about Meredith not as silly infatuation, as I'd feared, but as equal to the lines I attempted about my mother or the borderlands. Also thanks to Phaela, I had more enviable dresses and all the reading I could want. In this way, the weeks passed, King Emelia coming and going in the background of my life. I drafted many poems and fragments of poems-to-be, but for all my writing, I had forgotten my pledge to Marta—that I would post a weekly letter. Already, a month was gone, and I was a liar.

Dear Seventh Starlight Seeker,

Remember when I first woke at the monastery? I struggled with your names and veils. I didn't understand how you organized the sky. Your astrology was a language it took me a year to speak. A seeker and wanderer were the same to me. I was disrespectful and presumptuous and attempted to give you a new name for my own ease because we spoke most often. I said you looked like a Marta. You chastised me. I never called you that name again because I wanted you to keep liking me and thinking I was a miracle and savior. You doubted the elders. How could a girl of eighteen restore such a broken world? Here is the proof that your doubt was always correct: I never stopped thinking of

*you as Marta. Even now, writing this, I almost wrote "Dear Marta."
And now I've called you this forbidden name thrice. Now you know
I'm not a savior. I couldn't even do the least you asked of me. I couldn't
even write you this promised letter until now.*

*I've rambled this long to delay my apology. A savior never
apologizes, and I never did. There were times I wanted to hurt you,
and I'm sorry. I only wanted to know how much you cared about me
or if you cared. Because I wanted to see you hurt, you're not head cleric
anymore. I did that and I—*

I swept the page to the floor and laid my head upon my arms. The
glass pen dripped ink onto the fresh page beneath. Anne perched on
the edge of my desk. Her eyes sparked as if she might tease me, but
she only swung her feet and watched me fret. I set the blotched page
aside and began anew.

Dear Seventh Starlight Seeker,

*I hope I haven't worried you, though I know I have, and I am sorry.
How has the monastery been in my absence?*

*Life in the castle is everything I hoped for. We're allowed visitors,
and I wish you would visit me. The king has been lovely to me. I have
more than I could ever need. She even made sure my new dresses were
done in the traditional style. I'm learning from the royal poet and get
on well with my fellow poison girl. The food is—*

I swept the page to the floor.

Dear Seventh Starlight Seeker,

*I am sorry for breaking my promises so soon and with such ease. I'm
allowed visitors here in the castle and I beg you to allow me to correct
my negligence by hosting you.*

Yours,
Carlotta

—◆—

During my next session with Phaela, I hurried to her study with my letter in hand and asked whether she might post it. Her study's aesthetic followed that of her bedchamber—lurid red fabrics and bone-white furniture. The colors swallowed me whole, as if I'd entered a poisoned body to purge it. Phaela frowned when she saw the address and studied me for so long that I averted my gaze. Finally, she relented with a clipped "Very well."

I had no sense of how long it took letters to arrive to or from the castle and didn't ask, feeling that I had already asked enough in posting a letter to the monastery. I hesitated, said, "Meredith told me we could have visitors."

Phaela's lips quirked. "If your cleric were to accept your invitation, it'd be a first for us. Emelia would love to boast of a member of the clerical orders in her court, though given the friction between their doctrine and her mere existence, I deem it unlikely. At the height of the Retributionists' vitriol, she invited their head cleric to tea. Did you know this?"

I shook my head.

"They didn't respond to her directly, of course, but the letter stirred controversy. The head cleric framed the invitation as an attack against their order. Surely the king intended to poison him or lure him into a dread pact. There could be no other explanation."

"But Seventh Starlight knows me. Why would she suspect a trick?"

"Perhaps you have written a letter under duress. Perhaps you have been corrupted and are acting in accordance with Emelia's evil will." Phaela smiled at these last few words as though recalling a private joke.

"I promised her I would write. She expects to hear from me."

Phaela was solemn again. "To hear from you, yes. I don't want to see you disappointed when she declines to come here. At the least, it would risk her standing among her peers."

And yet Seventh Starlight had already cast aside reputation and responsibility simply to write to me. Did my attempt at an apology only burden her more? I thought of taking back the letter, but what else could I say? What other apology could I offer?

King Emelia did not come to the table that evening. Phaela was tardy. The table had been set, yet no one appeared to serve the food. Meredith, Beatrisa, and I waited. Eventually, Phaela arrived from the kitchen with a plate already prepared and set it before me.

"Emelia will be taking dinner in her study," she said. "I'll personally deliver it if you'd be so good as to taste it for her, Carlotta."

"Let us join her there," Meredith cut in.

Phaela gave her a sharp look, but her tone remained easy. "Emelia will summon you if she requires your presence."

Meredith shot to her feet. "But last time—"

"This isn't like last time." Phaela left my side to soothe Meredith, embracing her as one would a petulant child.

Meredith gripped her so hard the tendons in her hands strained. "You promise she is well?" she whispered into Phaela's shoulder.

"You trusted me back then, didn't you?"

Across from us, Beatrisa sat with a politely furrowed brow. "Is there a healer who can attend the king?"

"Your concern is appreciated as ever, but there is no need," Phaela answered, untangling herself from Meredith. "Emelia only needs her rest and sends her apologies. Carlotta, if you'd please."

The king's meal was a rare and unadorned cut of red meat large as the plate itself. It seemed such a primitive and graceless selection that I doubted it was meant for anyone, least of all the king. Obediently, I took up my utensils. The fork and knife were heavier and colder than before. I cut a sliver of meat, and it bled across the plate. Unlike the other meat we'd been served, this had no masterful sear. No sauce. Not even salt. It had already cooled as though left out after a drunken feast. How could something so poor be meant for King Emelia? It stuck in my throat as I swallowed.

"It is safe," I pronounced, looking up at Phaela with my own questions.

She closed the plate away in its cloche once more, the gleaming silver of it too fine for what it contained.

"Thank you, Carlotta," Phaela said, leaving us without another word.

Meredith glared after her with unshed tears in her eyes, her shoulders hunched against a sudden weight I couldn't understand. As soon as the onyx doors closed behind Phaela, Meredith snatched up her glass and clutched its stem in her trembling hand. Her jaw worked as though holding back some rude retort.

"Meredith?" I ventured.

Lost in her enraged study of the crystal's facets, she didn't seem to hear me. A rapid attempt to blink back her tears followed, then resolve. She smashed the glass upon the floor and with its shatter coughed up a laugh that broke her face into a jagged grin.

"Meredith," I tried again, but she was already making her own swift exit toward the courtyard. Shards crunched under my shoes as

I made to follow her, but she did not turn, and—in a reversal of our meeting on the castle wall—she didn't turn back, and I let her go.

We didn't see King Emelia for a week. Meredith woke later and later and spoke less and less, arriving to breakfast long after we'd been served, then appearing with her hair undone, then neglecting to change out of her nightgown. Her handmaiden trailed fretfully and apologetically after her, and Meredith barely acknowledged her. She picked at her food and would not look at any of us. Phaela witnessed this with strained patience but said nothing until Meredith begged one day to taste the terrible course of blank red meat Phaela had taken to automatically placing in front of me.

"Please," Meredith whispered, tugging at the lacy bell of the poet's sleeve. "I want to help her."

Phaela stared down at her a long moment. "You have made yourself sick when I have told you there is nothing to worry about. You're unfit to make such an important determination."

"Carlotta can taste after me," Meredith insisted. She squeezed Phaela's hand in hers, kissed her knuckles fervently. "Please."

Phaela's mouth quirked down. "What is the use if I must rely on Carlotta?"

Beatrisa's fork clinked delicately against her plate. We all looked to her as though she'd called us to order.

She folded her napkin into neat squares, unhurried as we waited on her. "Give the girl what she wants if you will not give her an explanation. We are all worried."

Phaela's brows rose, and she looked to Meredith as if seeing her for the first time.

"Your devotion to King Emelia and her privacy is admirable, but you forget the happiness of her poison girls," Beatrisa continued. "Meredith is as devoted as you and has suffered much through this past year."

Phaela gave a stiff bow. "I'm sorry, Beatrisa."

Two months ago, I would've thought the gesture forced and insincere. Having seen the servants and handmaidens bow to the king this way, I understood it was reserved for those deserving the highest honor—or when a mistake was so poor a simple apology would not do.

Phaela bestowed the king's plate to Meredith who sat up straighter, sniffling as she took up her fork and knife. Her eyes were permanently red these past days as though she had recently cried or was about to.

"I am sorry," Phaela repeated, petting Meredith's disheveled curls.

Under the long tines of Meredith's fork, the meat bled. I clenched my jaw and anticipated the taste. Too red, too iron rich, too cold. Meredith swallowed the bite and sighed. She closed her eyes and tipped her head back as though basking in a rare beam of sunlight.

"It is safe," she breathed, and Phaela stroked her hair once more before solemnly closing the plate away.

By the time I found her in the afternoon, Meredith was listless again, lost in the froth of her rumpled bedclothes and staring up at the ceiling. I didn't know what questions to ask or how she might receive them and so sat with her in silence. She would not let her handmaiden touch her, but I could sometimes coax her to sit up and allow me to brush her hair.

"You have such nice hands, Carlotta," she murmured.

"Thank you," I said, running my fingers through her hair and following with the brush. Despite her neglect, her curls were still as silky as the dresses we wore.

We had sunlight that day, watery and gray through the clouds but sunlight nonetheless. It streamed through her gauzy white curtains and cast a lovely sheen upon her hair.

Meredith's voice was miserable. "Last time the king was sick, I did not leave her side. Why does she not want me now?"

"Perhaps she isn't sick. Phaela hasn't said."

"And will not say. Don't you feel something wrong? Don't you feel the castle restless at night? I feel her pacing. I cannot sleep."

"You've been here longer than I. You're sensitive to it." I lay my head upon the hunch in her back and listened to the rise and fall of her breath. She found my wrists and pulled them around her so that I hugged her waist. Her sleeve had slipped down her shoulder. Its decorative bows sagged. I pressed my lips to her exposed skin.

"Please stay," she said.

I dreamed of beating my fists against an onyx door. It wasn't one I'd seen before—not the one that guarded the throne room or the great hall or the library. It was rough and unpolished like the mountainsides I was used to, and I wanted to escape. I didn't know what lay beyond, but I knew my life would be better if I could open it. To either side of the door and all around me was a barren landscape, but I could not step away from the door and peer at its other side. There was only me in the gray and the door that rose into the clouds.

I lifted my fist to beat my body against the rock once more, and a flash like untethered lightning sent me reeling back.

I jolted upright. White flashed at the edges of my curtains, but no thunderous rumble followed. Anne sat curled at the foot of the bed, her knees drawn up against her chest. In the flash, I saw she wore a nightgown identical to mine.

"Is that a storm?" I asked her, crawling out of bed.

Her black eyes followed me.

I threw back the curtains. There was no lightning in the sky. At the castle wall to the north, light erupted, flickered, and died, redoubling at odd intervals. It cast the courtyard in ghostly white, a soundless sheen there and gone. Above, the clouds were unhurried, and no wind disturbed the garden. I flicked the lock to the balcony door.

Anne screamed and threw her body between me and the glass. "Do not go out!" she begged, her eyes big in her face.

I staggered away from her. "What is that?"

"I don't know," she whispered and drew the curtains as though the light might hear us. "It's not safe to go out. I don't leave this room anymore. The last time I left this room when the castle was strange, I went looking for the king. Someone found me, and I woke here, and no one could see me anymore. Then you came. It was the first time I saw the king again. If you stay here, she has to come find you."

"Anne—" She slumped to the floor, and I joined her there. "What do you mean the last time the castle was strange?"

"There was screaming, but it wasn't a person screaming. Screeching. The worst sound you can imagine. Like someone scraping hot coals over your head."

I knew that sound, had heard it not so long ago at the monastery. "Do you know what it means?"

She curled tighter and pressed her hands over her ears. "I don't know where it comes from or what it means."

"It's quiet now. You're safe."

"Do not go out," she repeated.

"I won't," I said, but my promise didn't calm her. She curled tight again and hid her face. Searching for a topic to pacify her, I asked, "How did you meet King Emelia?"

Anne peeked at me, revealing first the glint of her eyes and then a full grin. She stretched long and swept herself up in a graceful arc, arms swanning over her head. In an instant, she was transformed. She twirled past me, leapt high, and landed with a bow.

"You're a dancer!" I exclaimed.

I'd never seen movement like hers. This was unlike our stoic dances in the borderlands, ceremonial offerings to the earth rooted in shows of endurance and strength. It was unlike even the women in the ballroom on the night of my arrival. Anne explained her art as an imported western dance. She'd traveled with a group of performers through the north, performing in new theaters every night until a bitter rival's jealousy turned treacherous.

Anne's arms floated down to her sides like clipped wings. "The night before my leading debut, she poisoned me."

I understood the shape of the story immediately. Why had I asked for it? What poison girl's origin would cheer them? Anne shouldn't have survived, but she did, and her survival was also a death.

"She was able to frame her attempt on me as heroic. Her deep concern for the reputation of the company drove her to expose me as a liar—but of course, I hadn't known I was anything but a girl. I was still sick from the poison when they threw me out. Of course everyone loved the scandal. That is how Phaela discovered me. She is so bright, you know, when you're hurting."

I nodded. I did know.

"I thought I would never dance again, but King Emelia was all the audience I needed." Anne drew herself up again, shaking off the memory like any good performer with a show before them. She danced to me on her toes.

"How do you do it?" I asked.

She looked me up and down, flirtatiously appraising. "I will show you."

No one came to breakfast the next morning—not Phaela or Meredith. I sat at the long table alone, the servants attending me with downcast eyes. Finally, Beatrisa arrived with apologies and complaints of poor sleep. We ate half our meal in silence, and I was adrift. Already I'd grown so used to the castle's rituals. It was meaningless to eat without the king and joyless without Meredith and gauche without Phaela. I poked at my rosemary potatoes and left my stack of flat cakes to dissolve in their syrup.

"All will be well," Beatrisa said.

I was startled to find her still across from me. I could not recoup my words and stared.

"I've seen the king in similar periods. She always recovers. When she does, she will need you more than ever. Her poison girls truly mean everything to her. Let that sustain you."

I could not be encouraged. "Why has she withdrawn from us?" I asked. Why did it feel as though the castle were emptying?

Beatrisa sighed gently. "It is not for me to speculate. I only know the depth of her care." She stood and came around the table to me. "Let's you and I endure for her, yes? Your portrait will be my best yet."

TWENTY-ONE

MEREDITH WAS NOT IN her bedchamber when I went to find her that afternoon. The balcony doors were open, letting in a chill and cleansing breeze from the courtyard. The bed had been made for the first time in days now that Meredith had finally left it. Volumes of poetry I'd strewn about were stacked neatly on the bedside table. The litter of nightgowns—I'd been able to coax Meredith into fresher ones, never a proper dress—had been removed. The brush we'd lost in the sheets had been plucked clean of her hair and returned to the vanity.

I sat at the edge of the bed. I thought of nothing and then, alarmingly, thought of crying. No present cause emerged from the morass of nightmares and fears and memories always at the surface, and so I decided I wouldn't cry in Meredith's clean and empty room. I took up a poetry collection from the table and read and waited for her. She never appeared. My chest began to hurt. Daylight dropped away, and it was only as my eyes began to strain that I realized I had never turned a page. How long had I skimmed the same words? After all this time, I knew nothing about the letters in my hands. I returned the little book to the top of its stack and shivered. The doors were still open, the curtains fluttering pleasantly. I went to close them.

The breeze died. The curtains fell. A hulking figure stood at the edge of the balcony, its menace wrong next to Meredith's little chairs. The knight's back was to me. It faced north where the mysterious light had flashed in the night. My pulse rose. I backed away, stumbling over something in my haste. A girlish yelp righted me.

Lenora stood wide eyed, her hands outstretched as though to catch me. "Are you well, miss?"

I breathed and nodded. Lenora didn't lower her hands as if worried I might fall while standing absolutely still.

"Did you not hear me?" she asked. "I've been calling for you."

I shook my head.

"The king has requested your presence. I'm to prepare you."

Lenora dressed me in red lace and painted my face until I looked wicked. I was delighted not to recognize myself in my shadowed eyes. Lenora had chosen a pigment for my lips that was so dark a red it was black by candlelight. I removed my scarf. It was night and the day's labors done. Only then, for the first time since coming to the castle, did I feel the irrelevance of the tradition's symbolism. But when had it ever truly been relevant to me? I had always been a farmer's daughter who understood my family's work abstractly. I never knew dirt under my nails. I would not think of home. I thanked Lenora for her help.

Anne sat at the edge of my vanity, swinging her legs furiously. Her eyes had gone black again, but her skin remained supple and glowing. She regarded me as if she wanted to bite me—her hands clutching the top of the vanity in some great show of restraint—and I was glad Lenora could not see or feel her presence.

When I stood to follow Lenora, Anne trailed after me but was stopped at the threshold as though I'd slammed the door in her face. I reached for her surreptitiously as I took the door handle, sculpting my expression into an apology. She watched my hand warily and held her own adamantly by her sides before relenting at the final moment and squeezing my hand through the gap of the closing door. The rush of undefined emotion I'd felt in Meredith's room redoubled, and I pushed it down just the same.

"King Emelia has recovered?" I asked Lenora as we walked.

"Not even Freda and Aline have seen her, miss. The staff know little about her state. Phaela has been attending her, so I'm assured she has all she needs." She patted my shoulder. "You will see her soon and soothe your concerns."

Black glittered at the top of the stairs. To either side of the king's doors, the knights stood watch, their attention straight ahead. Tension locked my shoulders as if there was some charge in the space between them. Lenora held the door open for me, and I hurried through.

"Have a good evening, miss," she said with a soft smile.

The doors closed. My eyes adjusted to the surreal and vast mirror shimmer of the room.

"Carlotta!" The mound of pillows on the bed stirred, revealing Meredith's glossy curls as more of her little embroidered pieces spilled to the floor. Her gown was a diaphanous shadow, billowing and sheer with nothing for modesty beneath. Satiny laces cinched the fabric at her waist for a dramatic flare from her full hips. Rubies ornamented its high neckline. She moved like a spirit native to this place, a guide come to welcome me. Her makeup was dark as mine.

I marveled at her. She grasped my hand and led me to the bed where the king waited.

King Emelia sat with her feet tucked under her, and yet her posture was just as cold and imperious as though holding court upon her throne.

I trampled an embroidered pillow and an open book on my way to her. Meredith pulled me insistently forward, but I cast my gaze back and down, disbelieving for a moment that I could have stepped on a book. I recognized the symbols inked across its pages but did not understand them here. They were part of clerical ritual, signs inscribed for breaking the grasp of evil energies. We would etch them into clay talismans and give them to the poisoned pilgrims I saved as a ward against further misfortune. I shook that image of my past away.

The king was not herself. Even in the gloom, the dark circles under her eyes were startling. The rich undertone of her skin had paled. Nothing bloomed around her horns, the vines barren but for two closed buds. Northern flowers naturally ended their seasons, but not with the king. Her garden was evergreen, perfect despite the chill and clouds. Had she passed the last week alone, watching her blooms wilt one by one? Had it hurt her? Tonight, she'd draped herself in a black shift, its shape so indistinct as to conceal the line and shape of her body. Even with her finally before us, she was hiding.

"My king," I began as Meredith delivered me to her grasp. I wanted to ask her about flowers and sigils.

Her smile was languid, but the heat in her gaze remained. "I've missed you both," she sighed, gathering us against her.

I missed her too. I missed her touch. I missed her scent. I inhaled the white warmth of her perfume and dared to kiss her neck. She held me tighter, an encouragement. Beside me, Meredith gasped. I glanced up. The king kissed her gently, adoringly, but had caught her by the neck, her thumb and forefinger pressing into the pulse points below Meredith's jaw, nails biting the skin enough to draw forth a bead of blood. Meredith made a little broken noise in the back of her throat but held obediently still.

A tight thrill of heat bloomed in my belly. I was slick. My flesh swelled against the ring, and I knew Meredith's bliss as my own. I let my head drop to the king's chest and fought to breathe. It would be overwhelming—the doubled pleasure of witnessing her and feeling her at once—if I did not hunger for precisely this. The king grinned, her gaze intent on Meredith as though watching for some telling twitch of her features. I swallowed, felt faint. I could not look away, mesmerized until the king dropped her hand. Meredith took a gasping breath. Her eyes were half lidded, her breathing ragged. She trembled and moaned, and I couldn't endure it. I wanted her touch or the king's. I was hot and couldn't think.

King Emelia held us both, helpless, against her. She stroked our hair and kissed our foreheads and said we pleased her, that we were such good girls. "I've devised a game for us. Would you indulge me?"

Meredith sighed, then hummed, attempting, as I did, to find her words. Her forehead against the king's shoulder, she nodded yes. She said, "Anything, my king," and I echoed her.

"Winifred," King Emelia called sharply, and Meredith's handmaiden emerged from the dark. I startled to see her, hadn't known we weren't alone.

The girl's face was red. She stared at Meredith with wide-eyed longing and came forward with halting steps, balancing a tray in her hands. Upon it, a jeweled dagger gleamed. It looked ceremonial, as if it had never known violence. I stared at its silver length on the gold tray, and King Emelia ordered me to stand. I did. My legs trembled, and I was hyperaware of the wet heat on my thighs, the swell and slick that demanded attention at even the slightest movement.

"Take the dagger," the king said.

I took it and suddenly didn't know how to stand with something so solid and sharp in my hands. The king observed me thoughtfully, and Meredith's gaze sharpened with anticipation once more. She curled against the king, her eyes flicking between me and her handmaiden. I held the dagger with both hands, its blade flat against my open palm, and turned it so that its gems caught the light. Its blade was narrow and vicious as a needle. I studied its dreadful point and waited for fear to settle. It never arrived, so I raised my eyes to the king and held her gaze. She smiled as though I had passed some test.

"Thank you, Winifred," King Emelia said. "You may go if you wish. Or stay if it suits you."

The girl hugged the tray to her chest. "I would stay if you'll allow me," she said.

Meredith smiled sweetly. "We would love to have you."

The girl ducked her head.

"Now," the king said against Meredith's ear, "if you'd be so good as to face Carlotta."

Meredith uncurled luxuriously, her legs sweeping over the edge of the bed, her back against the king. She stared up at me, and our eyes met before my attention briefly dropped to her breasts, her nipples sharp beneath the shadowy gown. The king gathered Meredith's curls up in one hand, tightening her grasp until Meredith straightened her spine, then pulling harder to expose the line of her neck. Meredith's throat bobbed. I thought of resting the blade there, flat beneath her chin, silver metal against gold skin. The king watched me, slid her hand against Meredith's inner thigh and encouraged her knees apart. I tightened my grip on the dagger.

"Now," said the king, "the rules of the game."

I had forgotten what we were doing, had forgotten this original purpose at all. I only knew Meredith before me, her back so gracefully arched, her throat bared and legs open.

"Carlotta, before you are permitted to touch Meredith, you must fully cut away her dress, starting at the neck. You must not make a mark on her skin." Again, she trailed her hand down Meredith's thigh, the touch of her nails eliciting a shiver from Meredith. "Understood?"

"Yes, my king," I breathed.

I studied Meredith's dress, its high neckline and cinched waist. These were the trickiest points. The fabric was otherwise loose and too delicate for resistance. But there, at her neck where the skin was thinnest, the dress hugged tight. It would be too easy to nick the skin. I stood over her, our lovely Meredith. She blinked up at me with her soft, familiar smile as though I prepared to recite a line of poetry instead of hold a cold blade to her neck.

"It is rude," she said, "to keep a lady waiting."

I pressed the blade under her chin as I'd fantasized and relished her little gasp, the fluttering blink and ensuing grin. I held the dagger there and let it warm to her skin. The king's smile was unseaming beyond the bounds of her lips, uncanny fissures in her cheeks revealing all those sharp teeth. She didn't hurry me, only watched like some bird of prey with Meredith in her talons. The room was quiet and sparkling. Behind me, I could nearly feel Winifred holding her breath.

I knew the depth of Meredith's trust in her soft, half-lidded gaze, and so I held it as carefully as the dagger and angled the blade. Its wicked point slipped easily between fabric and skin. Meredith was still but for the racing pulse at her neck and her quick breaths. She watched me work from the corner of her eye. The blade was mercifully sharp. It bit into the fabric at my first testing pull, and rubies clattered across the floor. Meredith sighed. I cut the dress between her breasts and set upon the laces like picking a lock. The gown fell down her arms and pooled around her hips with a whisper, and there I was kneeling before her.

"What do you want to do with her?" asked the king.

Meredith was beautifully aroused, her dark ring gleaming against her swollen clit, her wetness having dampened the bedclothes. So close, the scent of her was divine and primal at once. I admired the curve of her breasts from where I knelt looking up at her, how they trembled with each breath of anticipation. She'd grown so sensitive that a light brush along her thigh was enough to make her startle.

"I want to taste her," I said, my need so bright in the silence.

"Then taste."

Meredith whimpered when I ran my tongue along the wet seam of her, sighed when I flicked my tongue against her ring, cried my name when I closed my lips around her. She crossed her ankles against my back and held me close as the king held her, the three of us twined together as though this had always been our fate. She sank her hands into my hair, and as her pleasure shook me, I remembered that first time I'd been inside her, how she was beautiful then, too, as I'd saved her and pulled her out of death's hands. Meredith clenched around my fingers, tensed and then melted. My body followed hers, the magic that tethered us pulling me under with her. This was the inverse of a purge—the immersive ecstasy of falling into another with no fear of drowning. I didn't need to fight or resist. It was safe to be lost, and I collapsed into her warmth.

Above me, when the world came back, Meredith was limp and cradled in the king's arms. She made little satisfied sounds and tugged insistently on my hair. "Carlotta," she whined, and I rose to rejoin her, and it was easy to tangle our bodies together, the three of us one for a blissful and fleeting moment.

"Winifred," the king said, and it was as if the handmaiden's name spoke her back into existence. There she was, tense and quiet and wide eyed, her bottom lip worried swollen. King Emelia smiled graciously. "Come here, won't you?"

The girl approached the bedside, stared longingly at the wanton spill of us.

"Don't you think she's been good, Meredith?" the king asked. "Wasn't it a delight to watch her?"

Meredith's eyes gleamed, anticipating another game. "Yes, my king."

"Lift your skirts, Winifred," the king ordered. "You prepared as I asked? You wore nothing underneath?"

Winifred nodded meekly and did as she was asked. The king reached for her, slid her fingers appraisingly along her sex. Winifred gasped, her hands tightening in her skirts. The king's hand came away wet, and Winifred looked on in awe as King Emelia lifted her fingers to her mouth and tasted her.

"What shall we do, Meredith?" the king asked, her gaze intent on Winifred.

Meredith slipped eagerly from the bed and knelt before her handmaiden. She kissed the girl's feet and blinked up at her with that sweet look that had ruined me before.

"My lady . . ." started Winifred.

"Relax," said Meredith. "It is my turn to take care of you."

TWENTY-TWO

S CREAMS RIPPED THROUGH MY sleep. A searing warning. A scorching sound.

My own scream withered before it escaped my throat, a useless cry against such an all-consuming resonance. A white-hot knife had pierced my mind. I was hopeless. I was nothing.

Pain reduced me to prey. I was my most bare instincts. Curl away. Lie still. Hope that this torching wrath forgot me.

Suddenly as it had broken open the world, it was gone. My suffering went with it. I lay in the twinkling dark, breath too fast, heart too fast, anticipating a new and piercing pain. An agony so deep couldn't possibly leave me unscathed.

Around me, the warm bedclothes shifted. I was not alone and not in my room. I remembered. The past few hours were so distant now—the relief of returning to the king's bedchamber, our beauty and pleasure here. A moment of terror had stripped it all away.

Someone was sobbing. Winifred? I felt nothing. I was hollowed out. The primary instinct of prey was to flee, and I had lost even that. I lay still.

A shadow darted around the bed. I raised my gaze to the king. Though she had seemed listless before, she moved now with the cold efficiency of a huntress. She thrust her hand into the wall, and it was this new impossibility that made me sit up. The onyx rippled and congealed. Her arm sank to the shoulder. She twisted as though rummaging through a wardrobe, and when she grabbed hold of what she sought, the wall released her. A sword glinted in the king's hand, its black blade as long as I was tall.

"Stay here," she commanded. "Do not leave until I return." The fury in her countenance extinguished upon seeing Meredith, rigid and blank faced, squeezing crying Winifred in her arms. King Emelia's brow eased, her eyes widened, and written there on her face was a flicker of vulnerability I had never seen and would likely never see again—doubt and regret and maybe, maybe love; I wanted to see in her face something sacrificial, something that only a poison girl would aspire to, and then she closed it away and was impassive once more. She turned as though fleeing the revelation, and when I expected her to reach for the door, the onyx rippled once more, and she simply melted through.

We passed the rest of the night alone, Meredith, Winifred, and I. Eventually, Winifred's tears subsided. She turned her face to Meredith's shoulder and sniffled and allowed Meredith to rock her. Over the girl's shoulder, Meredith and I shared looks but did not speak until the first gray sign of dawn. The night had made us superstitious. Surely light's arrival meant horror couldn't come again.

"You're well?" Meredith asked softly.

I nodded. Asked, "And you?"

She nodded.

Winifred didn't stir. Had she fallen asleep in Meredith's arms?

Daylight grew, and the candles seemed to dim.

"What has the king gone to do?" I asked.

Meredith's voice was barely a whisper. So as not to disturb Winifred, perhaps. Or the silent castle itself. "She will keep us safe as we keep her safe."

"I heard those screams once before when Phaela found me."

"Those are the king's watchers."

"Watchers?"

"The black suits. They're occupied by sensitive but pained souls who have taken a liking to King Emelia. In her homeland, they are considered revenant pests. Whole forests become uninhabitable when they gather, and they are often driven out. But the king says souls are reborn this way when they are silenced in life. In death, when they sense something they dislike, their voices are relentless. Few can calm them."

Meredith told me the king's story of how she'd befriended these spirits, how she'd resolved to sit in the forest while they gathered about her and screamed. She didn't try to drive them away. She didn't shrink from them. At the end of a fortnight, they had worn through their sorrows. Some drifted away, but a few were curious and followed her. Her father was furious when she returned to court after disappearing for so long. But when he yelled at her, the watchers yelled back, and he could not reprimand her.

In the predawn light, in her murmur, it was as though Meredith related some storybook tale from memory—our king a gentle hero of misunderstood, albeit terrifying, creatures. The telling made clear how much Meredith adored her, in her downcast eyes and small smile. None of the rumors had prepared me for this.

"And tonight, the spirits have met something they dislike," I said.

"A breach of the castle boundaries is one of the few remaining things that will raise their voices."

"Was it not enough to take Anne from us?" Winifred asked angrily. So she was not asleep.

"It is most efficient to target those of us supporting the king rather than the king herself," Meredith said evenly. "She has so few vulnerabilities. Their choices are starving her or poisoning her, both of which have proven difficult. The route they've devoted themselves to of late is to first remove all us poison girls—"

"Please, stop. I cannot bear it," Winifred begged and fell silent again.

When King Emelia returned, it was without her sword. The sky was bright gray, and she was radiant once more—a cacophony of fresh red flowers in her hair. Spider lilies, yarrows, asters, dahlias, and other blooms I couldn't name grew impossibly together, the vines that adorned her horns spilling like ribbons through her braids.

"All is well," she declared.

Meredith was out of bed in an instant, throwing herself into the king's embrace. She heaved a dramatic, relieved sigh. The worry did not leave Winifred's features. She sat among the pillows, her legs tucked under her, and worried her lip as though there was much she wanted to ask but dared not speak until the king addressed her.

I dared. "What happened, my king?"

King Emelia looked up from Meredith's ardent stare, absentmindedly drawing her hand through Meredith's curls as she answered. "I found our intruder, ran him through with my sword, and devoured him." She said this as if it were apparent and rational, without shame or fear of judgment.

Meredith, still clinging to the king, cast a glance over her shoulder. Winifred's worried look settled on me.

I hadn't given much thought to what King Emelia had shared that night in the garden. She said she'd developed new hungers and cravings. I understood the bloody cuts of red meat. I understood, even, the chalice filled with my own blood. Borderland elders told tales of night-flying creatures who drank blood to regain their strength. They were stories to frighten children away from wandering after dark, but it meant such concepts were not foreign to me. The devouring that King Emelia mentioned was more than this. I struggled to picture it and felt nothing. I thought of wild dog packs with their prey, ribs torn open for the sun. I thought of cats with their kills. Tried to heighten the scale.

She will keep us safe as we keep her safe, Meredith had said. But for us, every new meal was a potential death. For King Emelia, it was a blossoming.

"Your new flowers are lovely, my king," I said. It was all there was to say.

She smiled genuinely at this, the big smile that showed all her teeth. I imagined those teeth closing around my throat. I imagined them rending flesh from bone. What would it be like to witness King Emelia advancing upon me with deadly intent and ravenous hunger in her eyes? Did the intruder know what awaited him should he fail?

"Who was he?" I asked.

"They are all the same to me," said the king. She brought Meredith back to bed, kissed her, and slipped her hand casually between Meredith's thighs. Meredith lay back on the pillows and hummed as the king entered her. "Winifred," King Emelia said lightly, and the girl startled. "Would you be so good as to tell everyone they are free to prepare for the day?"

Winifred nodded and stood hastily. "Yes, my king," she said breathily, her gaze lingering on Meredith before she turned to go.

The king hooked Meredith's ankle over her shoulder. "Sometimes they are mages sent by kings who do not enjoy having me as a neighbor," she answered belatedly, and I remembered my question. "Some, I speculate, are assassins hired by Retributionists. I devour them all, and when they never report back to those who sent them, the stories of my evil grow." She smiled at some private joke and sucked gently at Meredith's neck. I admired the soft curves of her as she lay beneath the king, was magnetized to her, allowed her to pull me in. "This world is ruined because men believe it is and make it so," the king said, her heated gaze finding me over Meredith's body. "Compared to the scale of their influence, I am merely surviving."

Breakfast would be late.

I returned to my room to find Anne huddled beneath the bedclothes, a conspicuous lump in the otherwise pristine bed. I called her name, and she didn't answer, so I peeled back the coverlet. She lay on her side with her arms wrapped around her knees. Her bones were sharp through her nightgown, the most skeletal I had ever seen her. Her hair had thinned to patchy coils against her scalp, and her skin was stretched papery over hollow cheeks. When I asked her what was wrong, she didn't acknowledge me. I sat beside her. At length, she uncurled and pillowed her head in my lap, exposing the bright-red stain across the stomach of her gown. My breath hitched. She bled on the sheets, and I watched them darken.

"Anne?" I tried again.

She said nothing. I laid a hand on her shoulder.

"I thought you might be dead." Her voice was a hoarse whisper. "I thought you'd be like me, and I didn't want to share this room with another like me." She shifted so that she could regard me with her hard black eyes. "I would've hated you for it. Truly, this time. Not the way I hate you now."

Anne's gown was a mess, the pool of blood growing beneath her. She didn't seem to notice.

"Are you hurting?" I asked.

She continued on as though she hadn't heard me. "The night of the screams, I was scared and went looking for the king as soon as it was quiet. It was a mistake to leave my room. A mage found me. He cut me with an enchanted knife so that King Emelia could not revive me. They'd learned from a previous attempt against us many years ago, long before I came to the castle. An assassin had mistaken Phaela for a poison girl. That is why she stays young, you know. The king saved her, but her magic cannot heal us. Phaela lives suspended in time so that she will not bleed out. I've heard the handmaidens say her wound still looks fresh as the day she was attacked." Anne watched me as I processed this. She rolled fully onto her back. The bleeding was terrible now. It would ruin the bed. I had never seen so much blood. "How was your night with the king?" she asked hopefully, as if I might have good news for her.

"Anne . . ." I started and found I could barely speak through the tightness in my throat. I didn't know why I would cry for her. She was already dead, had done little more than bully me. But then, there was the night of the mysterious light when she had begged me not to go out, when she had feared—as I now understood—that her fate would befall me.

The stain had reached me now. It was sticky on my thigh.

"Anne, you're bleeding," I told her because I was suddenly overwhelmed by this and her, the fact that there'd been a dead girl living with me all this time and I had not let myself feel anything about it, was unable to say anything about it, because death was all around me always. Since I was a child, I had prepared for it.

I couldn't move with Anne's head in my lap. It seemed wrong to move a girl who was dying, to refuse her comfort to maintain my own. I started to cry, and Anne sat up and embraced me, and heaven above, there was blood all over me now. The scent of copper filled the room. She was so heavy. Was she holding me, or was I bearing her weight? Her bones pressed into me, and her blood seeped into my pores, and I wondered again what my ma had felt as she was dying and whether she was scared or whether Da still felt the pain of the snake bite even though he was the snake and that's when Lenora appeared in the room and found me sobbing and screamed.

I insisted on dressing for the day and going to the table to perform my duties for the king. Lenora bathed me solemnly, her lips pinched into a thin line as streaks of red unfurled in the water around us.

"Miss," she ventured delicately. "You were just with King Emelia. How did you come to be so covered in blood?"

"It is Anne's," I said, and Lenora flinched and said nothing else.

The corridors were oddly empty, even taking account for the castle's small staff. How had the others weathered the intrusion? Were they all safe? Lenora walked briskly and flagged the first two women she saw on our way to the great hall. The three conversed away from me in hushed tones. Both eyed me uneasily and averted their gazes when Lenora's tone turned sharp. I did not mind. I was used to wary looks and furtive glances.

When I arrived, Meredith was already at the table sorting through the mail. Beatrisa was absent, but Phaela assured me she was safe and only taking time to recover from our harrowing night. Anne's ghost was everywhere—in the haunted looks of the staff and the hushed layer over the most minor proceedings. They had all been here the last time a night had ended in a woman's blood. They carried the weight of it in their bodies. For the first time, I was an outsider among them. While they grieved, I'd washed her blood from my skin.

I cast a sidelong glance at Meredith. Blankness had overtaken her again, the same as last night. I hadn't known what to say then and didn't know what to say now. I brushed her shoulder in what I hoped was a comforting gesture, and she gave me a distant but acknowledging smile. I joined her in testing and sorting the mail. After a night spent in helpless waiting, I was happy for a defined and familiar task to occupy me. Meredith blinked back to life at the sight of a plain white envelope sealed with black wax. I thought, with how she startled, that she'd uncovered a threat. Across the table, Phaela looked up from the little book she'd been annotating. I glanced between them. Eventually, Meredith extended the unopened letter to me.

"It's addressed to you," she said, a crease of suspicion between her brows.

Phaela set down her glass pen.

My hands were already shaking when I took the letter. Someone had written my name in a plain and blocky hand—someone, according to the sender's address, from the Restorationist monastery. It was not Marta's handwriting. I would know her slanted, cramped script. With Meredith's and Phaela's attention heavy upon me, I tore open the letter. It was short. At only a few lines, it could barely be considered a letter at all. I scanned it fast and read again, uncomprehending.

Seventh Starlight Seeker has been relieved of her veil and is no longer welcome at the Temple of Restoration. We have no information as to her whereabouts. Please do not come here or write again.

The words were a swift and sudden blow. *Relieved of her veil.* I had left her with an uproar, the elders herding her away. So her stepping down as head cleric had not been enough for them. Had the valley pilgrims acquiesced to her dismissal? Had Fifth Wanderer, always so close to her, done anything to protest the elders' decision? Or had he only made himself indispensable to Seventh Seeker in order to stay near me, to advise me toward his personal vision of restoration? From the moment he'd found me in the woods, he had tried to make me his.

Blaming Fifth Wanderer would be easy. I wanted to hate him as Da had, but my reasons weren't as noble. Fifth and I had used each other to our own ends and, ultimately, disappointed each other. My anger had nothing to do with Fifth. I was the one who'd promised Seventh Seeker I'd write and had failed to do so until it was too late. I'd asked her to give up her life without a thought. I disregarded everyone who tried to care for me, and now they were all gone from my life. I deserved such a letter, didn't I? I deserved these hauntings.

Crumpling it into my pocket, I avoided Meredith's questioning gaze. No one spoke. I snatched up a letter for the king. I hoped it poisoned me.

With Beatrisa unwell and King Emelia occupied with Phaela in her study, I had nothing to structure my afternoon. I sat cross-legged among the hellebores, slouching flamboyantly and with aggressive ease. It was the only thing I was grateful for that day—my loose dress and wool cape. Clothes hugging or pinching or stifling me would have made me likely to tear my skin off. I'd thought of returning to my room with the letter but dismissed the idea. I doubted Anne's blood had been left to soak into my bed, but I also wasn't prepared to see it cleaned and tidied as though my morning hadn't happened, nor the night that had catalyzed it. Most of all, I did not want Anne to appear to me, woundless and bright as though she'd never died. I'd seen it happen. I was her witness.

Perhaps I was the only one other than her killer who had seen her die. Is that all she'd wanted? A comforting presence in her final moments?

Both Restorationist and Retributionist teachings shared that the angel turned their benevolent gaze upon the righteous to soothe and accept their souls in death. For the rest of us, our souls were too lost for the angel to see, and so we were doomed to rot in the darkness of the evil earth, reliving life's sufferings—for eternity if one was Retributionist and only until the reunification of the heavenly and fallen angels if one was Restorationist. We thank the angel for their mercies! At the temple, I was told that clerics' bodies did not turn ugly and bloated upon death because the heavenly angel had looked upon them. At the advent of Restoration or Retribution—whichever one preferred—the fallen twin would find and raise these pure spirits back into life.

Within clerical doctrine, there was no room for restless spirits like Anne, spirits that had inhabited borderland stories for thousands of years, tethered to the in-between by love or lust or loathing. Most southerners accepted all as real—the restless and the doomed and the righteous.

Perhaps, for a poison girl's spirit—doomed and restless at once—a living poison girl was an angel who could soothe them toward peace. I hoped my seeing had transformed her.

I twirled a flower stem between my fingers and contemplated my new and blasphemous philosophy, darkly thrilled at how easy it was to make a new story. Was this what the Restorationists had done when they'd looked at the lasting pillars of Retributionist doctrine?

Da made agitated loops up and down my arms. The night had disturbed him too. What had he thought of the screams?

I tensed my shoulders against the sound of approaching footsteps. If Lenora had come to fetch me for something, I might snap at her.

Sweeping pearl skirts came into view. Not Lenora. Meredith rounded the patch of flowers and was drawn up short by my glare. I wanted to bite out something that would make her go away, and then I saw the glassy shine of tears in her eyes. I sat up straighter, my meanness draining into the soil. Everyone wasn't gone from my life. Like that, past and present separated.

"Please tell me you don't mean to leave us," she said. "Please tell me you're not returning to the monastery."

Her plea unbalanced me. "Why would I leave?"

"Because the clerics must be begging you to come back to them. That's why you haven't looked at me since you got that letter. And why you came out here to the garden instead of following me to my bedchamber as you always do. And now, because of last night, you've made your decision to leave us." She took a shaking breath and rushed on. "But King Emelia will keep us safe. You saw how she did. Please, if there is anything you need, you must tell Phaela or even the king. Don't give up on us so soon."

Meredith trembled as though my leaving would be the worst thing to happen to her—worse than the screams which had only numbed her, worse than approaching death. I went to her with the same urgency, uncomprehending but suddenly scared as she was. I crushed her against me and pledged that I wouldn't leave. I hadn't been thinking it at all. "I'm sorry. I'm here. I'll always be here."

Her hair smelled of rosewater and the golden oil that made her curls shine. She wore no perfume. I breathed her in, and the garden melted around us, and I forgot Da on my wrist. There was only her and her heartbeat against mine.

"Why would you not look at me? Why would you say nothing?" she asked.

"Because I was ashamed," I admitted, naming the emotion for the first time.

Meredith drew back to meet my eyes. I struggled to hold her gaze and told her how I'd left the monastery, how I'd cost Seventh Seeker her life there. I waited to see doubt or judgment in her eyes but never did. She received me with the same gentleness as when I'd told her about the borderlands.

"Rare to find a poison girl who hasn't done a cruel thing in pursuit of kindness," Meredith said, her smile rueful. I wanted to ask her what she'd done. "But your cleric knows you're here. Perhaps she will write once she has settled into life beyond the temple."

I didn't tell Meredith my doubts. Why would anyone write affectionately to a selfish, mean girl who had upended her life? But I allowed the suggestion to linger. This optimism was a gesture of Meredith's care most of all, and for the sake of the fragile warmth budding between us, I didn't want to cut it down.

Da wound curiously across the bridge of our linked hands. Meredith stilled and stared but didn't recoil at the touch of his scales.

"Oh!" she exclaimed, her gaze flicking excitedly between me and Da as if to add, *Look! See what small miracle has happened?*

"He's never willingly approached anyone," I said, as surprised as she.

His agitation from moments ago was gone, his spines flat as he curled leisurely over her forearm.

"Stunning," she murmured, raising her arm so that she could admire him. His scales flashed dark rainbows. He flicked his black tongue.

A sudden urge to snatch him back overwhelmed me. She was looking too closely at him, at us. I'd found him at the feet of my dead father! I'd found him at an open door at the end of a world. I'd found him because I was too absorbed in my own plight to help my father who labored persistently under grief. I didn't know what it'd be like for someone else to hold him so tenderly, as if he was as fragile as he was lethal.

"He's heavier than he seems!" Meredith commented.

Mystified, I said, "He's not so heavy at all."

"You're used to the weight," she said, extending her hand again so that he could wind his way back to me.

I returned him to the hellebores. "Has anyone ever left the king?" I couldn't imagine it.

Meredith gazed up at the castle and the tall, narrow windows of the library. Her expression turned solemn again. "I will show you something," she said.

We took the spiral steps to the glass case in the library that she'd encouraged me away from. We'd passed no one on our way, and the library was dark as it'd been during our first visit. With her own candle, Meredith lit a stub she found on a dusty ledge and handed it to me. As my eyes adjusted, all I saw in the glass was our reflected twin flames. The cabinet was a heavy thing made of the same dark wood the shelves were cut from and every inch ornately carved. Floral motifs dominated throughout, each species identifiable from the courtyard garden. In the crowning scene at the topmost panel, two women swam through the air to join each other above a flowering field, their forms arcing upward as though to escape the confines of the wood. Their hands formed a point. They would never touch.

Fabric lined the shelves behind the glass. It alternated stripes of color, and I leaned closer to see whether it had been dyed or sewn together, holding my candle aloft so I could see beyond its glare. Neither of my assumptions was correct. Upon closer inspection, ribbons and monogrammed handkerchiefs were set side by side as though they were a single cloth. The chain of a locket or charm on a bracelet glimmered atop the ribbons as I passed my candle over the arrangement. All the shelves but the last were covered this way. I'd never seen women's trinkets and ribbons behind glass as though they were treasured artefacts. I looked to Meredith's reflection. Though she maintained her composure before the display, the rise and fall of her chest betrayed otherwise. I inspected the initials on the handkerchiefs. *A. S.* was the very last before a stretch of bare shelf.

"What was Anne's kin symbol?" I asked.

"Spire," said Meredith.

The cabinet was a memorial. I observed it anew. I attempted a tally of the initials and lost count as my emotions rose.

"I came here with a woman who loved me," Meredith said to the glass.

I stared at her. She held the candle steadily and the flame did not flicker. The shadows it cast hollowed her face. I imagined Anne's gaunt body and hated how the image so readily leapt to mind. I never wanted to see Meredith so.

"When I told you that night in the garden about how Phaela had come to me—there were two of us. Siwan and I had known each other since we were girls. She was the daring one. Even for a poor girl, she managed to be scandalous," Meredith said with a flicker of a smile. "She confessed her love for me early. We hadn't yet completed our studies, and her parents disowned her. An illness swept through the cities and took mine. I was spared from shaming them.

"We went to Heledd's House together, and in addition to work, we found community there with the other girls. We were happy for a time, and then Siwan grew restless as she always did. We quarreled, often over trivial things that were easier to fight about than the real reasons we swiped at each other. Siwan hated that I hid who I was from my surviving family. They didn't know I was a poison girl or that I loved her or that I worked at Heledd's. I could tell they had suspicions. I had too much coin and too-nice skin for the work I claimed to be doing. I didn't keep a schedule like everyone else. And even though Siwan was careful to refrain from even the kind of affection that was common among ladies in public, anyone could see from the way she looked at me that there was something other than friendship between us. I think my family found it easier not to ask. There was nothing to be done about things they didn't know.

"Then Phaela came to us with the king's offer. Of course, Siwan wanted to go immediately. I asked her privately if she knew the fates of poison girls who served aristocrats. She only scoffed at me, said that everyone knows. But the truth was abstract for Siwan. She was here only for the ease and luxury. Siwan had never devoted herself to anything apart from me. When faced with the grim reality of this life, she couldn't stand it. She'd never known anyone who had died. Though none of us saw it, Anne's murder scarred Siwan. She begged me to leave with her."

Meredith paused for a long time as though at the precipice of a terrible secret, though of course I knew how the story must end. "I didn't want to go back to all my secrets in the Perch cities. Even more, I loved the king. I asked Siwan not to make me choose between them. Why would she insist we come here only to tear my heart in two? The choice ruined us. I knew Siwan my whole life. Now she will not return my letters. The very last one I have from her is vicious—a command to come home, a long screed about how my feelings for the king are false, how I had always been too timid to live my life and wouldn't have known the king if it weren't for her. She closed her final letter with a foretelling that if I stayed, I would die with no one to mourn me." Meredith swallowed. "Not even her."

I drew close to Meredith, rested my head on her shoulder and my hand upon her back. We watched our reflections again.

"Of all her letters, I've read this last one the most," Meredith said. "At first, it seemed to be written by an entirely different person, not my Siwan. I wouldn't accept it as her. But now I know why my heart is with the king, why I chose her. Siwan always had a sharp tongue. She would often leave me in tears, and I hadn't realized how much it strained me until I came here. I never have to fear that with King Emelia. I am at peace with her."

I smoothed my hand down her back. She let the tension in her shoulders drop and leaned into me.

"Please tell me you are happy here," said Meredith, her voice small.

I was not happy and had never been, so my unhappiness had nothing to do with this place, nothing to do with Meredith or the king. I was disappointed in myself and didn't want to disappoint Meredith too.

I nodded against her shoulder. I kissed her cheek. She turned so our lips met. She was sweet, and I didn't deserve her.

"Won't you come to bed with me? We have time before we're needed again," Meredith said. "You can read to me. Like you always do."

TWENTY-THREE

MEREDITH DREW FLOWERS AS skillfully as she embroidered them. I would finish a poem, and she would turn her sketchbook to point to a new blossom, its name scribbled beneath its petals. We sorted the garden like this. Meredith circled her sketches and traced an arrow to a destination on the scrawled map of the courtyard below, helping me name the plants that were still foreign to me. She lay across the bed with a pillow under her and her feet idly kicking the air, the flounce of her skirts gathered at the crease of her knees like clouds fallen to earth. I loved how her hair spilled across the coverlet as she leaned over her work, then the exhilarating reveal of her face when she'd tuck her hair behind her ear or flip it over her shoulder. Her hands were as animated and elegant across the page as a little bird flitting through the grasses, and I watched them with as much awe.

She was scratching away at her next flower when she said, "I worry this educational exchange is unequal. You're to read a poem in exchange for one flower, yet you watch me draw when you should be reading to me. Have you forgotten our arrangement?" she teased, looking up at where I lounged against her headboard.

Indeed, I'd forgotten my book in my hands. "My deepest apologies," I said.

She hummed appraisingly. A curl fell across her eye. She tucked it away and turned back to her page, and I lifted my book again. Cocooned in so many linens with Meredith at the center, I almost forgot the world beyond us or the lives we led. Then I settled onto my side, and Seventh Seeker's letter crunched in my pocket, and anyway, it was dinnertime soon.

Though we were early, King Emelia and Phaela had arrived to the table before us. Beatrisa entered the hall as we settled into our seats, casting a wary look up at the devils and their eternal war. Dark circles were heavy under her eyes. Phaela placed a sympathetic hand over hers as soon as she was seated, and Beatrisa acknowledged her with a grateful nod.

"I am sorry for last night," the king began. She was stunning as she'd been that morning, the only one physically renewed after the attempt against us. Her hair and flowers pooled on the floor around her chair, regal and red. A hound stood at her side again. Whether it was the one Meredith had named Rangford, I wasn't sure. I saw them so rarely and couldn't yet distinguish them from each other. The king petted its neck, bloody nails on black fur. "Have your days been kinder to you?"

We answered in turn as the food was set before us. I was disappointed not to have another surprise from the northern lakes but forgot my dismay when I saw what we were presented with: dark gourds halved, hollowed, and filled with chewy mushrooms and bright peppers; a heap of red pearled grain studded with sliced nuts and topped with a green, hairy herb; a braided loaf glistening with butter and larger than a babe; pale beans tossed with vinaigrette and slices of crunchy, watery vegetables that Meredith named *cucumber* and *celery*; roasted plums dripping with rose syrup, and finally, the king's favorite pomegranate soup.

"Considering the night we've had, I am happy to come to the table with good news," King Emelia announced as I rose to taste for her. "Earl Huxley's carriage shall arrive tomorrow."

At the sound of that name, I drifted to an empty place. My head and chest were light as though my body had lost its flesh. I could rise forever, up and through the ornate ceiling, through the gray clouds and out of the world. I thought of Da alone in the garden. I thought of Da alone in our parched field. I thought of Da alone on the magnolia hill. I clasped my hands, and my skin was so soft. It seemed to belong to another girl, one nicer than me. I went to the king, my head carefully bowed. I tasted the food without tasting it.

"It is safe, my king," I pronounced, and all seemed very quiet and very far away.

I took my seat. I could float away but I mustn't. Huxley would return to the castle, and I would befriend Delfina, and he would atone. He would be outed as the liar he was. I would make sure of it. The whole kingdom would know what he'd done to us. I would ruin him. His riches would be dust.

Meredith touched my arm. Her hand was warm, and her chair seemed suddenly farther than it had been before. She wore that gentle frown of hers, the one that didn't reach her brow or her mouth, a subtle tension around her eyes. "Are you all right?" she whispered.

"I am fine," I answered, keeping my tone soft as hers.

I picked up my fork but couldn't grasp it. I had forgotten how to hold it, or my hand would not obey me. It clattered startlingly upon the plate and then the table. Its fine polish gleamed. The tines were so long. I imagined pressing them into my skin and how it would dimple the flesh like needles.

"Are you well?" Phaela demanded.

I glanced up at the sharp urgency in her voice. She stood as though to remove the king's plate. I blinked at her, uncomprehending.

Meredith's grasp on my forearm tightened. "Are you sick?"

"I am. I mean I am well. I am not sick. I am . . ." I saw Huxley's face down the table as I had first seen him. That was the face my mother had seen every day until her death. My hands shook, so I clasped them tight in my lap. "I am . . ."

"Are you *poisoned*?" Phaela clarified.

Two nervous servants drew near her. Phaela had taken the king's plate. She was going to hand it to them.

"No," I said. There were tears on my face. I hated that. I hated myself for causing such alarm. I hated myself. "No, I'm not."

When our meal was done, Phaela summoned me to her chambers. I went, still numb. She never had lessons for me at this hour. She wanted me for something else.

I knocked, and she called for me to enter. The room was neat as always but for the papers strewn across the bed. She stood behind the chair at the vanity and beckoned me to sit. I met her gaze in the mirror's reflection.

"You worry me," she said. "And we need you at your best tomorrow."

I apologized. I was sorry.

She set her hands upon my shoulders. "I cannot tell if you fear Earl Huxley or if you hate him. There's something you've not told me."

There was much I'd not told anyone. I wanted Delfina on my side. She knew the truth as much as I and worked for the Huxley estate still. With her testimony, my story would have weight. I didn't want to accuse him yet. I didn't want my loss turned to baseless slander.

"He tried to court me into his service after my mother died," I said and waited for her reaction.

"I see," said Phaela. Her expression didn't change. What did she think of me?

"Back then, I wanted to go, but my da refused. The drought worsened, and the clerics took me in."

"Did the earl know the particulars of your gift?"

I shook my head. "I didn't even know fully, not back then."

"Do you regret not being able to follow your mother's path?"

"I want to be here," I said firmly. "I want to serve the king. I love her."

Phaela considered me, her stare cool. She went to the wall and pulled a little cord attached to a bell. It rang, and the room was silent again. I didn't know what awaited me and was offered no explanation. Phaela returned to me and drew her fingers through my hair. Her touch held no warmth. I missed the red woman.

Aline knocked and entered at Phaela's answering call.

"Yes, my lady?" she asked, her gaze landing briefly on me.

"I need help with my dress," Phaela sighed, tired all at once.

"Of course." Aline's eyes alighted on me again. "Shall I come back?"

"No. Carlotta has struggled this evening. I want to remind her of her devotion."

Aline bowed her head and didn't look at me again. She started on the buttons of Phaela's dress, and there all three of us crowded into the mirror's frame. None of us spoke, the only sound that of Phaela shedding her immaculate layers one by one. Aline was careful to set each piece aside on the bed so that nothing would be trampled or wrinkled. Without the assistance of the corset, Phaela's posture drooped. I'd never seen her so weary. She braced herself on the back of my chair and urged Aline to continue whenever the handmaiden hesitated. I felt I shouldn't be here or that I was witnessing something I shouldn't. Without her dress, Phaela was unarmored.

My breath caught at the sight of her chemise. Just below her waist, a menacing crescent of blood stained the linen. Aline, her eyes averted, helped Phaela out of the soiled garment. Unlike the other layers, she folded it tight so that the stain was packed away like a secret. But for the bloodied strips of fabric tied about her waist, Phaela wore nothing. Heat radiated from her like a fever. She continued to brace herself against the back of the chair. Aline's hands moved to Phaela's hair, and she nodded to the handmaiden. Unpinned, her locks tumbled down her back.

"Might I help with your bandages?" Aline asked nervously.

"No, thank you. Please have a good evening."

The handmaiden cast another uncertain glance my way but curtsied and left us alone. Phaela continued to evaluate my reflection, and I met her gaze just the same. She smoothed her hands through my hair again. I had never had an older woman to help me with my hair until I came here. All the times she'd made me pretty for the king, I'd believed she'd done it as a kindness—it was so easy to believe—but as with Lenora, everything was for King Emelia in the end. It had only taken them stating so several times for me to understand.

I didn't look at Phaela's bandage. It was a threatening vulnerability.

"My mother was the sole survivor of the attack that orphaned her," Phaela said. "That's how she discovered her gift. She was twenty and the last member of the aristocratic Mirrors line. Immediately, suspicion was cast upon her. Lords and ladies made her out to be a cunning murderess seeking her brother's inheritance. By the time the truth of it all came to light, her reputation was ruined. And what aristocrat would want to marry a poison girl? A distant male relative was found to manage the Mirrors estate. My mother took an untitled husband who was the youngest of four brothers and later signed a contract serving the very family her parents had hoped she would marry into.

"I lived a strange, undefined existence among the Stones, accompanying my mother but lacking her gift. Studying with their children but lacking a title. To publish my early compositions, I assumed the identity of one of their sons and naively hoped no one would discover me. The ensuing scandal was such that even the king took notice. In the midst of it all, I lost my mother. I wrote a poem for her, of course, knowing it would identify me. I had nothing left in the world and didn't care what fate awaited me. The Stones were relieved to throw me out without social consequence. The very day I gathered my few belongings to leave, a summons from the king arrived. I have been at her side ever since." Phaela abandoned the support of the chair to stand in front of me. Were the bandages redder than before? Or simply nearer—realer without the mirror as buffer? Beneath the heavy spice of her perfume was an aged, metallic scent. "Emelia made me. Before her, I was a disgraced daughter of a disgraced mother. The thing I was most proud of, my own gift, was diminished by scandal and my own lies. I had no place in the world. None of us here had a place in the world before Emelia." She stroked her fingers along my jaw. Her nails scraped my skin. "You say you love her. But this is what devotion looks like."

I let Phaela take my hand, let her place it where the bandage was knotted around her waist. It was made of a rough and common fabric, unfinished strips torn from something else. It did not match Phaela.

"Go on," she said.

I tugged at the knot until the bloodstained cloth slipped from her. It fell across my lap like a dead thing.

The cut was clean and deep, stretching hipbone to hipbone. It bled, though barely, the wound surprisingly tame for something that should have killed. Dark stitches zigzagged through it, neat and futile. The magic that had saved her also meant she could not heal.

"I want to see your devotion, Carlotta," Phaela murmured, palming the back of my neck and pulling me against her. My cheek pressed to her stomach, against the raw line and her feverish skin. "This is mine. Every day, I rise and I serve her through this pain because she has lifted me out of death. I still dream of my murder but am comforted by Emelia's strength and perfection. Whatever agony plagues you, however weak you think you may be, your focus on her cannot wane. Show me you are unafraid."

I placed my hands upon her hips, turned my face to the wound, kissed the stitches. Her blood stained my lips. I licked it away. She held me, and I, having met a strange peace, closed my eyes.

Down the corridor, Meredith waited in front of my door. "I was just coming to check on you," she said and stopped short when she saw the crust of Phaela's blood on my cheek.

I managed a smile for her. "Goodnight, Meredith," I said.

Her eyes widened. "Goodnight."

I closed myself into my room.

IV

HELL

TWENTY-FOUR

Earl Huxley, his brother, and Delfina arrived just past noon under a saturnine sky. For the occasion, King Emelia had selected matching black dresses for Meredith and me, and we accompanied her through the corridors like diminutive shadows. Delfina trailed behind with us. I tried to meet her with a cordial smile, but she kept her gaze trained on the lords' backs. I wanted to grab her and make her look at me—but I had already tried that once. I couldn't be impulsive with her again.

Meredith clasped my hand. We hadn't spoken much that day aside from pleasantries, and every time she looked at me, it was with the same soft concern as yesterday evening. While Huxley droned on about their recent trip to the northwestern kingdoms, his voice echoing down and around the stone corridors and assaulting my ears, Meredith smoothed circles against the back of my gloved hand with her thumb, silk against silk. I leaned into her gratefully and made myself forget Delfina. Meredith smelled faintly of the king's perfume. Fresh love bites adorned her neck. I wanted to press my lips to them.

We settled in the tearoom, Meredith and I naturally taking up a settee with the king, one of us on either side of her. My heart spiked when Delfina stood behind the brothers' chairs like a butler. There were plenty of seats for her. The king said as much, interrupting the eldest Huxley's monologue. The youngest at least had the decency to look chagrined. Delfina sat to the side, stiff on the edge of her seat. I could not hear the lord's story about the westerners' metals and the potentials for industry. I couldn't look away from Delfina, her perfectly blank face and perfectly straight posture. I hated Huxley in this room where Meredith and I had so often flirted or dozed or read or fucked. It was a fine room—imported scarlet rugs, big gilt mirrors, an alcove of tall windows for the gray light, more little seats to house Meredith's embroidered pillows—and his mere presence stained it.

The king rested a hand on my knee. I was grinding my teeth.

When the tea service arrived, I focused on the gold ribbon edge of the china, how it gleamed so primly, and on the tiers of tiny cakes and crustless sandwiches. Meredith and Delfina and I rose to our duty and gathered around the table between us. I ignored the lords and recalled instead what Phaela had told me, remembered her cold face and hot skin. Meredith and I compiled a sampling of everything on offer, taking our little bites and adding the treats to a small plate. Around its gilded edge, red flowers bloomed in delicate brushstrokes. Meredith poured tea for the king, and as it swirled amber into the cup and released its floral perfume, Huxley began to enthuse about its properties—another discovery on his travels and a gift to King Emelia. I sipped and found it lighter on the tongue than our usual selections. I enjoyed its clean, grassy flavor and hated that Huxley had brought something else so nice to us.

"My king." I bowed to her and offered the cup. "It is safe."

I sat demurely and watched the smooth blanket of clouds through the narrow windows, letting myself drift now that my obligation was done. I could not endure the lords' voices any longer. Neither did I have an appetite. I finished my own cup of tea and left the other refreshments. It was good to have the cup to hold, something with which to occupy myself.

Meredith opened her hands questioningly as soon as King Emelia's cup was empty.

"No, thank you, my dear," the king murmured, touching Meredith's shoulder appreciatively. She raised her voice to our guests. "We needn't bore our poison girls with what is sure to be a lengthy discussion. Meredith and Carlotta will likely retire to the garden or one of the sitting rooms until dinner. Delfina, you are, of course, welcome to join them, or the girls can show you to your room so you may rest after your travels."

Delfina inclined her head deferentially. "I'm happy to stay. As the lords' shield, I advise on any dealings that may pose a risk."

Blood rushed in my ears. Delfina was anything but happy. Anyone could see it, and what a shame to say otherwise.

Finally, Lord Huxley's gaze settled properly on me. I smiled sweetly, and a dark look crossed him, there and gone. He looked abruptly away from me as though refusing to see me could hide all his shame. I clenched my teeth, felt all my civility turning feral. Of course he had recognized me all this time—and was that fear? I hoped so. I hoped my presence was a blade at his neck, liable to slip any moment.

No rules existed against scouting young poison girls, but what he had done—finding me and my father in the vulnerable aftermath of my mother's death, tempting me away while refusing to dispense my mother's last wages—surely this was a stain upon his honor. That pay could've saved my da. We could've gone north. He could have lived. When Huxley peered at my face and back to the king, he wanted to know whether she knew. He wanted to know whether I had detailed his sins. What would King Emelia do to him once she knew? I basked in the possibilities.

Boldly and still with my veneer of sweetness, I said, "Oh but I would love to show you the garden, Delfina."

"I prefer to stay with the lords, if her highness permits me," Delfina said curtly.

Earl Huxley settled back in his chair, satisfied.

My stomach dropped. Why would she choose them? What had they done to her? What had they told her?

King Emelia surveyed the tension among us and said eventually, "Very well. There is much to discuss. Carlotta, Meredith, I will see you this evening."

I soothed myself with morbid fantasies: that Delfina had missed something in the food on offer; that the tearoom doors would open on Huxley writhing on the floor; that I would be fetched only to look down on his pitiable form and decline to save him; or that he would say something distasteful to the king; that both Huxleys would abruptly disappear; and that when we saw her next, the king's hair would be quite long and her flowers lush.

Meredith regarded me cautiously and didn't touch me, following quietly to my bedchamber and lingering in the doorway. I rummaged aimlessly through the papers and books on my desk. At the upper corner, the magnolia pod had dried and split open, spilling bright-red seeds across the white top. I would put them in the ground soon. They were ready.

"I know this must be so hard for you," Meredith began delicately.

"It makes me sick to be near him."

"Are they really so similar?" she asked, her expression and heart open to me.

And then I remembered how I had let her misunderstand me that day on the castle wall. He reminded me *about* my father; he was in no way *like* my father.

Trembling rage simmered out, and numbness washed in to replace it. Meredith and the door were suddenly distant.

"Huxley ruined my family," I told her simply. My voice was unfamiliar to me. These words floated up from my spirit instead of my lungs.

Meredith crossed the threshold and came to me, her eyes big with sympathy. Her voice was gentle. "What do you mean?"

"Delfina knows. I need her to talk to me. Then everyone will understand."

Now she frowned. "What does Delfina know?"

Oh, Meredith would not believe me. No one would believe me. There, already, doubt on her face. I backed away from her. My body was slow to follow my command.

Why wouldn't Huxley have paid my da? All his travels had enriched him. What was one poison girl's death allowance? I'd run my mind ragged over the question, but if others were to ask the same, I knew it would be with incredulity. An upstanding lord! Negligent on his payments!

"Carlotta?"

Had he assumed we were both dead these five years, that the dust that'd swallowed my da had taken me too? Did he never think of us on his travels? Was he not haunted by our fate?

"Carlotta?"

Meredith had drawn close again. I saw her hands on my arms but couldn't feel her touch. Comfort was so far from me! I didn't deserve Meredith or her kindness.

She guided me to the bed. "You must lie down. I will call for Lenora. She'll have a tincture to soothe your nerves."

I let Meredith pull the coverlet over me because I didn't know what else to do and it was nice to have someone guide me. The bed was overfull with all my skirts. I shook even as I tried to lie still and watch the ceiling. Meredith's pinched face left me. I couldn't breathe without her. My chest was collapsing.

Time slipped. Lenora brought a glass dropper to my mouth and murmured over me very sweetly. Meredith—lovely Meredith!—stripped my gloves from my hands, and I found a pleasantly dreamless sleep.

Something stirred in my hair. I roused. The room was all shadows and golden light from a few candles and the fire spinning in the hearth. The king bent over me. In her hands, she held the scarf I'd tied back my hair with. It seemed silly now. No farm woman would wear silk in her hair for a day's work, but Phaela insisted on matching my scarves to my dresses. I had never told her the origin of the tradition.

"I only meant to make you more comfortable," King Emelia apologized.

She settled onto the bed beside me, and I was happy to have her so near. I tried to move, to put my head upon her lap, or join our hands, but found my body heavier than I remembered. To even turn my head was an effort. I felt I had eaten a petal of luna.

"Don't tire yourself," the king said, smoothing her hand through my loose hair. "Lenora's given you a sedative is all."

"I am very heavy."

"Yes." The king frowned. "And Lenora was heavy handed in her dosing. Like many medicinals, octavia's mirror is poisonous in high doses. Lenora shouldn't have done it, but I understand Meredith was frightened and couldn't locate Phaela. I've warned them both."

I hoped she wasn't stern with them. And I felt guilty for scaring Meredith. "They only meant to help me," I said.

"I know, my dear, of course." The king kissed my forehead, and her perfume settled like a fog.

"Will we have dinner soon? Have you come to fetch me to the table?"

"No. It's quite late and dinner complete. Are you hungry?"

I considered all this. Perhaps it was best I'd slept through dinner and avoided Huxley. But then, had I fallen again in Phaela's esteem?

"If there is something simple and soft with not too strong a flavor," I answered.

"I'll send for Lenora." She tilted her head. Her expression was masklike again, sharp and impassive. "Would you tell me what upset you so?"

Unable to stand her scrutiny, I allowed my eyes to drift shut. I was still weary, after all. "I only wanted to talk to Delfina," I whispered.

"Yet she didn't want to talk with you. Why was that so frightening?"

"She didn't frighten me."

I did not want to speak with King Emelia on this, not yet, and she was drawing so near to my wounds. She would see them.

"Then what? So I might prevent it."

The mattress shifted, and the shadows across my eyelids darkened. I blinked to find the king now leaning close, her body caging mine, the coverlet tight about my shoulders where she rested her weight.

I shook my head upon the pillow and grasped for a sensible answer. "Phaela has told you my mother served the Huxley estate before her death."

The king did not breathe, did not blink. I couldn't see the thoughts behind her eyes. I saw nothing in her face and was unnerved. I imagined her opening her great jaws and closing them around my neck. Was this how she contemplated her prey before the kill?

Eventually, she gave a nod.

"I . . . never visited my mother there. I never saw her in all my life. When I look upon Delfina, I'm reminded of that, and it hurts me."

The king's lips parted, and there were all her sharp teeth. "Huxley never invited you to the estate?" she asked, her voice icy with disbelief.

"Only—" *After she had died, when I was meant to replace her and also die for him.*

I needed Delfina to testify with me. I needed her at my side for this. The king would not believe me! Huxley had only ever brought her gifts and compliments and good counsel. She had known him many years and developed her own ideas of him. I'd been with her a short two months, and Phaela already doubted my devotion. I couldn't accuse him here, alone, with her teeth so near.

My throat closed. Tears slipped down my temples, and I was distant from my body again.

Emotion reanimated the king's face all at once. My crying had startled her. She moved away.

"We will talk later, and I will hear you," King Emelia assured me. "Anything you have to say, Carlotta."

I nodded meekly, and the king rose. She didn't send Lenora as she'd said. She returned bearing a tray from the kitchen herself. On it, boiled eggs, halved, and a white bowl of steaming porridge that made me gasp on sight. I thought I would cry again. I would know this starchy scent anywhere.

I sat up in bed. My dress was a fussy mess of skirts all around me, but I didn't care. I stirred the spoon and put my hand over my mouth.

"Have the harvests returned?" I whispered to my palm.

The king stood at my bedside as though contemplating how to deliver news of an ailing relative. "Not as they were before. The northernmost regions of the borderlands have taken the maize inside glass houses where farmers have better control of its environment. They are small places, only a fraction of the size of a field, and more care to maintain. Very little is exported, but I thought you would like to have some."

I didn't know whether to feel hopeful or saddened. I was glad to have it again, but neither did I want a world where maize was so rare and expensive that one had to be a king to acquire it. It'd been such a humble grain before.

I spooned the polenta reverently into my mouth. Coarse ground maize, salt, and butter. Simple and warming. I licked the spoon.

"Thank you, my king," I murmured, wondering whether this was the last time she would show me kindness.

TWENTY-FIVE

O CTAVIA'S MIRROR SAW ME through the night, and I woke with a clear mind. The light around the curtains told me I'd slept long, but I didn't move from my bed. I knew what I must do.

When Lenora came to peer at me and found me awake, she apologized and asked how I fared. I lied and said my mind was still clouded and my body heavy. It was easy to lie, but I hated how repentant she looked and how she apologized again as though she'd hurt me.

"I hope the king wasn't angry with you for only helping me?"

"Not angry . . ." Lenora ventured. "But you know how many poison girls she has lost. Her grief is always just below the surface. My job is to show you the utmost care, and I failed."

"I'm the one who failed," I said, looking away from her. "Perhaps Phaela's suspicions are correct, and my temperament isn't suited to this role. You wouldn't have needed to calm me otherwise."

"You can't mean that!" Lenora started immediately. "The king is so taken with you. You must try, for her. We all do our best for her."

My heart twisted. I wanted so badly to need nothing but King Emelia and her approval. I'd gone on these weeks thinking my pledge to her was true—that there was nothing else I desired. But then Huxley had appeared and appeared again. My spirit was unquiet and would remain so, just as Da's had been for so many years.

And now I realized why he stayed.

I knew what I must do.

"You don't mean to leave us?" Lenora whispered when I was silent too long.

"I've grown a deep affection for the king and will stay as long as she will have me," I answered. It was truthful, though I wasn't sure how much longer that would be. "You've come to prepare me for the table?"

"Meredith served the king this morning, though soon there will be tea." Lenora's frown deepened. "The king said you must not taste for her if you've not fully recovered. She was strict about this. You're already weak by my mistake. If you were to be poisoned . . ."

"I see," I said. I did my best to look contemplative and disappointed. "Have they already gathered in the tearoom?"

Lenora squinted at the clock on the mantle. "Soon. They are due to meet at the next half hour. Though I would be happy to bring your tea to you here. And I'm sure Meredith would visit you after she's done with her tasting. Would you like food? Or perhaps a bath might be soothing?" Then she seemed to doubt her suggestion. "Though if you are ill, we should be careful of the stairs."

"I'll take my tea when Meredith is done," I said. "I'd like a short walk until then if I'm permitted."

"I can accompany you."

"I'd prefer to go alone if it suits you. I need to clear my head."

Lenora looked uncertain again. "Are you steady?"

I rose from the bed, careful not to look eager.

Lenora studied me for a long moment. "Then you must have a proper dress and cloak. It has turned cold again, and we cannot have you wandering the castle in your nightgown while we have guests." She cast the curtains open and tied them back as neatly as she always did, though today she seemed to linger over the bows.

Finally, she went to select a dress from the wardrobe. I watched the clock tick by on the mantle. I was losing precious minutes setting up this deception. My heart beat so fast I thought I might truthfully be ill.

I only needed to get to the garden and see Da. Then I would know my way for certain. Until then, I couldn't think of the branching paths I might take after. I would falter.

"Could I have one of the traditional dresses?" I asked, using fashion to calm me. "The one in red?"

Lenora brought the dress I'd worn the day of my first portrait sitting. I still loved it. Of everything I had here, it reminded me most of home. This was a good day to return to it.

I didn't need Lenora's help to dress, but I allowed her to help me anyway, allowed myself comfort in what had grown to be a familiar ritual. "Thank you for all your care," I told her.

She kissed my cheeks. "It is my pleasure." She tied my hair back with the matching scarf—she'd become as much an expert as I in the folding of the style—and even seemed ready to hold my toothbrush for me.

I declined graciously and brushed my teeth myself. As compromise, I let her take a washcloth to my face. I could've lost myself here for the sake of her kind and gentle touch. It would be easy to go on amid these comforts. How long could Huxley prolong his stay? I had only to grit my teeth through a few more dinners. But the thought kindled more heat in my chest. For once, I could give my family the devotion I'd so carelessly lavished on everyone else.

We walked together to the door, Lenora eyeing my bearing and keeping a steadying hand at my back. "Allow me to go with you at least part of the way," she asked. "I couldn't live with myself if you were hurt."

"I will only go to the garden," I said.

"Then I will help you down the stairs."

So she did, holding my hand as if I were a girl taking her first steps. I stored my frustration with my rage, pressing them down until they formed something glittering and hard as diamond. To Lenora herself, I gave only my tenderness and a grateful bow. She released me to the gray air and watched me go.

My mood colored the garden. It was smaller than before and the frost harder. Ice muted the flowers that day, but it had always been a place of stasis. The frost would thaw tomorrow or the day after as the castle's peculiar weather dictated, and the flowers would return to their springtime glory. Nothing could be allowed to die. Beyond the garden, we had already lost so much, and so the small things here—the things the king could control—must not be lost.

From among the bushes, a dark shape observed my passage. I paused before the red weigela and peered in at the hound. I had no pomegranate to offer and so it didn't acknowledge my outstretched hand. I continued to the hellebores.

Da emerged from his shelter at my approach, winding sluggish through the grass. It was too cold for him, and I was a neglectful daughter again. I went to my knees and gathered him up, shivering at the chill of his scales as I settled him around my neck. I welcomed the good shock and the glide of scales on skin. I drew the hood of my cloak and sat and breathed as the clerics had taught me until the snake's temperature met mine. Rejuvenated, Da stirred round my neck, raising his head to flick his tongue against my ear.

"I know now why you've stayed," I whispered. Our secret fogged on the air and was taken by the breeze. "You guard me, but anger also animates you, doesn't it?"

His tail slipped from around my neck to rest over my heart.

I took a breath. "I'll take you to Huxley."

My heart thudded, but Da's green stare was steady and sure.

I couldn't think of what would happen after my betrayal. This was the right path. This was the source of the restlessness that pervaded my life at the castle. I *had* been meant to come here; I had only shirked my purpose, and here it was before me again. Another chance. We were returning to the beginning, finally allied. Having devised my fate, I stood.

I didn't require poison. I only needed Da.

A hound stood sentinel at the top of the stairs. I'd never seen so many of them about—or was it the same hound, having moved as soon as I looked away? I pulled my cloak tighter and rested a hand over where Da hid in the bell of my sleeve. Though the king hadn't expressly forbidden his return to the castle, this was his first time within the walls proper since he'd lashed out my first morning here. I worried the hound might sense him and alert the king, but it remained as still and statuesque as ever.

The door to the tearoom was ajar. Men's voices murmured within. I didn't hear the king. I glanced down the empty corridor and stepped into the room.

Tea service had been set out on the little table as before and only awaited our tasting. Earl Huxley, his brother, and Delfina had resumed their positions so completely that it was as if they'd never left after our meeting yesterday. The lords carried on with their conversation and barely spared me a glance. I was not the king. I ducked my head and allowed myself a mad smile within the shelter of my hood. My heart rattled against my ribs. My hands trembled. My pulse thrummed in my fingertips.

I shut the door behind me. I locked it.

At the sound of the click, the lords finally saw me properly. Delfina frowned where she sat stiffly aside. Though I was the source of confusion, Earl Huxley looked to his brother as if for explanation.

I curtsied before him and rose into a state of calm. This day, I looked down on him and was satisfied. I asked cooly, "Do I look like my mother, my lord?"

Earl Huxley hesitated and looked again to his brother. For a man who commanded so much, he deferred when trapped. I felt the younger lord's gaze but did not look at him. I allowed my hood to fall and stepped to Huxley so that my dress swept over his boots. He flinched at this and peered around me.

"Where is the king?" he demanded.

Let him think the king would still arrive for him. I wanted him to behave until the final moment. I squeezed the key to the room in my fist. Da wound himself tight within my sleeve, scales slipping low on my wrist.

"Perhaps I look more like my father," I continued. "But only your messengers would know his face. You left him to die in the borderlands."

"That's enough, Carlotta," Delfina hissed. She stood and started for the door.

The betrayal pierced me. She couldn't free them—I held the key—but why insist on the protective performance?

I half-turned, torn between confronting her and keeping Huxley cornered. "What has he *ever* done for you?" I screamed.

Huxley saw his advantage and began to rise. A snarl ripped from me. I shoved him back down, and Da shot between us.

A howl tore the air. A shriek followed it. Someone laughed, and it was me. I let the evil mirth sweep me high on its current. I tripped back from Huxley and bumped into the low table. The china rattled. I pressed my hands over my grin and laughed and laughed while the lord scratched furiously at his neck where Da was steadily constricting. Swift strikes to Huxley's face had left him bleeding at the cheek and the jaw. Now Da's fangs were anchored in the lord's eye. His face was purple and ugly. Veins bulged in his temples. His good eye was bloodshot. The lord could do nothing but bare his teeth and wheeze and writhe like a beast. I watched him exit the world.

Little Lord Huxley screamed. An annoying, dreadful sound. *I* should be the one screaming. *I* was the one who had lost.

Behind me, the tea service waited like a relic from another life. I snatched up the nearest thing to me. I threw the teapot at his head. I was angry and wild, and it missed, exploding porcelain upon the wall and splashing hot black tea down the red paper. The brother scrambled from his seat, toppled his velvet chair, and fell. I followed like a prowling thing, plush carpets muffling my steps.

Though I had nothing left to throw at him but my own body and nothing to cut him with but my nails, he still backed away from me as from a feral borderland dog. He shook and gasped, then seemed to remember something. Fishing in his boot, he withdrew a knife as slender and menacing as a letter opener. He brandished it and continued his backward retreat, stumbling foolishly over a card table and sprawling again.

Bergamot perfumed the air. A shame. In better company, we could've shared a nice tea. I stooped to retrieve a long shard of porcelain and continued my advance on the lord. He had a trembling hand and a pen knife, and I had a shattered teapot and my fury. Is this how King Emelia felt when she hunted the men who dared intrude here? Did it always feel this high, like a good poisoning?

The young lord backed himself against the tall windows, and realizing this, sense returned to him. He finally held the knife steady.

I looked past him and out the windows. I felt the gray sky in my heart. Down in the courtyard, below the slate-smooth clouds, all the flora Meredith had meticulously named for me swayed obliviously in a breeze. It had been a lie, but I would miss tea with her. I would never have it again.

When I looked back at the lord, he shivered. I raised my shard and aimed for his throat, careless of the knife. I wanted blood, not safety.

I threw my weight at him, all the anger and grief I'd carried in my chest grim momentum. The shard struck true and broke where it met bone. He'd raised his arm against me—I felt it crushed against my chest—but it was nothing. He twitched once and was gone.

A tremor shook the floor. My breaths came ragged. I braced for pain but felt only the slip of blood against my cut palms, saw the white arrow of porcelain in the lord's throat, his blood burbling from the wound and mixing with my own.

There was no knife in my chest. There was no knife.

The room was darker, the sconces on the wall snuffed. I sat back on my heels and patted at my torso, bloodying my dress. The air behind me was dense and dark. I was done laughing. I was afraid. Something big had transpired, and I was small.

Haltingly, I turned where I sat on the floor. The king loomed. Shadow condensed around her, pooling along the floor and slipping down the walls to gather at her feet. She had come from shadow and wore it as easily as her dress. The castle groaned and shook loose its slumber. The walls crowded in to observe. Its consciousness pressed into my mind as an ache, and I was suddenly cold. The new dark had leeched all heat from the air. King Emelia said nothing, only regarded me. Her flowers withered and dropped their petals upon the floor, the misty edges of her shadows carrying them like leaves on the wind.

"My king . . ." I whispered and knelt and bowed until my nose met the floor. I pressed my bloody palms to the red carpet, let it drink of me.

She had usurped my chosen death. This was the only explanation that came to my frantic mind. She had usurped my death to punish me as she saw fit.

The shadows crawled to me, tendrils forming spidery hands that settled over my own. Cold, hazy fingers gripped my chin and raised me from my lowly posture. Steel glinted in the king's chest. She gripped its hilt and pulled it free. It clanged upon the floor between us, the blade wet with her blood. It was the young lord's knife.

The king's black skirts swept past me. Her shadows sluiced after her, dry flowers spiraling on their currents. She observed the dead aristocrat as though he wore a slightly unfashionable cravat that she had the good manners not to remark upon. The arrow of porcelain was still lodged in his throat. She knelt beside him and pulled it free. It looked like the chipped fang of a great monster fresh from the hunt. The king flung it away and bent closer to observe the wound.

"My king . . ." I started again, but a convulsion rocked her.

Her jaw unhinged, cheeks splitting and unseaming. A wet gurgle came from her throat. Her long tongue curled. Black bile spattered the lord's chest and dripped from her lips. The king put her hand to her mouth and heaved again. When she drew her hand away, two sharp black stones glittered in her palm. She wiped her lips and dropped one of the stones into the dead man's mouth. Then she rose. The elder Huxley faced away from me, slumped sideways in his chair. King Emelia took his jaw and dropped the second stone into his mouth. She stood watching him for a long time, the bottom half of her face and neck stained dark with blood and bile. Her expression wasn't a smile but blank contemplation, the long line of her natural mouth revealing inhuman teeth.

Across the room, she met my gaze. "How did it feel?" she asked.

The door was still closed and, I assumed, locked. The king seemed an apparition—unreal, ungrounded. Too suddenly present. Delfina sat in a corner, her manner as stiff as before. She avoided looking at me or the dead lords. She sat as though waiting or deciding, seemingly beyond the events at hand.

I looked back to the king and was honest. "It felt good," I answered.

The king nodded, neutral as holding court. "Now tell me what you would not last night. What did they do to you?"

Delfina looked sharply at me, her gaze wary.

Where to begin? That I grew up motherless when I had a mother? That Ma was planning to visit me, and I never knew? That they had kept her away from me and me away from her when I should have been permitted to visit all along? That they'd made me sweet promises with the intention of tearing my family further? That I was naive and silly and desperate and would have let them? That we'd been cheated of my mother's death allotment? That they left us to die? That my father did die? That they had lived on perfectly secure while thinking us dead?

"They ruined everything," I said, and for the first time named aloud what they'd done. I listed their sins blandly. I was burned down to ashes but had burned what needed to be burned. I remembered the beautiful horseman and told that story too. Perhaps, had I not ruined that invitation, I would have arrived to the castle not for King Emelia but at Delfina's side, claimed already by the Huxley estate. Perhaps I'd have lived on in ignorance and none of this would have happened.

My palms were slashed. I cupped my blood in my hands. Finally, I felt the throb of pain.

"Will you punish me?" I asked the king.

"For what?"

Delfina began to cry. I looked back to my palms. My hands seemed fitted to me like gloves, unflesh, detached.

The king went to her. "You both must rest," she said, helping Delfina to her feet.

I stood on my own strength and went to retrieve Da. All would be well now. We could go on in peace. I held my hand to him. He didn't stir. He was twisted wrong.

He was dead, a limp cord of black iridescence glittering at Huxley's throat.

TWENTY-SIX

WE NEVER BURIED MA. I didn't know how to bury Da, so I didn't. I left him on the desk with the magnolia seeds. I was gathering things to give to the earth.

Lenora screamed when she came to light my candles, dropping the tray of food she carried with a crash. She'd never met Da, and he didn't look so nice now. I sat up in bed and watched her leave. She didn't look at me and said nothing. She slammed my door. Had she meant it, or was she only scared?

A long time passed—or time seemed long—and she didn't return. My hands were bandaged and ached sharply when I flexed them, but I righted the tray and piled the broken dishes on it. The least I could do was help. Little of the meal was salvageable: a soup of roasted vegetables, its carrots and potatoes cooled and stuck to the rug; a roll of bread soggy in the puddle of broth. I tore the bread in two and nibbled on it in the dark. It would've been buttery and flaky when fresh but was now pasty and dense and stuck behind my teeth.

Da was gone.

Only then did it occur to me how hard it might have been for him to stay all these years, how much will he must've exerted to remain, in some way, present. Had living against the earth made it easier?

Da had scoffed at clerical doctrine that claimed the earth was filled with evil. The earth was where we went to gather strength. It was where we planted our ancestors. When I was a girl, he would gesture to the fields and the trees, would make sure I saw the seeds as they went into the earth. Up came beauty and life, and in the winter, all rested and gathered their strength. Truth was empirical. All one had to do was put their hands in the dirt. Why, as the clerics claimed, would it be a place of torment for anyone? The earth welcomed all.

A crack of light from the corridor burned my eyes, and I flinched away.

"Oh, miss!" Lenora exclaimed. She took the bread from my hands and threw it upon the tray with the broken dishes. "I knew I shouldn't have left you."

I didn't know which leaving she referred to. In the garden? In my room?

She guided me back to bed and made her rounds lighting the candles. She neglected the one on my desk.

"Please accept my apologies," said Lenora. "The afternoon has set us all on edge."

"I have set you on edge," I corrected.

She frowned as though I'd said something incomprehensible and clasped her hands before her.

"Poison doesn't trouble my body long. I lied so that I could be alone to kill the Lords Huxley. You must not apologize." I pointed to the desk. The motion briefly amazed me. The arm seemed to float. It didn't belong to me, but who else would it belong to? "My father, having his revenge, is dead now. He can do you no harm."

Lenora nodded slowly. I started to tell her about the magnolia too, but she stopped me. "You're in shock, miss. I will bring you more food, but should I send someone to keep you company in the meantime?"

I remembered the tea she'd proposed earlier in the day, the tea I'd thought I'd never have again. A little of the numbness peeled away. "Will Meredith come?" I asked hopefully.

Lenora blinked. "She is . . . occupied at the moment, but I can send another of the staff."

I shook my head. "No, thank you."

Lenora nodded again and stepped away, taking the old tray with her. As the door closed, I saw her motion to another woman who took up watch outside.

The days passed like this. Lenora would come to open my curtains or close my curtains and light the candles. Often, after she left, I would blow them out again and sit in the dark. She brought me meals and deflected my questions but stayed after dinners to let me tell her my memories of the borderlands or read her Ma's favorite poems. She changed my dresses and brushed my hair for no one. I didn't see the king or Phaela or even Meredith and became very useless. I let myself be docile. If the king had decided I should stay, I wanted them to trust me again. They never locked the door on me, and this was a good sign. Lenora and I progressed to morning walks through the courtyard and lunches alone in the empty great hall. Our meal done, we'd retire to my bedchamber again, and she'd braid the flowers I picked that day into my hair.

Da's eyes turned milky and his scales dull as though preparing for a shed. I wished it were so. Sometimes, when I sat writing at the desk, I would peer up from my paper and imagine him slipping free of his skin as he always had, renewed. Lenora coaxed me away from the desk when she visited. She didn't like me keeping Da and proposed one morning that I take him out to the garden a final time, but I wasn't ready yet. I was adamant that he stay with the magnolia.

I completed several new poems during my imposed rest. I wanted to have new material for Phaela when I next saw her, and I had much to write about.

Flower crowns were a girlish tradition foreign to the borderlands. Born after the wars, I lived in a time where flowers had already taken on their new and deadly meanings. But the poisonous varietals hadn't yet flourished so severely in the north, and girls who visited family there brought the trend to our schoolyard. The day they were discovered is one of my earliest memories. Scolding was unnecessary. By the time they'd been made to discard their crowns, their faces and fingers were swelling red. By the time their parents arrived, their skin was cracked and bleeding. Wariness heightened to paranoia. During our midday breaks, we stood close to the buildings, far from the woods that bordered the school. Some children cried if made to walk through tall grasses.

I once related this story to the king on one of our walks through the garden. We'd been quiet, and I'd slipped into memory. Most of my stories were morbid like this, but King Emelia didn't seem troubled when I told them. She tried to give me sweet things in return.

"Girls' imaginations weren't so different where I was born," the king had said. "We had crowns too, though the flowers were different."

We sat again by the pond where the spider lilies had taken over with their spindled red blooms. The king cut their stems with her nails, and I watched as she began to weave. Her hands were dangerous and delicate as a spider working in her web, befitting her chosen flower.

She'd crowned me and said, "You're safe here now, in this garden."

While I waited for Lenora to appear with breakfast, I disassembled the bouquet I'd picked yesterday and made my own attempt at a crown, spreading stems across my bed and picking my favorites. Lenora's crown would be white and blue.

When she appeared, it wasn't with breakfast at all but with news. Phaela would see me. After, the king had decided I should taste for her.

"What have you been working on?" asked Lenora, nodding to the flowers in my hand.

Stunned by the sudden news that I'd be reentering life in the castle, I'd forgotten my gift. I stood and bowed. "It's for you."

We found the door to Phaela's chambers closed when we arrived. Low murmurs drifted from within. I couldn't make out their words but recognized the cadence of Delfina's accent. Lenora stood politely across from the door while I wandered.

The corridors weren't so grand as before. Downstairs, the frames on the walls had gained a tarnish. Along the corridors of our private rooms, the floral reliefs in the stone were less lively. I held my hand to an arch, and the stone vines were slow to wake to my presence. They uncurled as if from a long hibernation, shedding dust as they looped to hold my hand. They didn't green.

Lenora was too far down the corridor for me to see her expression, but when I glanced up and found her watching, she looked away.

The red door opened as I made my return. Delfina was curtsying to Phaela and—smiling. She seemed a different woman entirely, her shoulders relaxed, lightness in her step. She thanked Phaela and stepped to the threshold.

Her smile faltered when she saw me. She ducked her head, and that's when I noticed the envelope in her hand, stamped red with the king's seal. She turned to go.

"I'm sorry," I said in a rush.

"Don't be," she returned over her shoulder and hurried away. Her skirts fluttered as she rounded a corner and was gone.

"Carlotta," Phaela called. She waited beside her desk.

Lenora inclined her head to me. Her flowers quivered in her hair, and she departed. I stepped into the study and closed the heavy door.

"Come, sit," Phaela invited, sweeping her hand toward the brocade shepherdess chair that I'd taken up during our lessons together.

I sat neatly and clasped my hands in my lap. At my left, the doors to Phaela's balcony were open. The sky was so bright and the clouds so thin that I almost believed the sun would break through. There was no breeze through the doors.

During our lessons together, Phaela always took the armchair opposite mine, but now she remained standing in front of her desk. Like the castle, even she was less vibrant—the red of her gown sober as old blood or rust.

"How are you?" she asked.

I considered my answer. "My father is dead."

Phaela's mouth pinched. "I'm sorry, Carlotta." Now she came to her chair. The rustle of skirts as she settled was the only sound in the room, then silence again.

"And I haven't seen King Emelia or Meredith. Why do they keep from me?"

"Two lords are dead, and all the aristocratic houses know the Huxleys' close dealings with the king. We've had to be careful in how we proceed, and it has exhausted Emelia. Her position as king is precarious, and we have few allies. We cannot afford to alarm, offend, or alienate more families, sects, or neighbors."

"You're so careful not to blame me. I was sure I failed you."

"Yes, well," Phaela began curtly. "You're rash and unsubtle and you've made a mess. You make *Emelia* rash. Yet you also make her happy. She wants to retain you."

"And you?"

"I would've killed for my mother, given the same chance." Her gaze drifted briefly to the shelves behind me. "I've called you here because we've settled our dealings with the Huxley estate."

I startled. "But I killed them."

Phaela rose. "They were due to visit a business partner to the south and rumored to be carrying samples of rare metals. The robbery was just beyond our borders. Delfina narrowly escaped. The carriage was found ransacked. Quite violent and tragic."

My mind spun, piecing together the story King Emelia and Phaela had woven on my behalf.

"Their wives are happy, of course, with control of the estate's assets. As long as they're secure, they've no need for their husbands and no reason to contest the holes in Emelia's story. Of what remains, a sizable portion to Delfina for early severance of her contract"—and here she paused to study me as though measuring my caliber—"and to you, for old debts unpaid." She handed me an envelope from her desk, one identical to Delfina's. "It is a significant sum more than a poison girl's death allotment. The Huxleys were exceptional. Your wealth rivals the holdings of a small lord."

I stared at the seal—a rose with outsized thorns curved as wickedly as fangs.

Phaela leaned her hip against the desk. "You could retire," she added, her expression inscrutable.

I stared at her. I stared at the seal.

It was too late for Da.

"The king told me there are farmers who haven't abandoned the borderlands. She said they're growing the maize in glass houses, that it's been costly. Give my portion to them. I've no need of it here."

"You mean to stay?"

"Yes. The king has given me everything. I'm devoted to her."

Now Phaela smiled, and there was the red woman again. She rang the bell on the wall and returned to me. "Emelia will be pleased," she murmured, pulling me against her. I settled my head against her hip and let her stroke my hair. Her touch was feverish, and I remembered her mortal wound and the useless stitches, so close. I closed my eyes.

All I wanted now was to see King Emelia.

Minutes later, a knock came at the door, and Phaela called our visitor in. She didn't draw away from me, and so I didn't stir from where I'd slouched into her side. One of the kitchen staff approached, a silver tray in her hands. Its cloche gleamed in the light as she set it on the little table before me. Fanciful filigree patterned the base. A rose formed the handle. Phaela traced the line of my jaw and down my throat, her nails tickling my skin as her hand came to rest on my shoulder. The servant removed the cloche.

Unlike before, there'd been no attempt to cook the meat. Raw on the plate, it looked like an emergency to attend to rather than something to eat. Its red and wafting scent would gag me. A heap of pomegranate arils drowned in a pool of blood.

My heart stuttered. I recalled what Meredith had said of the king's past illness, how she'd requested only meat and pomegranates. Then there was the castle itself, turning dull and still.

I looked from the servant to Phaela. "Is the king unwell?"

"She's wearied," said Phaela. "You'll taste for her, won't you?"

I looked back to the plate. I nodded.

Phaela placed her hand against my back. "Good."

The servant unfolded a napkin and offered me silverware. I took the fork and knife and focused on their weight. Meredith would do this gladly and without hesitation. I could do the same.

The meat was marbled with fat and bisected by a sharp bone. I couldn't guess what animal it was from or what part of that animal. Goats and chickens were all we'd had in the borderlands, and even those had become scarce in the final years.

The knife was sharp and the meat tender. My cut was nothing at all. A blade against air. My hands ached to balance the silverware, a dull throbbing deep in my palms. I felt the shard of porcelain in my hands again, how it'd broken on the lord's spine. A frisson of delight overrode the pain. I took the sliver of meat on my tongue and chewed thrice and let it bleed delicately in my mouth. My hunger woke. I dipped my spoon into the arils. Blood dripped down the handle and stained my fingers. I crunched the seeds in my mouth and licked the blood from my hand, relishing the taste of sweetened iron.

"It is safe," I pronounced.

Phaela bestowed a kiss to my cheek. "Good girl."

TWENTY-SEVEN

H UMMING DRIFTED DOWN THE corridor.

After my tasting, I'd been left to wander for the first time in days and was drawn to the sound. It brought me to Meredith's door. I flattened my hand against it until the line of my cut stretched and throbbed again. I traced the flowers carved into the wood. I made a fist and knocked.

The humming stopped. A pause. Shuffling and a shadow under the door. "Winifred?" she asked.

"Carlotta," I answered.

Another pause. The shadow withdrew.

My pulse rose. "Meredith?" I asked.

"I cannot see you right now," she said at length, her voice far away again.

I stretched my hands at my sides until the flesh screamed. "Why?" I asked and hated how my voice shook on that pathetic syllable.

"The king is *ill*, and I *know* it's because of you. We're sworn to protect her, and look what you've done!"

"I—"

"I cannot see you!" Meredith wailed, her composure finally breaking.

She began to cry, and I couldn't witness it. I turned from her room as though the lord's knife had landed in my chest as it was destined. I hadn't meant to hurt the king or Meredith or Seventh Seeker or Da.

Yet I had.

And wasn't it Meredith herself who had noted the pattern? That we poison girls were cruel in our search for comfort?

I lingered outside the door to my room. Why had I returned to the place I'd spent so many days immured? And still I pushed open the door, ready to close myself in again.

The scent of rot hit me full in the face, and I staggered back from the dark. It was an animal smell worse than the raw meat, and now I did gag. Earthy and pungent, it coated the back of my throat on every breath, slipped ominously into my chest. I tiptoed into the dark, but nothing lurked there that I hadn't welcomed myself.

Da was fragile with decay. I stood in the square of light cast through the door and studied the coil of him around the magnolia seeds. They were all red and vibrant while he was wasting away. I took him in my hands, and he peeled away from the desk with a brittle, papery sound, leaving behind a layer of graying scales. I tried to remember the exact day he'd lost his iridescence.

I looped him over my wrist, his body heavy and hollow at once. I took my time coaxing him into a suitable posture. He couldn't do it himself anymore. I scooped the seeds into my right hand and departed for the garden.

The wind had started up again, and I'd forgotten my cloak. I clutched the magnolia seeds in my fist and wandered the paths. Da's tail swayed limply, but he stayed put. I stood under a redbud tree and gazed up through its pink blossoms and thought of where a magnolia could grow tall and strong.

Movement above caught my eye. Meredith was stepping out onto her balcony, embroidery hoop in hand. Her hair was loose and immediately caught up by the wind. She combed the sudden assault of curls from her face and swiped at her damp cheeks with the back of her hand, each flick of her wrist punctuated with frustration. Around her, her white skirts flared; her shawl rose like wings on the wind. I didn't mean to watch her. I was going to turn away. But so many days had passed without a glimpse of her, and here she was now, wounded because of me. Eventually, Meredith won against the wind and her hair and looked out over the courtyard. She spied me through the redbud's flowers. She stilled. I turned as if I could run from her now.

Something crunched beneath my heel. I startled and lifted my wrist. It was bare. I looked down at my feet.

Da, I am so used to you holding on to me. How could I crush you underfoot? How have you left so completely?

I knelt to his serpentine body. I'd come to think of him as this form—snake father, snake daughter, girl born of serpents, crawled out of the dirt.

But he'd been a man, and I hadn't buried that man.

Now I've crushed your spine. You were always crumbling under the weight of me. I needed so much and never had enough, and now who can hold me?

I found the first stretch of clear sky. I held him like an offering. His eyes were too clouded to see, but I looked up for us. The sun was almost breaking through the gray.

Maybe I understood the appeal of heaven now.

In a few years, a magnolia would cover this view for him.

I'd brought nothing to dig his grave because when I decided to bury him, it was an impulse, as all my decisions were. I started to peel back the earth with a sharp bit of stone. Gripping it hurt my hands. I discarded it and clawed with my nails. I worked until they were ragged and split and still had only a shallow bowl of soil.

A sweep of white skirts appeared before me. I kept digging in the dirt. I pawed like the wild dogs, clawing at the earth as if I could scratch anything into nurturing me. The bandages across my palms soaked red. Meredith knelt, placed her manicured, clean hands over my feral, dirty ones. I froze at her touch. She flashed a spade and began to dig while I cried silently and watched the hole deepen and smeared dirt across my face. She dug the grave neat and long so you could stretch comfortably. I cried harder.

"Is there anything you want to say?" she asked gently.

"I'm sorry," I choked.

The tips of my fingers were numb from the wind and the cold earth. Flexing my hands hurt as though the cuts were fresh, hurt more than they had when Lenora first cleaned and bandaged them. I tried to hold Da gently. My hands were too numb to feel him. My heart was too numb to feel this. I lay his small body in the earth to sleep. To rest. To gather strength.

I pushed the pile of seeds into the grave with my ruined hands and watched them scatter bright over his body. I had to grow strong now.

In the end, it was Meredith who buried him.

TWENTY-EIGHT

MEREDITH AND I SAT on her carpet, a basin of ugly brown water between us. Winifred took it away, and when she returned with fresh water, Meredith set to scrubbing at my hands again, the splash and trickle of water the only sound in the room.

Winifred hovered. "I can do that for you, miss."

"If you'd bring ointment for her hands," Meredith said, never raising her eyes from her work. "Antiseptic for the cuts. And fresh bandages."

Winifred departed.

The little brush Meredith had chosen was soft under my fingernails. She swished the last of the dirt away and trimmed and filed my nails, the rasp of the emery board like a bitter sigh between us.

I didn't know what to say.

Behind Meredith on her bedside table, a bouquet of pink carnations wilted in a vase of dirty water. It was the only sign that anything was awry. Her dresses were all closed away in their wardrobe. Her vanity was neat. The bed was made. This was all Winifred's doing, I knew. Meredith would let herself go to waste over her worry for the king.

Winifred bustled in with Meredith's requests. "Shall I call Lenora?" she asked, handing down the supplies.

Meredith crossed her legs and deposited the bottles and bandages into the skirt of her dress. The glasses chimed when they kissed. "No need," she murmured and turned my hands in hers. "This will sting," she added to me.

Winifred took up the basin and left us again.

I watched Meredith's face as she treated my hands, but she wouldn't look at me. She rubbed oil into my cuticles with her thumb, massaged lilac butter into my skin. Every touch was an act of devotion, and yet a sour frown twisted her mouth.

"What happened, Carlotta?" she asked finally.

"I killed the Lords Huxley."

Meredith startled and met my gaze at last.

"I brought Da his revenge."

Her hands were squeezing mine. My palms ached anew.

"But Earl Huxley was our emissary to King Marcus. For the trade agreement, Carlotta! For the water!" Meredith added when I stared blankly. "Arga would be Vinstrum's first true ally in a century!"

I thought my heart had found rest with the knowledge that Huxley had been excised from the world by my own hand, but a familiar heat simmered in my chest. "Why conduct trade dealings through a liar and a thief?"

Meredith blinked. She noticed our hands again and released mine from her crushing grasp. She glanced over the bottles and bandages in her lap as though surveying perplexing and foreign objects. Selecting a wrap, she reached for my hand again and set her attention on binding my wounds.

"What happened?" she asked again, in a whisper.

I recited the same lines to her that I'd given the king. It was easy now. Was it relief?

"My Carlotta," Meredith murmured and drew me against her and let me pillow my head in her lap. I sank against her, let go all my tension.

The light was changing. Darkness settled as if it'd been with us all along.

"But why has the king fallen ill?" Her voice was so small and injured. I remembered how she'd lain listless for days, lost without the king's gaze to warm her or her hand to guide her. I longed to soothe her, but now that she asked so plainly, I was unsure.

I flexed my hands and felt the sting. I'd stabbed young Huxley. His knife, at the moment of my attack, had disappeared. The king had arrived in a veil of shadow. The knife had been in her. I'd watched her remove it, watched it fall. Her flowers had wilted, whether from the exertion of materializing herself or accepting an injury on my behalf. Perhaps both. She'd put stones in the lords' mouths.

"I . . . don't know," I admitted at length. I recalled to Meredith how the hounds had appeared in my path that afternoon, how I'd locked the Huxleys into the room with me. I told her everything as I remembered it.

Meredith frowned and sighed but didn't withdraw her soft hand from my shoulder. "If King Emelia turned her eye upon you and still let you proceed, then it is as good as her blessing. You couldn't have taken Huxley's life if she didn't grant it. And if she took a blade for you, then it is because she could empower *your* power. As to these stones you mentioned, I've no guess." Meredith's touch slid down my arm and returned to my shoulder. "A royal poison girl has never done this sort of thing, you know."

I nodded against her.

"I have nothing, not even revenge. The king is everything to me. She's my life."

I turned to meet her gaze. "She's *my* life," I insisted.

"No," she said. "We are different. But you're still my favorite girl."

Meredith and I had migrated to her bed by the time Lenora came to find me. We'd discarded our dresses and lay skin to skin in the dark, the small lights of the night sky limning our shapes. It was good not to speak for a time and to be understood. Now the world had come back.

"If you'd follow me, miss," Lenora said from the threshold. "I'll leave you to dress." And the door closed again.

As if in defiance of Lenora's request, Meredith clung to me, pressing our bodies flush together. I loved all of her softness. I pressed my nose to the warm crook of her neck and breathed her in. She hummed and rolled on top of me and kissed my throat. My breath caught at the heat of her against my thigh.

"If only you'd not ruined your hands on a terrible man," she breathed.

I kissed her, and she sighed, and I opened my mouth to her.

Lenora knocked again. The door cracked. "Please, miss!" she urged.

Meredith startled upright. "What's wrong?" she called. A realization lit her face. "Is it King Emelia?"

"I need Carlotta."

Meredith was on her feet and across the room all at once. "Can we see her?" Meredith asked, drawing Lenora into the room. "Is she well enough to receive us?"

"I can assist you, miss," Lenora said to me.

She picked a chemise from the floor. It was Meredith's.

"Leave the dresses, simply take us to her," Meredith begged, hovering at Lenora's shoulder.

"I understand this is a sensitive matter for Carlotta alone," Lenora admitted.

I paused with my rumpled dress in hand.

Meredith's frantic gaze found me across the room. "But you will tell me how she is? You must promise," she said.

I promised.

"We all share your concern, miss," said Lenora. "But you must let us go."

Meredith ducked her head and stood against the wall with her hands clasped to her chest. She watched me dress as though I were her only hope. When Lenora ushered me forward, she followed us into the unflinching light of the corridor still wearing nothing at all.

"Give the king my love, won't you?" she said, falling into step with me.

I promised again.

She followed us up the stairs. We passed a pair of maidservants with baskets in their arms, but neither so much as blinked at Meredith, nude and unshod, her curls a wild mane.

The black doors of King Emelia's bedchamber opened at my arrival. Lenora curtsied and left me. I stepped through alone.

I'd never seen the curtains around the king's bed drawn. No one greeted me. No one seemed to be here at all. The candles glittered unattended. The discarded books on the floor had multiplied since my last visit. I bent to them. There was no mistake as to what they were now. These were theoretical magics from Retributionists and

Restorationists alike, the works of extinct angelic cults tossed in among them.

"If you sit there reading, you will be a long while. I should know," the king's voice came from beyond the curtains.

I crossed to the bedside but didn't presume to look within. "Meredith longs for you and misses you, my king. She sends her love," I said to the velvet curtain.

"Meredith is a lovely girl." A pause. "Has she told you of Siwan?"

"She did, yes," I said, surprised by the king's mention of her former poison girl.

"Witnessing Meredith's heartbreak stirred me to anger I didn't know I could feel. I have never known hate or jealousy for a human, but Siwan squandered a lifetime with Meredith and turned to hurt her in the end, all their history honed to a weapon. I have always been able to let poison girls go when they decide it is their time to go, but Siwan— I wanted to eat her."

I let the king's confession hang in the air.

"Many girls have come to me. I can see the glimmers of how they might blossom if taken into the castle. Occasionally, as with Siwan, I am wrong. Most often, my instincts are correct. Some girls, though, still surprise me." Behind the curtain, the linens rustled. "Remove your dress. There is a blindfold beside you. Put it on and come to me."

Meredith had been right not to bother with our dresses after all. I let mine pool on the floor around my feet. To my left, I found a red strip of silk tied to one of the onyx stalagmites that grew up the sides of the room. I knotted it behind my head and entered a rich, personal darkness. Feeling into the velvet folds of the curtain, I found the gap between them and presented myself to the king.

The linens rustled again, and I felt the king's presence upon me like a storm cloud—dark and total, a force with enough wrath to unmake me. Her hand grasped mine, and I startled at her cold touch. She kissed my knuckles, her breath ghosting over my skin. I shivered. My skin tightened. My nipples pinched. The king turned her attention to them, the length of her tongue a heated contrast to her skin. A slick pulse throbbed between my legs. Withdrawal crashed upon me belatedly and all at once. It'd been too long since she'd touched me. Her hands braced my hips, and she sucked my nipple into her mouth, bit gently with those teeth. Lightheadedness swept through me. My knees were weak. Wet tickled down my thigh.

"My king," I gasped.

My pulse shook my chest. She'd ruin me like this, without even touching my clit.

Sensation doubled and melted. A breath sighed at my ear. It wasn't the king's. Distantly, elsewhere, Meredith felt my pleasure and touched herself. I knew well the press of her fingers, how she'd slip through the seam of me.

The king pulled me down on top of her, and I was momentarily stunned, jolted out of the meld between my ring and Meredith's. I shifted and found the king's thigh between mine, felt her skin against the slick core of me. Then her lips were on mine. She kissed me as if she meant to break me. I wanted her to. Her hand closed around my throat. I moaned into her open mouth.

"Go on," she murmured against my lips, a devious undercurrent to the words. "You two want to rut against me. I can feel it."

A hot wave crashed over me, a twinned fever. Meredith urged me forward. I clutched the sheets and released myself to chase instinct, let myself grind against the king's thigh until pleasure mounted and I was only my need for release.

The king threaded her fingers through my hair, nails rasping along my scalp. "Look at you," she purred. "A little permission and see what you become. I love seeing pretty girls undone like this. Beneath all the lace and ribbons, your instinct is simple and pure." Her grasp on my throat tightened, cutting off my breath. "That's enough now."

I was on my back in an instant, panting and dizzy. Her breath was ragged against my neck, and I knew immediately that she had only to snap her jaws and I would be gone. I lay frozen under the threat, and still my body ached for her, still her thighs parted mine, my wet center open for her. A low growl hummed in her chest.

"My king," I whispered. I tipped my chin back, bared my throat to her teeth. "Do you mean to eat me too?"

I raised my hands slowly as though approaching something wild. I found her jaw, and she didn't pull away, didn't bite. I rested my thumbs against her lips and traced wider to her cheeks, along the line of her true mouth. I tested the pad of my fingers against her rows of teeth. I chose a point and pressed until it broke the skin. The king sighed, her tongue sweeping to catch the blood.

At once, she withdrew, and I lay where she'd pinned me, my legs still open. Beyond the curtains came small sounds I couldn't identify. I waited patiently for her. She'd saved me, and I could be good for her now.

In the silence, I felt her regard me, the familiar weighty shadow of her drawing near. She settled above me again, palmed my ass and traced her nails up the back of my thigh. Capturing my ankle in her hand, she guided my leg over her shoulder and bent close. Something chill and hard teased my opening, and I tensed. My ring woke to it with the ache of something long lost, and I realized they were one and the same, both cut from the castle's onyx. I reached for King Emelia, for reassurance. She was kind and let me have my arms about her shoulders.

She kissed my lips, my throat. "Relax. I will be gentle," she soothed.

She slid into me, and I drew a breath, let her sink into me and fill me until our hips met. I shivered from the cold length of her, the novel sensation of being so full and spread. She withdrew slowly and thrust in again. I clenched around her and let my head fall back.

"Good girl," she murmured and found a rhythm to take me apart.

I moaned, gasped her name, reveled in the wet sound of my own cunt. My heat warmed the length of her, and her pace came harder. I opened myself to it. I let her fire build mine. I loved being hers.

Tension shot through me, then a blooming warmth. She fucked into me as I came, and I dug my nails into her back and gasped against her shoulder, her collarbone sharp beneath my lips. Such a delicate bone. I thought of biting. I bit. The waves of my orgasm receded, leaving me limp and sensitized, but the king didn't slow her pace. I whimpered.

"My ki—"

She covered my mouth. "It isn't time to beg. Be good, my dear."

Her command was enough to elicit a shiver. A new surge of heat found me. "Yes, my king," I said and let her use me and glowed with the honor. King Emelia had never sought her own pleasure with me.

When she came, it was with a hiss and stillness. She was buried deep, our bodies flush, a mess of slick between us. She didn't move, and I waited.

With the cool air of a command, she said, "I want you to free me," the same as though she'd asked me to taste for her, to kneel, to open my legs.

I struggled to answer. How should I move my body to serve her? "How do you mean, my king?"

"Before I accepted you into my service, I asked if there was anything else you desired. You said there wasn't. But you were wrong. Now I have granted you your great desire. I wonder if you would grant mine."

My thoughts cleared. "Tell me, and I will do it," I swore.

She slid out of me, and I gasped. I was hollow without her. Her heavy shadow withdrew. I lay still again, my body wrung out. I thought I heard a metal clasp, an unbuckling, followed by the slip of fabric on skin.

"I want to leave this place. And now must, since my emissary is dead. I want you to free me of my father's pact so I may act fully in my role as king of Vinstrum as I choose it. I never found a worthy cursebreaker. For so long, I labored to be my own. Now I have you, and you have shown me what I need, a girl equal parts vicious and tender."

I started to say I was not this girl. I wasn't tender. I wasn't even vicious, only rash, as Phaela had said. And how should I know, better than the king herself, how to break a curse? I worried at the immensity of her request and also of failure. But she had asked me to do this great thing, and she wouldn't ask me if I weren't worthy.

"How do I do this?"

"You asked why I wore no crown. It is with King Eric in the castle's heart. I can go there, but the pact set forth by my father and my predecessor ensures I cannot reach the crown. I need you to take it from him. Once I have it, I can break the command that seals me in the castle's walls. I can resolve the pact and close the door on my father."

"And when you are free from here . . ." I began, thinking aloud, "you can also return home?"

The room was quiet, and I couldn't feel King Emelia near me. I sat up. I reached for the blindfold.

She captured my wrist. "No. If I close the door, the door is closed."

I was startled. I'd never thought seriously of returning to the borderlands, but to have the route closed to me completely would be another tragedy.

I tried to clasp her hand in mine. Did I seek comfort or offer it? "You'd never go back?"

She pulled away. "Go back so I can be another pawn in his court? Go back to sitting demurely at his side forever? Go back to being ridiculed and punished whenever I stray from his plans for me? No. I will do what he's said for once. I will stay here, and I will make his punishment my freedom. I can survive being hated by many so long as a few love me. Do you understand? At home, I am neither hated nor loved. I see this for what it is now—granting me the figurative crown while stripping away any tools I might have to improve Vinstrum. It is exile. It always has been. Do you understand?" she asked again, a manic breathlessness to her speech I'd never heard before.

"Yes, my king," I said. I spoke softly. "I understand." I reached into the space before me, but there was only air. "Won't you let me see you?"

"I am not fit for your eyes."

"You are always beautiful, my king."

"Not now."

"Then let me touch you again."

Her hand found my cheek. She turned me toward her, pulled me against her beating heart. She wore something soft now. I curled into her.

"May I ask you about the books?" I asked. "Why keep the work of clerics?"

"They claim to have ways of cleansing or setting a boundary. I tried to turn it to my own use, but the law that keeps me here doesn't break. It is not the same language and will only answer to its own riddle."

"You've tried this lately?"

"I've tried for decades and recently, yes."

"And it hurts you to speak this language?" I asked, picking up her metaphor.

She stroked my back. "Sometimes my articulation is clumsy."

"A fortnight ago ..." I hesitated. "There was a light that woke me. After, you didn't come to the table for a long time. And your meal requests became ..."

"Yes?"

"You'd hurt yourself, hadn't you? Trying to break the pact?"

Trying to break from your father's control with the words of people who hate you.

She was quiet. Her nails trailed down my spine. "Sometimes my articulation is clumsy."

My heart swelled. I put my arms around her. I held her, *hugged* her. She turned rigid at my touch, then eased into the embrace.

Who was there to hold the king?

"I will save you," I said to her chest. "I will save you, my king."

TWENTY-NINE

I PAUSED TO CHECK the sky again. The sun was directly overhead, and the rows of maize threw no shadow. It was a day so hot that the sky seemed bright white rather than blue, and as I sweat through my dress, I looked up past the hairy antennas of the maize stalks to check that the sky's color was indeed still there. I felt the humidity at my temples, in my armpits. Each breath was heavy with water. Sweat dampened the hairline of my scarf, but today I was happy. The husks were green, and the silks were mature. I'd been checking the ears every day.

I stepped to a stalk and chose an ear at eye level. Peeling back its husk, I pressed my thumb into a kernel, checking ripeness. It broke open with milky juice.

Da slithered from under the shelter of my hair. "That's the start of the harvest season," he declared proudly from his perch on my shoulder. His voice was full and deep as I remembered it. He flicked his black tongue and nodded to the king. "Look closer, see here."

King Emelia was beside me, though I didn't remember when she'd arrived. She wore the dress from the night we met, the one that revealed the long length of her leg with every step. She didn't sweat at all. Her braids were gone, replaced by a full cascade of luscious red flowers. They trailed down the row of maize, all the way back to where we'd come from the house. She nodded to what Da was saying about the maize.

"You've strong hands," Da commented. "Grip the ear like—" He could not grip anything. He sighed. "Carlotta, please demonstrate for me."

"I think I understand," the king said, a glint in her eye.

In a flash, she reached past me. She grasped the ear. She twisted; she pulled.

The stalk snapped like bone.

Like a small spine.

There was no field, no sun. And Da was gone.

I was alone. I was in the king's bed. The curtains were open.

It was a dark day, the kind of foreboding the castle liked to entertain but that never committed to tearing open the sky. The candles burned on and dripped their wax. The hearth fire, needing no fuel to snap and hiss at, was silent. Everything was eerily silent. Unlike my room along the servants' corridor, there was no murmur of conversation beyond the door, no passing laughter or pattern of footsteps.

My blindfold was twisted over a mound of pillows, one of them painstakingly embroidered with all the flower specimens the king grew in her hair. I smiled to feel Meredith's hand near. The dark sheets were littered with papery red petals in various stages of disintegration. Beside me, I found a black tangle of leather, some kind of belt or garter I didn't recognize. I reached for it and found it weighed down by an intimidating wand of onyx. I dropped it. It seemed like something forbidden. I hooked a cautious finger around one of the straps and raised it again. Pieces of the night before fell into place.

I slipped the wand from its harness, trailed a finger down its glassy length. Memory rekindled old heat. I brought the stone to my lips. I kissed its cold surface, closed my eyes. It had all the weight and sacredness of a temple artefact, and I knew how to handle the sacred.

"My king," I whispered to it. "My king."

The room was different and the same when I opened my eyes. I'd invoked King Emelia as the clerics entreated the angel, with simple chant and a heart of sacrifice. Her shadow was with me.

"King Emelia," I breathed over the stone.

She heard me and answered my prayer, and I was blessed to be swollen and slick for her again. I lay back. I opened my body in offering.

My palms ached when I flexed my fingers to angle the wand inside of me, but it was a good ache, like something earned through dedicated labor. The castle's chill drew close again, bringing with it the spirits I had met the night King Emelia pierced me. I knew the cold trail of their fingers down my body, their kisses at my neck. They welcomed me back into their grasp with a sigh, and I echoed it, closing the circuit of our pleasure.

"Carlotta?"

I opened my eyes. Anne bent over me, her painted lips inches from mine. Her breath was icy. Her gaze burned. I reached for her.

"Carlotta?"

The vision of Anne cleared. The voice had driven the ghosts away.

A figure stood at the foot of the bed. Too short to be the king. Too thin to be Meredith. I blinked her into focus. Lenora clasped her hands and took a long breath. "I'm to escort you to the table now, but . . ." Her gaze dropped from my face. She noted the spreading damp beneath me and swallowed. "Please continue, miss," she said, her prim voice breathier than usual. "King Emelia would want you to finish."

With the castle's energy tuned to me, it was easy to slip back into its currents and into the arms of the ghosts. Liquid black cocooned our rapture. Onyx facets refracted our bliss. Anne put her fingers in my mouth. She raised her brow. I sucked obediently until she hummed and let her head fall back. She stroked along my tongue, and I worshipped her skin, the bitter floral taste of her. I'd lost the wand though I didn't remember when. A girl's hand filled the ache in me. I moaned around Anne's fingers, and she withdrew them to choke me with her slick hand. An eager glint lit her eyes. She cast her gaze to the girl who fingered me, and her thrusts came harder. Anne's grasp tightened. She strangled my moan. The ghosts converged with their sighs and kisses. My head was light.

Anne bent close again. "Let me hear you," she murmured in the king's voice and released me so I could scream.

The room snapped solid. The wand was in my hand, inside me. Dour light fell across the bed, and there was Lenora, still waiting patiently, a flush to her chest.

I licked the wand clean, appreciating the mild salt of my own body with the same attention as when King Emelia asked me to taste for her. I lay back on the pillows and waited for my heart to calm, for will to return to my muscles. Lenora stepped to the side of the bed where a robe cut from the same red silk as my blindfold had been laid out.

She held the robe open for me. "It's beautiful witnessing your bond with King Emelia and the castle grow."

I rolled my head on the pillow to look at her properly. She spoke to me as the clerics did to the pilgrims. *The angel's eye will find you. Their blessings will flow.* Oh, to be suddenly a pilgrim! And of King

Emelia! I smiled at the thought. I went to Lenora and slipped my arms into the robe.

Our king had requested blood this morning. As soon as the servants whisked away our empty plates, Phaela set a tray bearing two chalices and a thin knife between me and Meredith. The tray and glasses were the same style as the ones from the night King Emelia had claimed me. Was the knife the same one Meredith had held?

Beatrisa had joined us for breakfast and was now our audience. The conversation that morning had been polite—how did we sleep and how was the king's condition and what an especially petulant sky we had today! Only Meredith had smiled knowingly upon seeing me. Beatrisa avoided looking at my hands or looking at me in any way that could be mistaken as looking at my hands. We didn't acknowledge the sudden disappearance of the Huxleys, my long absence from the table, or the connection between these events. If anyone else had seen me digging a frantic grave in the garden, she didn't remark on it. When I was addressed, it was as a beautiful girl deserving of the king.

I was happy to be back at the table.

Phaela took Meredith by the wrist first and set a chalice before her. As Meredith had done for me, Phaela made a precise cut at the soft skin of the inner elbow. Meredith sighed longingly and watched her glass fill. We observed silence while she completed her offering. Beatrisa watched all this with a ladylike fascination. Now, with bloodletting, the conversation turned earnest.

"Forgive my question if it is too private," Beatrisa began, "but why must they bleed?"

"Blood from her poison girls is physically as well as emotionally nourishing for Emelia, though she commands it rarely," Phaela answered, her expert eye on the veins at the bend of my elbow. "We don't want to place undue strain on their bodies when a potential purging is strenuous enough. For Emelia to subsist on blood alone would require too many donors, and so her diet necessitates careful variety and moderation."

"Unless," Meredith spoke up, "there is a pathetic man to devour." She looked to Phaela. "If Carlotta killed the Huxleys, why is the king weak? Why didn't she eat them?"

Phaela clicked her tongue and seemed as if she wouldn't answer. She flicked the tip of the knife across my skin, and my blood dripped into the waiting chalice.

"To mend the situation," Phaela started, "Emelia needed to know what the Huxleys knew. Extracting memory from a dead person is taxing work. By the time she was done, the meat was not fresh, and anyway, magic spoils the taste—at least, this is what she's told me."

"The stones," I said, understanding now.

"Yes," said Phaela.

I'd filled my chalice, and she began to wrap the cut. I looked thoroughly broken with all my bandages.

"The Huxleys were never initiated into the castle, of course," Phaela explained. "Emelia needed to integrate them, in a way, to make their memories hers." Phaela took the tray and inclined her head in an apologetic bow. "I should deliver Emelia's meal while it is vital. Thank you, girls."

My desk had been cleaned while I was out. The debris from the seed pod had been swept; Da's scales had been scrubbed away. I smoothed my hand over the corner, then braced myself against it as a wave of feeling overcame me. I squeezed my eyes shut. I wanted a nap.

I almost missed the envelope set squarely in the center of the desktop, but its placement was too intentional among the haphazard piles of books and scraps of paper. I turned it over. It was white, unmarked, and unsealed, the flap tucked humbly into the envelope. My heart sped. I opened it.

Cursive bubbled across the page, its loops rounded and stout. I didn't recognize the handwriting.

Dear Carlotta,

I am sorry for leaving without relating any of this to you in person, but as you understand, it has been too long since I have seen my family. I am going back to them now thanks to you and more secure than I could ever have dreamed.

I'm not sure how much you know of the lives of contracted poison girls. As I remember it, Priscilla was careful to keep these things from her letters to you. The pay is why we all do it. Despite the risk, it is better and easier on the regular than taking work as a maid, but it is still lucky to find a secure position in a stable household. Your mother, like me, was lucky. So as you can see, our luck is very poor.

Earl Huxley lied to me about you. I knew they were lies, but I accepted them because it was made clear that anything else would jeopardize my contract. He told me that you had schemed to become a poison girl in your mother's place and sought to frame him because he refused to take you in. I'm sorry I couldn't be seen with you.

I would like to tell you more about Priscilla when we next have the chance to meet. You were correct. We worked closely together. We started at the Huxley estate the same month—both of us part of a new crop of girls brought in after three had died within a few months of each other. Priscilla was always talking about how you were growing and what she could send you next. She was the gentlest among us and always with a book or her own notebook. She was the kind of person to be amused by the antics of small animals and did not flinch at blood. You do look like her.

It's well known among us that the king doesn't require contracts and that she is extravagant when it comes to caring for her girls. I hope your arrangement brings you happiness, but if you ever quit the castle, please know you can come to me.

With love and apologies,

Delfina

I read the entire letter twice over and lost track of how many times I skimmed the paragraph about my mother. I looked like her. She didn't flinch at blood.

I was relieved to know her memory was safe with someone who still lived. I hadn't buried her with Da.

I took the letter to bed, lay on my side to read it again, and fell asleep like this.

Dreaming of my mother in the flesh was rare, and when I did, it was always as a voice calling me downstairs only for her to be long gone once I arrived. Or it was a hand braiding my hair that, when I turned to look, had belonged to no one, and I was alone in my room.

Usually, I dreamed of paper.

I was running through the stalks. The sky darkened with one of the rainless storms that tore through the borderlands during my final days there. I hurried to make it home before the heavy winds blew in, but my pockets were overfilled with Ma's letters. With every step, one of them escaped and was snatched away by the air.

Lightning flashed across the sky. The roof of the house was in view. Years of letters spilled from my dress and floated up to the sky. I screamed and tried to snatch them back, but without my hands to shield my pockets, more pages flew away. I grew frantic. I leapt at the sky. I flailed my arms. My pockets were emptying, empty—

And then Ma's hand was in my hair. I whirled to face her—hoping that if I was fast enough this time, I would catch her. Hoping that she had come to replace her letters. Hoping that she could save me from the coming storm.

Meredith startled back from me, her hand frozen over the pillow. I didn't remember sitting up, but I was. My breath was fast and the room unsettled as a dream. I scrubbed my hand across my eyes.

"I'm sorry," I whispered.

"No," said Meredith. "I didn't mean to scare you."

Delfina's letter was crumpled under me. I smoothed and refolded it along its original lines.

"Are you . . ." Meredith began and then decided on a new question. "Is there anything you need?"

I shook my head.

She sat beside me, and I leaned against her. She settled her arm around my waist.

"This," I said.

"Hmm?"

"I needed this."

Meredith stroked my back.

"Why have you come?" I asked.

"We'll have dinner soon." Her eyes sparked. "And there are rumors the king is up and about."

The table was set and our food presented, but Meredith would not eat. She stared longingly toward the doors of the great hall as though she could will them open and have the king step through on the strength of her wishing alone.

All of King Emelia's favorites were served—pomegranate soup, bitter sprouts glazed with cactus nectar, dark salad greens drizzled with sugary red pepper sauce, hearty slices of roasted honey ham, citrus slices in syrup. The menu was overwhelmingly sweet when served together, and even Phaela took only polite small bites.

"I've delivered your portrait to King Emelia," Beatrisa said to me. "I'll depart in the morning."

At the mention of the king, Meredith's burning focus was diverted from the door to Beatrisa.

"In the morning?" Phaela exclaimed. I thought, for the first time, I might see her pout. "It's the first you've told me."

Beatrisa winced delicately. "We decided only recently. King Emelia thinks it will be for the best."

Phaela let her silverware fall to her plate with a dramatic clatter. "And what decision was this?" She wadded her napkin in her lap. I'd never seen her so angry. "*I* was never informed. For the best of *what* ? What is to happen?"

Meredith grinned bitterly, her eyes alight with triumph. "Now you see how it is! You see how it feels."

Phaela cut her eyes at Meredith. Beatrisa's shoulders slumped.

"*I* have cared for Emelia for *decades. She* tells me *everything*," Phaela hissed.

"And now she has told Beatrisa!" Meredith giggled.

Phaela closed her eyes and massaged her temples. "All this sugar has given me a headache," she muttered fiercely.

"Phae . . ." Beatrisa started, but Phaela did not raise her gaze. "You know best how King Emelia is. She won't be vulnerable with too many at once. She isn't choosing any of us over the others. She is acting as she feels will keep her safe and give her time to think. Let us not quarrel"—and here she looked pointedly at Meredith—"especially while our king is ailing."

"You all don't see her when she's ill. You don't know how it shakes you. You don't know . . ." She shuddered. "You don't know how scared I have been."

"We're all scared," said Meredith. "We all say it all the time. And yet you hold yourself apart from us as if you don't feel it."

"I must be strong for Emelia and carry out her orders when she cannot," Phaela said as though this was a line often repeated.

"We're all strong for her," Meredith retorted. "You scout us poison girls. I'd think you know what it takes."

"Yes," Phaela whispered as though in defeat. "I know."

"You wish you could taste for her, and you cannot," Meredith continued determinedly. "It is the one thing we have that you don't."

"Meredith . . ." Beatrisa warned.

"But you fantasize about it, don't you?" Meredith barreled on. "You're not your mother, no matter how much you romanticize her sacrifice. You don't actually know what it is to live as a poison girl."

Silence.

Meredith bristled as though ready to fight, but Phaela only said, "You're right," waving her hand as if to dismiss her own jealousy. "You're right and I am sorry." She covered her eyes.

We exchanged glances. Phaela never cried. What would we do if she did? We startled at her sharp inhale, but she only lowered her hands and drew herself up again.

"I'm sorry, my loves," she said with that humbling bow. "I've shamed my mother."

Meredith screamed. She shot from her chair. We startled again, and there was the king herself standing in the arch of the great hall's doors and Meredith throwing herself into her arms.

THIRTY

T HE HEART OF THE castle was as much a place as it was a memory or a feeling, King Emelia explained to me, and it was a hungry heart. It did not like to let things go. It did not forgive or forget. It was and wasn't King Emelia. It was a lurking force that had coalesced around her, born when King Eric pledged his blood to the pact. It was solace and horror, its range as expansive as the memories it hoarded.

She told me all this while the moon presided over the garden and said, "The heart will endeavor to speak to you. You can be kind or cruel as you please, but you must not reply. You must not so much as cry out. If it hears you, it will try to keep you."

Meredith stopped picking at the grass and stared up at the king perched on her stately rock, as serene as though it were her throne. Phaela paced steadily under the willow's boughs. I nodded where I sat at the king's feet.

"Carlotta might not come back?" Meredith blurted.

"She will come back," the king promised. "I am telling her how."

Phaela shook her head. "We cannot risk losing another poison girl. And what a bad end it would be."

"You haven't seen her as I have—fury and poise at once, to meet fate unflinching," said the king. "She's the one I've waited for, and I cannot wait longer. Carlotta will navigate the heart. She can."

Meredith placed her hand on my knee. Her eyes were full of the moon. "You're certain?"

I took her hand, but I met Phaela's gaze. "This is my devotion."

Lenora took extra care with me the next morning, asking exactly how I wanted my hair and what I wanted to wear, all of her usual efficiency left to soften. She spoke little and lingered over every task, delaying handing me over to the day.

"You dress me as if it's the last time you'll see me," I said to her. "You braid my hair as if it's the last time you'll touch me."

"I'm sorry, miss," she said. "It's not how I mean to do it. I'm only thoughtful." She smoothed her hands over my shoulders and stepped back to study her work.

I'd ruined my favorite dress—Lenora said the blood had set too long—and so today I wore green, its hue deep and vibrant as a magnolia leaf. It was one of Phaela's hybrid creations, a breezy southern silhouette styled with northern aristocratic sensibilities: taffeta in place of linen, a wide bell of lace for the sleeves, a ruffled hemline as a nod to their conventional layers and flounce.

Out in the corridor, Meredith waited for me with Winifred, whose dark suit emphasized her height. She looked like a shy boy escorting Meredith to a dance.

"King Emelia said to wear what we like," she said when I looked too long.

"I know." I smiled. "I was admiring is all."

Meredith's hem was very short at her knees and trailed in the back. Phaela's style fit her well. She was rarely in black, though upon drawing closer to kiss her cheeks, the fabric shimmered plum.

There was a feast that morning and, around the great hall's table, a few more women in fine suits. All the castle's residents were here, a new gathering for the ceiling devils to observe and the first time I'd seen us together in one room. Even the hounds were in attendance—three lounging about King Emelia's chair—and the watchers at the door.

Though the table was only half as full as it had been during the poison girls' feast, the room was twice as loud, full of compliments and giggles. A girl had brought a lyre and sat at the end of the table strumming, rousing a brave group into a dance by the hearth. Others lined up to bestow little gifts on the king: a knit shawl that Phaela eyed critically but withheld comment on, a clay vase painted with red flowers, a wooden statuette of a distinguished hound. King Emelia invited the girl to pet one of the inspirations, and she bowed to it and tentatively stroked its large head. Though the hound gave no indication that it noticed the girl at all, King Emelia smiled and said that Cecil was very happy to meet her.

The king had done well styling the day as one of spontaneous celebration. Our beloved King Emelia finally free of her predecessor's shadow! Free to wander the world as she wished! It was momentous.

Except the task was not yet done.

Only Phaela and Meredith were not entertained, the former tense and the latter jittery. After tasting for the king, Meredith had promptly downed two glasses of spiked citrus only to bemoan that it had no effect on her. Across the table, Phaela cut her already cubed potatoes into even smaller pieces. I couldn't eat at all.

The king inclined her head. "You have doubts?"

Meredith's and Phaela's stares burned.

"No," I replied at once. "Never, my king."

She nodded solemnly and stood. Immediate, reverent silence fell.

"I've gathered you all," said King Emelia, "to honor Carlotta's journey to the heart of the castle." Everyone looked to me. I kept my gaze on the king to steady myself. "Boundaries may shift and old spirits visit. Be calm and know that I watch over you here."

The king beckoned, and though we went to the onyx doors hand in hand, I felt she carried me. Watchers flanked the tall doors, their suits gleaming in the great hall's festive light.

"Remember," King Emelia murmured, "your exit is this door, though it may not be where you expect it."

I nodded.

"The old king may be strange. He may threaten you. He can do nothing."

I nodded.

"Once inside, speak to no one, not even to me."

I nodded.

She looked me up and down. She kissed me. She delayed as if I was something sweet, her hands cupping my face, her soft hum against my lips. I never wanted her to let me go, and then she did.

King Emelia closed her eyes and felt the air before us as though groping for a handhold in the dark. She frowned. Her fingertip found the seam between the onyx doors. She planted her palms, one on each side, and braced her arms as though she meant to shove the doors open.

Under her touch, the onyx metamorphosed to a new vermillion stone, colors shifting like a disturbed bottle of oil and water until there was only the oil. The watchers turned their heads to me by inches, the simple motion stuttering and halting. I found my wide-eyed face in their helms, and my reflection was true for the first time. King Emelia's hand came to rest at the small of my back, her question implicit. I nodded again. She looked to the doors, and they swung open to an engulfing and absolute darkness, the red stark against it like a beacon.

I looked up at King Emelia, but she was looking into the dark.

"Nothing within can hurt you," she said. "It is only as dangerous as a nightmare."

The king did nothing to urge me forward. She didn't take her hand away. I realized she would wait as long as I wanted, that the first step must be my own.

Like a character in an ill-fated myth, I looked behind me. The women stood in tight pairs and groups, now murmuring, now uncertain, their revelry spoiled. Meredith's gaze locked with mine, and she was on her feet in an instant and running to me. She crushed me against her, and I felt her wild heartbeat against my chest and the rush of her breath at my ear. There was nothing left for her to say. We had said it all last night as we fell asleep and this morning when we woke in each other's arms. Our kiss was the opposite of the king's savoring restraint—fingers snagged in hair, fists clutched and wrinkled taffeta. When we broke apart, it was like weary fighters conceding to a stalemate.

I needed to go, or I would never go.

I started for the door, determined step after determined step. I braced for cold when I crossed the threshold into the dark but felt no change at all, no indication that I'd breached such a solid boundary, and that was the more shocking thing. Someone gasped, but when I glanced back, the great hall was gone and the door vanished and nothing around or above me but black.

I walked into the nothing for a long time. The floor seemed not to have changed, for my heels clicked upon it the same. I met no walls or doors. I had no indication of where I should go and grew restless. I knew what prey must feel scuttling along the floor of the night woods where any taloned thing might lurk behind or above, observing and plotting to strike. My arm grew tired. I had no other strategy but to walk with a hand before me. At first, I'd feared running headlong into a wall. Later, I feared I would never meet one.

Then the dark started to slither and rasp.

After so long in silence, I froze. Prey instinct gripped me tight. My first thought was to turn back or to move wide and avoid the source of the noise.

Only as dangerous as a nightmare, King Emelia had said. It was comforting and unnerving at once. Nightmares were neither lethal nor kind.

Susurrations filled the air, the source growing larger or nearer. Both hands out in front of me, I took a tentative step forward, another. The floor was the same. Another step and my breaths came faster. My heel caught something soft. A body that snapped under my weight. That hissed in pain. An arrow of memory pierced my chest. I lost my balance.

I pitched forward into a sea of writhing, scaled bodies. I flailed. They crawled over my face. They smothered me. I feared I'd fallen into a pit and would never claw my way out. Though I tried to shake them off, they were all around. They drowned me. Their anguish whipped them into a frenzy. I'd hurt one of them! I was an enemy. I clenched my teeth so I didn't scream. My breaths became another hiss on the air. A snake threatened my neck, wound tight in a warning. Instinct said to dig in my nails, to fight. But Huxley's purpled face flashed into my mind. I pictured his doomed and ugly struggle against Da. *I'm not him!* I wanted to scream. *I didn't mean it! I am one of you!* I couldn't die this way.

I lay still. Stopped struggling. I opened my hands. The mass of snakes slowed. They slithered over my palms, testing, questioning. *Breathe, dear girl.* I did. The snake that had my neck calmed and slithered away, and there was no pain. The mass reformed, gathering below me and moving as one. They carried my body.

I hoped they would accompany me through the heart. I imagined the comfort of their lithe tumult around me, scales glinting dangerously.

I missed Da.

My snakes dispersed one by one into the dark, leaving me on my back. They had carried me as far as they could. I blinked at nothing and listened until I could hear them no more. When I stood, I expected more aimless walking, but my hands immediately met a wall. No, a *door*, a handle. I tugged.

Gold seared my eyes. Squinting against the light, I stumbled into the throne room as it had been my first night at the castle. Music was a vibrant, incomprehensible sound after so much silence. My senses were stymied. I stood with my hands shielding my eyes only to realize I'd intruded on the dance when a woman snatched me up and whirled me around. She held my hands and wouldn't let me shrink. I was dizzied by the light and her laugh. The dancers dragged me through the steps and turns like a ragdoll, but none of my partners seemed to mind. They held me and handed me down the line as though I belonged. At the end of the dancers, I staggered away into the crowd before they could catch me again.

Women were crowding around the dais. They traded thrilled whispers behind their hands and fans. Anne—vivid and alive—sat in the king's lap, bathing in the attention of King Emelia and the onlookers. She sighed, her head falling back against the king's shoulder. King Emelia seemed not to notice their observers at all. Her regard was for Anne alone. Slowly, under the golden light, the picture of them came together.

The king's hand was hidden beneath the white folds of Anne's dress, a scandalous twitch of skirt drawing the eye. Her eyes were downcast, reading Anne's every expression and sigh with the same serious assessment given to any matter she might attend to as king. Her lips were at Anne's ear, murmuring. I wished I knew what she said. I couldn't hear Anne's answer, but I knew the shape of the words in her mouth. *Yes, my king.*

Like the other women gathered here, I couldn't look away. Even here in the castle's heart, or perhaps because I'd ventured into the castle's heart—here where Anne was so achingly alive—my ring knew her pleasure as my own. My skin was hot. My pulse rose. Her moan grew in my throat. I pressed my hand to my mouth, bit down on the palm of my glove. I swooned. A woman caught me. She let me lean against her.

The woman nodded to Anne. "She's stunning, isn't she?"

I could only nod.

The woman smiled, her eyes sparkling in the light. She considered me. "What a beautiful dress." She traced the line of my shoulder, her touch questioning, and let the fabric slip down my arm. "May I?"

While I watched Anne, the party had grown heated. Laces and ribbons were loosened. Hair spilled free. Gowns slipped low. A group of women tangled on the dais steps, lovingly posed as though their pleasure was a gift to the king.

I glanced back to the throne. Anne stared at me, the blur of passion receding from her face. She frowned. King Emelia, noting her distraction, followed her gaze. Anne tilted her head as though trying to place me, and I hated the moment she did. She shook her head as if she'd witnessed a horror or else wanted to deny one.

If I were here, she couldn't be alive.

Memory withered her. Her eyes glazed black and hard. She pointed a vicious finger at me. Her face contorted. "Get her out!" she howled, her mouth a slash of white teeth, then a void. "Get her out!"

Music crashed to an end. I felt the vastness of the room again, how high its ceilings, the walls widened by the beat of silence. Our party roused from its indulgent languor, dozens of black eyes turning to me. The woman who held me, her grasp once soft and teasing, clawed into me. I wrenched away from her.

"Throw her out!" the women chorused together. They rose in eerie unison and turned on me. "Throw her out!"

I expected a swarm of manicured hands to descend, but the party stood frozen and unblinking, their attention sharp as a knife. The air was brittle. I backed away. Their stone eyes followed like glinting black mirrors. Anne broke into great heaving sobs. Her anguish was thunderous. King Emelia cradled her and pointed solemnly. I followed her direction to where a humble wooden door had materialized by the dais. Chaos broke out.

I ran for the door, threw myself heedless into whatever awaited me on the other side. I slammed it shut. There was no doorknob and no lock. Bodies slammed the door as each woman reached it, rattling it in its frame. I imagined them piling up, women trampling each other in their frenzy. There came a final fleshy thud, and the door rattled once more and then was still. Faint crying was all I could hear from the other side.

Guilt chased me. I hurried from the sound. The king's door had brought me to the courtyard at night. It was serene and empty, unchanged but for the giant magnolia blooming at its heart. I rounded the tree once, twice. I loved the dense certainty of it, the white musk of its flowers. Its broad branches swept the ground, and its leaves were big and sturdy as those of the tree on the hill, the one we lost to the drought. I settled beside it and rested my forehead on my knees. I took hungry breaths of the cool air.

A small thought took root in the back of my mind—*I want to go home*—and I snatched it up like a weed. I had no way of knowing how long my journey here would be, and any thought of going or being anywhere else could do nothing but lead me to despair. Where was the heart of the heart? How would I even know when I was close? It was too soon to think of going back. I brought my fingers to my lips and remembered Meredith's kiss. Through the trees ahead, I could just spy her balcony.

The way to her room hadn't changed. At my passage, the castle bloomed, dark leaves unfurling and flowers opening in the stone, but I found no comfort in them. Moonlight was strange through the windows, overbright despite the eternal layer of clouds, washing everything ghostly. None of the sconces were lit.

Meredith's door was ajar. I pushed inside.

In a large bed rested a small woman, the blankets pulled up to her chin. My breaths came fast. She was exactly as I'd first seen her—which meant she was dying again.

I touched her hand and found her cold as before, but when I hovered my hand over her chest, nothing stirred within, not breath or blood. I pressed my palm flat to her breastbone. I curled my fingers to draw the poison. Her body didn't meet me, didn't recognize me. I crawled into bed with her. I put my ear to her chest. She was quiet inside.

My breath slipped out of me, and I forgot how to draw another. I lay with my head pillowed on her silent chest and couldn't move. A breeze from the balcony stirred her curtains. I watched them billow.

The king stepped through, her gaze cutting to me. Its bright clarity burned. Her resolve brought me upright. She was not sad.

I glanced back at the woman in the bed. Of course. I could only grieve her because she had lived. I remembered our Meredith who I had left breathing and warm on the other side of a red door, our Meredith who lived. I shivered to have forgotten her so fast, to have fallen helpless to the heart's folding of time and memory.

King Emelia pointed again, out at the corridor from where I had come. I gathered myself and did not look back.

All the castle's familiar places were where I remembered them but without people. In Phaela's study, an annotated volume was open on the desk. I nearly disregarded it and continued on—there was always a marked-up book on Phaela's desk—but the erratic handwriting was unlike her. It scratched across the page without care for what was being overwritten. I peered closer and saw the truth of it. These weren't marginalia. This was a volume of poetry haphazardly repurposed as a journal, its stanzas all scrawled over with unrelated notes. I bent closer. It was hard to read the handwriting layered on top. I brought another candle to the desk.

3.16 – Emelia will not tell me what sort of girl she wants, only that she is tired

3.23 – I worry Meredith is not eating as she should. She says we must not cook meals specifically for her, that she will eat as Emelia does until the king's condition improves

4.2 – How often I have wished I could simply be Emelia's girl

4.7 – I've presented Emelia with a preliminary list of suitable candidates, but she refuses to see it

4.30 – Winifred says Meredith is bleeding from her nose and mouth

5.5 – Emelia is very low

5.9 – It is too risky to go on this way, with only one girl

5.27 – Winifred says Meredith is covered in bruises. I cannot let this diet continue

5.28 – Meredith's temper persists despite her growing illness. She refuses to see reason on her diet

5.29 – At Emelia's command, Meredith has been convinced to one small plate of vegetables

6.29 – I fear I will lose them both

7.1 – If I can just find the perfect girl

7.3 – Intriguing rumors from the valley. I have added another candidate to the list

7.15 – Emelia says my blood will not do, given my condition

7.16 – If I can just find the perfect girl for Emelia

Here, the quality of the journal deteriorated further, the remaining pages scrawled with a frantic echo of the last entry. The pen nib gouged into the pages so that they scarred and curled.

Shrieking tore the air. Lancing pain threw me back in my chair. White heat pierced my ears. My mouth stretched on a silent scream until my jaw ached. My eyes stretched wide for some horror I couldn't see. Then quiet and collapse. I breathed against the desk, great heaving breaths as though I'd drowned on my own air. The journal was under my palm.

Another scream came, this one human and afraid. I staggered upright and went for the door.

Anne again, down the corridor, bleeding. She pressed a trembling hand to her nightgown, then held it up to her face as though disbelieving the blood. Our eyes met. She beckoned to me with her bloodied hand and turned the corner. I followed hesitantly, keeping the trail of her blood to my right.

No mob of poison girls waited for me, just Anne. She pointed to the door of my bedchamber. I placed my hand upon the wood. She nodded eagerly. I was weary of opening doors, and how could I trust her? She saw my doubt and set her hand beside mine. I steeled myself, and we pushed into the new room together.

A great red hall soared. It had no ceiling, only red extending forever, its far end just as obscure. Its confines were as silky and mesmeric as the door King Emelia had opened for me, and a frisson of recognition told me I was finally, finally near. The door behind had vanished, and there was only the high polish of the stone and the gold veining through it. No chandeliers or sconces lit the space, and yet it was bright as daytime, the light diffuse and coming from nowhere. Anne twirled in circles, her arms outstretched, gown flashing white, red, white, red. She skipped soundlessly ahead. Her gown fluttered about her ankles, the soft white of it hypnotic in this hard, lifeless place. I trailed after her. Not even my footfalls echoed.

Anne gestured ahead and to the left. She slipped into the wall and disappeared. I ran to catch up with her, and as I neared the place where she'd vanished, I saw the arch cut into the stone, indiscernible from a distance. A smaller space was hidden within, organized like a gallery. Gold frames of identical sizes faced each other, each with an onyx pedestal beneath. Anne raced to the end of the hall and turned back to watch my progress. Each frame held a portrait of a woman. Each woman posed against the dark backdrop of the throne. My breath caught. Anne waved me forward, but I couldn't hurry. This place was a memorial. Throat tight, I drew close to the first portrait. *Lilian Needle* was carved into her pedestal in a strong, angled script. I looked up into her face—the keen glint in her eyes, the impish quirk to her lips. Her braids were piled high and ornately arranged, rings winking in her hair like gems in a diadem. If someone had told me she was a past queen, I would have believed them. On the pedestal with her name, a shapely black vase shone. I looked down the line. Every pedestal had one. Not a vase, then. An urn.

With their frames mounted at King Emelia's eye level, the high perspective lent the poison girls an air of overseeing guardians. I took my time with the portraits, studying every face and honoring their memories with what time I could give. Anne joined my side when I reached hers. Beatrisa had not only captured her likeness but her restless energy—chin tilted just so, as if she prepared to spit a retort. The Anne beside me hefted her urn. I startled. She opened it and stuck her hand inside.

"Curious how little a body burns down to," she said as though she'd found a forgotten ribbon at the back of her wardrobe. Her hands were a mess, all ash and blood. The grooves of her name were dusted white.

Behind Anne, two last portraits faced each other across the hall. Meredith looked down on us. The king had dressed her in a white gown with a high collar, its lace fanning up to the drops of pearls at her ears. Her lips were brightly rouged, a single focal point of color in the entire composition. Her countenance was uncommonly grave, something of her withheld. And then I remembered Siwan.

Meredith's pedestal was bare but for her name.

"Aren't you going to look at yours?" Anne asked behind me.

I shook my head. It was enough to know that King Emelia foresaw grief in the joys of first meeting, that she stockpiled memory the way others prepared for storms or failed harvests. And mustn't she? Even if we met no misfortune, we would die, and she would survive us.

We returned to the main hall, and Anne carried her urn out in her arms like a doll. We passed other alcoves, all of them filled with treasures and curiosities. In one, a pale tree grew up from the stone, its bark smooth and pale as ivory. Shards of light scintillated in its leafless branches. Another housed only a jar of sharp teeth on a plain wooden table. By the shape, they seemed to be the king's own. In yet another, blue flowers floated preserved in drops of glass. Their petals ranged in hue from darkest midnight to nearly moon white, their shapes carnivorous. Anne tapped one with a finger, and it bobbed and spun. King Emelia had lamented that the plants from her home wouldn't root in our soil. What existed here in the heart seemed to be all she had saved. I imagined her carefully gathering cuttings and seedlings for her departure only for it to have been in vain. Instead, she nurtured the flora of a land that wouldn't do the same for her.

We had gone on so far in silence, Anne and I the only people in this carefully curated world. Now, a rattling breath stirred the air.

I looked to Anne, our eyes meeting as a flower drifted past. She pressed her lips into a thin line and held her urn tighter. I left the sanctuary of the flowers first, stepping into the exposed main room.

In the center of the hall, in a gilded throne that had not been there prior, sat a wizened man covered in a shroud of liquid gold. He breathed as though in the grip of a hacking cough, like fluid filled his lungs. Gold bubbled around his nose. It thinned like a drum over his gasping mouth, dripping from the point of his chin onto the fur trim of his cloak. He was wretched in his finery, coughing then groaning, slouching then pushing himself upright, ragged nails scraping at the gleaming armrests. His skin was thin and wrinkled along the backs of his hands, tendons and bone protruding like a corpse that had been picked over and had no meat left to scavenge.

Around the throne, growing up through the red stone, weeping luna thrived.

I crept to the old king. Flowers brushed my legs. Anne kept her distance, hanging back by the alcove. When I'd drawn near enough to see the crest on the king's brooch, he startled and grew still, though I'd made no sound.

He spoke with a voice hoarse from disuse, droplets of gold scattering like spittle. "You're not her." He tilted his head. "Or him."

I rounded the throne, watching him think from a distance as I grasped for my own plan. My task had become a riddle. How did one retrieve a melted crown?

When King Emelia first told me its fate, I assumed it had killed its wearer, that he had burned and suffocated under the symbol of his power. Instead, the unfulfilled pact had preserved him for years of torment. I never wanted to meet the sort of man who could do this. He didn't seem like the kind I could kill.

"You've come to steal his power for yourself?" King Eric said next and wheezed a laugh until he choked on the shroud. He doubled over gasping, then threw himself back and slouched again. It didn't seem he could stand. His hands never left the armrests, as though trapped in invisible bonds.

I was glad I shouldn't speak. I didn't want to be lured into a conversation with him. I circled closer and finally stopped before him. The flowers swayed on a breeze I couldn't feel. The king twitched, turning an ear to me as though he'd heard something.

"A servant?" he whispered, then laughed again. "A poison girl! Imagine a poison girl wearing the crown of Vinstrum!"

His amusement brought on another fit of coughing and gasping, splattering me with gold. I wiped my hand down my dress, and the gold smeared, reforming into a bead in my hand. It shot back to the shroud like something magnetized, rippling into the molten flow.

Eric recovered enough to sneer. "Who would listen to the likes of you?"

I forgot caution. I caught him by the throat. I sank my fingers into the gold. It burned, so hot that at first I felt nothing, felt powerful. Eric roared and thrashed. He was a hollow and cursed man, and I held him easily. The gold chose me. It melted up my arm in a devouring wave, burning away weakness and imbuing me with light. With this second skin, I would be radiant. No one could look upon me, beautiful and dangerous as the sun.

THIRTY-ONE

I ROUSED IN THE dark of the throne room, alone. The golden high had faded. Anne's party had long ago dispersed if it was ever here at all. This seemed a different iteration of the room in a different time. Onyx shards littered the ground at my feet, the black casing of the throne shattered to expose the bones beneath. Here was the original gilded throne on which Eric had sat, its back and seat upholstered in plush velvet. In my hand, the crown had remembered its first state, so gem encrusted as to be grotesque. I wanted to pry them loose. They could fuel a small economy in the borderlands, all of us trading the same glittering handful back and forth and laughing at our fortune.

A crunch at the foot of the dais made me turn. Meredith stood gazing up at me as though risen from the dead, still dressed in the flower-embroidered gown. She started up the steps heedless of the glass. Her bare feet bled dark prints on the stone. I backed away from her, but she only smiled, taking the crown from me and settling it upon my head.

"There," she breathed, but all I could think of was the shroud and breathless torment. "Would you make me your queen?"

I backed away from her and toward the steps. I had the crown, my prize, King Emelia's salvation. I must find the way out.

Meredith blinked, and her eyes were black stones. Her smile fell. "My king?"

I hurried down the steps, slipping on the glass in my haste. If I stayed for her, I would lose my Meredith. I needed the red door.

"Please don't leave me!" Meredith cried. "Don't leave me!"

Her pleas chased me, amassing and layering to a disembodied crescendo. I shielded my heart and pushed the great onyx doors and was blessed with silence.

My feet met grass. The garden, again. The castle had become recursive, all its entrances and exits attuned to the places I had given the most power.

It was a pleasant evening, evincing that rare and perfect balance of warmth preceding summer. An easy breeze brought the scent of promise and night-blooming flowers to me. Something like a truce loosened the air. I took the path by the hellebores. There was no magnolia this time.

Where it had been, a white iron table had been set out with two chairs. One was empty. In the other sat a woman I had never seen before. She wore her hair loose, the glory of its full and coiled length drawing the eye to her round face, the heart shape of her lips and flat borderland nose. I took the chair across from her as she finished pouring her cup of tea. She welcomed me with a grateful smile, and I saw the delicate gap between her teeth. She poured a cup for me. Its plume of steam was earthy and grounded with none of the floral or citrus embellishments I'd grown used to in the castle. One of the king's little flames drifted near, and the tea flashed a rich red.

Around the woman's shoulders, a shadow moved, uncoiling. It took all my restraint not to cry out. Da flicked his tongue at me and slithered down the woman's arm. I held my hand out for him, and he met me as he always had, winding up my arm to perch on my shoulders. The woman smiled again, this time to cover the saddened look that had crossed her. She sipped her tea, eyes downcast as though preparing herself to face me again. But I couldn't stop staring at her, a woman I had never seen before and yet recognized like my own face in a broken mirror, the features changed but familiar.

How was Ma here? How did the castle know she was mine? How did it know a face I had never seen?

Then I remembered what Phaela had said. The king needed Huxley's memories.

She was the Priscilla that he saw.

The realization punched through my chest. I clenched my teeth. I felt ill. I wanted *my* ma. I wanted to cry like a child. It was all I'd ever wanted to do, to cry and scream for her and have her appear like so many other mothers did for their children.

She saw all this. Doubt creased her brow.

"I'm sorry," she said. She made her voice soft. "This was the only way I could come to you."

She spoke as if she were real, as if we were having this meeting truly, the one I'd longed for my entire life. But she was only my own longing and fear reflected back to me as everything in the heart had been. She was nothing. She was a cruel trick.

I pushed to my feet. My chair toppled into the grass.

"*Please*, Carlotta, for once, quit storming about," she snapped.

I almost scoffed at her. My retort burned on my tongue. I glared.

She took a calming breath. "I would like to have tea with my daughter," she said and gestured to the table. There were little biscuits now. There was a small bouquet. Her sad smile returned. "My daughter who I am proud of," she added as if it might sweeten me.

I righted my chair in a huff, stabbing it upright and falling back into my seat. Da didn't enjoy all this. He slithered back to the table and curled around the heat of the teapot.

Angry tears stung my eyes. There was nothing about me to be proud of.

"You have survived. You have fought. Made all the desperate choices you thought would save you but didn't. Clawed your way through a comfortless world and demanded comfort. You have asked politely and impolitely. Taken what wasn't yours and what was. Sacrificed yourself and others. Sank into despair and yet here you are."

Where was here? What was I?

Ma raised her hands, her smile wide like the moon, and gestured to the whole expanse of the garden, the sky. She had the conviction of the clerics, but I was tired and the crown heavy. I dropped it to the table and rested my head in my hands. The steam from the tea drifted up to warm my face, reminding me I hadn't yet tried it. I took a sip, and she eyed me approvingly.

"Good, isn't it?"

I nodded.

She stood and came around the table. She pointed at my lap. Folded papers slipped out of my pockets and spilled into the grass. We gathered them up, and she returned to her chair to read, waving a bobbing flame close to the page. I thought they might be our letters, but as I pressed them flat on the table, I found all the poems I'd written at the castle, half drafts and fragments among them. She smiled or frowned over them, taking her time and humming. At one, she laughed.

"You must treasure this girl!" Ma beseeched. "If she reminds you of the moon, it is the least you must do."

I blushed and watched her read every line. I knew when she came to a poem about herself because she would put her hand to her chest and press her lips together and set the page aside as if it had singed her fingers.

In the end, she only said, "It is getting late. You should head home." She finished her tea. "May I keep these?" she asked, indicating the poems.

I nodded. I wanted to ask whether I might see her again.

Ma poured another cup of tea for herself, shaking her head as she did. She stirred sugar into her cup, and her laugh was bitter. "I am not myself, as you've said. I think it is for the best if we part ways here, yes?"

My throat was tight. I took the crown up again and stood to leave but didn't know how. I wanted her to hold me, just once, even if she wasn't real, and I didn't know what that meant. I had always been desperate.

Had Huxley known Ma was amused by small animals and did not flinch at blood? Did he know all her favorite poems were about death and dying, as though she were trying to make sense of what she knew was coming for her too soon? Did he know that she, like me, hated for her hair to touch her ears? Did he know that her family was so poor that as a child she went without shoes in summer? Did he know that she and her sisters played in a lake that she only later learned was full of cottonmouth vipers, that none of them were ever bitten, that she never saw the danger lurking there in the water? Did he know about the magnolia?

What did any of these little facts make? Who had known her more?

Ma saw how I tarried and finally stood. She opened her arms to me, and I flinched. She waited. With her arms like that, with her face so solemn, she looked like one of the king's many statues—a figure from myth doomed to longing, always waiting and hoping and never receiving. I stepped to her cautiously because I had wanted this for so long, and now I was afraid it wouldn't be as I dreamed.

But Ma was warm, and she held me just as I wanted to be held because of course she did, because she was literally everything I had imagined. She squeezed harder at the end, just as Da would before letting go.

Then Ma let me go.

I wandered away from her and felt her gaze on my back. When I was sure I wouldn't see her, I looked behind me. I looked at the sky. I clutched the crown until it hurt my palm. Then I continued on as I always had.

Where the southern courtyard door had been, red shone through the leaves. I broke into a run. It felt good to run toward something instead of away.

I broke through the trees. And stopped.

The clerics believed I had been blessed with a vision of the angel. When I related to them what I had seen in my final conscious moments, they asked whether I remembered what the angel's face had looked like. I said I didn't. When I set out from home, I had been parched and starving and half mad. How could I have remembered a face? And if I didn't remember a face, wasn't it likely that it was one of them, veiled as they were? But the clerics said a feature of angelic visions was that the seekers who were blessed with them could never recall a face.

Now, I saw the face.

Guarding the red door, the angel waited with their arms crossed over their chest. They wore a robe the same as the clerics, the white of it so brilliant that I thought it glowed. Its majestic billow didn't follow the wind, instead moving according to its own forces. Where I expected a cleric's humble laces, there were no shoes or feet at all.

The angel floated. And the face was not a face. No eyes, no mouth or nose. Their head was bulbous, pale, and papery, wide at the crown and cinched smaller at their neck. I didn't understand their crinkled skin or what had happened to it. They didn't seem to notice as I crept near, but when I tried to sidestep them for the door, their wings snapped open at once, blinding me with the radiance of their feathers and rebuffing me from the door.

They rustled as they uncrossed an arm, and it was the sound of childhood harvests, of the restless wind harrying the maize stalks. I understood the nature of them. They were a doll made of husk grown large.

The angel themself was so fascinating that I didn't notice what they offered to me until the wind carried the unmistakable scent of weeping luna between us, and I finally saw the bloom tied to the end of their arm. I recoiled. I shoved past and pushed the door. It didn't open. I pounded my fist against it. Wasn't the king on the other side? Wouldn't she be waiting for me and hear? But my fist made no noise against the stone. There were no handles; there was no keyhole. I felt I'd met a wall. My hope ashed. A pit opened in my stomach.

The angel rotated to me and drifted nearer. They held the luna to my face. I shook my head and beat my hands against the door. My eyes stung. My throat tightened. I wanted to scream my frustration and couldn't. King Emelia wouldn't abandon me here. She wouldn't.

I slipped the crown down my arm so that it dangled at my elbow and set all my strength against the door. If this was a final test of will, I'd win it.

Again, the angel proffered the bloom. I gagged and held my breath. Its scent sickened me now. How had I ever cultivated it? Lain so many nights under its branches? Spent so much time dreaming with its aura in my head? It was cloyingly sweet as though to disguise the acrid sharpness of the poison beneath.

I didn't want it near me. And the door wouldn't open.

I shoved the angel, gritting my teeth against a scream I couldn't release. Their husk body crumpled and crunched under my palms, but though they floated, nothing moved them. I imagined tearing the luna from where it'd been tied around their frayed wrist, of grinding its petals beneath my heel. I felt the violent release of it in me. I grabbed the stem. Then noticed their other arm, still crossed. In it, a different white flower.

I pointed to it. The angel uncrossed their arm, raising the second flower as though in question. I nodded; I reached. I pulled the magnolia bloom free of the twine. Its petals were perfect, a sturdy and open cup silky as porcelain. It trembled in my hands. My hands were shaking. I was shaking.

Holding the flower aloft, I fell wearily against the doors. They opened, and I spilled into daylight—true yellow daylight. The crown slipped away from me, rolling into a ray of sun and glittering as it went.

MY DEAREST CARLOTTA,

 Of course I forgive you. I wouldn't have sent that first letter if my heart held no love. I may not be a cleric anymore, but I can't seem to stop believing in the stars. They foretold a personal reckoning, my own restoration. Now I am returned to the borderlands and remember myself. I am tending to those who remained. My labor in the water gardens is so physical as to be spiritual. It suits me.

 News of your poisonworker council has made it to the borderlands. I'm proud of you, my girl. It takes strength to step into the light and to call others to you. My intuition about you was always right. This work will be a struggle. I know firsthand how enduring belief is. But you will improve the lives of many if you succeed, and that possibility alone is worth the fight.

 Color is returning to the south. I will bring some cuttings and seeds for King Emelia when I visit. I believe you when you say you love her, but are you happy? Forgive me this motherly concern. You write with such a solemn hand.

 Yours,
Marta

Dear Marta,

 I am happy, yes, but I am also prepared to bite. The lot of poison girls must improve. I do this for my mother who is gone forever but also for Meredith, still here, who slumbers at my side as I write this.

 The land around the castle is also in bloom, and King Emelia walks free in our new landscape. Picture the baby deer, fresh in their bodies and unsteady on their legs, testing to see if the earth will bear them up. That is how King Emelia first ventured beyond the castle. Every day, the flowers are more beautiful, and every day, the king gathers a new bouquet for me and Meredith. We identify new species whenever we take our walks, which is to say the old flowers are returning, ones I've never seen before. The king is eager to explore Vinstrum after her strange exile, and the three of us will soon disembark to visit our new allies. Chief among our list of places to see, however, is the borderlands. Please stay where you are. I am coming to you.

Acknowledgements

Thank you to my editors Sarah Mesh and Maggie Morris for the invaluable insight and cheerleading. Maggie—you've been editing my books since my debut, and I wouldn't have it any other way. Your understanding of my voice puts me at ease. Thank you to Elaine Ho for saying yes to illustrating another book of mine and for the stunning King Emelia and castle. I worried it was excessive to ask for a second demon lady cover, but your excitement over the Artemisia Gentileschi reference reassured me I was right to ask. Cass, your typography is so incredibly sharp and thrilling. Absolute perfection at first mock.

Thank you to Lana for the energizing first read and brainstorming calls. Thank you to Chloe at Thistle & Verse for being with me since my short fiction era and loving the story that inspired this novel. All my gratitude for your sharp-eyed beta read.

Thank you to the online SFF magazines that published my short stories and poetry before I could call myself a novelist: *Fiyah Magazine*, *Strange Horizons*, *Beneath Ceaseless Skies*, *Baffling Magazine*, *Uncanny Magazine*, *Fireside Magazine*, and *Mermaids Monthly*. I've been circling the images and themes of this novel for five years, and you gave me the first stage for my ideas.

And as always, thank you, dear reader, for spending time with my work.

THANK YOU FOR READING!

Visit TamaraJeree.com to join the newsletter for

- exclusive epilogues
- early cover reveals
- lore & news

About the Author

Tamara Jerée is a fan of women with sharp teeth. Their short stories have appeared in the Shirley Jackson Award-winning anthologies *Unfettered Hexes: Queer Tales of Insatiable Darkness* and *Professor Charlatan Bardot's Travel Anthology*. Their debut novel *The Fall that Saved Us* won the 2023 Indie Ink Award.

Join the newsletter at https://www.tamarajeree.com/

instagram.com/tamarajeree